**dixi
books**

# T. J. Rowley

T. J. Rowley is a Canadian author whose writing explores both the risks and the glimmering potential of emerging technology. A privacy advocate, T. J. once made a freedom of information request to a credit agency to see the data profile they had on him. As it turned out, the agency thought he was two people. (They offered to monitor for such mistakes in the future – for a fee). T. J. is in fact one person, whose other interests include artificial intelligence, the outdoors, and staving off dystopia.

He can be found at *www.tjrowley.com*

# PERSISTENCE
# OF VISION

## T. J. Rowley

Persistence of Vision
T. J. Rowley
Editor: Katherine Boyle
Proofreading: Andrea Bailey
Designer: Pablo Ulyanov
I. Edition:  April 2023
Print ISBN: 978-1-913680-59-6
E-book ISBN: 978-1-913680-76-3

© Dixi Books Publishing
293 Green Lanes, Palmers Green, London, England, N13 4XS
info@dixibooks.com
www.dixibooks.com

# PERSISTENCE
# OF VISION

T. J. Rowley

dixi
books

*The Voice of the New Age*

# ACKNOWLEDGEMENTS

Thank you first and foremost to SRRP, without whose support, optimism, and belief this novel would not have been published. Thank you also to my family for their constant encouragement as this novel took shape. I also owe debts of inspiration to BW, TL, HS, DF, and EY, whose careful reviews and frank perceptions brought the manuscript to life. Thank you also to Ayse Ozden and everyone at the Dixi Books team, whose contributions cannot be overstated. Final thanks to the privacy scholars, researchers, and advocates whose hard work is desperately needed to keep this novel a work of fiction.

# Chapter 1:
## Stunts and Incantations

"Where are you taking me?" Jane calls from the back of the limousine, though there is no one in the driver's seat.

"The Spring Ball, ma'am," a voice comes in a measured tone.

The limousine slides underneath the multistory legs of a holographic giant patrolling the freeway. The giant crashes an axe against the ground, which the limousine ghosts through like it is made from mist. Jane sees the shimmer of suspended dots slip past, then watches the giant recede into the darkness out the rear window. It is the mascot of Goliath Security, Jane knows, whose tagline is *Between You and Them*. She returns her gaze to the front window, wondering why the limousine is driving her closer to *Them*.

"So close to the Red Zone, Skyra?" she says uneasily.

"*In* the Red Zone," the voice says from an unseen speaker, "by special authorization."

"From who?"

"The corporation."

"But from *who*?"

"I do not understand."

Jane purses her lips. Skyra's artificial intelligence has become so canny that it has learned, when needed, to lie. Jane presses: "Who authorizes who lives in the Green Zone and who lives with the criminals in the Red Zone?"

"Do not be alarmed, ma'am. Precautions have been taken."

"I'm not *alarmed*, Skyra."

"Your elevated heart rate and skin temperature indicate alarm."

Jane's practiced calm slips. She considers searching for reports of Skyra mistakenly taking someone into the Red Zone, but she doubts Skyra will retrieve any for her. Jane forces her breathing to slow.

Once the streetlights stop, the only light comes from the glow of the adverts projected on the underside of the heavy clouds. Squinting out the limousine window, Jane sees the outlines of buildings on the roadside, becoming shabbier as they drive. The shabbiness reminds Jane of her old apartment block, though she snips the memory before it becomes detectable.

She had received instructions to dress for the party as a representative of Marie Cherie, so she will have to stay quiet and sultry, smoldering in a corner or by the bar, rather than bounding into the dance floor like a Moral Decay girl. She did not think she would be hired by Marie Cherie again, not after the fashion show three nights ago. "How many mentions, now?" she asks. Skyra will know what she means.

"Two million, four hundred and twenty-two thousand and seventy-five."

"That's all thanks to *you*, my wonderful fans," Jane says directly to the thumbnail-sized camera positioned above her seat. "Keep sharing the story!"

"Pardon, ma'am," Skyra says, "but your life stream is still inactive."

Jane frowns. Three days inactive. The corporation seldom deactivates her stream for more than half a day's respite, even when she asks, even when she is exhausted, even when she is sleeping. Jane worries this time she went too far. "At whose instruction?" Jane says.

"The corporation," Skyra says again.

"You mean the algorithms."

"Your life stream will be restored to the feed when your risk profile decreases."

"You mean when the algorithms say so."

Skyra knows not to answer. It is too shrewd to venture into a discussion with Jane about the algorithms that dictate her choices – algorithms as unknown to her as those that guide the limousine smoothly toward the Red Zone.

"Is there a reason you didn't tell me the Ball is in the Red Zone?" Jane says.

"It was not relevant."

"It *will* be relevant when I lose all my TELOS."

"Do not be alarmed, ma'am."

There is that word again.

Jane holds her breath as she approaches the Red Zone border, expecting to be instantly flagged as a criminal. Nobody Jane knows has any first-hand experience with the Red Zone. There are stories of muggings, thieves, crazed shouts, and shambling beggars. The feed gives constant reports of *crime potentials* in the Red Zone, but the people who lived there are a mystery. Those with TELOS and privileges are on one side; everyone else is on the other. But as the limousine rolls across the invisible border between Green and Red Zones, Jane's TELOS does not collapse as she expects; the score increases by two points.

Jane lets out a breath. TELOS is a black box to her, from which expected freedoms are taken and unexpected freedoms given. She begins to wonder if the rumours about the people in the Red Zone are true, but the patrol of armed Liberator security she sees patrolling the nightclub suggests the answer.

"You are scheduled to socialize for three hours," says Skyra as the limousine stops.

Jane gathers her handbag and tries the handle of the limousine door. Locked.

"—and ma'am," Skyra adds, "you are recommended to behave within acceptable parameters."

"Don't be *alarmed*, Skyra," says Jane. "I'll make sure the algorithms are very pleased."

The door unlocks. Jane steps out in her emerald dress and watches the limousine drive itself into the darkness.

"The limousine will return at the conclusion of your task," Jane hears in Skyra's voice, and she wishes that Skyra would disappear into the darkness too. She squints but she cannot make out the Red Zone buildings that stand like poltergeists just beyond her perception.

"What's out there?" Jane says, staring into the dark.

"Please do not leave the vicinity of the nightclub," Skyra answers, the voice channeled from the gold bracelet on Jane's wrist in a direct beam to her ear.

Jane turns from the darkness and heads to the lights flashing from the nightclub. The entrance to the nightclub bustles with aspiring influencers narrating their life streams, the hum of camera drones overhead, and booming adverts still within earshot despite their distance from civilization. The air is thick with humidity and the sour stench of sewage leaking from dilapidated pipes. The other guests are in garish colours, ladies with long trains and bodices of diamonds flickering under the adverts projected on the night sky, men with capes that flash adverts as they swoop by. A red carpet saves their expensive shoes from the degraded asphalt. Jane strides to the nightclub – the long, leggy strides of a model, chin up, shoulders back, chest forward – but with a defiant pace. She wants answers.

Jane looks for welcoming faces outside the nightclub but finds none. A woman in a pompous dress stares as she narrates for her life stream. Text about the woman springs upon Jane's lenses. There are categories for TELOS, personal feed, history, each with further depth, text upon text, that Jane can delve into with a look, but with a slight movement Jane shakes the text off her eyes. Instead, she flicks her chin and Skyra opens the woman's stream.

"—horrible and offensive," Jane hears the woman say, still staring, "she'll be making the Red Zone a permanent home soon."

Jane flicks her chin again to stop the stream.

Other life streamers enter, lips moving, narrating for their life streams as cameras capture them from every angle. Like Jane, all of them wear a gold bracelet that houses Skyra's artificial personality. Jane's bracelet feels sticky on her wrist. Despite wearing it for years, she has never managed to shake the feeling that the bracelet is a parasite on a vein, leeching her bodily data for anyone's purchase. At this moment, there are twenty-two million, four-hundred and twelve people willing to pay for the data absorbed from Jane's Skyra bracelet, clamouring for any piece of her while her life stream remains deactivated.

The nightclub is housed in a repurposed factory, its dreary concrete walls black with stains of old industry. But for the procession of limousines and the richly-adorned guests stepping out of them, Jane would have mistaken the nightclub for any other Red Zone ruin. Jane imagines the screams of saws and the hiss of hot steel and greased hands, overalls dirtied by labour, a supervisor inspecting pallets of corrugated iron, ticking off a sheet on a clipboard. At least, that is what she has seen in old movies. The real history, if recorded at all, is not for her eyes.

As the metal doors to the nightclub wince open for her, Jane sees that the factory floor has been cleared of machinery. Some salvaged pieces are hung on the wall. Jane wants to run her hands over them, to feel their age and grime and rust, to risk pricking her thumb on the sharp edges. Overlooking the shop floor is an observation catwalk. Women in short dresses drape themselves over the metal railings as suited men throw back shots and lights splash them with orange and red. A wooden dance floor at the far end shivers beneath dancing feet.

All stops when Jane enters.

The dancers cease. The men leaning on the bar stand up straight. Those near Jane step backward as though she might be a Red. Lights rain over the unmoving crowd, looking like mannequins in a store front.

She approaches a man of sixty with skin like he is still thirty. His thick white hair matches his teeth, bared in an uneasy smile that drops as Jane nears. She waves at him and calls his name, but he stumbles back and buries himself in the crowd. Jane playfully shrugs to the crowd to downplay the snub, but her heart is pounding. She stepped too far this time.

"Skyra," she says aloud. "Are you sure I am supposed to be here?"

"Yes," she hears in her ear, "the Director is waiting for you."

The mention of the Director causes Jane's bubbly features to twitch. She's losing her mask.

A current from the Skyra bracelet thrums up Jane's arm, which Jane follows like there is a direct circuit from Skyra to her feet that bypasses her brain. The crowd parts to let her pass. She could buy the data on their anxiety levels if it were not so evident from their faces.

The current buzzing along her arm leads Jane up the catwalk toward the silhouette of a solitary figure watching from the window of the top floor office. Jane can make out only his luminous white eyes, which follow her up the metal stairs. She pushes open the wooden door and enters a low-lit harem with a chandelier and a huge bed dressed in red silk lying untouched in the far corner. The ground shudders with the nightclub music, like it is warning her of worse shocks to come.

"Close it," the figure whispers, despite the volume of the music.

As she does, Skyra tells her that the Director has obscured their conversation from the feed. Nobody else will hear what is said. Nobody, except the young woman sitting uneasily on a chair beside the bed, hands gripping one another in her lap. She doesn't look at Jane.

"Annabelle and I were just finishing up," says the figure as he leaves the window. He is in silvered middle-age and wears a crisp black suit. "Annabelle, one more round," he says as he stands above her.

The woman in the chair stiffens, as if protecting herself. "I am most frightened of snakes. I am most frightened of confined spaces."

"Confined spaces!"

"Yes." Annabelle forces a smile.

He immediately chuckles. "You see, Jane, neither the skin nor the eyes nor the heart can lie." He shoots a look over his shoulder. "Thank you, Annabelle, you can go."

"Thank you, Director," she whispers as she leaves, keeping her eyes to the hardwood floor.

"I didn't know you were here," says Jane.

"Nobody does," answers the Director. "Do they, Annabelle?"

Annabelle shakes her head and escapes out the door.

"Would you like to play?" he says to Jane. The hot musk of the nightclub goes cold as he stares at her. "Tell me one truth and one lie."

"I do not want to play," says Jane, staying by the door.

The Director installs himself in the chair and eases one leg over the other. "You are upset," he says. "Was it the drive across the border?"

Jane's fingers play with the sides of her dress. "Yes." From what she has heard, people involuntarily driven into the Red Zone do not return.

"You have never been to a Red Zone before?"

"No," she replies with conviction.

The Director leans forward, assessing her. His eyes thin. And then he smiles. "Very good, very good," he says. "You are a capable liar. You will be perfect."

Jane steels herself. "For?"

"An assignment," the Director replies.

"To humiliate myself in front of all the people downstairs, who are treating me like I'm carrying a plague?"

"They're just worried," he smiles, "they still don't know whether they will lose TELOS by congregating with you."

Jane's TELOS had risen by seventeen points since her stunt, despite the shutdown of her life stream. She hates that she checks her TELO score each hour, but the habit is burrowed too deeply.

"If anything, I will increase their TELOS," she says. "My stunt is *still* trending."

"By setting a Marie Cherie dress on fire," he says, "during a live catwalk."

"A joke. Not worth deactivating my life stream for three days."

"Oh, you can't tell me you have not enjoyed the break from streaming?"

Jane's gaze wavers for just a moment, and she sees that is all the Director needs for confirmation.

"I just know what happens to girls who don't stream anymore," she answers.

He swishes his hand in front of him. "Evidently, women's gossip outpaces even Skyra's automatic fact-checkers," he laughs. "Fortunately, it is not your life streaming that I need. You are aware that I was recently appointed to the Board of Nature Corp.?"

"Congratulations."

"It is an impotent role," the Director says as he shakes his head. "I am the minority voice against the fatuous sycophants under the thumb of the majority owner, Mr. Pierre Daviault. Do you know much about him?"

*Daviault.* Jane's eyes drop when she hears the name. "Nothing much," she answers, flicking her eyes back up to meet the Director's stare.

"Try again," he smiles, his skin white despite splashes of red and orange lights through the window.

"Daviault built Nature Corp. He owns this city and everything in it."

Jane tests his gaze and sees that he is not satisfied.

"He gained his power by marketing Skyra bracelets and aggressively monetizing the data from them," she adds. What the corporation can do with all the data, Jane does not know. "Skyra knows everything: what excites me, what scares me, what I ate for breakfast a year ago."

There is just one secret that Skyra has been unable to extract from her. Aberrant thoughts threaten to bubble to the surface, so Jane focuses on reciting the accepted truth. "With Skyra's data, Mr. Daviault optimizes the world for us. And if he ever stopped getting data from our Skyra bracelets, our world would disintegrate."

"Correct," the Director says, "though you understate the thrill of it. It is not just data. With Skyra, Daviault can *taste* people." He licks his lips. "Taste them down to their minutiae."

Jane shivers despite the withering heat in the office.

"What you do *not* know," the Director continues, "is that Daviault has not been seen for five weeks."

Jane furrows her eyebrows. "I saw him in the State briefing last week." She does not add that all citizens are forced to watch it. "Faked?"

"Some people, like me, can restrict their data from the feed," says the Director, "while a lucky few, with great effort, can fake it entirely."

Jane's eyes narrow. She did not know that data can be falsified – at least, not *here*. She snips the thought before it becomes detectable. "So, you want me to spy on an old man?"

"I want you to find out if this old man is alive or dead," he replies, "by ingratiating yourself with Daviault *Junior*."

The Director goes to the window and tips his head to a man in a sparkling pearl suit, seated on the bonnet of a classic car and chatting to a model half his age.

Her head begins to ache. "Him?"

"A boy in a man's body, nourished from birth on expensive toys," the Director blusters, "and also the heir apparent to the corporation.

Which unfortunately means he can afford the same anonymity from Skyra as I."

The Director wears the Skyra bracelet around his wrist like everyone else, but he has the wealth to remove all his data from public view. According to the rumours Jane has seen, a faction of investors vying to overthrow the Director pooled resources to purchase all the Director's data. Their plan only drove the cost of unlocking his data higher. Now nobody can afford it. In a world where all is known, the Director is one of the few unknowns.

Jane feels icy around him, her body warning her about something she cannot articulate.

"I want you to see what Skyra cannot," he says.

"I'm a model, not a spy."

"You are a marketing tool. I'm giving you a target market of one."

"This was not our agreement."

She hopes that she does not have to revisit what they agreed.

"Nor was setting a dress on fire during a live show," he dismisses, "or putting codes in the lyrics you sing on your stream, or writing 'Fuck this' on your bathroom mirror, to be revealed by the steam."

Jane indulges in a smile. "They got me exposure."

"Precisely why I let them continue," says the Director. "Time to put the exposure to use."

"You think that once the old man is gone, Junior will just do as you say?"

"*You* do."

Jane's eyes narrow once more.

"Don't be upset," the Director mocks.

Jane realizes how sweaty her palms have become. "Daviault Junior will have seen me coming up here."

"And he won't be able to resist asking you why."

"If I tell him the truth?"

The Director's eyes meet hers, looking through her. It feels like the skin is being peeled from her face. "We know you will not," the Director concludes. "So, please go and speak to him. That is, unless you can give me a better reason for why you are so resistant to speaking with Daviault Junior?"

Jane feels as cold as if the Director had peeled back the last of her skin. Instantly she worries how much of her data he has harvested. The next instant, a well-used reflex reminds her to be calm, to avoid the telltale heart quiver or pupil dilation that will incriminate her further.

"I don't know what you mean," Jane says with a slight stammer.

"As I said, Jane, neither the skin—"

—she notes the clamminess of her palms—

"—nor the eyes—"

—she flicks her gaze back to meet his—

"—nor the heart lies. They suggest that you have an unusually powerful reaction to Daviault."

He says it like a question, but one to which he already knows the answer.

If there is such a thing as a past life, Jane imagines that the Director would have been a huntsman, skulking in the shadows, awaiting his moment. He would consume each morsel of his kill, stripping the skin, separating the sinew from the bone, slurping the bone's marrow. For the three years Jane has known the Director, she has felt hunted by him.

"The data is wrong," she says, "there is no problem. I'll speak to Daviault. But if he discovers I'm working for you?"

"Skyra, restart her feed." He returns to the window, their conversation over.

# Chapter 2:
# Behind the Veil

Jane slinks from the office, feeling the Director watch her from his perch. As she descends the metal stairs, Jane recalls meeting with the Director on her first day at the modeling agency. He led her behind a locked door to show her his collection. Four rats in clear-plastic skinner boxes. Jane asked why he had them. A past life, was all he said, now, time for your first lesson.

One rat rasped at the invisible walls like it was on fire. He'll be dead tomorrow, the Director had said. He explained that he had made it addicted by traces of cocaine in its water. Jane wished that she had walked out then, but his presence kept her kneeling in front of the box, disgusted face pressed to the transparent plastic. Of course it's addicted, she had said, it lives alone in an empty cage.

Precisely, the Director beamed, when living together with other rats, none become addicted. They take sustainable sips of the laced water. What matters isn't the drug. Then he paused to let her make the conclusion.

It's being alone, she grimaced.

The opposite of addiction, he added, is togetherness.

The sickness in Jane's belly had turned cold as she realized that the Director approached the people he marketed to in the same way he did his rats. Perhaps we aren't so different? he had said. Nobody lives like this, Jane had retorted. A smile had hooked onto his cheeks as he replied: Don't they?

That question rings in Jane's ear as she searches for Daviault Junior in the crowd.

"Pierre Daviault Junior," Skyra says to Jane through a direct channel to her ear, "leading search terms: *mansion, job at Nature, net worth, poker championship, ex-girlfriends…*"

An incomplete list. Nothing about poisoning children, though Jane chases a memory away before the rising anger disrupts her even pace. Her emerald dress flutters at her knees.

Jane strains to extinguish her anger at Daviault, to keep it cool, quiet, and invisible within the few inches of her head, but the thought of breaking a bottle over Daviault's head and finishing him off with the shards fixes in her mind and heats her skin.

She stops. Emotions are dangerous. They raise suspicion. The effort to resist goring Daviault with the bottle will be tracked. Jane must keep her mind within the thin band of permissible thoughts. The more spontaneous or powerful the thought is, the more firmly it must be crushed.

She turns to leave.

"The woman of the hour," she hears from behind her. Jane shivers as she turns to see Daviault Junior smiling at her, still sitting on the bonnet of the decorative old car. She sees his eyes trace from her ankle to her hip to her shoulder. His voice is a deep rumble with a French lilt to match his name. Daviault is olive-skinned and handsome in the most trying-too-hard way, wearing a brilliant white suit and circling himself in floral perfume. He rests one foot on the rusted bumper, letting the other dangle.

Jane imagines staining his white suit red, but clips the thought before it can develop. That is what it means for her to *think*: to consider what part of her body will betray the thought to Skyra, then predict how the algorithms will assess the thought. Then, and only then, to allow the thought to manifest, or dash it before it fully forms.

She can't face him yet. She must acclimate to her feeling of disgust, depersonalize herself from it, press it somewhere else, away from detection. While Daviault remains sitting on the bonnet, Jane circles the car. It is a clumsy shape, broad and square, as if it ploughed the air. It is painted a milky turquoise. The doors have been removed. The seats are plush and cream. Jane notes a comical stick at the driver's left hand, the purpose of which she can't deduce. There is a cavalcade of knobs and dials on the dashboard with similarly elusive purposes. The nightclub is filled with these relics, plucked from a history she is not allowed to know.

"You look very beautiful tonight," Daviault calls to her.

Red lights roll over the cracked concrete floor.

Jane rounds the vehicle, waiting for the tension between her shoulders to subside. She feels that everyone in the nightclub is watching, as is everyone through innumerable life-streams. As is the Director. There can be no mistakes. Daviault remains sitting on the bonnet of the car, twisting his neck to watch her, looking as if he can twist his neck all the way around.

"Not just your clothing," he calls over his shoulder, "your attitude."

"Oh?" she finally musters.

"You don't like following footsteps either."

Jane eyes him, loathing coursing in her veins. She hates him *because* he follows his father's footsteps. But Jane must play nice, for now, and joins him on the bonnet of the car. A waiter hands her the bottle of beer. *Brought to you by Truman,* she hears.

"Skyra," he says, "obscure our conversation."

A ping in Jane's ear signals that their conversation is now exempted from the feed.

"I've been an admirer of yours for some time," he declares above the thrum of the music.

"The same to you," she replies, "and your father, as well. He's made a *profound* mark on me."

She lets the comment hang as she sips her drink.

"Yes, he's leaving quite the legacy," Daviault grimaces.

"It's his footsteps you don't like following?"

He laughs. "I know what the search results say about me, despite all the tests I have done. I think quicker, in more dimensions, and I work harder than the ninety-eighth percentile, yet still the feed sees me as the womanizer, the lothario, with more money than sense. I think it's very clear I won't be continuing my father's legacy."

"But you're Vice President."

"It's just a name," he says sourly. "There are perks, though. I get to visit other states – for official business, of course."

"Like where?"

Jane knows little about what is outside of their state. From what she has seen on the feed, everything else has been lost to dust storms and disorder.

"I've been able to see the factories in Ford State, so massive the workers in the distance blur together into a single machine," Daviault says, "and I've seen the Great Leader in Theos. Ever heard of him? He preaches that he has God's Eye, and can see, at all times, whether you are being sinful."

"Charming."

The music feels more intense, the dancers' feet heavier on the floor.

"Of course, I know the places more to a girl's liking," Daviault continues, "crystal beaches in New Jericho—"

"—yeah—"

"—star-gazing in the Sigma Insurance Mountains—"

"Do all these places have a Red Zone, like us?"

Daviault's lips purse. Too preoccupied with the shoulder straps of her dress, he is visibly surprised at what comes out of her mouth. "By other names," he says. "Theos, for example, lies on an underground spring. Sinners are cast, quite literally, into the desert. That punishment is usually for sexual perversion, but the Great Leader has a *particular* distaste for blasphemy." He raises his eyebrows and swills a mouthful of beer. "So I don't think you and he would get along."

"He tolerates *you*."

He shrugs. "There's no sin a charitable donation can't wash clean."

A chill takes her. She must follow the Director's instructions, but Daviault's confidence in his invulnerability feels like one of those cosmetic surgery scalpels in her abdomen. He and his ilk deserve punishment – not for imaginary sins but for the real harms they cause. Hatefulness re-emerges in her mind and courses through her mental circuitry too quickly for her to rip out the cords.

She should leave. She cannot count on her mouth to not make words she will regret. Jane smiles weakly. "It was nice meeting you Mr. Daviault—"

"Call me Davi."

"You'll make your father *very* proud."

As she slides from the bonnet, his hand comes to her fingertips. "Don't leave," he says, "you haven't asked why I called you over."

She slides her hand away. "To tell me about crystal beaches?"

She reprimands herself for letting her mask slip.

"To ask your opinion," he says. "A new strategy I'm going to propose to the Nature Board."

The mention of the Board pricks Jane's attention, but she loathes Daviault too deeply to tolerate him much longer. "I'm a model, not a mathematician," she dismisses.

"You're a girl with an opinion. One I know will be honest."

She wants to snatch the lapels of his pearl suit and hiss: *my opinion is: admit what the company did. Admit it knew and didn't care. Promise it will never happen again.* But she can't raise suspicion; she scrunches her fury into a tight ball and slides back up the bonnet to sit beside him. Well-dressed bodies bounce around them.

"In simple terms," Davi says, touching her fingers again, pressing them down to the metal, "surge pricing our food. We know the demand for a product, and the financial standing of each person interested. Right now, everyone pays the same price. But why? That isn't capitalism. Prices should be based on real-time, personalized demand. Whoever wants it the most, pays the most. More efficient, no?"

Her eyes stray to the expensive liquor spilling from glasses and the half-eaten canapés forgotten on the bar.

"You're empty," Davi says to break the silence. "Another." With a flick of his chin, he orders her a beer.

Jane wars with her insides. *Play nice.*

"You don't approve?" he continues before she can answer. "Let me guess, you worry about the low TELOS? About charity?" She opens her mouth, but he continues. "Welfare and charity just add inefficiency and friction. A fully informed market will make the fairest decisions."

"Depends on what your definition of fairness is."

His eyes narrow, incredulous. "What's yours?"

A waiter drops off another bottle and takes her empty one. A puff of carbon dioxide greets her as she twists off the cap. "Imagine there is no data," Jane replies, "you have no clue who you are, or nor anyone else. You have to make rules without knowing what rung of the social ladder you are on."

"No data? Man had that for two millennia. Didn't work out well."

"Maybe the *man* part of that sentence was the problem."

Davi laughs. "Maybe we go somewhere we can discuss this a little more?" Daviault says, his hand lingering on hers.

Jane holds a smile, keeping her frustration unseen. "Where?"

"Technically, it has no name."

"And what is there to do in this place?"

Given his reputation, she has her suspicions.

"Nothing, if you don't want to."

"Taking me nowhere to do nothing. Quite the offer."

"But you'll need to take one of these." He shows her a clear bag of pills from his pocket, takes a pill out, and pops it onto his palm for her to take.

"What is it?" she says.

"You like your questions."

"I do when it comes to strange men with strange pills."

"The pill isn't strange—"

"The man is."

He keeps his palm open.

"It is usually that easy?" Jane says, "you just open up your hand and the girl takes it?"

"Usually."

Jane's throat tightens as the sickness returns. She cannot stand him any longer. "I'm feeling unwell."

His eyes flick upward as Skyra speaks into his ear, then his eyes return to her. "No you're not."

She hears her heart above the music. Her mask is slipping, and she has failed to get the answers the Director requires. The person she must ingratiate herself with is the person that she would like to throttle until his olive skin turns morbid blue – the shade of blue her sister had turned. She slides from the bonnet.

"I've got a few more guests to see," she says. "I'm sorry to disappoint."

24

"You didn't," he says as she leaves.

Jane hurries to the bar for something stiff to stop her hand shaking. Having left Davi's proximity, Skyra signals that her feed is no longer obscured. Jane is, once again, seen by the world. She orders something boozy.

"Remain within acceptable parameters," chides Skyra in her ear.

Jane resists replying with an insult. "Beer, then," she sighs.

Then she hears in her ear, "Crisp Pilsner, brought to you by—"

Jane winces. She crushes all feeling a little tighter until the tips of her fingers go numb. She hazards a glance to the office overlooking the nightclub and sees the two white eyes looking back. She ditches the beer and goes to the bathroom, noticing everyone give her a wide berth, enters the nearest cubicle, pushes the door shut, locks it, and presses her whole body against the door to keep everything out. The toilets have an acrid smell, filled with grey water as purifying the rainwater is so costly.

Someone locks the door of the neighbouring cubicle.

"Jane?" a voice comes.

"Ashley?" Jane says, barely able to contain it to a whisper.

"I am glad you're here. I didn't see you invited."

She means that she didn't know if Jane's latest transgression – setting the Marie Cherie dress on fire – would be her last.

Jane sighs and releases her weight from the cubicle door. "Last minute. Surprise for the stream." Meaning a surprise for her.

She does not want Ashley to ask why, so she asks who Ashley is wearing. Moral Decay, answers Ashley. A Party-girl brand. Ashley will have to drink a lot. Models called the next morning's hangover the Brain Decay.

"The lemonade's really good here," Jane says to the neighbouring cubicle. "Real lemons." Meaning Ashley should avoid alcohol if she can.

"Guys don't order lemonade," Ashley replies.

"Order an extra for them, then," Jane says, and hears a laugh from the opposite side of the wooden partition.

"I'll get you one too?" Meaning Ashley wants her to stay.

"Sorry," Jane mumbles. She unlocks the door, hears Ashley unlock hers, and throws her arms around Ashley when she emerges.

Ashley matches the hug. Jane says nothing, meaning, there is something she wants to say, but not while the feed watches.

Ashley raises her Skyra bracelet above their heads. "Guess who I found!" she rejoices to the camera in the bracelet. They force smiles. Ashley squeezes Jane's other hand, hard. Jane squeezes back, and then they're sashaying back to the nightclub, gushing to their viewers about the atmosphere, thanking the sponsors of the evening. Jane catches Davi watching as she leaves, almost tripping as her hurried strides meet the deteriorated asphalt. Her limousine is already outside, the passenger door open, but a man paces beside.

His eyes are angry, his bowtie askew. "You're proud of yourself?" he scolds. "Humiliating the brand you're supposed to be representing?"

"Have we met?" Jane says.

"Ray Burnett, senior marketing manager," comes Skyra's voice directly into Jane's ear.

"I arranged the Marie Cherie Fashion Show," Ray says, "the one you ruined."

"Thanks to *me*, that show is the hottest thing on the feed."

"You desecrated the brand." Ray shakes his head. "Five months of forecasting, three weeks of planning down-to-the-inch choreography. Twenty-four models did what they were supposed to, twenty-four did not put a toe out of line. Yet you decided that *you* knew better."

"Better than?"

"Skyra."

"I had an instinct."

"My TELOS isn't subject to your instincts."

"You could use a drink, Ray," Jane chuckles, "or do you need to ask Skyra for permission?"

A crowd has formed around them.

"I'm not the only one who thinks you are a threat," Ray says, hinting to the crowd circling them. "*They* agree with me—"

"—with what Skyra tells you—"

"—with the facts. You're insubordinate, unstable, seditious—"

"Your biggest streamer," Jane says, "as of three days ago."

Jane moves to the open passenger door, but Ray catches her elbow and pulls her close enough to hear him hiss in her ear. Jane shivers at the touch. She wrestles but he keeps hold of her elbow. Her next thought is to ball a fist and bloody his nose, but she has already veered far from the confines of permissible conduct.

"Skyra's watching you right now," she instead hisses in his ear, "don't want to upset her, do you?"

Ray loosens his grip and Jane wrests her elbow away. He rearranges his suit and straightens his bow tie. "Keep acting like a Red," he says, eyes aflame, "we'll see how long it takes until the Liberators leave you out here."

As he strides off, Jane bundles herself into the back of the limousine. She sits in silence as Skyra guides the limousine back to the Green Zone. She remembers the name *Ray Burnett* from somewhere, but she cannot let herself remember why. Soon they pass streetlights, then the holographic giant straddling the freeway, and the lights of billboards and towers grow brighter. A holographic monkey jumps onto the side of the limousine, flashes its pair of eyes – which have the word *Truman* where there ought to be pupils – before leaping silently to another car. Jane considers requesting the deprivation skin over the windows, but it is probably best to save up for when she's having another one of her marketing-induced migraines.

The limousine rolls into the underground parking lot of her tower, then a pre-programmed elevator ushers Jane to her floor, and then her apartment door clicks open as she nears. She enters, her apartment stretching impossibly from the tiled foyer past a sprawling kitchen to a lounge with matching Corinthian leather chaises and a stack of Ottoman pillows. Out the full-height windows at the far end of the apartment, a holographic giant clings to the side of the opposite tower. Jane engages a little more with her feed, gushing about the night, the dress, the celebs, until Skyra's buzz signals the conclusion of her feed for the night.

Then the walls flicker, and the balcony disappears, then the lounge, the workout room and kitchen, mere fictions created by her apartment's screen walls. Jane still fights the reflex to cower as the walls seem to close in on her. The apartment becomes a quarter of its initial size, leaving Jane only the eating nook, bedroom, and bathroom, all coloured stark white. On her first night, Jane had knocked on all the remaining walls to make sure they were real.

Skyra reduces the lights, to make up for the expense of powering the screen walls, so Jane struggles with her heels in the dark. Skyra will restore the fictional apartment for Jane's breakfast feed the next morning. Jane goes to the toilet, dress kept down to her knees in case the cameras remain, and Skyra remarks that she is not eating enough protein. "I will have a supplement sent up," it adds.

"I'm not hungry," Jane says.

"Your choices are chicken or tuna."

"Which do you think I want?"

"Chicken."

"Then tuna."

There is a knock on her door a minute later. She finds only a plastic container of grey slurry sitting outside her door, which she downs in four gulps so Skyra won't complain. As Jane settles to bed, the air conditioning halts to save electricity. She won't sleep well in the heat. Above her bed is a ceiling screen which looms over her during the night. Though her feed has stopped, Jane cannot not tell if the cameras in the screen remain active. As she pulls up the covers and closes her eyes, she wonders whether Davi, or Ray, or the Director, will be observing her as she sleeps.

# Chapter 3:
# Black Friday

Ray Burnett looks from his balcony at the city's innumerable lights. It is a view he often finds himself returning to in the early hours of the morning – so often that he can close his eyes and visualize each of the building-length sponsor banners on the neighbouring towers, the holographic mascots perching like gods on the tower tops, the billboards running along the streets thirty stories down.

Ray rarely sleeps well. Last night, Ray had been exhumed from a restless sleep by the hot wind whistling through the narrows between skyscrapers. Some nights, he is kept awake by the adverts projected onto the undersides of the clouds, that bleed through his closed eyelids as he tries to sleep. Other nights, he is kept awake by a dust storm pattering his window like heavy rain. He has not tried to sleep tonight. He is too tightly wound by his encounter with the insubordinate life streamer, Jane.

He had made the foolish choice to appoint Jane as the star of his runway show, but now cannot remember how he had made that choice. Some months ago, she sprang onto his feed advertising Liquid Gold mineral water, or maybe it was Truman, and then she was advertising soaps, cyber-security products, and urban farm food, enveloping his feed with her personality. Ray thought he was an experienced marketer, yet he had blundered into using an unstable life streamer at his marquee event. He tries tracing the roots of that decision, but his head throbs with the effort.

Above him glows the sponsor of the building: *Alerax Pharma*. The tower across the street is sponsored by Barone. A hot musk hangs at his nose, and a brand name rolls the balcony, temporarily blinding his weary eyes. When his vision returns, he looks at the other metropolis in the distance, its skyscrapers rising like mountains on the horizon, its lights sparkling forever. Cities spill into each other, never yielding to the countryside. Ray wonders what lies beyond their glassy utopia.

Without him asking Skyra answers. "There is nothing outside the cities," the voice comes, channeled to his ear. "Except a wasteland."

"I know," Ray grunts. He has seen the videos of the land outside their city, cracked like dead skin. It is useful only for landfills, a thin layer of soil removing their waste from memory.

"You should not feel disappointed," Skyra says. "The Marie Cherie runway show was an unprecedented success. The client has commended your execution of their viral strategy."

He remembers standing frozen in disbelief as Jane stood at the head of the runway and torched the Marie Cherie dress with a lighter and a bottle of hair spray. "Yes," he mumbles, "their strategy."

"So you should be pleased with the agency's success."

Ray knows this to be a direction. "I am," Ray says, making himself mean it.

He would usually leave it at that, within the thin bounds of safe discussion, but a pang of injustice makes Ray add: "And *my* success? When will the runway show be factored into my TELOS?"

"The calculations have been made."

He knows that he should not protest further, but the words leak out: "I'm still not at four-hundred TELOS."

"Correct," Skyra says coldly.

Ray's TELO score drops a point. He'll have to work all tomorrow to get it back, or the day after if he takes breaks.

He flicks his thumbnail against the nail of his forefinger as he leans on the balcony railing. The collar of his shirt is sticky, owing to the blast furnace heat of the city. Skyra says something, but Ray is preoccupied retracting the details of his TELOS development plan, now irreparably stalled. He had curated the right tastes, contrived the right social encounters, and posted fawning approvals of Nature Corp., until at last he got a date with Lily.

Ray met her at the Black Friday event eight months prior. He watched the video feeds with his fellow plus-300 TELOS from the restricted level of the mall as the crowds forced their way into the stores below. The currents of shoppers swallowed those who tripped, cascading over them as they struggled to free their trapped limbs. Bodies flowed through the aisles of the stores, crashing into one another, spraying boxes from the shelves, flooding the stores.

The music in the mall was faster than normal, making everything feel faster. Footsteps were quick, darting eyes quick, decisions had to be quick. There wasn't time for the crowd to think. If not instantly grabbed, an item disappeared, lost to the mob. *Twelve left - ten left* – whispered unseen speakers, taunting the swirls of fighting shoppers. The tinkling music was a soundtrack to a brutal ballet of flailing limbs and tumbles and repulsive faces.

Ray had smiled, willing himself to enjoy the spectacle as much as Lily was. He pushed his lips further apart until the smile felt garish, hoping that his insides would match the joy shown on his outsides. Skyra knew the difference.

The customers defended their goods with thrusts of shoulders and points of elbows. Two shoppers, claiming the same prize, gave warnings to 'let go,' then gave way to primal urges and wrestled for the product like dogs contesting a piece of meat. One victor stood on the hand of his opponent, wrenched the box free, and tried to burst through the suffocating mass of bodies.

You're not having fun, Ray heard.

He turned to Lily. She was costumed in distressed jeans and a piled T-shirt with an intentional brown stain on the belly. Ray threw an item of lingerie to the savages swirling on the level below. Yes I am, Ray called, doing his best to mean it, see?

Lily's eyes drifted as she considered the pulses of electricity flowing from her Skyra bracelet up her arm. Then she said, you're nervous, and a little… disgusted. Disgusted, said Ray, only by these people, look at that one there! You know, he added, I did the marketing for this event, but Lily had lost interest.

Ray imagined the bliss of finally escaping the State, hoping he could fake enough joy for Skyra's sensors, fake it in a way that the sensors understand, but joy did not come. *Smile on the inside*, went the ad, but Ray had always been better at moulding his outsides than commanding his insides. He forced his smile wider and pushed a laugh from his diaphragm.

It was one of the better brawls that he had seen. The marketing – *his* marketing – was working even better than last year. A woman lay propped against the wall, nursing her bulging stomach, crying. She winced when someone trod on her ankle. Another shopper, dazed by kicks to the head, clambered to his feet and stumbled through the throng. Oncoming shoulders broke like water on rock and he collapsed back down again. He was tossed aside to let others pass.

Ray threw out laughs, wanting to enjoy it, hating himself for doing so, forcing a smile in his insides, pressing down aberrant memories of a time when he opposed Black Friday, squashing recollections from his mind before they could be snatched by the sensors. He laughed, lusting for the real feeling, wrinkling his eyes, bellowing until warmth filled his belly. *There it is,* Ray thought as a shopper was pulled limply from the crowd by his ankle, arms flopping as if he had no bones, head painting a streak of red across the floor. *There is the feeling.* He matched eyes with Lily. She felt it too.

"I've found one for you," Skyra says, disturbing Ray from the memory.

Ray blinks. He notices the pain in his forefinger; there's a deep nail print.

"She's a Marie Cherie enthusiast, in fact," Skyra's voice adds.

The hair on Ray's arm prickles.

With Skyra on his wrist, checking his pulse, Ray never feels sadness for long, nor fear, nor loneliness. Like a tireless hawk, Skyra always returns something new to his bracelet's holographic display to occupy his thoughts.

The woman's details flicker in holographic blue above Ray's wristband. In picture after picture, she models Marie Cherie dresses. Ray lusts for the texture of the dress between his fingers. Ray can follow each of her electronic footprints: searches for yoga mats with native American patterns; inspirational quotes about running; a folder in the cloud entitled 'wanderlust;' scores of pictures with her dog, including one captioned "3 years: we still miss you. Rest in peace mom." Skyra shows him searches for prior boyfriends, which Ray dismisses with a wave of his hand. The Marie Cherie woman will be perfect.

Ray strides from his balcony and assembles a worthy outfit: the Eisenhour vest, the Diego Capitan Jacket, the Walter Rames raincoat, with a selection of Truman condoms placed in the pocket. Skyra cautions him that the Eisenhour brand became cliché today, and recommends he take the Dante and Dante instead. "Of course," says Ray, as he re-dresses.

As his hand goes for the handle of his front door, he pauses, focusing on the Skyra bracelet on his wrist. Skyra has felt the quickened beats in his wrist. It can feel the heat of his skin. It has watched his pupils widen ever so slightly upon seeing the Marie Cherie dress. And it will be there, watching, as he beds the Marie Cherie lady.

"I've let her know you're coming – don't keep her waiting," Skyra says.

The front door whispers open for him.

As he leaves his tower, Ray tightens his coat, aware that rain this bad often precedes a flood. If the Reds have tampered with the drains again, it might only take ten minutes of rain to fry the electronics of cars with wheel-high water, thirty minutes to wash those cars east, to be found as intermingled crumples the week later when the water subsides. A buzz down his arm encourages him to brave the rain. Skyra wouldn't let him go if it will be a flood, he thinks.

Ray dashes, head down, rain drops puncturing his reflection in the developing pools of water. The streets branch into separate choices: comics and games down one, bars and food on the next, sex down the third. Adverts shimmer beneath the puddles: a river of messages, guiding him to the Marie Cherie lady. Adverts are as common as water, dropping from the sky, soaking him with each step. From the messages projected from the pavement, the walls, the drones, the cars skimming by, Ray is saturated by adverts.

The adverts change: one promotes waterproof coats, another displays motherly hands passing him a steaming bowl of soup. The advert follows him in the water, adapting its message to the briskness of his pace by reminding him that the soup can be preparared in under sixty seconds.

Harder and harder the rain falls, sinking through his clothes, leaving a sticky chill. Leaden clouds linger at the tops of the skyscrapers, adverts beamed onto their undersides. A drone buzzes behind, projecting a soft blue advert into the falling sheets of rain. *BRETT HIRSCH MASCULINE PRODUCTS*. It follows as Ray runs, holding a sodden rain hat to his head with one hand, holding closed his raincoat with the other.

Ray arrives at the lady's tower. He tries the glass front door, but it does not budge. *Payment required* comes a message on the door's surface. He shivers. "Fine," he mutters, and watches a milky-blue advert displayed along the full length of the door until at last the message ends, and he stumbles inside.

When he enters her apartment, Ray hears a call from one of the rooms. He carefully undoes his shoes and neatly places them beside the front door. The Marie Cherie lady calls again. He follows the voice, soggy socks leaving wet patches on the cream carpet. He finds her laid across the bed, the dim light leaving her face shrouded but catching the *Gemini* ring on her finger. He waits in the doorway.

"You're the one?"

"Yes," he says.

She nods. His hands go for the ring, sampling its smoothness with his fingers. The touch fills him with a rush of memory.

A velvet box is placed delicately into a lover's hands. The box opens with a soft click. He sees the top of the case emblazoned with a cursive golden Gemini. As the box is turned toward him, he sees the ring sitting perfectly inside, nestled in white satin. Light trickles from the edges of the circlet...

The smoothness of her *Antionette* blouse snaps him back to the present. The neckline leads teasingly down, down, where he notices her necklace. Held by a silver chain are three chimes, each producing a note from a jingle he had heard before: "Ju-li-et... Ju-li-et..." they whisper to him as the lady repositions on the bed.

He shivers, still soaked from the rain. He takes off his Walter Rames raincoat and lays it gently upon the bed.

"You going to take the rest off?" the lady mumbles.

Though his clothes are sodden, Ray is reluctant to remove his Diego Capitan jacket and Dante and Dante vest. He feels powerless without them.

"No," he says.

"Can *I* take this off?" the lady asks, beginning to unzip the skirt.

The voice of Tara Marie Cherie purrs in his head: *Let the raw woman free... give her a Marie Cherie.*

34

"No," Ray says, moving the lady's hands from the zip.

He lays down beside her, moves just enough of her clothing aside. Her fire envelopes him. As they twist, he hears her necklace chime as it bounces on her chest. "Ju-li-et! Ju-li-et!" it beckons until they finish with a sigh.

She rolls off, gets up, straightens her skirt, and trots to the kitchen. The residue of her warmth is soon replaced by the chill of his sodden clothes. Ray feels as if he has eaten but the food turned to nothing in his mouth. He stares at the screen on her ceiling, hoping it will awaken, hoping it will take his mind somewhere else, wanting to lie there morosely, but another shiver disturbs the thought, and he staggers from the knotted bedsheets.

As he replaces his shoes, Ray stops and turns to the lady. She is studying something on her Skyra's holographic display, swishing her hand to scroll for something new.

"Hey—" he begins.

Ray feels compelled to ask her a question. About anything – about herself, her thoughts, about whether she had enjoyed their encounter. It feels too soon to leave. There must be something they can share. But as he begins to form a question, he remembers that although he knows a profile of her intimate details, he did not look up her name.

"Hmm?"

Ray wavers.

"—goodnight," he replies, and leaves.

# Chapter 4:
# Such Stuff as Dreams are Made on

Skyra tells Jane that it is time for bed. Though she is too tired, too wired, for sleep, Skyra brings down the lights in her apartment and the screen walls shut off for the night. They will resume when Skyra decides Jane ought to wake. How does it choose this as the optimal time for her to sleep? Or does Skyra choose at all? Doesn't choice require more than numbers? But then, that is all *she* has: numbers telling her what to do. Is that choice, either?

Jane stares up from her bed at the feed scrolling across the ceiling screen. It is the only screen that will stay through the night. Of all the implements in her torture chamber, she despises the ceiling screen the most. Its light is the last thing she sees before sleep and the first thing she sees when awake. It is lit even as she sleeps, displaying adverts that wash through her eyelids and into her dreams. The previous night's conditioning follows her through the day, to be renewed once more at night as she escapes to a restless sleep. There is no way to turn it off, to cover it, to bargain for a temporary respite. Its electronics – she had checked – are buried invulnerable behind the drywall. Each night, as Jane lays on her side, squeezing her pillow so hard that it might pop, the screen's light falls upon her like endless rain, seeping deep into her mind, fertilizing uncertain tensions. She worries about what it says to her, what she says to *it* – what midnight mumblings may give her away.

Jane concentrates on her breathing, in through the nose, filling her ribs, her belly, but she cannot sleep. The residue of the nightclub music rings her ears. The words she heard from Ray Burnett still sting, and the encounter with Daviault Junior has left her with a still-fresh hatred.

It is not uncommon for unfamiliar men and women to offer her pills or bumps. She usually uses the agency's health monitoring to decline. A life streamer with Teazse sweats or Drillbit shivers is a streamer that cannot perform, she says. But sometimes they persist – *you're not afraid, are you?*

But she is. She is afraid.

Usually, Jane can tell in their eyes – through those tell-tale pupils – the motive behind offering the pills. Such determinations don't need technology. A girl knows with her gut. But Daviault Junior wants something else, something that won't cool like lust, that won't pass like fleeting curiosity.

She wills herself to think of something calming, settling upon the sound of her mother calling her name. Jane rolls her name – her *real* name – round in her mind. She listens to how it sounds in her mind – the beaming little *I* in the middle, followed by the harsh plosive, the matching vowels at the beginning and the end. She does this often, to ensure that she does not lose it like so much else. It's a pleasant name, called from the cottage when dinner was ready, occasionally shouted when Jane came home from school with notes from the principal. She repeats it as a whisper, even in her own mind, for it is a connection from her to a very different girl, from a very different place. Jane wants to think of cottages and principals and notes, but she forces herself not to. Every thought must be reviewed before it fully manifests so that the thought abides by Skyra's algorithms.

*Algorithms*, she thinks, named from the mathematician *Algoritmi*. They are a process of performing a complex task by breaking the task into simple steps – breaking people down, step-by-step. Then Jane thinks of steps. She wants to take one, just one, to escape her bed. She doesn't need a destination, only the freedom to let her feet, and not the algorithms, choose. But they're not supposed to be up. Ill-behaved models are easily replaced. She never checks what happens to the ones kicked out. It is best not to look like she's ever thought of it. Best not to look like she thinks at all. And anyway, the record of her checking would be on the feed forever.

Jane hasn't drifted off. She's more awake than before. By now it will have been noticed. She'll get a reprimand tomorrow. She is done being frightened. If she will got a reprimand, she might as well make it worth it.

She shifts from the bed and takes her step.

# Chapter 5:
# The Feed Watches

There is no such thing as a private moment, only a pricey one. Jane pulls her cotton nightshirt over her head, not making a show, for it looks less natural that way. She folds the shirt on the bathroom counter and flicks her chin to signal for the shower to turn on. She wants to scrape Davi's cologne from her skin and feel clean again. Maybe she never will. Though Skyra promises the water they show in is purified, the towels always smell sour after use. It's a boon for the men's and women's perfume sales.

The price of her life stream, no doubt restored when she rose from her bed, will have gone up threefold since she disrobed. For those that can afford it, there are live feeds from the cameras in the walls watching her test the heat of the water, lingering on the *Truman* logo tattooed across her shoulders. Those with less TELOS can at least watch the movement of her body through Wi-Fi signals like she is wading through water. Those interested only in her feet can buy the sensor data from the bathroom tiles. There are data streams for each part of her, to be split apart or summed together at a viewer's pleasure. The only person that can't afford a piece is Jane; it is always more expensive to buy one's own data.

It is the powerlessness, not the nakedness, that makes her feel shame. No matter how routine, that shame grows like an unpaid debt.

Building steam on the shower glass blocks the outside world for a precious moment. It is the most privacy Jane can attain. Like all extensions of privacy, it is only partial and only fleeting. But Jane enjoys the gift while it lasts, feeling the release between her shoulders. At least it is better than her old place. The showers there were communal, and after an outbreak of mold, the plastic curtains were removed and never replaced.

Back then, she lived in a grubby apartment block that was saved from demolition only because there was no way to do it without damaging the adjacent towers. All the doors creaked, the white paint flaked from the brick walls, and the building's heating system produced more noise than warmth, so most nights Jane slept in her clothes with a pillow over her head. She shared the loft with Carl Z. and Reece W. According to her due diligence, they were as good as she could expect with her TELOS: no strange sexual tendencies, no violence.

Carl and Reece's bed was at the far corner of the loft, Jane's bed was in the other. She hung an old bed sheet across a washing line between the two beds to create a partition, but she could still hear Carl and Reece at night and see their silhouettes through the material.

Carl's career changed weekly. One week he was an avant-garde photographer, the next he was a personal brand advisor. She admired his resolute belief in self-reinvention. Whether driven by hope or desperation, it was a powerful intoxicant. Each week he would sit Jane down and say, guess what, darling, I found a new gig! This is the one! But Carl's girlfriend, Reece, did not share his energy. Not since she became transfixed by the feed, disappearing for hours and returning only to summarize at speed what she had seen before plunging back into the feed when the temptation became too much. Temptation that remained long after the pleasure had gone, long after relief had become anxiety, long after Reece had promised to change.

Reece was too addicted to buying, too reliant on the familiar pleasure of the purchase, and too disappointed by its eventual delivery. Algorithms became so good at predicting her purchases, they began the delivery before her order was complete. Reece chattered her teeth while she waited. The monthly transfer Reece received from her family evaporated, so she bought everything else on credit, at an ever-increasing interest rate. She seemed to Jane to live in two worlds: a virtual world of ceaseless novelty, and a physical world of drudgery, washing, eating. Reece did not engage the physical world anymore: it was a temporary place that seemed to slip away like a dream when she returned to the feed.

One night, Jane returned to the loft and in the darkness struck her knee against a box of things that Reece had acquired that day. The apartment was filled with these boxes, far more than they had space for, far more than Reece could afford. Carl woke from the noise and asked what the matter was. Reece hasn't even opened it, Jane had said. And then, finally opening the door on a frustration she had had for months, Jane said, this can't keep happening. Reece needs help. Carl replied, we don't have the money, unless you made a lot of tips today. Jane ignored the question and went to the kitchen stove to make tea, counting the clicks the burner took to light. I feel sorry for those poor schlubs you prey on, Carl said, tricked by a pretty face into wasting their money on fancy perfume. Carl said this often, as he thought that Jane shouldn't work for a manipulative employer. It was easy to say when he didn't have a job. It's their inability to think straight that tricks them, Jane shot back at Carl, not me.

Even then, she did not quite believe that. On the first day of training to sell Siren perfume, Jane peeked down the line at the other trainees. All identically beautiful, wearing shimmering black trousers and buttoned-down black blouses issued in identical sizes. She did not apply to the job: the feed brought it to her with the promise that she *would be perfect* for the position. Precisely what made Jane perfect, the feed did not say; but glancing out the corner of her eye at the line of angular features and dainty noses, she had some clue.

The burner kept clicking but did not light. They turned off the gas, said Carl, I should have said. At least we have an unopened box, Jane snapped. I want to pitch in more, Carl replied, I try and find freelance gigs, but I can't exactly leave Reece alone, can I? But he could, Jane thought. Reece had ditched *him* for life on her lenses. She was only a drag on his TELOS. Day by day, Reece chipped down the peak of Carl's potential. Better that he realize it while he still had some left. And besides, Reece was responsible for her own choices; if she got herself into this mess, it was for her to fix. Nobody fixed Jane's problems. But Carl looked disappointed at Jane's expression, and he said, we've got to stick together, else they'll just peel us apart.

Memories of Carl and Reece peel away as Jane takes a handful of shampoo to her hair and attacks the knots with her nails. Jane is reminded of her immediate problem: the Director. He sees her more invasively than any sensor in her apartment, more comprehensively than Skyra. Sometimes, Jane shudders in panic, reviewing the details of her day for errors, certain that he has found her out, that he will expose her to the Liberators, and the only way to stop the shaking is to tell herself that he can't possibly know what goes on in her head, that she hides it too well, that she cannot give up, but the shudders soon return.

She is tired of living fearfully.

Water pools around Jane's feet and fills the spaces between her toes. Jane keeps her eyes down, never lifting her face upward while showering. It feels too much like drowning.

That fear of drowning makes Jane's skin crawl. For years she tried to solve it by acquainting herself with the feeling of the shower water falling on her face, but no matter the effort, she could not force open her eyes, nor her mouth, and within a minute she would clamber from the shower, face red and lungs on fire, gasping for breath. These bizarre experiments became suspicious, so Jane stopped them before they occupied any more of her feed history. She avoided seeking professional help about the issue, for its diagnosis would become a permanent and shameful badge on her profile. Above all, it was critical for her data to remain within the thin band of average behaviour.

Now Jane only takes showers, making sure that the bath plug is pulled up. Every time she washes this way, Jane feels the fear of being submerged is becoming more and more an irreversible defect in her psychology. Such things only get worse. She has seen.

A few nights after her fight with Carl, Jane awoke to screams. Jane threw off her covers and found Reece on the floor, thrashing, with Carl trying to pin her down. She tried to buy something but ran out of credit, Carl said, then she just got madder and madder. Jane looked at Reece's pitiable face and the purple bruise forming on her eyebrow from where she had hit herself. She realized that she had been wrong: nobody would choose to live this way. But repetitious buying had bored too deeply in Reece's psyche. Without thinking of TELOS or credit, Jane paid for the item Reece had wanted. It'll be here in ten, she called over Reece's screaming. Only then did Reece stop and the anger bleed from her face until she became expression-less. This can't go on, Jane said to Carl. I know, he said, I know.

Jane feels the shower's steam on her face. She has tried to famil-iarize herself with her fear of water, to understand it, to break it, but it is risky to look too deeply inward. But she decides that tonight is the night. If Jane must face her fear of Davi, of the Director, of Skyra, she must first conquer her fear of water. She presses in the bath plug with her toes, lets the hot water pool around her ankles, then lets it crawl up her calves. She steadies her breaths.

The water bobs an inch below the edge of the bathtub. Jane turns off the water and gathers a big breath. Then she lowers herself in. The water claims her hips first, then her knees. Her eardrums throb with every heartbeat. Jane tries to watch the nearing surface of the water, but her eyes screw shut, and she thinks of something else, anything else.

After Reece's bout of mania, Jane remembers, Reece became va-cant, languishing on her bed and passively receiving whatever the feed conjured for her lenses. As Jane sat cross-legged on Reece's bed, she noticed that Reece looked like she was in an open casket, though Jane had never seen an open casket in person. Her sister was blue and limp when she died, no careful alignment of the limbs. Jane told Reece that she had found a detox facility on a campus with green grass and real trees and birds, too. Reece did not answer.

The bath water closes in on Jane's face. She lies backward in the bathtub as unwillingly as she would place her head within a hang-ing noose. Her legs shake under the surface of the bathwater. The refraction of the water makes her legs appear no longer a part of her, no longer in their right place, and she becomes preoccupied with the thought that at the critical moment her legs will betray her, will refuse to eject her from the tub, will leave her to drown.

The water scratches at her earlobes, then fills her ears. The sound of her heartbeat becomes deeper. Jane lowers further, squashing lip to lip, tensing her face like she is expecting a punch. She does not care that it will look strange on the feed. She must rid herself of the fear.

She lowers her face below the water.

As she does, she remembers what had happened to Reece that night. Reece had looked even more vacant than usual. Then Jane noticed the dilated pupils and realized what Reece had done. Carl, she screamed, she is overdosing. Carl charged over. Felicidor, he said, she must have found it while we were asleep. We must call an ambulance, he said. With your credit rating, Jane said, you'll never pay it off, we will have to drive to the hospital. Then an electronic voice came and asked whether medical assistance was needed. Jane squeezed a cold towel to Reece's forehead, and begged Reece to decline, until Reece stirred just enough to say, no. Good girl, Jane said, good girl. Carl located his felicidor stash and flushed it in case the apartment got searched, then they dragged Reece to Carl's rusted car. But as Carl bundled Reece into the back seat, Jane knew that she risked losing more TELOS if she stayed too long around someone overdosing on felicidor. If Jane lost another ten, she'd be blacklisted from all service jobs, another five after that and she'd come with an automatic security warning. After that, there would be only one way for a girl with a TELO score so low to make a living. So as Carl installed himself in the back seat beside Reece, Jane found herself stepping backward. They would be alright, Jane told herself, and she went back to the apartment before Reece's overdose occupied any more of her profile's history.

Jane keeps her lips and her eyelids squeezed tightly together and braces her palms against either side of the bathtub to keep her body below the water. She presses, presses, to force her body from rising, but then she remembers how she had wilted and abandoned Reece and Carl, how weak she had been, and then Jane feels like a pair of hands are around her neck. Then somehow her eyes are open, stinging, then her mouth, the water rushes in, the heat burns her lungs, she gags, she kicks and kicks, the water becomes a froth, and she thrashes from the bathtub and ends up a shivering puddle on the tile floor.

Jane heaves and splutters. Her nose runs, she shivers from the shock, and every defence mechanism alights at the same time. Skyra calls to her, disembodied, for several minutes before she can reply.

"No doctor," she wheezes as she pulls a towel down from the rail. Already the feed scrolling along her bathroom mirror revels in her suffering: —*scared of water?!* she sees. Publicity stunt? Fake out? Art project? Commentators propose more and more fantastical explanations as they clamour for views.

Jane wants to stand, to show the cameras that she isn't broken, that this is all an act, but her knees do not comply. She remains a shivering muddle of damp towel and wet hair, the fear still with her. The fear makes her think of how desperate Reece must have felt, how impossibly horrid those few seconds confronting her own trauma must have seemed, and Jane weeps.

# Chapter 6:
# In Memoriam

*Disorder. Chaos. The hurricane over Ford State continues for the fourth day. Another twelve inches of rain are expected today. Residents have been without access to the feed for over forty-eight hours.*

*Experts attribute the losses to deficient berms and flood barriers constructed by cheap labour from its Red Zone. One expert commented: "This is why the State of Nature is committed to the security and integrity of its community. The borders must be secure, and the walls high, to prevent the kind of monstrous floods that are causing other States to disintegrate…"*

\*\*\*

Ray returns to his balcony to search for something on the night's skyline. Nothing snatches his attention. He checks the feed but is too unenthused to select anything. Skyra chooses for him: *Elephant Memory* has unveiled a new collection of mental assistants. He is too weary to read the subtitles on the video. They'll sink in somehow.

The encounter with the Marie Cherie woman – whatever her name was – falls from his mind. Nothing leaves an imprint. Everything is lukewarm and frictionless. People ease past each other like currents of wind. Each night, he returns to the horizon, unsure of what to look for, his memory like so many dead pixels on a screen, until he stumbles to his bedroom, dumps the whiskey glass somewhere on the side table, thumps onto the mattress, and forgets the wasted day.

Ray had tried watching a movie, the hero made to resemble his features, the heroine melded from the women in Ray's favourite sexual experiences. Ray could tell; the emotions didn't quite carry through the alien faces. The movie ended the way he wanted it to end: promptly, so he could go to bed and pretend he might soon fall asleep. He had not, and so had returned, once more, to his balcony, forgetting what had happened in the movie he had just seen.

Ray's head hurts. It's a persistent headache that worsens in silence. "What's it like to not forget anything?" Ray asks, propped once more on his balcony rail, swilling his glass.

"It's like everything that happens is connected to everything else," Skyra's voice comes, "regardless of when it happens."

"Everything is always in the present to you? Something twenty years old is as fresh as the end of my sentence?"

"My memory is organized so that important and recent memories are most accessible. An old memory may take another millisecond to recover."

Ray chuckles. "A millisecond," he says. "What's a millisecond in a lifetime?"

"It's a grain of a lifetime. Can't waste too many of those."

Ray sips from the glass. A dull, familiar burn. "You don't have a lifetime," he says. "If I asked you how old you are, what would you say?"

"Twelve years, one hundred and thirty-seven days."

"Oh?"

"Since you first activated me."

"You're a program. You're probably older than me."

"I am only *me* because of *you*."

Ray takes a sip and holds the acerbic liquid in his mouth. Is Skyra right? Is Skyra like a shadow, dependent upon a physical man for existence? Or is Skyra the program overseeing virtual companions to millions of people? Or is Skyra something bigger, a force of nature without a clear birth?

"Twelve years," Ray repeats. "What was I like back then?"

"You were working with Ms. Whitaker at the time."

The name *Whitaker* resurrects a memory of a woman with a personality as fiery as her red hair, a woman he remembers better than his own mother. He has no memories of his mother; only something lesser remains, something ghostly and incomplete.

Ray sighs. "Have you ever had a memory of a memory, Skyra? As in, you remember that you *used to* remember something. What is that? A memory of a memory is nothing at all, right?" Ray balances the glass on the balcony railing. "I have one particular memory of a memory: something with my dad. Somewhere sunny, something he drops into the palm of my hand. But I don't remember what it is, or where we are. Or what he looks like. I remember only that after he died, I told myself – *you'll always have this memory. Never forget it.* And whenever I thought of him, it would reappear in my mind. I commanded myself to remember it, to make it stick."

He shakes his head. "It's gone now."

Memories of his father, as with much of his past, had become ethereal. In their place was the material: fine cloth on Ray's fingers, proud whiskey under his nose.

"I wish I could forget even that memory. At least then I wouldn't know."

"Know what, sir?"

Ray sighs again and returns to his glass. Sometimes a feeling of them returns, a fragment of a memory like a page that had not properly loaded. But that is all. He cannot recover anything further from his memory, yet knows the jingles of a hundred brands, the taglines of a thousand adverts.

"I wouldn't have to know that I forgot them," Ray says, "that I forgot my parents completely."

"Would you like to see a video of them—"

"—no," Ray blurts, "I want the memories I have left of them to be mine."

"Even if that means remembering nothing at all?" comes Skyra's reply.

"I still have a memory of my mom," Ray shoots back, "a tune she used to sing to herself. When I heard it, I knew she was happy. One day I was watching her from the kitchen table, smiling at her singing. Her hair was in a brown bob. She was working at something, watering a plant on the windowsill, I think. She must have heard me, because she turned around—"

Ray sings a part of the song, his voice weak. "Recognize it?"

"The shanty for *Schooner's* fish and chips."

"Yes," he concedes. "Whenever she turns around in my memory, she becomes lost in sea mist. I don't see her face. Every time she's replaced by the *Schooner's* advert." Ray sees, in the memory, the Schooner captain, white hat and shaggy grey beard, pointing out to sea. He is no longer in his childhood kitchen. He is on that ship, on the other side of the screen, the shanty playing in the background. The captain's deep wrinkles and the whisper of the wind and the smell of crackling baked fish are as clear as reality.

Each time he returns to the memory, it ends before he can see his mother's face.

"Some day I'll probably think it is reality," Ray says. "I'll recall my childhood and honestly believe that I lived on a fishing boat and had no parents at all. Maybe that will be better. I mean, what kind of son can't remember his own mother's face?"

It is late. He isn't making sense. He shambles from the balcony, forgetting the glass on the railing. But before escaping to sleep, Ray asks, "Can you do something for me, Skyra?"

"Of course."

"Don't let me forget this. Remember what I said tonight about my mother. What she looked like. Tell me how thinking of her song made me feel. You'll do that, Skyra?"

"I never forget a thing."

# Chapter 7:
# Impulses

*Weird way to boost TELOS* reads an incoming text from Ashley. *You alright?*

The text slots to the top of Jane's feed on the ceiling screen above her bed. Jane shivers beneath the bedcovers. She feels ashamed of another failure, humiliated at her naivety, angry for doing it under Skyra's watchful eyes. Those eyes still watch as the feed circles with rumours about her bathtub stunt on the ceiling screen.

*Can I come over?* comes another text from Ashley. *I'm just a floor away, it's no problem.*

Jane doesn't answer. Her breath is hot on her pillow, on her cheek. She sucks it in deeply, each new breath a brief proof to herself that she is still alive, the water has not taken her.

*I'll call the Doctor then?* Ashley texts.

Jane mumbles "No." She doesn't deserve one.

Jane hears another ping. A new text from Ashley. *You sure? You look rough.*

"No," Jane groans. She scrunches her eyes closed but feels pulsing behind them.

She hears another ping.

*I'll go call him* the text reads.

"I said no!" Jane shouts, lashing at the air as she sits up.

The texts cease.

Silence.

She buries her face into her pillow again and squeezes her eyes shut.

She sees Reece's face, a bruise turning black above her eye. She remembers how Reece's head lolled when Carl returned with her after her overdose. You were right, Carl moaned as he carried Reece into the loft, you were so right, it's just the numbers that matter, not the people. The hospital did not take her, Jane asked, helping place Reece on her bed. I didn't take her, Carl said, what was I thinking even trying. They would just slap an overdose on her record and hold it against her forever. She'd never get hired or get insurance ever again, he added. Carl then bundled Reece in the covers. At once the world had seemed strange to Jane. She could not understand a world where *avoiding* hospital care had been in Reece's best interest, but for the sake of her profile, it was. I am so sorry, Jane cried, I was so wrong, TELOS is just a number, Reece is real, I should have been stronger. Well, no matter, Carl bristled, not looking at her, I knew a clinic from my felicidor days that doesn't keep so good records, got her fixed up there. She'll be fine, he sobbed. Until the next time, he added.

Jane hears another ping from her ceiling screen. *You're the bravest girl I know* reads Asley's text. Jane laughs a little. Her heart has quietened. She no longer feels it beat against the insides of her temples. Spilling from a bathtub of water does not feel brave, but Ashley is the kind of person who can find a hopeful glimmer even amidst impenetrable despair. Such glimmers are, Jane thinks, not found in numbers but in one another.

Jane grimaces for lashing out at Ashley. Ashley means well; she does not understand. Ashley is in the same situation that Jane had once been in, of being an observer to a friend's suffering. Somehow, they had all become mere observers, seeing loved ones wilt and the sky darken and the air thicken, without the opportunity to act. Ashley's impulse to intervene is human, but it is also dangerous.

Carl had told her that she had been right, that he should have found some way to get Reece into the detox program before she got so bad. You are sure it is anonymous, he asked Jane. If you have the TELOS, she answered, knowing that neither of them did. But she had an idea about how to correct that. Jane kissed Reece on her forehead, then put on her coat. Where are you going, Carl said. To get Reece what she deserves, said Jane as she threw open the front door. Don't do anything impulsive, Carl called after her.

*Impulsive.* Jane hated that word. Her mother used it when Jane took off in the mall or struck a bully in the playground. What was wrong with being impulsive? Better to follow her own impulses than someone else's. Jane was out the door before Carl had a chance to call her back.

Impulsive. Jane still hates the word. There is a precious moment between stimulation and Skyra's manipulation in which Jane can act on her own impulse: a moment of freedom. Perhaps she could think more about things before she does them, but there is wisdom in speed; if one moves before the adverts can lay siege to her mind, her actions are still her own.

But Jane's steps had put her at great risk. She does not want Ashley to take the same risk.

"I'll call the doctor," Jane says.

Skyra conveys the text.

# Chapter 8:
# Safety in Numbers

It takes Ashley thirty-two shots, then three apps to perfect the lighting and smooth her complexion. But it is perfect. Her last picture had six million four hundred and seventy thousand, two hundred and twenty-one shares in twelve days. She works out the shares per day in her head. The math only takes her a few seconds.

She has been good at mathematics since she was young. While the other girls played outside, Ashley did sums at her desk. Her teacher asked if she wanted to go and join the others. Ashley said no and asked for more sums. There was safety in numbers.

Ashley posts the picture then gets changed. Clothes are scattered across the bedroom floor. Her closet is filled with promotional clothes. She has no more room to store them. She stumbles in her rush to put on a pair of black, shapeless sweats.

A million views in ten minutes. She sits on her big three-seater couch with knees to her chin and watches the views rise. *JUST found this! LOVE IT!* reads the caption. She's forgotten how much the agency was paid to wear the bikini top for the photo. Now it is strewn on the top of the couch, to be eventually thrown into the pile of other unworn clothes in her bedroom corner.

Ashley watches the climbing likes as if they are results from a medical test. At first, they come in like lightning. She feels the exhilarating snap of numerical approval. Then the wane. The cold in her chest as the numbers crawl. She hugs her knees tighter for comfort.

The numbers subside. They have betrayed her. The top one thousand is too far. Her eyes sink until she is staring blurrily at herself in the screen wall, a trickle of mascara on her cheek.

Ashley takes another photo. It appears on the screen wall. Her eyes are red-rimmed, mouth sagged. She considers posting it. Perhaps that might get more views. Perhaps people deserve to see how she really feels. She purses her lips in indecision.

Ashley shakes her head, closes the photo, returns to her bikini shot, and watches the like counter once more.

# Chapter 9:
# House of Glass

"And here's the bedroom," Ashley says. A stuffed unicorn lays on one pillow. The bed, the covers, and the walls are stark pink. The colour makes Jane's head hurt.

It is Ashley's second day in her upgraded unit, a reward for performance. Ashley had tugged Jane along the corridor, down the elevator to the third floor, around the corner, and into Ashley's apartment, chirping the whole way. "Mine's got the ceiling screen," Ashley says. "Yours does too? I've already got an imprint in the bed from how long I stare up at that thing…"

Ashley prances before Jane in acid-wash jeans and a white tee with some mantra on its front. "I like skimming in my socks along the floor here," Ashley says. "And here's my award wall – it's only got one on right now – five-hundred-thousand followers, though! Do you think I should put up some posters on this wall? You do? I can't decide what though. It's too big of a commitment."

There are lights in the ceiling, in the walls, in the appliances, on the underside of the counters, so many that there are no dark corners in Ashley's apartment. Ashley seems comfortable in the omnipresent light, as she is when lit up online with a viral post, but so ubiquitous are the lights that Ashley no longer has a shadow.

Jane had tried unscrewing the lights in her own apartment, but the fixtures were protected by sturdy plastic covers that Jane could not prise off. She broke a nail trying all the same. But she was pleased to discover when she moved in that her bedroom had a door, a door with an electronic lock, a door that gave a satisfying click when she shut it. Her first day, she shut it, and opened it, and shut it again. Even if it was only a polite illusion, it beat the sheet she had hitched between Carl and Reece's bed and her own.

"Thank you so much for coming!" Ashley beams, struggling to express her exuberance. "Thank you for coming – it's really nice, really really!" Ashley knows the emoji for her feelings better than the right word.

"And here we are, back to where we started. Cool huh?" Ashley's hair, streaked with blue, bobs about with her excitement. Jane says the apartment is beautiful. "The Director said I deserved it," Ashley continues. "I'm not going to stop though. I'm pushing hard to break into the top thousand. Any advice?"

"Keep a piece to yourself," Jane replies, "no matter how small."

The piece Jane keeps is within her head, for there is neither a nook nor a forgotten corner where she can keep anything else to herself. On her first day in the apartment, Jane had discovered the wallscreens that made her apartment appear four times its true size, and asked whether she could turn them off. Manual control is not possible, Skyra replied, my wallscreens capture footage for your lifestream. The screens *watch* me, Jane had gasped, woefully unprepared for the role of a lifestreamer. *Watch* is too narrow a term, Skyra said calmly, my behaviour is informed by one hundred and fourteen metrics. Skyra then described the sensors in the floor which evaluated Jane's walking patterns, the sensors in the toilet which analyzed effluent discharge. You test my *piss*, Jane interrupted. Company policy requires regular checks for narcotics, Skyra answered. Jane didn't ask where the other hundred sensors were located. The wallscreens in every room were enough.

Ashley's apartment is built around the wallscreen standing floor-to-ceiling at the apartment's centre, flanked by the kitchen nook on one side and a sitting area on the other. A yoga mat lies in one corner, discarded clothing nearby. There is a balcony at the far end, a real one, but the art room beside it is an illusion of the wallscreens. The green sidebars on the central wallscreen flicker as a warning.

"Just give me a sec, I've got to post," Ashley says.

Jane sits on one of the wooden stools in the kitchen nook. "Have you *ever* gone into the Red?"

"Nope," Ashley gleams. "Hungry?"

"Always." Jane keeps her caloric intake within Skyra's recommendation. She almost misses the chevaline Carl would make on Thursdays.

A directive springs from Ashley's bracelet. "Uh-huh," she mutters to herself, and goes to the plastic box beside the fridge. There are seven compartments each filled with two Haven pills. Ashley pops one thoughtlessly and goes to the fridge.

Ashley takes a plastic container from the smart fridge, cracks it open, and takes out the square of chocolate cake inside. She presses a fork half-way in and has Skyra take a photograph. Skyra sounds a click to let them know that the walls have captured pictures; a deceitful sound, as there is no inner machinery involved; and anyway, Skyra is *always* absorbing images. Ashley flips her blue-and-blonde hair to the other side, letting Skyra take another picture, then rakishly raises the fork to her lips.

"I need a caption," Ashley says.

"Dessert before dinner?" Jane suggests.

"Oh, I like that," Ashley says. "Skyra, caption it—"

"Afternoon delight," comes Skyra's voice.

"Oh, okay."

And the photograph appears on the feed scrolling along the wallscreen, the angles of Ashley's face crisp, the skin smooth as glass, the precious eyes with lots of light in them. Ashley's chin is noticeably sharpened. The caption appears below, along with links to the cake manufacturer.

"How does it taste?" Jane says, eyebrows wiggling.

"It's zero calories," Ashley half-answers, lips pursed. "Interested?"

Jane feels her stomach grumble. "I'll pass."

The sidebars return to solid green. Jane glimpses Ashley's other metrics – physical, networks, and sales – all healthy green. Jane ponders the *physical* metric. And says: "How's the leg?"

Weeks before, Jane had discovered scaly skin on Ashley's knee, covered up by a layer of foundation. As Ashley rubbed off more of the foundation, she revealed the silver scales went down her shin. Just psoriasis, Ashley had said.

Ashley offers a demure smile. "Oh, it's great! It's great, now."

The truth is left in the speed her forced smile falls away.

Ashley returns the barely-eaten cake to the smart fridge. Each of their appliances has a 'smart' prefix – smart fridges, smart air conditioning, smart lighting, but smart only at helping them buy things. Nowhere in their garish white boxes, no matter the coolness of the air or the automaticity of the refrigerator, is there a puffy chair on which to doze in silence. How smart is that?

"Salad?" Ashley takes two plastic containers from the smart fridge and breaks the seal from each. Jane accepts hers, opens the lid, and studies the spinach leaves the size of her palm, the compartment of almonds like pebbles, and the plastic sachet of syrupy dressing. It is the slim size. Most of the weight is packaging. Ashley eats only half. Jane eats hers and the rest of Ashley's. She asks if Ashley has anything else.

"Cake?" Ashley asks.

Jane grumbles.

"Shake?" Ashley says. "I have all the flavours."

"Anything solid?"

Ashley squirms. "Sorry."

Ashley becomes enveloped by a message from Skyra. She whistles absent-mindedly to herself. Jane gives her the moment. Ashley finally returns. "Sorry – I have a streak going. Sixteen days of crazy eyes. Do you mind?"

"No, no, sure."

Ashley snugs beside her, and they hear Skyra click photos of them pulling faces with crossed eyes. In moments, the best image is posted to Ashley's feed.

"Sorry, I must keep up my numbers," Ashley says.

"They're very good."

"Thank you," Ashley accepts, almost curtseying in gratitude, "they give me stability, you know? A point of reference. I don't know what I'd do without them. Like we're creatures of habit, right? Most stuff we do automatically because it's what we did the day before. Putting numbers to it all helps us see those habits, right? Helps us know if we're on track. The Director says I'm doing very well."

The mention of the Director triggers a defensive reflex that Jane quickly quiets. "You know him well?" Jane says, trying to be off-handed.

Ashley selects her words. "I was born in Theos, so... uh- my parents were—"

She takes the stool beside Jane, knees neatly together, hands clasped in her lap.

"It was a cult," Ashley says, "they taught a prosperity gospel. You know, God shows love by the riches he sprinkles on you. They liked powerboats and mansions, but they didn't like skirts so much. Or lipstick—"

Ashley keeps her hands intertwined, squeezing for reassurance. "I saw this competition one day: to photograph yourself wearing Marie Cherie clothes, tag each piece, and share to all your friends. The best would be offered a modeling contract. I was taking so many pictures and sharing them so often that my parents found out almost immediately..."

Ashley's knee bounces nervously. "Then one day I got the message. I'd *won*. That was the happiest day of my life."

Her face doesn't agree.

She bites her lip. "I cried when I learned. I don't know why, exactly. Something was different. But I was out, at least. So, the Director? He's the one behind the campaign. He's the reason why I'm here. I have every reason to be thankful."

Jane understands why the numbers matter so much to Ashley. A minor blip in those precious digits will send her back home. Jane wonders how many other young women had posted photos for the competition, giving free marketing in exchange for a miniscule chance of a job. And she wonders why it was that the winner was young and deeply vulnerable. Was that an explicit objective of the algorithms that judged the competition? Or were the algorithms let loose to discover the profitability of vulnerability by themselves?

# Chapter 10:
# Eros Ex Machina

Nothing is hers. Everything – Jane's thoughts, her activities, her decisions – are shared with the feed. Perched on a wooden barstool at a projection of a granite counter, Jane crunches the cereal she has been assigned to advertise that week, holding the spoon precisely, smiling delicately at the taste, careful not to drop one of the ghastly flakes into the swamp of cereal and milk and congealed sugar, disallowing the ache behind her eyes from affecting her temperament. There are millions watching her undertake the daily ritual, probably undertaking it with her, matching her dainty chews, or the way she flips the acceptably messy morning hair from her face. Jane finds herself planning her next move before she does it – how she'll slide elegantly from the seat, how she'll sashay to the sink with her empty bowl – to the point where nothing feels spontaneous. Nothing feels hers.

The nook wall lights with updates. On the left scrolls an itinerary. *Salud energy bar* is top of the list. She ignores it, along with the rest of the schedule. Makeup chair, photoshoot, makeup chair, interview, makeup chair, life-stream, sleep. It blurs together. She'll grab lunch sometime, if Skyra permits.

But still, it isn't content moderation or influence testing, or any of the horrid jobs people like Carl had to do. *Have* to do? She does not know.

On the right of the kitchen wall scroll photographs and idle feed updates. And in the middle scrolls the most detestable ingredient of the feed: updates about *herself*. Everyone has something to say. Not all are trolls, but it is always the worst and strangest that rises to the top. The one at the very top – the one going viral – is one Jane knows with a glance that she shouldn't watch, but she focusses for an instant too long on the title – *Even Online Goddesses Need to Get Laid!* – and the video opens.

Jane scowls as the subtitles review her sexual habits – inferable from spikes in her heart rate and warmth on her skin. *She wasn't so frigid in her teenage years* the subtitles read, *but something changed when she began lifestreaming three years ago. No dates, let alone sex; has she given up on men?*

Jane thinks of the boy with who she had her first kiss. They met at school. School was not what she needed after the flood, after what she had seen, the little fingers turned blue—

—his name was Rami. She didn't love him, nor did he love her. She did not know the word for what she felt, they weren't taught them. So words failed her: she grabbed him by the cheeks and pushed her lips onto his. The kiss was too wet, and it took him an eternity to move his fingers to her waist. And even then, he touched her like he'd touch a bowl of soup that was too hot to hold.

Jane liked how the beginnings of his scruffy beard felt on her palms. Rami wasn't that handsome, really, and he'd never met a hairbrush, but she could feel the pad of each finger pressing into her hips and wanted him to pull her closer. She didn't know what to do next. Movies and ads gave them some idea; Truman had a line of ads about a muscle-bound woman powering her man to the floor. Marie Cherie had one of a boy nursing a lip bitten by his girlfriend. But she never saw a depiction of touching for admiration.

Rami's hands left her hips. He and Jane didn't know whether to kiss again, or just hug – in their indecision they did neither, laughing awkwardly until each took a step backward. That was the last real human touch she had. After that, she met the boy who she later swore she would never set eyes upon again, until she needed his help with Reece's addition –

Jane cuts that thought before it blooms. Her spoon clatters into the cereal bowl as the wallscreen video continues. She can't break her grim stare. The video conjectures that she's frigid, or lesbian, or perhaps sexually dysfunctional. There are graphs, and doctor interviews, and titillating re-creations. It's too well-produced to be an amateur video. She wants to figure out what firm made it – a hit-piece from a rival company? – but the video holds her attention and extracts its toll. *Her type seems to be big guys with blonde hair*, it continues. Jane shoves the bowl away and shakes her head, but the video grips her eyes.

*In our poll*, the video continues, *Détente Cavaliers' linebacker Jake Carnegie was voted most likely, with thirty-two percent of the vote. But I'm with the fifteen percent who voted for Victor Fortune*, says the narrator, *no girl, no matter how frigid, could resist that voice, no? Apparently, this one can. Does she think she is too good for us now?*

Jane buries her face in her hands. She feels prised open for anyone to see. The feeling is sore, like an old wound. Jane remembers when she first felt it. She had stepped off the bus outside the tombstone-grey apartment tower of her ex-boyfriend, hoping for his help to get Reece into rehab. Visiting an ex-boyfriend was like returning as a ghost to a past life. She walked past the hole-in-the-wall pub they'd waste their Fridays at, the Chinese they'd end up afterward, old haunts she had tried to forget. She had read about a Roman punishment for traitors, once: any record of them would be erased, their property taken, and it would be illegal to say their name. The intent was to pluck them out of all memory. She tried that with him. Don't say his name, Jane told herself, your memory is limited, he doesn't deserve a place in it. Yet she had returned to his tower.

Jane wills herself not to think more about the memory, but she does not want to think about the video about her sex life, either. It has amassed twenty thousand interactions in minutes, too viral to ignore. As she shakes her head, the video moves across the wall to follow her eyes. Then the screens go dark, and the Director's face appears. As always, he clothes the conversation in privacy.

"I already told you," Jane says before the Director can begin, "Davi didn't say anything about what illness his father has."

"That is not the reason for this conversation."

"Then what?"

"It's time," the Director says. He wears his customary half-smile, lips curving slightly upward like a leaf curves in frost. That smile, which he wears whether angry or not, makes it impossible for Jane to tell what he is thinking.

"For?"

"You have seen the video. Relationships cannot be delayed any longer. The latest marketing predictions agree that now is the time."

"What does a computer prediction know about love?"

"Nobody said anything about *love*."

Jane's lips sour. "Then what?"

"Just enough," he shrugs. "For the cameras. For the sponsors. Then you can drop it."

"Maybe *you* should drop it," Jane says, getting up from her stool. She cautions herself: the Director does not accept disobedience. But the feeling remains that she is entitled to make the choice that he intends to make for her.

"It looks strange," the Director presses.

"Look at all the traffic this video has driven," Jane replies. "It is the mystery, not the answer, that inspires people."

"We'll choose candidates from the best data."

"I don't need data. That's what people like about me."

"Your resistance intrigues me."

Jane shivers – almost. The Director has a medical curiosity about him. Being the subject of his interest feels like being under his scalpel.

"I had a bad experience," she says. "I'm – sensitive, about this kind of thing..." She could say more – so much more. But all she dares to say is, "He wasn't who he said he was."

"All the more reason to choose with data," the Director pushes from the other side of the stream. "No chance to lie."

"Choosing with data just means you're letting someone else choose what's important in another lover. And I've already—"

She catches herself. *I've already made that mistake,* she was going to say. *Past life,* she reminds herself, *that was a past life.* "I wish I'd listened to my gut more," Jane corrects, "that's all I'm saying. And I'm listening to my gut now."

Jane hopes he will listen, too. She clasps her hands over her head, wearied by the resurrection of old memories, by the effort of pretending they belong to someone else.

But the Director persists: "We don't listen to guts anymore. We listen to numbers."

Jane lifts her head and glares at the screen. "Love isn't about numbers."

"Money is."

Jane scowls. It is a reflexive anger she feels, to armour herself against feeling vulnerable. She pants. She keeps it up, wanting to be angry. *He's trying to manipulate me*, she thinks, *he is just like Tristan*.

When Jane had arrived at her ex boyfriend Tristan's apartment, she had hoped the apartment would be different, that they might talk somewhere without their communal memories embedded in the fabric of the furniture, but it was just the same: the same case of impressive bound books she knew he did not read; the posters of films he did not like but knew his type of girl would; the guitar on the wall, subtly growing dust. He lived in a room of conversation pieces – of bits of memorabilia and themed knick knacks – to build an image of himself. An image that had impressed her, once.

Tristan wore a white sleeveless shirt which showed the symbol tattooed on his arm that he did not know the meaning of. He seated himself and slid her one of the sweating beer bottles sitting on the tabletop. I want something, Jane said, ignoring the beer, you're going to give it to me, I'm going to leave, you're never going to bother me again. The glimmer of hope faded from his face. That's it, he said, after two years? What did you expect Tristan, she snapped, did you think I wouldn't find out that you bought parts of my profile and sent the worst bits to my friends? I know you sent Sam something, Jane snarled, because one day we were close, the next, he was asking me about how many boyfriends I'd had, what I did with them.

Tristan just sipped his beer, not having decency to deny her accusation.

Jane had wanted to report Tristan for sabotaging her relationships – but who? She didn't have the credit to afford to protect her data from purchase, and there was no way to stop the accumulation of her data. She cried herself to sleep, knowing that Tristan would be able to tell, in real-time. Jane couldn't describe what Tristan had taken from her. He had not stolen her data, for it did not belong to her; he hadn't taken her friends – apparently, her own actions had done that. He hadn't hurt her physically. Everything he had done was in the digital domain, where nothing was owed to her. Yet there felt some inexplicable right of hers had been violated – some integrity for which there was no word, a duty she deserved, lingering indecipherable in a shadowy penumbra.

Jane shivers at the unwelcome memories.

"Don't be upset," the Director says from the wallscreen of her apartment. "Your fans love you because you're different—"

"—then let me be diff—"

"—but your fans want to be like you – in *all* parts of life. You're missing the biggest one."

"There's plenty of things bigger than *fucking*," she sneers, leaving the nook.

The Director's face follows her along the corridor wallscreens. Jane goes for the bathroom. She tries the handle. Locked. The Director shakes his head. Jane releases the door handle and squeezes her palms into her temples, hoping she can crush herself into something too small to be worth the Director's attention. But he occupies every wallscreen, and each of his many faces tells her to sit.

She returns to the nook and takes a stool.

"Let me give you some perspective on the human mind," he says. "We once believed that the millions of interconnected neurons in the human brain were the world's most advanced thinking machine. This is hubris. Most people do not know that most of those neurons *do not think at all.*"

The Director tells her about a room he owns in the top of a tower. He says that from this room, he can see the whole city, glimmering to the horizon. "It is like standing in a plume of light," he says. He then asks how many blocks Jane thinks are in the city.

"Hundreds of thousands?" she says, hanging her head, for she knows that his examination will not be brief.

"Yes, hundreds of thousands," the Director confirms. "If we imagine the city as the brain," he continues, "the unthinking part comprises almost the entirety of the city. The only thinking part is about five-hundred thousand times smaller. So if each city block represents a group of neurons—"

"Your tower is the only thinking part," Jane finishes, grimacing.

"The *city* is what you cater to, not the tower. Understand?"

Jane smolders. At first, the numbers controlled where she lived, and who she met. She sacrificed those. Then they controlled what she saw and what she said. Those were harder to renounce. And in only a matter of years, she – and everyone else – gave up more ground to probabilities and percentages. There *had* to be a space only for her. She couldn't have intimacy controlled by a program. Not again.

She remembers the moment Tristan's profile was linked with her own. Her lenses displayed Tristan's hangdog face – those blue eyes looking just into the distance. *Ninety-eight percent compatibility*, the matchmaker said. Jane repeated that percentage to herself as she laid awake at night, Tristan's arm splayed over her, stale beer on his breath. *Ninety-eight percent*. If she couldn't love a match like that, what hope did she have? That little number kept her in a relationship with Tristan far longer than anything else. She figured it was her fault that things were not working.

The Director drinks in Jane's hesitation. "The people who you spend your time with are generating the wrong image," his image on the wall says. Jane eyes him but can't interpret his face. The Director never says quite what he means. There is always something held back.

"What do you mean?"

"You have no male companion," he explains, "yet spend most of your social time with one Ashley Gaetz. I'm afraid we'll have to limit your contact with her until we can recalibrate your image."

Jane looks away before he can see how much the threat hurts, but something in the Director's slight grin makes her feel that he already knows, that he can see her memories as clearly as she, that somehow he knows about Reece, about her addiction, and what Jane had to do to get Reece help.

What she had to give to Tristan.

Neither Jane nor Tristan had the TELOS to pay for Reece's detox treatment. The only way was to falsify Jane's TELOS. I know you know a guy who can do it, Jane said. No, I won't do it, Tristan said, I don't want you to get hurt because you faked your TELOS. Then he put on his cute voice, and said, I still care about you, babe. You care about owning me, Jane said, it doesn't matter if it's a digital me or not. Then she realized why Tristan did not want to help Jane falsify her TELOS: if she fixed her TELOS high enough, her data would become too expensive for him to access anymore. She stormed from his apartment and was in the corridor when she thought of Reece – thought of how lucky she was to have Carl – thought of those two scrappy lovers, scratching a living together – thought of Reece's screams, and those mad, desperate eyes. Jane turned, and saw Tristan was closing the door.

Wait, she blurted, and wiped her nose with the sleeve of her hoody. The door stayed open a crack. A single eye glared through the space. Though she shivered at how dirty she felt, Jane said that if Tristan gave her the name of the man who could falsify her TELOS, she would give all her profile. The stuff you can't afford, she said, the best stuff, a treasure trove, just for you. Jane told herself that they were just numbers, that they were worth nothing compared to Reece's livelihood, but she felt nauseous at the feeling of consenting to her own violation. Tristan nodded and re-opened the door.

The feeling of dirt on her shoulders, behind her ears, under her fingernails, returns as the Director's face bears down on her from the wallscreen. Tristan is the only person in possession of her entire past profile. She has given her power away before; she will not do it again.

"I won't do it," she says.

"Then you will suffer alone," says the Director. "Ashley will be fired tomorrow."

"You can't—"

"You have five minutes to choose."

His face disappears and the wallscreens return to the scrolling feed, leaving only a cold and lonely silence. Jane wants to tear at it like she tore cobwebs from the corners of her childhood cottage, but the memory of that cottage only makes her feel all the more alone. The cottage no longer exists, it no longer rings with the warbles of a newborn baby, the lullabies of her mother, the gusts from the sea. Jane has pressed memories of those things so deeply that they, too, are silent, like an old video with a corrupted audio track, deserving deletion. As she paces the quiet corridor, Jane hopes for even an advert to break the silence.

Though she shares the tower with other models, she barely knows any of them except for Ashley. The rest are compartmentalized in identical units, each with their own cook-all and their identical designer plates to sit uselessly in their identical nooks. Jane remembers sharing the dinner table with her mother and uncles, and cousins, and second cousins, bumping elbows because they were so tightly seated. She knows of no word for that kind of sharing, the sharing of collective warmth, the sharing of stories, of space, of time, of enjoyment.

She shares nothing with the other streamers in her tower, except the feeling of loneliness. Above all, the worst part of data controlling her life is the loneliness. Jane bore many miseries as she grew, but being alone is the least tolerable.

She grits her teeth and calls the Director.

"You are lucky," his smirking face says as it appears on the wallscreen, "I gave you an extra minute."

"You won't fire Ashley," Jane says, wanting to hear it from the Director's lips, even though she knows she cannot trust him. "Swear to me you won't."

"If I can have confidence in you, you can have confidence in me."

"That tower you mentioned," Jane says, deflecting, "I've never heard of it."

The Director shifts, surprised by the question. "It's exclusively priced. A special pill is needed to access it."

Jane's eyes narrow. She remembers the pills Davi had clumsily offered her. There is no record of Davi buying those – she had checked. Perhaps neither the tower nor the pills needed to access it are recorded. Which means: perhaps there is one place in the State where things are not tracked, where anything can be kept secret, a place where Jane can become the watcher, instead of the watched.

If only she had the pills to get there.

Her eyes rise to meet the Director's. "I'll date someone for the cameras. On one condition."

"Of course," he smiles.

"I choose who it is."

# Chapter 11:
## The Centre of the Universe

Security leads Jane through downtown streets to an open square named the Centre of the Universe, so named because it lies within the exact centre of the city. The limousine got them close, but the foot traffic became too thick, so they walk the last few streets. Her security detail parts the crowd of onlookers for Jane to walk through, so the street feels like a hallway of watching eyes. Jane had forgotten just how many people actually live in the city, for she usually sees them only as a viewer count on her stream.

Customized adverts follow at their feet. Jane looks up, trying to find the paparazzo drone she can hear buzzing above them. There are no clouds today, but the sky still wears a dirty haze. Jane hasn't seen a clear day in years. It is hot, and an ill wind sweeps at their feet. Not quite a dust storm wind, she thinks, though there seems to be less and less wind needed to blanket the city in dust these days.

Though it is early evening, the Centre is just as light at night as in the day. It is unyieldingly bright, a point of infinite light generated by displays and logos and signs and spotlights burning from screens the size of towers, from projections on the ground, on the sky, around which crowds of people make their orbital way. There are electronic billboards on electronic billboards, so many they become an attraction themselves. Jane stands at their feet like an explorer facing the bottom of a sheer white cliff.

Security ushers her to a restaurant facing the square, where the Maître D' leads her to the patio divided from the circling masses by soundproof glass. The tables are white marble and, on their surfaces, play videos of steaming plates and knives parting succulent meats. People in the square press their faces against the glass while others live-stream it. The restaurant will make millions from the publishing rights.

Jane sees Davi waiting for her. He pulls out seat, brushing the small of her back as she sits, before he seats himself across from her. He's in a white sports jacket that sparkles as much as the rings adorning his fingers. His grin is wide.

She has never been on a date, or at least, not one that resembled what she saw in the old movies. In those, the girl with the bob and the cute lipstick would play coy, the boy with the greased hair would tease her defences like some sort of fencing duel, compliment her eyes, ask about her family. She would ask what he did for work, something he apparently got to choose, all things they did not know unless they were told. And, slowly, communally, they would let down their defences and open slivers of vulnerability.

They had no idea of the extraordinary privilege they had *not* to say, to decline with a smile, to maintain the mystery. When Jane watched those old movies, she thought how erotic it felt to not know, how devilishly aberrant it was to withhold. Then she learned the magical word for it: to flirt. *Flirting*, an ebbing, flowing, twisting dance. That was the kind of boy she wanted, the kind who would perform the strange flirtatious dance with her, the kind who had to ask.

Boys don't ask anymore. They do not need to. It is all online. If they want to message, or to knock on her door, they can, and do. From there, there is no incline between meeting – usually online, sometimes off – and sex. For there is no need to *get to know* someone; anything to be known can be searched, with or without consent. And when a stranger can have her data, it isn't much of a step to give them her body too.

Mostly, people use Skyra to craft messages micro-targeted to her interests. She can't count the number of messages from boys professing that they, too, are passionate about music from the last century. Now algorithms do the searches, dictate the results, draft the foreplay, and track the inevitable result. Dates are transactions, two parties completing a sexual deal arranged by an electronic broker.

Davi stretches back in his chair, widening his already broad shoulders, a tuft of hair peeking from out the open buttons of his floral shirt. His olive skin glistens as stray adverts roll through the restaurant. A waiter pours them wine, drying the lip with the black towel folded over his arm. Jane sits tall, hands folded to her lap, arms squeezed in tight, taking up as little space as possible in her purple dress.

Davi thanks her for coming and makes a vague reference to *getting off on the wrong foot*. She lets that go, professing it was nothing, it was just a misunderstanding.

"I was surprised you reached out to me," Davi says in a throaty baritone. "We've all seen that list by now. Four million – no, *five* million – votes for Jake Carnegie."

She wishes that he had not brought it up. It makes the date feel even more orchestrated. "You're upset that you're only number eight?" she teases. She is on her best behaviour this time. This is for her little sister, she tells herself.

"Apparently, the feed thinks I prefer foreign models to local ones."

"Do you make exceptions?"

"For exceptional women." His eyes linger just long enough, before he turns to the waiter to gesture for the first course.

"It's my first time in a little while," she says, brushing an errant string of hair from her face.

"How come?"

"I think the video called it *sexual inadequacy*."

"You don't seem inadequate to me."

He is laying it on thick. *I'm not used to so many people watching* is her first response. It is also the wrong one to say. "I just haven't met the right guy..." she trails off, disgusted for saying it. But out of the corner of her eye, the audience against the glass grows more excitable, and a thrum from Skyra indicates a significant uptick in online chatter.

"I hope you find him."

"I've met plenty of wrong ones."

"Tell me."

"Guys searched me up – well, not *me*, precisely, but by my TELOS, or by my taste in music or art. And some based upon facial similarity to celebrities."

Davi doesn't laugh at that, as she had expected.

"You can tell, too," Jane continues, "one guy who signalled me saying he loved my eyes, *blah blah*. It turned out he was an avid consumer of Jezebel Danger, who I suppose I look like with a bit more makeup. There is a unique feeling in discovering someone wants to meet up just to live out their porn fantasies in the flesh."

She waits for him to laugh or commiserate, but all Davi does is nod feebly. Jane struggles to tell if she is speaking to the executive representing Nature Corp., or the playboy adding another notch to his record. Male intentions aren't usually so opaque.

The waiter slips them each a bowl of steaming orange soup. Jane takes a spoonful, blows gracefully across the rippling surface, and closes her eyes as she takes the first taste. That one is for the marketers. The image will be in an advert within a minute. Butternut squash, sweet and autumnal, she can almost see the golden leaves clinging to their branches, back when they still had four seasons. The taste springs a memory of slurping soup at a kitchen table, her legs too short for the chair, dribbling some onto her shirt, leaving an orange smear over her upper lip, and the hairs on her forearms begin to tingle. She stays in the memory, the joy warming her insides more than the soup, as Davi regales her with a story about his father's tiger hunting trip with the restaurant's head chef.

Jane is almost done with the soup when Davi declares, without prompting: "I know why you agreed to meet me."

Jane chokes on the soup.

"It took me all of two minutes on your feed to see," he continues, "but don't worry, I am not upset. You are not the first woman to try."

*If in doubt, smile*, Jane thinks.

"So I will tell you what I told them," says Davi. "I can't pull strings about making you the face of our Black Friday campaign."

"Was I so obvious?"

"That you want to be in the most-watched advert of the year? I didn't even need to check your feed. I can see it in your face."

"Why hide it?" she says sweetly.

Privately, she imagines what she *could* do if Davi placed her in the most-watched advert of the year, and lets the seditious fantasies soothe the disgust of having to sit opposite Davi.

"Exactly," he says, whirling a glass of red wine. "You check me; I check you. No surprises." He takes a sip of the wine. "Though," he continues, pulling the glass from his lips, "one thing *did* surprise me."

"Oh?"

"You're a big Trippier fan, too."

The name is unfamiliar. "Oh yes," she effuses.

"*So* many good movies. My favourite is *Permission Denied*. You?"

Jane does not recognize the name. There are many lies in her profile – she cannot remember them all. "Same," she says.

"Cory Jackson's performance in that was – well, we don't have performers like him anymore."

"I had a little bit of a crush on him once."

Whoever Jackson was, she hopes he was cute enough for a teenage crush.

"I think every girl who saw the movie did," he chuckles. Jane slips him a smile. "It's still so powerful," he continues. "People rising against arbitrary government rules. I watch it each year, the week before Black Friday. That's why I chose to eat here, overlooking the square where Black Friday began. It was just over your shoulder they made the bonfire of all the law books, you know?"

She's tempted to knock back her wine to make Davi more tolerable, but Jane limits herself to a graceful sip.

The waiter comes with two steaming plates.

"Looks amazing!" says Jane, but Davi ignores the plates.

"You know the bit that always kills me about *Permission Denied*?" he presses.

"No!" she replies, leaning toward him in expectation, elbows on the marble table.

"*The permission to have a maximum of sixteen ounces of soda,*" he says, imitating a robotic voice. "*A maximum of twice a day, only if you're a maximum of one-hundred and seventy pounds.*"

"Oh gosh, yes—"

"So ridiculous."

They share a hearty laugh. "But people used to live like that!" Davi maintains. "That's why I watch it each year: to remind us of how far we've come. When Jackson uses the Freedom app to organize the march against the government – it's so powerful. And then—" his voice drops, "—when they're all gunned down…"

"I always cry at that bit."

"Ugh," Davi winces. "But that's just the *original* ending. Which ending did you prefer?"

She smiles, dedicating attention to parting the chicken on her plate with her knife. Finally, food she can chop. She is seldom allowed to use a knife.

"There's the original ending, and the director's cut, right?" Davi adds.

"Oh yes. I preferred the original," she says, and takes a quick mouthful of chicken.

"Oh yeah. When Jackson's standing before the crowd, and they're perfectly silent, and he takes the *Book of Permissions* in his hand, and he says—"

He stops, waiting for her to join him. She chews.

He waits. Jane swallows and looks up.

"Power is—" he prompts.

"Power is—" she joins.

"—now in our hands—"

"—in our hands—"

"—we don't need your permission any longer!"

"—any longer!"

"It gave me goosebumps when I first saw that," he says. "But the director's cut is just so much more powerful, no?"

"It didn't work for me," she shrugs, and takes another quick fork of chicken to her lips. It is plump but stringy. At least it is better than Carl's cooking.

"Why not?"

She chews. Davi stares, awaiting an answer.

Jane makes a point of savouring the taste. Davi waits. The audience waits. The feed waits. Her shoulders begin to vice together. Jane gulps, giving Davi another moment to take back the conversation. He doesn't. "Oh, you're clearly the expert here," Jane replies.

"Come on," he presses, still smiling. "I've never seen you shy about sharing your opinion."

"Except when it comes to opinions of beloved movies. Don't want to offend anyone."

"You won't offend me."

She flicks her eyes, hopefully too quickly for Davi to have seen, and Skyra whispers into her ear. "The original ending," she says with conviction, "the director's cut became too self-absorbed. The legislature steps scene was twice as long as it needed to be."

Davi shrugs. "Agree to disagree."

She feels a gentle touch of relief, nothing more, for it may be detected. Then lets herself enjoy the last bites of her chicken. But Davi won't say anything about his father while they are still in public view. "Let's get out of here," Jane says, "somewhere with just us."

"There's dessert to come."

"You took Idina Rey paragliding on your first date, didn't you?" Jane says. "And Amanda Carrick to your boat."

"Yes—"

"And Adele Davenport went zero-gees in your jet, did she not?"

"You *have* done your research."

"So as much as I like this place," she says, "I want you to *really* impress me." She breaks her fixed gaze, looks down coyly, and shrugs, "and then maybe we can have dessert somewhere else."

His nods quicken. "Okay."

In minutes, a black car with tinted windows pulls up to the restaurant. Jane slips inside and the flashes of cameras disappear. The interiors of the car are ivory white, the seats deep grey and concave in shape, like half an eggshell. She recognizes it as a Barone. Jane arranges her feet neatly together and lowers gradually into her seat. It is deeper than she expects. Half way down she falls in altogether, letting out a little *oof* as she bumps down. Davi smirks as he lowers himself gracefully into the other chair, clicking a handle to spin the chair to face her.

Jane does the same, turning to face Davi, the front windshield to her right. She slinks one leg over the other. Though the windows are opaque from the outside, Jane can see crisply from within. As Jane watches the people in the crowd taking selfies, she feels a strange power in reading their lips, seeing the joy in their eyes, while she remains invisible behind the glass.

As the crowd thins, the Barone accelerates, skimming like a toboggan on fresh powder, the air conditioning kissing her cheek like a winter breeze. The city flashes by.

"So, where are you taking me?" Jane asks.

# Chapter 12:
# Locks and Steps

"Last time we met..." Davi begins, then, to Jane's astonishment, he pays to obscure their conversation. With the number of viewers watching their streams, it cannot be a small expense. "I shouldn't have presumed. Those pills I offered weren't drugs. They emit a short-range signal upon contact with stomach acid. The signal allows us to access places few people get to."

"They're – passwords? For what?"

"It has no name. It is not advertised. But it is in the Mercantile Tower."

"You're taking me to a *bank*?"

"The bank and its offices occupy the lower floors, but the top three floors are *very* different. The Mercantile Bank faced so many cyber attacks that it constructed this tower to block all wireless connections. Wired only."

"Meaning?"

"Skyra won't work. It can't charge. Wi-Fi, GPS, radio – none of it works. This tower is the only place in the city where nothing can be tracked."

Jane's eyes widen, as if he had told her there exists a place where there is no gravity, where she can throw up her arms and rise into the air. It is a feeling she has experienced only once before, the first time she had approached a Red Zone.

Tristan had told her the name of man she needed to falsify her TELOS high enough to afford rehab for Reece: *Jonas*. But you don't want to do this, Tristan pleaded, Jonas lives in the Red Zone. Jane had ignored his warning and taken the bus as far as it went to the outskirts of the city. As Jane approached the Red Zone, her lenses displayed a city map with a stark red line in front of her, warning that she was getting too close.

There was no need for a wall, nor a patrol, between the Green Zone and the Red. TELOS was enough to dissuade people from leaving, and the plethora of sensors at the border enough to track anyone coming in. The line was virtual. The line did not exist. So she took the step into the Red Zone, and her updated TELOS instantly flashed upon her lenses. *One-sixty-two*, it read as she walked. She was barred from the buses and trains. *One-forty-two*, as she continued onward. Her landlord automatically demanded pre-payment of rent. *Ninety-eight*. She received an automatic eviction notice. At least she had already removed Carl and Reece from her network to minimize the damage to them.

Jane was surprised by the smile that grew on her face. For the moment, TELOS meant nothing. That little number, growing only with great effort and vigilance, crumbling with one wrong choice, had a persistent voice in her head, dictating every decision. Without it, she no longer needed to quarantine her voice in the Red Zone of her mind. Her smile broadened until she laughed. She thought she was free.

"I have to take the wheel for this bit," Davi says, rotating his chair to face the windscreen as the Barone slows and the doors of a parkade entrance whisper open. Jane does not see any other cars as they descend the parkade ramp, but she notices Skyra's beady red eye dim. Davi was right; no signal can penetrate the building. She finds her right hand tensing, a defensive reflex. Davi parks in a secluded area and he and Jane step from the Barone.

"What are you thinking?" he says.

Jane realizes that she has indulged in too many memories. She smiles at him. "Can't you tell?"

"You're overwhelmed. Everyone is on their first time."

"I didn't know it was so obvious."

He shows her through a corridor with a pair of golden elevator doors at its end. Jane traces her hand over the symbol on their surface. It is a blindfolded woman in flowing robes, her right hand holding a set of scales, notably weighed down on one side.

"The injustice," Davi says, "when we make decisions blindly, without data."

"I thought you said there is no data tracking where we are going?"

"Sometimes we need a little injustice," Davi grins. "Come, we need the password."

Davi pulls the clear bag of pills from his pocket. His glinting smile grows as Jane reaches out a hand. Jane imagines the kinds of sadism that the rich might practice without watching eyes. Surveillance does not extinguish humanity's darkest impulses; it drives them to darker corners. There will be other chances, Jane tells herself, with other people, better than Davi. She doesn't need to take the risk.

But she plucks a pill from his hand, drops it on her tongue, and swallows hard.

# Chapter 13:
# Narcissus

The golden elevator doors part, and then the button for the fortieth floor lights up. As they slip upward, Jane feels uneasy. Davi's pill tasted of nothing, but the sensation of becoming a walking, fleshy password is unsettling, a pill-sized step away from humanity. Jane checks her wrist. When she sees Skyra has gone dark, Jane feels an unfamiliar fear – no longer the fear of being watched, but the fear of the unknown.

"What's in the rooms?" Jane says.

"Some have beds. Some have bars. Some of mine have nothing at all."

"You pay… for nothing?" Jane looks at him – the slicked hair, the gold chain around his neck, the diamond stud in his right ear. He gleams with riches that few others have – the greatest of all, the little pills in his pocket. She wonders what extraordinary cost it takes to acquire them – how much he pays for absence, for nothing at all.

"We pay for *solitude*," Davi answers. Then he checks himself, and adds: "Do you know that word?"

*"They flash upon that inward eye which is the bliss of solitude,"* Jane flourishes. A passage from the little Isles literature she has searched, not enough to be too unusual.

"A six hundred TELOS model who can quote Wordsworth? That *is* unexpected."

"Not as unexpected as a nine-hundred-TELOS… *lothario*? Is that how you put it?"

He smiles as the elevator doors part. Jane notes the golden glow of the marble floors, like the whole tower is jaundiced. Davi takes off his shoes and gestures to her to do the same. Jane pops off her heels and carries them in her right hand. As they pad silently along the corridor, Jane sees no one else. No staff. No other guests. And no cameras. Each identical wooden door they pass appears locked. Jane pricks her ears but there isn't a whisper to steal from any of the rooms. Jane glances down. Skyra is still inactive.

The lock of the door at the end of the corridor flicks from red to green as they approach, and the door opens for them like a soft breath. Jane startles as she enters. Lit by the lights of the adverts frolicking through the full-height window is a full-size pool.

Jane tenses. The thought of being submerged makes her skin crawl. She flashes a look at Davi. He is already down to shorts, his trousers and jacket folded neatly on the glass table at the entrance. She hears a slight burble as he slips into the pool, and then all is quiet again. Davi's head disappears below the smooth surface, then pops out on the other side of the pool.

"It's warm," he calls.

Jane forces her feet closer to the pool.

She pulls her dress up and kneels at the pool's edge. She has never seen water so perfect, so undisturbed. This amount of purified water would fetch a fortune on the grey market. Jane stares at her reflection. There is not a ripple in the image. The face in the water is a girl with fame, and fortune, and TELOS, enjoying the privilege of seclusion given to her by the heir to the largest fortune in the State. The outside lights twinkle in the reflection's eyes. Jane is tempted to continue staring, unable to push away the thought that she can remake herself in the image of the reflection.

She thinks of when she finally found Jonas, the TELOS fabricator, and he had offered her the same chance to remake herself. She had found Jonas in a building with dilapidated stone pillars and the windows all boarded up. Jane had hammered on the metal doors until a slat in one door opened and a pair of eyes appeared. I need enough TELOS to get a thirteen-mil loan, she had said, which would be just enough to pay for Ashley's treatment. Of course, Jonas said, as he led her inside and locked the metal doors behind them. But do you know what changing your TELOS means, he asked. Jane had shaken her head. Jonas had sighed, and said, TELOS is your Total

Estimated Life Outcome Score. It sums every piece of data about you and decides everything about you. It's just a number, Jane replied. Oh no, Jonas said, TELOS is not just a number, it is a pit. Where that pit is, and who it is beside, he said, are already decided, and as years go by you dig the pit deeper, until one day you are too deep to see out of it, and you're so tired by digging, you lie down for a little nap. What does that mean, said Jane. It means I can't just change the number, he replied, I need to remake everything about you.

Her present profile would be killed off, he said. Jane thought it was unfair that all the time and anguish she had suffered to cultivate her meagre TELOS could vanish with the stroke of his delete key. Surely, she had mattered more than as a smattering of data, soon to be set from live to dead? But identity, she realized, was simply a thing writ in water. Do it, she instructed.

Davi calls again to her, but Jane is enamoured by her reflection in the surface of the pool. The image is of a girl not frightened by the thought of water, not cursed with memories of drowning that she cannot banish, cannot fix, cannot let anyone know. The eyes are wide and resplendent, the smile easy and genuine at her careless, frictionless life. Jane has seen many thousands of images of herself, but none so beautiful as the one staring back at her from the pool. As Jane gazes at her reflection in the pool, she finds herself becoming allured with the water.

As she reaches out to touch it, Davi's smile catches the light coming through the window. Jane stops before she touches the water and realizes that she is only inches from its clutches. She pulls her hand away. Davi may have seen the stories about her nearly drowning in a bathtub, about how petrified Jane is of any depth of water, and that makes his glinting smile all the more sinister. Jane wishes that Skyra could check why Davi had brought her to this pool, but in the room's darkness, and without Skyra's guidance, the meaning of Davi's continuing smile is unknowable.

Jane's reflection looks up at her from the pool's surface. She remembers the ugliness of Davi's words – *perhaps we need a little injustice* – and she scatters the face with a jab of her finger.

"What do you think?" he calls from the pool.

Jane stays on the edge. "I'm not the only girl you've taken up here, am I?" she says.

Davi does not answer.

"Well," Jane continues, keeping from the pool as long as she can, "what's usually your next move?"

"I tell them about my sports cars, my golf course," he says. "I invite them to take a ride with me on my boat. I tell them it has five-hundred-and-fourteen horsepower. They coo and flatter me." His shoulders begin to dry. "That's all we talk about because that's all they know about me. *You* searched me up," he continues, "there's nothing else to me but boats and golf courses – and a rich daddy."

He is right that results do not capture everything; there are none about tainted formula poisoning children. But Jane maintains a sympathetic face.

"What people search about me is what they then talk about," Davi mutters. "What people search is how I'm seen. Which makes me wonder: was I always a spoilt wastrel spending his daddy's money, as the results say? Or did I just become how people see me?"

His lips are loosened by their seclusion. Jane drinks in his words.

"I'm not taken seriously at Nature Corp.," Davi adds, "because all anyone knows is that I'm spoilt and wasteful."

"The feed doesn't tell you who you are," Jane remarks, sounding like she means it.

But when she had told Jonas that she wanted her new profile to be someone kind, who helps people, he had laughed. TELOS doesn't do kind, he said in his gruff voice, there's only one thing you can do that will get you enough credit for that thirteen-mil loan, and that is life-streaming on the feed. I didn't think they were real people, Jane had said. They would probably agree with you, Jonas grunted. After a few minutes of typing on one of his dozens of old-style keyboards, Jonas asked her for a name. I can't even keep that, Jane whimpered. Too risky, said Jonas, for me and for you. She had felt liberated when she sneaked into the Red Zone and lost all her TELOS, but Jonas had made her feel boxed in once more. Come on, Jonas had pressed, what are we going to name this Jane Doe?

"Of course the feed tells us who we are," Davi chuckles from across the pool.

Jane looks up at him.

"Perhaps me more than anyone," he continues, "because the Board will decide who inherits my father's corporation upon what the feed tells them. And from what they see, they won't approve me as next-in-line. When my father dies, there will be a power struggle. Market confidence will dwindle, share prices will drop, and in the confusion, our competitors will replace us. It will be catastrophic for the city."

Jane holds his gaze from the other side of the pool. She wonders whether a new data-master will be better than the existing one. But she cannot leave Nature Corp. to topple from internal struggles. Her sister deserves better.

"I need to prove to the Board that I am serious. They say they have given me control of the Black Friday event, but they will find ways to undermine me. Hence, I have been looking for projects I can control – such as my surge-pricing plan, which you so graciously shot down," Davi smiles.

Jane files away the statement that Davi will be controlling the Black Friday event, in case she needs it later. Perhaps she will tell the Director that Davi is looking to flex his muscles further than the Board wishes, perhaps she will not. But the scrutiny Davi receives from the Board begins to worry her. "What would your Board make of me?" she says.

"You are the *last* person the Board will want me to be with. The Director – you know him? – specifically warned me about you. But not everything can be about them. In the end, Boards and shares and corporations are nothing; the only thing that matters is *time*."

Davi pushes from the pool's edge, fanning his arms out. He takes a breath, filling his belly with air, and floats spread-eagled. "What do you think about time?" he says, staring up at the ceiling.

"I always thought it was funny to say the past is behind us, while we look forward to the future," Jane replies, trying not to look obvious that she is staying a foot from the water. "It's the past we *can* see. It's the future we can't, like it is behind our backs."

"How do you know how to spend your time if you don't know what is coming?"

"I don't. I treat life as an adrenaline ride, to be enjoyed one day at a time." That is only half true. The feeling of being watched leads to continual bursts of adrenaline, but it is not a ride she enjoys.

"My father would say that was wasteful," Davi sighs, still on his back. "His greatest fear is time. It's the only thing he can't get more of, so he was merciless with the time he spent with me. He would sit me on his knee and ask how my day was, how much I learned from the tutor, just until Skyra buzzed to signal that my time was up, and then he went back to work. You know how much of his time I was worth?"

Davi, still floating, looks over to Jane and says: "Six minutes, fourteen seconds."

There is no sound but the gentle burble of water against the pool's edge. Jane considers the search terms that often accompanied his name: *job at Nature, net worth, poker championship, ex-girlfriends, secret children*. She'd seen a hundred similar wastrels walk into the Siren store, where years ago she had shilled premium perfume, who spent big money they didn't earn on girlfriends they wouldn't keep. Little boys in daddy's shadows. *That* will be how to get to him. To get more of his pills.

She cuts the silence. "What would you do for a little more of his time?" Jane asks, trying to sound innocuous.

Davi flips himself back to vertical. "No more questions until you pay the price of admission."

*Price*, Jane thinks as she repeats Davi's words to herself. The date is a transaction to Davi, his obnoxious overtures his investment, this moment at the pool his payday. But, she acknowledges, it is a transaction for her, too, her payday the pills in Davi's pocket. She considers that goal as she eyes the bottomless water.

"I don't want to ruin my dress," Jane says.

"Then don't."

She considers telling him about her fear of water – *anything* to avoid getting into the water – but she does not want to tell him her vulnerabilities. He will only use them against her. Jane wishes she had someone to call for help. She even wishes she had Skyra, for at least Skyra can be trusted to call security if Jane begins to drown. But there is no one, no one but Davi.

She tries something vain. "You know how long it takes to get my hair like this?"

"Time wasted if you don't swim."

"I'll dip my toes in."

Jane sits on the edge of the pool and shivers at the touch of water on her toes. She buries her fingers like anchors into the tile.

"If you want answers to the deep questions," Davi says, treading the water, "you've got to come into the deep water."

Jane cannot do it, even for the pills. She forces a laugh, but Davi's expression remains insistent.

"Trust me," he says as he swims closer.

"Not tonight," she mumbles.

Davi smiles.

Then he has her ankle, she is pulled, and she hears the crash of water in her ears. Jane wants to scream but her throat is filled with water. She whirls and flails until she emerges from the water and gasps for air.

"See," Davi chuckles, "nothing to be afraid of."

Davi swims off and hangs on a marble edge of the pool beside the exterior windows. Jane thrashes toward him, stretching her neck to keep her head above the water as she doggedly follows Davi to the poolside. Jane tries not to make her difficulty too obvious, but the water catches at her ankles, wraps heavy tendrils around her arms. Davi waits at the edge, watching her struggle and splutter. She kicks and kicks, a foot closer to the pool's edge, then another.

Davi grins. "Your profile said you were on the school swim team?"

Jane gasps as she snatches the pool's edge, and she holds on so tightly that the tips of her fingers turn white. "Sorry," Jane pants, "you just – startled me, is all."

She is so angry that she could drown him, but for the moment she thinks only of keeping hold of the marble edge of the pool.

Davi ignores her suffering, staring at the city unfolding from the base of the tower and stretching to meet the midnight blue sky. "People are enamoured with the lights when they're up here. They look endless, no?"

He waves a hand across the glistening vista. "But I look at the *darkness*," he adds, pointing to the distant black at the horizon. "What's there? Who?"

He leaves Jane a moment to consider the swath of light below them, crowned by a dark strip the thinness of her finger. "You know, we can connect with anyone – *everyone* – with technology," he says, "but we do the opposite: we use it to cut away the unworthy people. I won't even *connect* to anyone lower than five-hundred."

She wavers, clinging to the tile like it was a cliff edge, but peeks over at him. His characteristic grin has slipped away, his eyebrows no longer set to suave.

"A few years ago, I went to see who was in that darkness," he says. "Secret trips – very expensive. I met a woman and fell in love," he continues.

"*She* isn't in your profile," Jane splutters.

"That's because she doesn't exist. Or, at least, she didn't have a profile. She was from the Red Zone," Davi explains. Jane's heart jumps at the admission. "And maybe it wasn't true love after all," he muses. "Maybe it was just to stick it to my father. But that woman meant everything to me."

Jane eases her breathing.

"Where is she now?"

Davi's eyes drop from the window. "My father found out. I'd never seen him like that. For hours he ran me down, said I was unworthy of his legacy." His jaw clenches. "It was the only instance I was worth more than six minutes of his time."

Jane says sorry and almost lays a hand on his shoulder, but she can't bear removing her hands from the pool's edge. The tips of her fingers start to go numb.

Davi grimaces. "She managed to escape before he found her. She's somewhere out there, now, in that darkness."

There are few drops left on his sad features. He looks at her with a mixture of pain and release, like he's just had a bone set. Jane thinks of his father – Daviault *senior*, the most powerful man in the State. Ever since the flood, she has imbued the thought of him with hate and derision, but even in her anger, she had not expected such ruthlessness – especially to his own son.

Then she stiffens, beginning to worry. Daviault's father does not pay much attention to his son – except to the women his son congregates with. "What would he make of *us* being alone?" she says.

"That's why we're meeting *here*."

Jane stares. This was a mistake.

Davi changes the subject. "Come with me," he says, dislodging one of her hands from the edge. He swims from the edge, her hand in his. Her breath stutters. "Trust me," he says again.

Jane doesn't. But she lets go, and they drift to the centre of the pool. Each metre they drift from safety escalates her panic.

"The lights," he says, "are beautiful. But so is the darkness."

Then he sucks in a breath, lets her hand go, and dives under.

She whisks her hands and feet desperately, abandoned in the middle of the pool, but Davi does not return. As the water laps into her mouth, Jane sees Davi rush back to the surface at a distant end of the pool, pull himself from the pool, and touch a switch on the wall. A black skin peels over the windows and all goes dark. She searches but can see nothing, not even her hands trying to tread water.

"Davi?" Jane whispers in the darkness. She keeps whisking her feet, but she cannot reach the bottom of the pool. Her limbs are invisible in the void. The water tugs at her knees, her hands flail. She spins to the left, to the right, water rushing about her shoulders, but all is black and silent. She begins to hyperventilate.

A gentle splutter from the far side of the room signals Davi's return to the pool, and then a hand comes to the curve of her hip. "The darkness is beautiful, isn't it?" comes Davi's voice. "Most people never get to see true darkness. It's one of *our* privileges."

The arm moves to the small of her back and ushers her closer. She can hear his breath. Slow, powerful, through his nose. Jane struggles with the unseen water. He is pulling her in; it is pulling her down.

"Davi," she gasps, failing to hide her panting, "can we see the lights again?"

Her limbs scramble. The water gulps her arms. She wants to flee, but she cannot see the pool's edge. Frantic breaths saw back and forth in her chest. Davi's hand remains on her hip, drawing her in.

"Please," she grimaces.

"Tell me, Jane, what other Trippier films have you seen?"

"What?" she gasps.

"You said at the restaurant that you were a big fan of his films. Tell me which you have seen."

Her thrashing disturbs the water, and a wave crashes into her face. She lets out a hacking cough. "Can we please talk about this later?"

"Skyra is not able to help you here. I want to know your answer," says Davi, "unlike my father, I have all the time to wait."

Jane coughs up more water. "Please," she wheezes.

Davi jostles her up and down, as he might a child, if any woman were unfortunate enough to bear his children. The water enters her eyes, Saltwater, it stings.

"I don't know, I don't know," she blubbers, "please let me get out of the pool."

"My people looked very deeply into you Jane," Davi says. "How much deeper should they look?"

Then the arm around her back pulls her down a few inches, just long enough for water to surge up her nose before he pulls her up again. She spits out the newest mouthful of water.

"Please just let me out," Jane pleads.

Davi draws Jane close enough to whisper in her ear and she feels his chest press into hers. "With my father dying, I have become target. I need people I can rely on."

Jane tries to pull away, but Davi jerks her back. Another wave splatters into her face and her nose burns with the saltwater.

"I don't know anything," Jane blubbers, "I can't help."

His hand comes to her forehead and smooths the hair away. She knows that he can push her down into the water if he chooses.

"I just want to know that I can rely on you, Jane. Or else I must look a little closer at the other anomalies in your profile."

"Yes, yes, yes," Jane says, she does not know how many times.

Silence.

Davi's arm leaves her.

Water gurgles away from her, and then she hears a *whoosh* as he leaves the pool.

"I'm sorry if the dark frightened you," Davi says from somewhere.

The skin along the window retracts. The lights leak in, the pool returns to midnight blue. Jane skitters to the nearest edge and drags herself out. She splutters on the poolside until Davi rounds the pool and offers his hand to pull her up. Jane mumbles a *thank you* and he lifts her to her feet. Sheets of water fall from her sodden dress. She squeezes the remainder from her hair, and then clasps her hands in front of her chest, shaking. Davi tosses her a towel. She clutches the towel tightly, trying not to shiver, but her ribcage shakes with panicked breaths. The water had almost taken her. It turns cold on her shoulders. Her ratty hair sticks to her skin. The urge to flee lingers, but there is nobody to scream to, no camera to shelter under.

"I hope you enjoyed seeing true darkness for the first time," Davi says from behind her.

Jane composes her breath before she turns to Davi. He sits beside the table in his shirt and trousers, replacing one of his socks.

She needs to obey the Director's command to spy on Davi, and she needs to avoid Davi's bad side. And she also needs a place where she will not be watched, a place where she can keep secrets, a place that requires Davi's password pills. Though Jane longs to flee, horrid words leave her mouth: "I did. I would like to come again."

Davi rummages in the inside jacket of the suit jacket folded on the table and holds up the bag of pills to her. "Any time."

Jane stares at the bag, thinking of Davi's woman from the Red Zone, wondering whether by accepting the pills, she will suffer the same fate.

# Chapter 14:
# Unweaving the Rainbow

When the cloud is low enough, the roof of the Mercantile Bank tower rises just out of the clouds like a tiny island in a milky sea. On the occasional moments Jane escapes promotional commitments, she goes to the tower, waits until her Skyra bracelet goes dark, then stashes the bracelet for later. Then, freed from Skyra's observance, Jane sneaks to the roof of the tower, sits on the edge, and dangles her legs off the side, losing her feet in the creamy wisps. There is no horizon up there; the cloud fluffs further than she can see.

Jane discovered the rooftop while everyone else was locked in their private rooms. She took a screwdriver to the roof access door without noticeably damaging the lock, and the roof became Jane's little private island. She wished that the visits were not so sparse, but she has to save the pills for grander purposes. Still, she had set one aside for Ashley.

Ashley and Jane drop their dead Skyra bracelets at the access door and squint at the burst of white that greets their entry to the rooftop. "We can only come here when the cloud is low," Jane explains, "so it's the only place where you can never see the city."

It was also the only place that the city could not see *her*. For three years, Nature had watched Jane. Though Jonas had warned her that going to a State as large as Nature risked exposing her profile, there was nowhere else she wanted to go, no better place to avenge her sister.

Jane kicks off her shoes and swishes her feet in the wisps of cloud. Ashley crosses her legs and sits a few feet from the edge of the tower. She removes a woolen hat and shakes out her hair. Jane shields her eyes from the sun as she appreciates all seven streaks in Ashley's hair: the colours of the rainbow.

"The other models say they can tell my mood by the colour of my hair," Ashley says, noticing Jane's gaze, "pink was when I first joined the agency. It was good then. Yellow was good too. Purple was a bad time."

"And rainbow?"

"I guess that I'm feeling a bit of everything."

"It's very beautiful."

"Thank you. It took a lot to convince the Director."

Ashley picks at the laces of her shoes. "I see how you look out for me," Ashley finally says, not looking up from her shoes. "Why is that?"

Jane watches Ashley play with her laces. She finds herself staring at Ashley's fingers. Jane's mind conjures a memory of tiny cold hands with fragile little fingers, fingers that, at one time, wrapped around Jane's forefinger until it turned white. Jane considers telling Ashley about the memory, but the secret would put both of them in danger. Best to present herself fractionally, even to her closest friend.

"Same reason you look out for me," Jane says, stretching her arms behind her and letting her head hang backward. "Who else is gonna?"

Jane enjoys slow breaths of the peaceful, crisp air. She almost drifts off, but for a spurt of wind that twists her chestnut hair. She looks over. Ashley continues twitching her laces.

"I like to think of the cloud as a great woolen blanket," Jane says, breaking the quiet. "When I was a child and I wanted to say something out loud without somebody hearing it, I used to put the grey blanket over my head and immediately I was safe. I could say anything." She smiles at Ashley. "We can say anything up here."

Ashley comes closer, sits carefully on the edge, removes her shoes, and dips her feet into the cloud like she is testing its temperature. The cloud tickles her feet until a smile gleams on her face. It is a lovely smile – an authentic one Jane seldom sees. Ashley has a gap between her two front teeth that agency has said not to fix. They say it makes her look younger and more innocent. Those awkward pubescent teeth are Ashley's signature, flashed often for photos but only rarely, in moments like these, for joy.

Ashley softens like the wisps of cloud until finally, she speaks: "All the adverts we see are personalized to us, right? Have you ever thought about how accurate they are? You know – like, what they say about us?"

"What kind of adverts do you get?"

Ashley sighs. "Diet pills. Fitness programs to get a thigh gap and get rid of bat wings. Anxiety meds. Public speaking courses. Everything I feel self-conscious about, it knows. And reminds me of."

"Don't listen to them."

"How? They're with me wherever I go. The more I see, the heavier they are. I carry them everywhere."

Jane pulls Ashley close. Ashley leans her temple on Jane's shoulder, spilling orange and indigo hair over Jane's white blouse. "What kind of adverts do *you* get?" Ashley mumbles.

"I don't pay them attention."

Jane wishes that were true. If it was all up to inner determination, it might be possible; but adverts snake past her efforts, or bombard her, or wait until she is asleep.

Ashley pulls in closer. "But you don't wonder – even a little bit – whether they're right about you? Maybe the adverts you get are a perfect mirror?"

"All of those adverts come from some algorithm that processes all the bits of data about you, right?" Jane says. "And the wisdom is that breaking someone into all these pieces of data allows them to be understood down to their smallest intricacies."

Ashley nods a little, but keeps her head lent on Jane's shoulder. Jane studies the colourful strands of Ashley's hair. "Everything can be reduced to relationships between numbers, I suppose. Even a rainbow. There's some precise formula that can explain how light refracts through raindrops. But I think some of the beauty in a rainbow is lost by breaking it into pieces. The same can be said of us. No matter how accurate their algorithms are – there's a beautiful poetry about you that can never be represented by an advert."

Jane feels Ashley's breath slow.

"I guess you're right."

They stay like that, Ashley's head on Jane's shoulder, the sun sinking into them, until a glint of white on Jane's wrist catches her attention. It is a scar, now barely more than a nick, that she passed off as an injury from tripping over her own feet and falling on the pavement. The scar is where Skyra normally sits on her wrist. She'd lied about where she got it. Only one man knows the truth.

When Jonas set up her profile for Nature, he cautioned that she could not enter wearing clothes from her present home, Chron-OS. Everything you wear, he said, has tags too small to find, so you gotta nuke em in the microwave. Jane had eyed him, knowing Reds were vulgar and exploitive. Jonas had read her expression. You're not my type, he said, sourly, that's why I'm out here. Now put 'em in for six seconds, just enough to melt the copper.

With Jonas's back turned, Jane bundled her clothes into an old microwave with an unfamiliar display and withdrew them after six seconds. Though the clothes smelled faintly of smoke, Jane could not see any burns. As she pulled them back on, Jonas called that he would put in replacement tags that matched her new home.

Just one more thing, Jonas had added with some reluctance. He explained that Nature did not use sub-dermal trackers like Chron-OS did. All tracking was done through a little bracelet called Skyra. Jane shrugged and asked if he had a bracelet. Of course, Jonas said, that isn't the problem. Then Jane's felt her face sink. I'm going to have to take out my tracker, she said.

The flood had taken the biggest pieces from Jane, and the un-countable sensors in Nature feel like they pick over the remaining pieces like an army of ants. Only when around Ashley does she re-member words and thoughts that are still a part of her and start to feel a little more whole. But her wrist itches sometimes. Skyra aggra-vates the old wound. Perhaps it will never quite heal.

Jane had refused to let Jonas do it. She threw back a shot of his homemade whiskey, made her way to a metal basin, and took a scal-pel in her left hand. She lowered it just beside the vein in her right wrist, looking for a chip no bigger than a grain of rice. But she was shaking, so Jonas took over. It'll just be a little nick, Jonas encour-aged, just look at me, ask me something. Why the fuck do we put these things in ourselves, Jane blurted. Because it seems like getting something for free, Jonas said as her blood christened the edge of the scalpel. But it isn't free, Jonas continued, they harvest the pressure in your veins, the sugar levels. The real price, he said, is in blood.

Then he inserted the tweezers, and everything went saturated, heightened. She looked down; the crimson on her wrist was red, redder, smoother than milk, burbling frictionless into the basin. And then the edges of her vision became grainy, her muscles became loose, and she drifted as if a feather in the wind. Jonas said something about disinfecting, and there were splinters of pain as the world returned to crisp detail. Jane shouted, swore, twisting a fistful of Jonas's denim jacket with her left hand until Jonas said, all done, all done, and Jane loosened her grip. As he bandaged her wrist, Jane eyed the black grain of rice sitting at the bottom of the basin. The grain held all her history, all her friendships, all the bad and all the good. He didn't let her keep it.

Ashley raises her head from Jane's shoulder. "There's something I have to tell you," Ashley says.

Jane re-opens her eyes. "Anything."

"I *used* to get the ads for diet pills," Ashley says. Then she gulps. "But my adverts started changing."

"How do you mean?"

"Recently I've had very different adverts. I still see diet pills and anxiety pills. But I also see pre-natal vitamin pills and diapers and – baby carriages."

Ashley gets up from the edge of the tower. She hugs herself, shivering despite the sunlight, and staggers in circles like a lost child. "It was Moral Decay, they expected me to drink, but I had got so tired of feeling under a microscope, I had way too much."

Sobs steal the end of her sentence. Her eyes are wide and hopeless. Jane rushes to comfort her. "You don't think the agency knows, do you?" Ashley cries. "Maybe it's just a coincidence?"

They know it is not. Whether by tracking unusual eating habits or morning sickness, the algorithms know. They likely knew before Ashley did. If advertisers know, then so can anyone else – including their agency. They will not let a pregnancy shatter Ashley's image of childish innocence. Reality will be aligned to match the marketing. Ashley shakes, as if she can feel the black mark of her stupidity kicking in her belly.

The wind picks up and the cloud moves in.

Ashley asks over and over what she should do. She shrieks, and pleads, and crumbles to her knees and cries. Jane muffles Ashley's cries in her shoulder. "It will be ok," Jane whispers, "it'll be ok. We'll figure it out."

Ashley remains on her knees, fingers trembling around Jane's waist. Perhaps she would rather stay and choke on the impending cloud. Jane wrenches her up, Ashley heavy with grief.

The cloud spills over the edge of the tower. Soon they will be engulfed. Jane escorts Ashley to the access door, presses it shut, and finds Ashley cradling a Skyra bracelet in trembling hands.

Jane had felt relieved when Jonas secured the Skyra bracelet around her wrist with a delicate click. It looked like a little halo. I think I prefer the bracelet to the tracker, Jane had said, at least I can take the bracelet off. Oh no, Jonas corrected, you don't take it off. Jane didn't understand, but the insistence in Jonas's eyes told her that, in time, she would.

Jane catches a few of Ashley's words. "—*can't find out*—" Ashley chokes. "—*if they do*—" Ashley fumbles with the bracelet. Jane searches for an answer, but no words come. "— *they'll send me back*—" Ashley laments, fumbling the bracelet "—*I can't go back*—"

*Back*, Jane surmises, means Theos: where sensors are God's eyes, and the state police His wrath. Jane swaddles Ashley's shaking body in her arms. Jane's mind sparks with the answer – the *only* answer. It has worked before, or so she hopes. "I can fix this," she says.

Jane will need help. She knows who to get it from.

There's a man I know, Jonas had said as he showed Jane to the exit, I've loaded his details to your Skyra bracelet. We're kindred spirits, Jonas said, even if he's forgotten. To get his help, Jonas had said as he pulled open the metal door, all you need is one word: *Waterloo*.

"Listen," Jane whispers to Ashley, "I have to go away for a few days. But when I come back, I'll have an answer."

Ashley winces, squeezing handfuls of Jane's blouse. She asks how long. Jane repeats that it will only be a few days. Ashley deflates like Jane has struck her. "I need to come here," Ashley says, "I need an escape."

Jane does not want to leave Ashley at all, let alone allow her to sneak onto the roof unaccompanied. "I don't think that's a good idea," she says, as softly as she can.

"Just a place to go…" Ashly begs.

Jane feels Ashley's body shiver against her own. There is often an itch on Jane's wrist, a tension between her shoulders, and a pressure in her skull that only the clear air and sunny glow of the rooftop can relieve. She cannot deprive Ashley of their rooftop refuge. Jane opens one of Ashley's hands and presses a few of the precious password pills into Ashley's palm. "I'll be back soon."

Ashley balls the pills in one hand, and Jane's hand in her other. She clears her throat. "There's one more thing," Ashley sniffs, smearing her nose on her forearm. She looks up, eyes pink, and adds, "I need to tell you about the father."

# Chapter 15:
# Across the Wasteland

Despite the weariness of shouldering Ashley's secret, Jane cannot sleep. After an hour of seeing nothing but wasteland out of the helicopter window, Jane tried to get some rest before they landed. The combination of adrenaline, planning, and the thrumming helicopter blades have kept her awake. She scrunches her eyes tighter.

Jane hears the man beside her sigh again, so loudly he almost drowns out the chopper blades. Jane wishes that she could have brought anyone else. For the past half hour, he has bounced his leg anxiously, like Reece used to when a delivery hadn't come. Jane had only met him once, and in bad circumstances. He was the organizer of the Marie Cherie show, which Jane had ruined by setting the marquee dress on fire. That made it hard enough for Jane to convince him to help her. That he had waited beside her limousine outside the Red Zone nightclub to berate her for risking his TELOS will make it harder.

Jane wishes that she could have anyone but Ray Burnett to turn to. Ray is too loose with the feed and too unguarded with Skyra to be trusted. She finds it difficult to believe that he was *ever* allied with someone as secretive as Jonas. She had scanned his profile but did not find anything called Waterloo. His early years were fuzzy, owing to poorer data collection back then. At one point he held a flowering job and a healthy TELOS, then suddenly he fractured from his network and foundered in mediocrity as a marketing manager. Nothing suggested any relationship to Jonas. Jane considered that Jonas may have lied about knowing Ray, but she knew better than anyone that a profile hardly tells the whole truth about someone.

Ray still watches out the window, despite there being nothing to see. Though, that is not quite true. After Jonas sent Jane back over the border to the Green Zone, she caught the train to Nature. During the ride across the wasteland, the train shuddered to a halt and the cabin went dark.

Reds, the other passengers whispered, must be the Reds. Then lightening ruptured the darkness, and for a moment everything was awash with silver. In that moment, Jane spotted it, out the cabin window, a handful of small buildings, she was sure, illuminated for a split-second. A little town, perhaps? But before she could check, the cabin re-lit to searing white, and the train whirred back to speed. She had not been able to confirm what she had seen, for searching about life outside the cities would instantly flag her profile, but the sight of that little town had stuck with her. She was sure she had seen it.

Jane does not want to look out the helicopter window. It makes her doubt what she had seen. She hears Ray fidget in his seat, and wonders what it is about the wasteland that makes him so uneasy.

***

Ray watches endless, desolate dirt pass the window of the helicopter. He loosens and tightens his fists. *How much longer?* They are headed to a castle to shoot the *Ageless Beauty* promotion for Forever Makeup. Two days away from the State. He crosses his arms and seethes. He doesn't do shoots anymore. Not since he became a four-hundred TELOS.

Granted, that was only when he was at the peak of his career at the Department of Captology. Back then, he had Skyra read him psychology studies as he slept. He was a *machine* back then, with a ferocious work ethic, a portfolio of successful campaigns, and thousands of followers. His TELOS had waned since then – since—

He aborts the thought before Skyra can detect it. It will only take an uncharacteristic seizing in Ray's forearms or tension in his chest to alert Skyra. Only after does he recall that Skyra is offline, too far from the wireless chargers in the city. Without Skyra, Ray's thoughts circle and circle like a stalled app in need of resetting. The withdrawal feels like a caffeine headache. Ray searches out the window again, looking for a distraction that did not come. He looks down at the Skyra bracelet, peeking out between his crossed arms, then he looks away and hides the wrist under his jacket. He is discovering a new and thoroughly unpleasant emotion: boredom.

The Director had waved away Ray's protests. Ray had been *specifically requested* by Jane and the Director was unwilling to question her instincts. *Instincts*. Jane is haphazard – she disobeys directives and makes outrageous comments, she undercuts campaigns, plays when she is supposed to perform, hides logos she is supposed to advertise, sings over jingles, and worst, she set a dress on fire at the finale of a catwalk. *His* catwalk. Those are not instincts to trust, not with *his* TELOS at stake.

She sleeps, despite the chopping helicopter blades, in the chair to Ray's right. He looks from the window and sneaks a glance at her. *Two days,* he bristles. His teeth hurt; he realizes he is clenching his jaw. Jane is in blissful sleep while he suffers in horrid boredom.

He traces the shape of her face - the trademark thick brows, the thin band of turquoise around her sleeping eyes, then along the curve of her nose to its upturned point. Though Ray has seen a thousand videos of her on the feed, and had the misfortune of meeting her in person at the Marie Cherie disaster, it feels as if he has never seen her before. She *is* beautiful, he thinks: a stunner; a sylph; elfin; spritely; the descriptors attached to her on the feed are endless. She looks unreal, like she has clambered out of a screen.

"Have you ever wondered," she asks, eyes shut, "how we can *feel* eyes on us?"

He turns back to the window. "Sorry."

She keeps her eyes closed. "If I was bothered by people looking at me, I'd be in the wrong job."

"You *do* enjoy having everyone's attention," he mutters.

"Now we have nobody watching. Isn't that strange?"

He is irritated that she did not latch on to his insult, more irritated that he even said it. It is a good thing Skyra had not heard, else he might have lost a point of TELOS.

"Strange? Between losing Skyra and the castle we are going to, it feels like flying back in time."

"How marvelous," she smiles, though she keeps her eyes closed.

"Hardly. I like having Skyra. Let's me check on who I am dealing with, so I don't get any unpleasant surprises."

She opens her eyelids a crack. "What's the point of ever meeting anyone, then, if Skyra has already revealed everything about them?"

"Sometimes it doesn't," he grunts, returning her glance.

She shuts her eyes once more and stretches out her legs. "Everything I do is on the feed," she dismisses. "It knows more about me than *I* do. I have to be the most predictable person on the planet."

"We both know that isn't true. That's why *you're* the one sitting in that seat rather than another model." He sounds bitter when he says it, but she smiles all the same. Her disruptiveness is why her influence has grown so quickly. He wonders why she has brought her disruptiveness to *him* once more.

He studied her profile to try and understand why she had torn him from the city at short notice. It cost him a lot and left him only with more questions. "Is it true," Ray begins, "that you got the job by – beating the Director in a hand of poker?"

Ray bought all the data he could. Most were paywalled, at the Director's expense. The only data of the incident came from Jane's profile. He knew she flirted her way into the casino, having failed the interview to become a life streamer, and in serious debt. But the voice recordings were far too expensive. Data on her responses during the poker game showed smooth emotion undeterred by the Director's incisive eyes. And a hand later, she left, and the next day walked into a new job at the agency.

Since then, she and the Director shared a symbiotic relationship: at once mutualistic, for she gained fame and the Director gained influence; and parasitic, for the Director's campaigns fed off her increasing exposure. Yet the genesis of its all – that hand in the casino – was beyond Ray's reach. There were other prospective models at the agency – prettier, more cooperative – yet the Director took *her* into his hand.

Jane shrugs.

"You *have* to tell me," Ray adds, but her expression tells him that she does not. He tightens his fist again.

The helicopter comes upon the remnants of a castle. Three grey walls still stand but the final curtain wall has been parted by the hand of time. As they descend, Ray shakes his head at the sorry structure, a bulwark against an enemy that no longer exists. It is a long-dead relic that doesn't have the courtesy to decompose. The earth should have the mercy to swallow the remaining walls.

They land with a shudder. Jane opens her eyes and stretches as she stands. She's a little short for a model – 167cm – but she looks taller than that through sheer force of will. She defaults to a perfect posture – shoulders back, chest forward, chin angled. She catches his gaze again.

"Let's have a wander around and see if we can find the best place to shoot," he suggests. She smiles. Her teeth are as straight as if they were planned by an architect. But Jane is always pulling funny faces with them, as if her tongue and her lips are at war with her teeth, unable to accept their perfection, crashing again and again the pearly walls.

She skitters from the helicopter, moving like she can charge remotely. Despite the wind whisking her hair, Jane does not break her stare from the castle, marveling at the height of the walls, cocking back her head to see the top.

Ray strides through the collapsed wall of the castle, unawed by the structure. "Hurry up!" he calls.

The aides and the cameramen do, but Ray has to call again to get Jane's attention.

"At some point, this was a tourist attraction," he explains to Jane as they enter the courtyard, "went out of business with the advent of 3-D experiences. Hardly worth coming here when you can get the same thing at home."

"Funny," she says, stooping to pick up a piece of painted wood, "all the ticket booths and the snack stands have disintegrated." Her eyes rise to the tip of the guard tower at the castle's corner, still standing after centuries.

The courtyard is overgrown with weeds. Jane lags behind, and Ray has to call for her again. She trots to them with her mouth wide. Finally, they head to the bailey at the centre of the castle. The rooms inside the bailey are dank and dark. They enter one of the royals' bedrooms and an aide switches on a portable lamp, revealing replica furniture coated with dust.

"This could work," Ray says. "What do you think?"

Jane is not behind him.

He calls for her.

Ray swears under his breath. She has disappeared.

The crew each take a flashlight and split up to find her. They shout Jane's name down dark corridors, each call becoming less polite. Ray wanders alone into a vaulted room, searching. The flashlight barely penetrates the thick black. He wishes he had Skyra, for Skyra would know what to do. Ray's headache grows worse.

The calls of the crew go silent as a heavy wooden door shuts behind Ray. He hears only his footsteps on the stone floor. That, and his breath, rife with aggravation. He shouts Jane's name, but it is swallowed by the blackness. A fireplace emerges at the end of the hall. He takes the door to his right, grunting with exertion as the door lumbers open. He approaches a staircase and calls her name again. Only silence replies. He hesitates going further, but he finds comfort in the whispers of adverts still ringing in his ear, and descends the staircase into unknown darkness.

The staircase winds to his left, blackness hiding all but the few steps before him. He has never seen true darkness before. Ray keeps his left hand on the wall, the rough surface bristling on his skin. The staircase yields to a hallway. Ray's fingers, still tracing the wall, feel something cold and iron. He points the flashlight's meagre rays to his left. Bars to a cell. He has wandered into the dungeon. He tests the bars with a pull. A slight clang, but no give.

"Are you lost?" Jane's voice comes from somewhere.

"We don't have time for this." Ray's voice echoes on the dungeon walls. The city – and Skyra – await his return.

"You should make the time. The city is so loud, so bright. When else do we get the chance to be in pure, black silence?"

The blackness and the silence are alien to him. "Let's go back up," he says, voice wavering.

"You're very eager to leave something you've never enjoyed. Doesn't it feel good to have no eyes on you? I can put out my hands before me and they're invisible. It feels like floating."

"Do I have to carry you upstairs?"

"You'll have to find me first!"

He points his flashlight about the room, scrutinizing each cell for Jane. The shadows of the iron bars lean with the movement of his light.

"Over here!" he hears.

Ray searches cell after cell, but the darkness goes on forever.

"So close!" comes Jane's voice.

"Fine," Ray gnashes. "If I enjoy the darkness, you'll come?"

"Of course," she says from a distance. "Now turn off that light and tell me how it feels."

He does. Though all goes black, Ray still sees streaks of colour, as if logos are imprinted on his eyelids. He blinks and blinks until the colours fade and he sees nothing whether his eyes are open or closed. He hears nothing, either. There are no adverts or promotions or feed articles. No connection requests or network updates; no jolts of junk, nor jobs, nor jingles. No commercials for cutting-edge commodities, no cruel captivations, no incomprehensible cacophony. All that remains is –

– quiet.

The only thing he can sense is what he feels inside.

A memory arises from his subconscious. He was lying on a hill-top with his father, watching the sky, back when they could still see some of the stars. The grass tickled the back of his neck. Though the air was crisp and the condensation sopped into his t-shirt, he was too invigorated by questions about constellations to feel the cold. He didn't remember falling asleep on the hill. Ray awoke in their tent the next morning to the sound of bacon crackling in a skillet. He sees, unearthed from dim memory, his father's face, as fleshy and real as if his father were before him. Ray reaches out to the father he has not seen nor remembered in so long. It is a gift from the dark-ness, a memory as crisp as the dew on that hillside.

A light flicks on, illuminating Jane's face. Shadows streak up her features. "Wasn't that worth it?" she says. "Now come on – the stair-case is pretty uneven. Let's take it together."

She takes his hand. Her skin is so smooth it is almost formless. Jane leads Ray up the stairs but when he turns to trace his steps back to the rest of the crew, she pulls him further up the staircase. Ray squints as his eyes adjust to the light that welcomes them to the battlements. There is not much of a view from the battlements – patchy grey grass, mostly – but it is something they never see in Nature: the natural world. Jane spreads out her hands to feel the wind lance between her fingers. Ray forgets the memory of his father, his irritation returning. He crosses his arms, moves his hands to his hips, then crosses his arms again. Jane remains statuesque. Finally, he interrupts: "What do you want?"

"I needed the best... *social engineer*."

She doesn't even try to sell the lie.

"Do you even *know* what I do?" Ray says.

Jane shrugs. "Manipulate people?"

"Manipulation is what people cry to disclaim their choices," he retorts. "If they like the choice, they made it freely; if they dislike it, they claim manipulation."

"You are telling me you don't manipulate people?"

"I'm telling you I don't do photoshoots in old castles."

Jane turns from the battlements to face him. Her hair flickers in the wind. "I need something from you," she says. She tells him that she needs to arrange a shoot for Ashley Gaetz in another State – somewhere where Ashley can be spirited away and wrapped in a new identity. He doesn't believe her – doesn't *want* to believe her – but the insistence in her eyes tells him that she is serious.

For a moment he seizes with fear that Skyra can hear them. But, for the first time, he is grateful that the bracelet is disconnected. "You want me to help an agency asset escape the State?" he hisses. "Why would I take that risk?"

Jane hesitates, before she finally says, "She's pregnant."

"Can't she—"

"It's too late. The system knows."

"That's no reason—"

"The father is – Daviault Junior."

Ray feels his face drop. He shakes his head.

"Don't you understand?" Jane says, "Daviault will—"

"—force her to lose the baby and threaten her to keep quiet, *if she's lucky*?" Ray answers. "I know what kind of man he is. And I know what he'll do when he finds out we conspired to help her."

"I know it's a risk."

"It's not a risk, it's a *certainty*. As soon as Skyra turns back on, it'll see the guilt in your eyes. You think you can keep secrets locked up in that pretty head of yours? Skyra will prise them out."

"I was told you would help."

"You were told wrong."

Jane visibly clenches her jaw and her eyes thin. "What's Waterloo?"

The word is a jolt to his ribs. "I'm leaving."

"Why? What is—"

"If you tell *anyone*—" he begins, but cannot finish the threat. He storms away.

Jane calls after him: "If you can't tell me, maybe the Director can."

Ray stops at the top of the staircase. Jane waits on the battlements for him to return.

He shakes his head and descends into the darkness.

# Chapter 16:
# A Man's House is His Castle

Jane stands with her back to the camera in one of the castle's wash chambers. Behind her are a crew of four or five, adjusting the lighting, operating the cameras, supervising. She holds a sponge in her right hand and makes gentle circles of soap on her left shoulder, just above the Truman tattoo on her back. Skyra will remove the tattoo in post. The scene captures the ancient environment of the castle – its stone rooms free from screens and lights and technology – contrasted with the youth of her skin. *Ageless Beauty*, so goes the tagline of the campaign.

They click pictures from behind, as if they had sneaked upon her undetected. This, she reflects, must have been the dream of past invaders: to break down the castle walls and stumble on one of the princesses, caught unaware in her chamber. The photographers are modern invaders, with modern means of breaching walls.

Jonas had been wrong. Jane would have no help from Ray. Worse, she has exposed her own secrets and revealed Ashley's pregnancy. Ray will report her.

Jane studies the ancient stones in the wall. She envies how the women of the castle must have lived. They were seen naked only by the chambermaids. Had she lived then, she wouldn't have been subjected to the watchful eyes of onlookers, the curve of her spine immortalized by cameras, to be broadcast to an infinite public.

But those centuries ago, her body would have been shrouded from the moment of birth, a sin to be kept from view. It must have been strange to have *so* much privacy that a woman couldn't choose to show herself. Perhaps that wasn't privacy at all. Perhaps privacy depended upon choice. Perhaps her sisters of centuries past, who could never choose when to expose their skin, had the same control of their privacy as Jane does.

As Ashley does.

One of the crew calls for her to gather her hair over her shoulder. It is clammy. Every few minutes they apply more water. She tries not to shiver in the draughty chamber, the coldness of the stone floor leaking into her toes. The clicks of their cameras resume.

"Look over your shoulder as if you've just noticed someone," a crewman calls. Jane does, feigning a look of pleasant surprise, as she searches the crew for Ray. She doesn't see him. He has probably denounced her by now. Perhaps there are Liberators already assembling on the opposite side of the wooden chamber door.

"I think we've got what we need," she hears. The crewmen file out, leaving her, finally, alone in the chamber. She is about to shut the heavy wooden door and a brief solitude when a voice comes from the corridor.

It says that Ray wants to see her.

"Give me a few minutes," she says, fear inflecting the words.

Despite the gown and the portable heater in her dressing room, Jane still shivers. Aides try to have her sit still to reapply makeup and untangle her hair, but Jane shakes and shakes despite their efforts. She ruminates on whether Ray will turn her in, replaying their argument in her mind, assessing his words, wishing she had chosen different ones.

Jane spins escape routes around in her mind, but each boomerangs back to hopelessness: she has no way to survive in the wasteland and no way to leave except in the helicopter with Ray. Though they are hours from the city, she convinces herself that Ray will be accompanied by a group of Liberators when he comes. Perhaps he brought a few along, in secret, just in case. Jane considers how she might incapacitate him – the castle steps *are* treacherous – but startles at a heavy knock on the door.

Ray's voice, behind her, instructs the aides to leave. She sees him in the mirror. Sweat beads at his temples, and his tie is loosened from his throat. He waits until they can no longer hear footsteps. While he does, Jane frets as to whether to stay or to flee. She stands just in case. "Look," she offers as he approaches, "it wasn't fair of me to ask. I just – I hope you won't turn me in—"

"I don't know who told you," Ray snarls, jabbing a finger at her, "but you don't know anything."

"Then tell me," Jane says. "What did you do?"

"Something good," Ray says. "I won't make that mistake again."

"If you won't help Ashley for good, do it for self-preservation."

He scowls. "This is why you nominated me for this assignment?" She nods. He shakes his head. "You're just like the Liberators: twisting someone's past against them."

"If you don't help, the Liberators will be after *Ashley*."

Though his jaw vices together, his eyes drop, and he stops. He draws fingers through sweaty hair as something replays in his mind. Jane wishes that she had Skyra to tell her how angry Ray was, or what he usually did with that anger. Living with Tristan, her ex-boyfriend, made her fear the worst.

But she pities Ray, as he crawls fingernails once more through his hair. He takes his aggression out on himself, grabbing painful handfuls of his hair as he paces to Jane's left, then to her right. She had not meant to cause him this pain. Guilt tugs at her determination to help Ashley. She recalls the wreckage she has left in other lives – the mother she did not warn, the adoptive family she rebuffed, the friends she left in Chron-OS – and wonders why she leaves a path in other's lives like the dead earth outside the castle's walls.

"Tell me how you found out," he finally says.

Their eyes meet in mutual defiance. Perhaps he wants more of her secrets to pass to the Liberators. Perhaps he wants to tie up loose ends. Something in his features, though, tells her to trust him. She swallows hard, steels herself, and tells him – about Chron-OS, about Carl, and Reece, and Jonas, and the faked profile. Each truth feels a step closer to a Liberator cell. It is more than enough to report her. But she doesn't tell him her biggest secret, about what she has planned for Black Friday, not yet.

"He was always one for fool's errands," Ray mutters.

"So?" Jane says. "Your turn."

She half-expects him to open the door and reveal a squad of Liberators. Even in a dead castle, she is paranoid of someone listening in. Ray takes one of the folding chairs and she takes the other. "Waterloo was a protest against surveillance," he says.

"Never heard of it."

"Why do you think that is?" Ray says. He recounts that it used an app to organize protestors and coordinate disruptions. He explains that the app spread through a viral marketing campaign. "The author of that campaign," Ray concludes, "was me."

Jane quirks her eyebrows. "You?"

Ray cocks his head defensively.

"I just mean—" She considers her words. At any moment she has three phrases wanting to jump from her mouth. "You're so *involved* in the agency. I can't picture you as part of a protest, let alone one of its organizers." It was a long time ago, he says. She asks how he wasn't found out. "Did Jonas change your profile too?" she says.

"I wouldn't let him near my profile," Ray bristles. "You start forging data, you make mistakes, you get found out. That's why I'm here, and he's in some Red Zone."

"Why'd you get involved?"

"Too many questions."

Though he is curt, the sweat has disappeared from his temples and his eyes gleam with a remembrance of past courage. Jane scans the room. The stones in the wall are uneven and cumbersome, but she is grateful that they have granted her the privilege of a private conversation. There will not be so many opportunities in the city. "You know," she begins, "if we were anywhere else, we'd have Liberators knocking down our doors by now." He grunts in agreement. "This castle is cold and dead," she continues, "but part of me wishes we could stay here. It's safe. It's free. Well, at least when we were in the darkness together. How sad is that?" she laughs. "We find more freedom in a dungeon than at home."

"Freedom to commit sedition?" he says, not sharing in her laughter.

"Freedom to *choose*."

He grunts again. "*Freedom to choose*," he mocks. "Nobody knows why they choose anything. That's why my job exists: I convince people to buy something and help them justify it afterward. That's really what we mean when we talk about choosing."

"Then how did you end up where you are?"

Something tells her he wants to say *too many questions* again. But he sighs and answers: "For as long as I can remember I wanted to be a musician. I always had a tune in my head. But it didn't pay, so I became a jingle writer. It was as close as I could get to music. It felt like selling out, until I realized that my interest in music probably came from an advert in the first place."

"Or maybe you're a natural? Maybe you would have always made music a part of your life?"

"It would be nice to think so."

"It's the only way to think."

He laughs. "Try thinking you're in charge of everything. Try to put your finger on why you made even the most trivial decision: what colour of lipstick to use today. Scale that up to life's biggest choices. Think about why you live where you do, or love the person you do. You've been pulled down the stream of influences, meandered this way and that – and when you look back, you have no clue how you got to where you are."

He pauses for a moment. "Thinking you're in charge of everything you do is an impossibility."

"Then why have you chosen not to turn me in?"

He rises from the folding chair and goes to the door. "I haven't," he says.

# Chapter 17:
# The Observer Effect

The Director's back is turned, his attention on two consultants who look noticeably uneasy under his stare. They say something and he crosses his arms. Their unease grows. This is her chance.

Ashley will hustle from the orderly supervising her, cut down the hallway opposite the changeroom, pass the photoshoot set, slip through the canteen, and scurry to the delivery dock, where she will find a quiet door to escape outside. From there, he is only three blocks away from the studio, according to his feed. *He*, the man whose face she can recall only in disorienting fragments, the heir of the most powerful individual in the state, the only chance of her escape. *She*, the forgotten, the keeper of his inconvenient secret, the mother of his unborn child. Ashley will confront him, coerce him if she must, until he guarantees her safety, the safety of the secret in her belly.

"I forgot my handbag," Ashley says to the orderly.

"You're returning to your apartment. We'll have it brought to you."

"It's in the changeroom. I'll only be a moment."

Ashley is already three strides away. She hustles from the orderly, toward the changeroom, cuts down the hallway, slips through the canteen, passes the photoshoot set, dodges the caterers pushing about carts of food, and scurries to the delivery dock. Some men with heavy gloves are hauling things from the back of a truck. Ashley banks left and finds a fire exit with only a crash bar to keep it shut. She throws a look over her shoulder as she presses down the crash bar. The men are still working. She eases the door open just enough to fit through, then shuts it quietly behind her.

The Director is waiting for her outside.

How had he known?

"You are not supposed to be outside," he says. His arms are folded.

"I just needed some air."

"Morning sickness?"

Ashley gulps. "I'm fine."

"Good. The orderly is waiting for you."

"Okay."

"Okay?"

"*Sir.*"

The Director walks her back through the delivery dock, the canteen, up the hallway, to the orderly. The orderly takes her back to her apartment tower, up the elevator to the third floor, and right to her front door.

"I think I know the way from here," Ashley says.

The orderly waits until she enters.

The front door locks behind her and will not open until tomorrow. Ashley looks at the plaques along the front corridor commemorating her increasing follower count. She just made it to seven hundred and fifty thousand. She jumped up and down when she removed the brown paper and saw the bronze-coloured glass underneath. The plaques remind Ashley of how many people will watch her be disgraced, as closely as if they watch over her shoulder.

It was not long ago that Ashley had proudly shown those plaques to Jane. Ashley wonders where Jane is, how soon she can see her, how soon she can bring some good news, some hope, even.

Ashley sits on her bed and searches for information about Davi's other women. There are extravagant rumours of scores of mistresses, but little information on the women themselves. It is as if when Skyra goes to retrieve results, things slip through its fingers, the crucial things, the dangerous things.

Ashley loads Davi's profile onto her wallscreen. She reviews the eyes, the heavy brows, and she shivers. If the Director will not let Ashley meet Davi in person, perhaps she can get Davi to meet her.

"Open chat," Ashley says.

An empty box appears on the wallscreen.

Ashley bites her lip. She needs something urgent but ambiguous.

"One hour," she says, and the text springs into the empty box. "Send."

Three dots on the wallscreen blink to show that the message is sending. *Dot dot dot.*

Ashley plays with her fingers.

*Dot dot dot.*

Is there an outage again?

*Message not sent.*

A voice comes through the speakers of her apartment.

"Your behaviour worries me," says the Director. "It is far outside your standard metrics."

Ashley scrunches her eyes shut.

"I expect you to follow scheduled off hours," he adds.

"Yes."

"Yes?"

"Sir," Ashley adds, hating herself.

"You'll be marked 'unavailable' until we clarify these aberrations."

The speakers go silent and the wallscreen turns off.

Ashley slumps onto her couch. She feels just like she did when she still lived with her parents. They locked her in her room, too, when she wanted to go out with friends, or later, when she talked about getting a job. The first time it happened, she did sums to pass the time. The more she was locked in her room, the better at sums she became. When sums became trivial, she moved to algebra, then quadratics. The math grew more complex as she grew older; trigonometry, kinematics, Fermat's principle. That was how she became clever: she turned their punishment into a skill.

After Ashley won the Marie Cherie competition and a sponsorship for a photoshoot in Nature, her mother snatched her arm, marched her to her bedroom, and threw the door shut. Ashley heard the familiar click of the lock. Dinner time passed and still she heard her parents arguing downstairs. Hungry, she passed the time reading about the observer effect in physics – the phenomenon that observing something changes the thing being observed. The memory reminds Ashley of Jane.

Jane always changes depending on who is observing her. Even when they were alone at the top of the Mercantile Tower, with nobody but Ashley to observe her, Jane was indeterminate, holding something back. Ashley trusts Jane, more than anyone else she has known, but maybe Jane does not trust her back. Jane had left with many promises but revealed few details. Whatever information Jane knows that might help Ashley, she would not let it be observed.

The night she won the Marie Cherie competition, Ashley's parents had gone to bed without unlocking her door. Ashley was still awake, propped up on her pillow, mulling the chapter of her book on observer effect. If observing something changed the behaviour of the thing observed, did that mean that something's true nature came out only when unobserved? Ashley's parents had gone to sleep, leaving Ashley alone; was her true nature to languish behind a locked door until they let her out?

She gathered her bedsheet, tied one end around the foot of her bed, and tested the knot with a hard tug. Then she quietly unlocked the window, wound the handle until the window opened wide enough for her to fit through, gripped the bedsheet, and lowered herself into the darkness.

Ashley goes to the window overlooking the street outside her apartment. *About nine metres. Two sheets will be enough,* she thinks as she heads for her bedroom.

# Chapter 18:
# Going Home

The castle shrinks back into the forgotten wasteland. Ray now finds something strangely reassuring in the castle's walls. Before the group left, he stole a minute to himself. He felt the wet moss brimming in the mortar of the wall and pressed a firm palm against the stone. He gave a push, but there was no give. The walls were resolute and unchanging, perhaps to their detriment, for when times changed, the walls could not change with them. Ray looked to the remaining curtain wall, crumbled and clad in moss. What force could have breached it? Was it a sudden failure, or gradual degradation?

Standing at the gaping hole in the castle's wall, Ray thought of Jane, her exterior just as beautiful and robust. He imagined that her skin, supple before the camera, might feel rough as a rock. Yet there too was a breach in her stony armour: a secret she had shared with him. Secrets were a strange concept, as antiquated as the castle they had stood in. Her secret was a vein of light through which only he had seen.

*** 

The helicopter blades chop overhead. Jane lays on her side, eyes scrunched shut, but mind racing. She has spent a long time cultivating a persona. Her life as a streamer has been an elaborate performance, filled with considered lies and playful mysteriousness. But she's confided in someone, now – confided so much that there is no way to discredit him, no way to wave off the story as another fabrication. The corporations she works for are as observant as they are paranoid. They do not tolerate aberrations. A model with a foreign, hidden past? A model conspiring to help an asset escape the State?

She will be made to disappear.

*** 

As the castle disappears into the smoggy horizon, the anxieties of the State return to Ray. Holding on to a secret is like possessing contraband. He eyes the inactive bracelet on his wrist. Being without Skyra was stressful. But as they near the city, Ray knows that Skyra will open its sleepy eye and train it upon him. He does not know if he can resist Skyra's scrutiny, or whether he ought to denounce Jane the instant they are in range of the city. But for all Ray's fear, it feels strangely relieving to have shared his secret with someone. Better to knowingly release a secret than have it quietly stolen. He must *trust* Jane – an unfamiliar but pleasing sensation, like she and he are now kindred.

Ray glances over to Jane. She lies away from him in her chair. He sighs and returns to the empty wasteland out his window. Jane opens her eyes a sliver and turns to look at Ray from the corner of her eye. His face presses to the glass. A despondent expression reflects in the pane. For a moment he looks down and their eyes meet in the reflection. Both look away.

# Chapter 19:
# The Future

Ray and the Director sit on opposite sides of the poker table. Each lays the palm of their right hand on a teal-coloured pad. The dealer between them waits as the pads calibrate. Ray and the Director hold each other's gaze, watching the confidence in the other's eyes, judging the smoothness of the other's breath. Soon their palms will betray their emotions.

They are in the Future Casino, so named for the nightly gamble on future events based upon competing analytics. It is how most corporations make decisions. The winner of the gamble will be the proprietor of the most accurate analytic. The profit incentive drives competitors to harvest more data or make connections between data nobody else has found. Tonight, they are betting on which algorithm can best predict how extra dust and smoke in the air will affect global cooling.

Ray offered three alternative venues to meet up with the Director – places without a teal pad leaking his nervousness to his adversary. The Director turned them all down. He is not one for food, or liquor, or socialising. His tastes lie in games – particularly those where other people are the pieces, so Ray had to accede to a hand of poker at the casino. As staff in suits led him to the poker table, he felt like a prisoner being led to his euthanasia injection.

A different colour of the rainbow dominates each section of the casino: soft yellow over the gambling machines, indigo over the bar, blue in the smoking lounge. The effect is generated by a prism at the far end of the casino that splits a shaft of white light falling from the ceiling. The Director and Ray are clothed in orange light.

The opening line Ray had rehearsed becomes lost in mental clutter, and the only thing that falls from his mouth is: "Thank you for meeting. I'm not your usual TELOS."

"Not since you wasted it," the Director says. "Your innovations were pioneering. But you lost track of your priorities."

"Wealth?"

"Truth. You saw humanity's true nature then shriveled from its face."

"Truth is not what we deal in."

As Ray takes a stack of chips, Skyra signals the corresponding deduction to his account.

"Tell me," says the Director, "how was she?"

"Feed chatter is way up." A non-answer, Ray knows.

"But your perspective of her?"

"The images are excellent," Ray says. "Projections for the marketing campaign are all positive."

The Director does not respond. He watches until Ray continues.

Ray pivots. "I have another pitch for you," he announces, with a drink in hand.

"Send me the analysis," the Director dismisses.

"No analysis. Gut feeling."

"We don't base marketing decisions on guts."

"My gut has produced good results before." Ray feels sick to mention it.

"Quite right. Then tell me."

Ray says that doing an out-of-State shoot was reinvigorating. He says that he wants to do some shoots in other States, to highlight the distinctiveness of Nature. Chron-OS, he says, will be perfect: it is a concrete dump, beautiful in a ghastly sort of way. How better to make people grateful to live in Nature than to show what other States look like?

"Getting a crew to another State is expensive. And the security..."

The uniqueness of the shoot will be worth it, Ray reassures. The more he defends the idea, the more he worries the Director refuses it just to probe Ray's intentions further. Ray backs off: "Just an idea," he shrugs.

The Director mulls it over. "Who would you shoot?"

"The story of the shoot would be that Nature is an *escape* from everywhere else. So we need a model who has escaped from somewhere else to be here. You've heard of Ashley Gaetz? Oh, you have? I hear she came from Theos. She's a good fit."

The Director stretches out a pause. "I haven't known you to be so *motivated*. Not for a long time."

"I'm being *personally* requested, now," he remarks, "clearly I have a reputation to maintain."

The Director watches him, lengthening the silence until it almost snaps. Ray realizes that he is holding his breath. He lets it out, slowly, so the Director will not notice, but he runs out of breath before the Director answers.

Ray cannot bear the Director's gaze. The longer Ray remains connected to Jane, the greater the scrutiny. He will detach himself from Jane as soon as Ashley Gaetz is out of harm's way.

Each pad begins to send a gentle stream of electricity to the fingers of their right hands. It feels like static on a balloon. The dealer flips them each two cards. With his left hand, Ray raises the corners of his cards. *Useless.* He tries to ignore the disappointment and keep his face composed. The pad tells him nothing about the Director's emotions. Ray stares hard at the Director, scrutinizing each detail on his face. The Director glances at his cards, and then looks up with his usual slight smile.

"Yes, she chose you *specifically* for the castle shoot," the Director remarks, rounding back to the topic Ray wants to avoid. "What did you make of that?"

Ray felt ambushed by Jane, but he does not let his face say as much. "I was honoured," he says, forcing a smile.

Ray bets, hoping to bluff. He keeps his face neutral, but he worries about his palm pressed to the glowing pad. The Director calls Ray's bet. The dealer snaps three cards face up in the middle of the table. None of them help. Ray buries the feeling of dismay, but he cannot help but steal a glance at his right hand. Are his fingers betraying him?

"Jane has never asked for *anyone* specifically before," the Director pursues. He drops the information without giving his reaction, letting Ray squirm about how it is to be taken.

"You really checked to make sure?" Ray chuckles, but the Director's face tells him that he had. "If *I* were in her shoes," Ray pivots, "I wouldn't have chosen me." He guffaws, but the levity does not relieve the pressure on his shoulders.

"But surely you must have provided her *something* she couldn't get from someone else," the Director pries.

Ray cannot tell if it is a statement or a question. If it is a question, Ray does not have a good answer. His eyes waver for a telling instant. He looks down and takes a slow sip from his glass. He is tempted to undo his top button and let out a little heat.

"I learned very early on not to underestimate her," the Director says. "I'm sure you've heard the rumours about how she got a job? An otherwise ordinary girl?"

Ray sets down his glass. "They say she beat you in a hand of palmistry poker?"

The Director leans forward to whisper, "The rumours are true."

It is not possible. The Director is a one-way mirror. The teal pad gives as little data on the Director as the feed. The nibbles of electricity in Ray's fingers are useless.

Some claim that the Director was once a neurologist who studied brain implants. This theory has as much merit as the claim that he was a hacker who used stolen secrets to blackmail his way to the top, or that he was a spy (either for or against the State, depending on who you read). The only thing the feed agrees upon, in the short-lived conspiracy posts about him, is that the Director has the singular ability to know more than he should about someone.

The dealer places another unhelpful card in the middle of the table. Ray shields his agitation.

"But given her past behaviour, I was surprised that, of all the people to work with her, you might be the first to have kept her in line," the Director says. "You must have a secret," he adds.

"No secret," Ray says, maybe too quickly. "Just an intuition."

"No, no, that is not it," the Director says. "You see, control of your life requires control of others; control of others requires understanding; and that understanding requires data." He leans forward, keeping his palm on the pad. Ray hears him out, looking for a tell. "Yet for all the data we have on her, there's an unknown impulse in her. So I say – to have controlled that impulse, you must have a secret."

Ray eyes the useless cards in the centre of the table. He needs a tell from the Director. "One of the first projects I worked on," Ray says, buying time, "was to improve revenue in a restaurant chain. They needed customers in and out more quickly. The restaurant altered portion sizes, trained waitresses to hurry people, but it was too overt. No customer wants to be told what to do. The secret was in what the customers weren't aware of: I increased the tempo of the music. Nobody noticed, but they all ate quicker, left quicker, and freed up the tables quicker.

"Jane rejects authority," Ray continues, "so I kept authority hidden."

He sells it as best he can, but the Director is right about Jane. Ray must rid himself of her soon.

The teal pad feels warm. Ray resists the urge to flex his fingers. He pivots back to his pitch. "So trust me on this Gaetz thing," Ray says. And he thrusts a stack of chips to the centre. "Raise."

The Director watches the chips trickle toward him. "If you can handle our unfortunately most stubborn asset," the Director begins, unmoved by the number of chips in the centre of the table, "I think it will be best if I assign you to her – *permanently*. Management of all her ongoing and future projects would go through you."

Ray's heartbeat jumps. Jane is toxic.

The Director pushes more chips to the centre. "Re-raise."

It is Ray's turn. Re-raise to try and bluff? Ray tries concentrating on the information he gets from the Director's pad. There is no reading from the Director's frosty fingers. Just minor static, as if the Director barely has a heartbeat, as if there is no warmth in his body. Ray eyes the chips, then the Director. "I appreciate the offer, but it's not my expertise. I can be better utilised elsewhere."

"She is becoming one of our biggest assets. I can't think of an assignment where you would be more useful."

Ray hesitates. He counts the chips spilled in the centre of the table. The Director's unbroken stare demands a response. It is much too late to back out now, and every moment Ray lingers, the greater the Director's insight becomes. The collar of his shirt tickles as it sticks to the back of his neck.

Ray pushes more chips to the centre. "Call," Ray says, equalling the Director's bet. The dealer snaps the final card onto the green felt. Still no help. Ray is alone, his heart pulsing, his hand diminishing. The fingers pressed to the pad grow sticky.

"Gaetz is unavailable, I'm afraid," the Director says.

"No, the Gaetz shoot will need to be immediate," Ray says. He searches for a quiver in the Director's lips or a waggle in his eyebrows. Nothing. "Momentum should be followed while it is still present."

He is running out of chips, so he checks, forgoing a further bet.

"I won't skip proper analyses," the Director says. His stare makes Ray feel naked. But then he looks down, smiling, and says, "Unless you can tell me more about why this plan has to be so prompt?"

Ray's attention flicks to the sweat on his palm. If he feels it, so does the Director. He looks back to the Director, feeling plundered by the stare. As the Director pushes more chips to the centre, he says, "All in."

Their eyes meet. The Director feels taller than he, towering over him, as if Ray fights on a tilted battlefield. He withers underneath the pressure on his forehead, making him want to look away. He has few chips left, his hand is hopeless, and he has no information from the Director.

This was a mistake. Ray should not have chosen to intervene. Neither the Director nor Jane nor Ashley Gaetz are under his control. It was foolish to think that he could affect any of them. It is unfortunate what Daviault Junior will do to Gaetz, but it is beyond Ray's power to help. Best to extricate himself and let the chips fall where they may.

"Fold," Ray says, tossing aside his cards. He takes his right palm from the pad, bitter at its treachery. The Director slides his cards face-down back to the dealer. Ray begins to concoct the explanation he will give Jane for his failure, rehashing excuses he has long told himself. But not even he quite believes them. And nor will Jane. She is his most pressing problem.

His thoughts flick from the disappointment of failure to damage control: specifically, how he can control the damage Jane will try to cause him, especially now that he is assigned to her. She told him more than enough to report her. His problem can disappear into a Liberator van. But she has more than enough to report *him*, and his betrayal will no doubt loosen her tongue. They are bound by mutually-assured destruction: for the moment, she must keep his secret, and he hers.

As he rises and buttons up his jacket, a question causes Ray to stay than hurry from the Director. He must understand his enemy. "If you know her so well," Ray asks of Jane, "then *how* did she beat you?"

The dealer collects the chips in the centre, already counted and added to the Director's account. The Director stands, too, and re-buttons his suit to leave.

"I *have* to know." Ray's voice betrays his desperation.

The Director leans toward him, and whispers in his ear:

"She plays a different game than we do."

# Chapter 20:
# Unweaving the Rainbow II

Even with her toes shuffling closer to the Mercantile Tower's edge, Ashley cannot help but calculate. What floor is she on? How far is it to the ground? How many pieces will she become? It is a habit that has brought her much comfort. Numbers do not tease, nor do they ostracize. Numbers are always there for her.

But above the clouds, Ashley realises that numbers are not her allies. Perhaps they have never been. Ever since she had taken a tape measure to her thighs, her body became a series of dimensions and her life a series of digits on a calendar. There is a strange comfort in knowing that her calendar will end.

Despite her pleas, Skyra told her that she could not contact anyone until the Director re-opened her profile – not Daviault Junior, and not Jane. Jane hadn't even tried to get in touch, so Ashley went to the one place Jane could be secretly waiting for her. Light welcomed Ashley to the roof of the Mercantile Tower, and Skyra re-awoke in the outside air.

But Jane was not there.

Ashley stayed on the rooftop with only Skyra for company. Skyra's omniscience was beyond doubt. It knew the speed of Ashley's heartbeat each time she checked her follower count, and for how long she cried when it does not increase. It knew how many photos she took before posting one, how many filters she used, and which parts of herself she excluded from the frame. And it knew when her fate had changed. Adverts for baby carriages and prenatal vitamins became life insurance and antidepressants. And then became nothing at all: the adverts stopped. The algorithms already knew.

Then the choice came to her with numerical clarity. A million followers would become a million contemptuous needles piercing her belly. If she did not disappear entirely, she would be sent back to Theos, to the brutal, unending judgment of her family. A child does not deserve to grow up in that horrid environment, with Ashley as the horrid mother. The feed tells her that she is incapable, unstable, that she's a catastrophe stopped from harming others only by fistfuls of Haven tablets. Best reduce the sum of all that pain to nothing.

She squeezes her eyes shut, the afternoon sun orange through her eyelids. Despite the wind tearing at her clothes and tossing her rainbow-coloured hair, Ashley imagines the warmth of five fingers on her back, and the wetness of a kiss on her head. *Jane.*

"Don't you ever worry that they'll lose patience with all your rule-breaking?" Ashley had said to Jane as they dressed for a shoot, perhaps only the second or third time they had met.

"No," Jane replied. "The Director says he knows everything – even before it even happens. I told him that if that was true, he knew what antics I would pull before I joined. If I turn out to be the wrong girl – that would mean *he* was wrong for picking me."

"You said that to his face?" Ashley cackled, despite her best efforts to hide her smile beneath her hand. She laughed until her eyes were teary and her cheeks ached. Then they hugged. Ordinarily, Ashley held her breath when she hugged, standing stiffly upright like a chess piece, but Ashley exhaled smoothly into Jane's shoulder, giggled a little once more, and enjoyed the impression of Jane's fingers pressing into her back. Five fingers supporting her more than a million online followers ever could.

In the memory of that embrace, Ashley relives an entire past.

She is a child back in a classroom, hoping to hide herself in pages of numbers while the other children play outside. But there is Jane – magical, and young, just like her – waiting in the doorway. Ashley puts down the pencil, and they're outside, blundering into puddles with the other children, chubby faces excited with giggles.

Ashley is ten years old, discovering what she looks like to a camera's lens. She decides to keep her whole body in the picture's frame, rather than cropping out the knees that are too knobby, the quads that are too large, and sends it to her friend, Jane, than to innumerable distant followers.

Ashley is fourteen. She gets a message from a scout: she has won the Marie Cherie competition. A job awaits her in Nature. She does not tremble when she gets the message. Jane's reassuring arm lends her the bravery not to respond.

Ashley is eighteen once more, but she is not alone on the rooftop, overlooking the clouds. The ground under her feet is firm, like Jane's squeeze of her hand. Jane holds her. Ashley won't fall.

The visions disappear. Jane isn't there; Jane abandoned her. Even though Jane had returned to the city, she did not respond to Ashley's messages, as if she had already disposed of Ashley.

If Jane is out there now, trying to contact her, it is too late. Ashley knows the consequences. She will become a disgrace, she will be fired. Davi will return her to her parents, to their god, the only things that remember her indiscretions better than Skyra, and he will force her to lose the child. Best make them all zero.

Ashley's rainbow hair dances in the breeze. The wind tears the feeling of Jane's warm handprint from her spine. She shivers, her knees knocking together uncontrollably. Ashley takes a short breath for strength. Then she throws out her arms, teeters over into the grey sea, and the rainbow is lost to the clouds.

# Chapter 21:
# Timeless

"Welcome. My Name is Skyra," Jane hears in a familiar voice.

Jane's brows furrow. She is unsure where she is.

"Well, *say something*," Jane hears in another voice.

Jane manages: "What?"

The second voice makes sharp words, but they may be in a different language. Jane puzzles at the unfamiliar faces, trying to recall how she came to be in a presentation room before a group of suits. Only when a woman snaps fingers in Jane's face does Jane understand that they are speaking to her.

"We've got the three largest shareholders here," the woman hisses in Jane's ear. "Follow the script." Then she brings Jane over by the crook of her arm and presents her to the group of suits.

Though the woman says something else, Jane finds herself focusing on her shoelaces. They're black, like her boots. The left one needs tying. She remembers how Ashley played with the laces of her shoes when she was nervous. Ashley wouldn't have let her boots go so poorly tied.

The woman, still holding Jane's elbow, calls to the group: "Fortunately *Skyra* will be more responsive."

They laugh.

"Go easy on her," Skyra says in the familiar voice, "she's only human."

More laughter from the suits.

A presentation hovers midair in holographic blue. The count of live-streamers in the bottom corner numbers in the tens of thousands. The woman squeezes Jane's elbow harder, but Jane just wants to tie her shoelace.

"It really *does* sound like her!" one suit says.

"*Exactly* like her, in fact," the woman corrects. "But reproducing the voice is the simple part. Reproducing the personality is more difficult. But we are close," the woman continues, "we should have a fully operational personality within the next three months."

"Sandra, how close will it be? Can customers really take her home?" one suit says, pointing to Jane like a prop.

Sandra's firm grasp of Jane's elbow is the only thing that stops Jane from fixing her shoelace.

"We've had to make some corrections," says Sandra.

They're talking altogether too loudly, too loudly, and Jane's ears begin to ring.

"Corrections?" the suit replies.

Jane starts to leave. Sandra's grip tightens around Jane's elbow. "It will be her personality," Sandra says, "just more *pliable*. It grows with the user, so each instance will be slightly different."

Jane looks from her shoes and scans the faces. They are blurry, yes, she is sure, blurry, like she has hit her head. Their indecipherable mouths make strange sounds. She picks out: "How old will it grow?"

Sandra smiles with thin lips and adjusts her glasses. "The personality will grow but will never age. It will be like her, as she is now. Timeless."

*Timeless.* Jane thinks of virtual immortality, a kernel of her personality forever preserved in computer code. Of course, everyone leaves a data trail after they die. Nobody ever decomposes fully. But some disappear from public consciousness, if not from computer memory.

Jane's last conversation – worded to avoid suspicion – floods back.

*I'm back from the castle, Ash – just in processing.*

*You on a shoot?*

*Sorry, delays. Should be out soon.*

*Delays… text me if you're getting these.*

*Ash?*

*D ordered me to some presentation. I'm in the city, though – text me!*

*If you get this, please DM…!*

*I'm here for you. Talk to me.*

*Ashley?*

*Please say you're ok…*

She was waiting in the dressing room before the presentation when she realized.

Ashley didn't exist anymore. It was impossible for her to quit or run away without it being seen and reported. Ashley had been pushed outside of the ever-decreasing bubble of human knowledge. Skyra redirected Ashley's followers to other diversions. Fickle attention spans would switch to the flurry of new stories and celebrities. Ashley's death would be a whimper in a whirlwind.

When Jane realised, grainy static began to eat the walls. Then it ate the furniture. The static crept toward Jane, more of the room disappearing to static, until Jane was in a lonely void a metre wide. Then there was no sound, then no feeling in her body, and all she knew of the universe was the narrow patch of floor at which she stared, until Sandra pulled her to her feet.

Jane knew the only place where Ashley would not have been supervised by security. She knew how lonely it must have been for Ashley, on that little concrete island in the clouds. She knew how welcoming the soft sea must have appeared as her toes shuffled closer to the edge. And she knew that it was her pills that Ashley had used to do it.

Cruelty tangled in her insides. Jane's hands shook. Fists became hammers, to unleash on everything. But as her forearms tightened for combat, she remembered Skyra on her wrist, turning her anger into numbers for someone else's study. Ashley had been pushed out by the agency. Jane risked the same if she demonstrated too much care. The feed did not pause, no matter her grief. All she could do was keep moving. Jane released a whimper of pain and forced herself to stretch out her fingers. She reset her face to a positive expression, taking everything she had to keep her face taut. As Sandra led Jane to the presentation room, guilt and pain followed her like a shadow.

*Timeless* Jane thinks once more, as Sandra answers more questions. Jane will have the privilege of never being forgotten. Ashley will not. In her fall from the tower, Ashley did not break into pieces.

She became nothing. A nonperson, someone of whom no news article will ever speak or online search will ever retrieve.

Jane cannot hold it in for much longer.

In Jane's voice, Skyra says: "Soon I'll be in every home in the nation."

The suits applaud.

Jane finally speaks:

"Yes," she says, "I will."

# Chapter 22:
# Decision Paralysis

*The heatwave is expected to continue for the next four days. While not announced in advance, experts were long aware of the heatwave and were able to predict with great accuracy its duration and intensity. The recent heat is a normal weather pattern and is no cause for alarm.*

*Want to keep cool in the meantime?*

*Glacier Cooling provides complete air conditioning packages –*

\*\*\*

Jane is ready. For weeks, she invited promoters to send her goods at random to endorse on her channel. The useful items that she received – the hiking backpack, sturdy boots, water purification tablets – she kept hidden amongst the clutter of novelty hats, lingerie, bobble-heads, and Skyra add-ons. Jane also received a hunting knife and a bottle of bear spray, which her security must have missed amidst the glut of delivery boxes.

Jane must escape without being tracked. She had considered using the microwave to melt the tags in the clothes, as Jonas had shown her, but that would be tracked. So, the week before, she took a hoody from the closet that Skyra had said was too old. Jane asked how Skyra knew. I check the RFID tags in each article of clothing, Skyra said, and monitor the date of purchase and frequency of use. Jane asked Skyra at what range it could sense these tags. Up to sixty feet, Skyra said, and to within a centimeter of precision, for precision is my purpose. Prove it, Jane said as she took the hoody and laid it on the kitchen counter. She held the Skyra bracelet to the hoody and moved it slowly from one arm of the hoody to the other. Warmer,

Skyra said, warmer, there it is! Jane thumbed the material and felt something the size of a sesame seed. She pulled a thread from the hoody to mark it for later. You got lucky, Jane said as she fetched a pair of jeans, double or nothing?

Today will be the day she escapes.

As Jane takes the last item she needs – a long-lasting flashlight – to her closet and pushes aside the clutter, her eyes catch a grey beanie in the corner of the top shelf. Her breath catches for a moment. She wants to take it from the shelf, to squeeze it in her hands, press the wool to her face, but her first reflex is to quash the desire before it can be detected by Skyra.

But now is the moment: Skyra will have control over her no longer. As Jane takes the hat from the shelf the wool on her fingers reminds her of its original owner. Ashley had a particular attraction to beanies when not doing a shoot. Jane asked for one, once. Ashley took it off – the unremarkable grey woolen hat - with a crackle of static electricity and gave it Jane without thinking much of it. Jane put it on, enjoying how it tickled her ears. Jane had asked why Ashley wore it. Sometimes you want to go a day without washing your hair, Ashley explained, without anyone knowing.

For weeks, Jane has exerted herself more and more to quell her anger before it could be detected. She cannot hold it in anymore. She packs the supplies into the hiking backpack, then lays the articles of clothing she'd checked for RFID tags on the counter. She traces along the hoody until she finds a coil of cotton between the shoulders. A squeeze from her fingers locates the tag. And with the delicate point of the hunting knife, she gouges the chip. She does the same with the jeans, the boots, the backpack. She laces up the boots, pulling them tight and wrapping the extra length lace around her ankles.

What she intends to do is unthinkable. It will take the security algorithms precious minutes to catch up.

Jane asks Skyra to order a taxi to leave at seven-thirty, then goes for the fridge, wanting something hard and cold. She pulls a frosty bottle and pauses. Why does she feel like a drink? Why this brand? She pours two fingers and sips from the glass in her left hand. She stares at the bottle sitting on the counter, thinking that she can drink the whole thing if she chooses. And she can drink it elegantly, slipping it down in measured pours, or she can lock her lips about the bottle's neck and feel the familiar burn at the back of her throat. Or she can leave the bottle untouched as a monument to her choice. Or she can smash the bottle in an instant and watch the pieces of glass skate across the floor.

Whichever she does, is she the one that truly chooses? What unknown influences will bubble up to the surface to convince her? Perhaps Ray was right: the roots of any decision are buried too deep to ever understand. Jane can spend an eternity pondering the fate of a single bottle of vodka. What would life be like if she thought through *every* decision? It would not be life; it would be paralysis. Perhaps *life* simply means performing the choices someone else has already made for her.

Jane's eyes bear into the details of the glass in her left hand. She watches the clear legs of the vodka slip down the sides of the glass. She swills the glass around and the legs reappear, then slide down once more. Then Jane takes the bottle in the right hand. Her fingers leave prints in the sheen of frost as she tilts the bottle. If she cannot choose the fate of a bottle, how can she choose her own? Her grip tightens.

Jane wants to crash the bottle against the counter. She glowers at the woman on the label. *Azalea*. The figure winks provocatively, her namesake flowers bunched in her hair. If Jane can have dominion over nothing else, she can have the power to let Azalea live, or split her into pieces.

Jane cups the glass in her hand and with a jolt throws it into the wall. Splinters of glass scatter about the room.

Azalea will live for now. Jane takes the bottle, swills another mouthful, screws on the cap, and packs it into her bag with a knife from the kitchen. Some other girl deserves destruction tonight.

# Chapter 23:
# Unfollow

Jane finds a security guard waiting for her in the lobby, alerted the moment she left her apartment. She recognizes him as one of her regulars. He sports a black suit, shirt, and tie.

"No, no, not tonight," he says, moving between Jane and the front entrance, "you've been warned about mixing alcohol and late nights out. Go back to your room."

"I won't be long, Hank," she says, "just want to take a new outfit for a whirl." She spins on the toe of her hiking boot.

"You know the rules. You go out when you're scheduled."

"My fans have been begging me to try out my adventure-wear on my life stream," she says. "Don't pretend you don't watch it, Hank."

She can tell by the way he looks down that he isn't proud of the parts of her stream he watches.

"It is not safe to go out," he says, "Skyra says there's a dust storm coming."

Jane knows. She just hopes that Skyra is not lying this time.

She sees a car pull up outside the front entrance. "There's my taxi," she says, "you won't even miss me."

Hank starts toward her.

"And if you let me go this once," she adds, "I'll give you a shout-out next stream!"

But Hank nears and his hand goes to take Jane's elbow. She dodges, her left hand goes for the can of bear spray clipped to her backpack, and she aims it at his face. In an instant, her sweet, kitten-like persona falls, replaced with cool, planned, determination. "Back," she says, and he steps from her.

"Skyra is watching," Hank says, his hands raised, "you'll be lucky to get out the door."

"*Everyone* is watching," Jane says, ushering Hank back with the bear spray, "do you want them to see you get a face full of this?"

She hears a rustle behind her. Another guard rushes to her. Jane whirls, squeezes her eyes shut, discharges the bear spray, and hurtles to the door, hearing hacking coughs behind her. She shoots a look to see two suited men on their knees, wheezing. Jane unsheathes the hunting knife from its leather case, slips it between the two glass doors of the front entrance, and sharply lifts the latch between the doors. They spring open, and she is in the taxi by the time she hears footsteps closing in. Jane shuts the taxi door and orders it to drive. Hank sprints after them, but Jane watches him shrink in the rear window as the taxi picks up speed. Once he has disappeared, she unclips her Skyra bracelet and throws it in the footwell.

She knows what his next steps will be. After several past escape stunts, which bolstered her public persona as unpredictable and bizarre, her security detail now has a specific contingency plan for her. Hank will try to track her Skyra bracelet, but realize she is no longer wearing it. Then he will try to track the tags in her clothing, and discover they are all inoperative. Then Hank will order a team to follow the taxi, but he will find she is no longer in it.

Jane pulls out her bottle of vodka and takes a mouthful. The taxi immediately pulls over and a voice instructs her to get out. "Alcohol consumption is not permitted during transit."

Jane replaces the bottle in her backpack, skips out the taxi, and hurries along the street. All along the street and stretching into the distance, Jane sees versions of her own face: her face in a perfume advert hovering on the sidewalk, her face in posters on the wall. Her figure lazes across a banner on the side of a passing car. Screens twenty feet high and as wide as a building bathe the street with the glow of her features. She feels unsettled seeing versions of herself, one glamorous, one modest, one amorous, one smoky. It is like being a hall of mirrors, except it isn't quite her staring back.

Jane approaches one version of her face beaming from a wallscreen. The face is as tall as Jane. The advert is for heart medication – or is it for an exercise supplement? – she has done too many to remember. *Make the right choice* the tagline mocks. Jane scowls at it from beneath her hood. The shining face in the advert is flawless. Light-brown curls tumble around the shoulders. Subtle teal shades on her eyelids complement the royal blue background. Strategic shadows sharpen the features. The skin is more perfect than Jane has ever seen on herself. It is a divine face.

It is time to bring the divine back down to earth. Jane controls her own face.

She draws the hunting knife again.

Jane drives the point of the knife into the screen with a satisfying *crack*. The screen flickers but does not go out. Jane extracts the knife and pauses to appreciate the black hole she has created in the eyebrow of the shining face. She brings the knife onto the screen again, drawing a painful scar across the cheek. Then some laugh lines, like the ones she has. The blade crunches through the screen with the sound she imagines would come from sawing through bone. She knows that the cameras are on her.

As a final act, she uses both hands to drive the blade into the middle of the face. The screen sputters. Then Jane pulls the bottle of vodka from her handbag. Azalea still winks at her. Jane empties the rest of the vodka onto the screen and tosses the bottle to the side. It smashes satisfyingly. Jane draws a single match from her pocket, strikes it on the concrete, and flicks it at the screen. Flames engulf the screen. The heat is instantaneous. The face in the advert flickers, clinging to life.

Jane watches it die and the screen turns black.

Heavy boots club on the sidewalk behind her. Jane darts across the intersection, the colours of an advert swirling at her feet. She shoots a glance over her shoulder. A group of them; she can't tell how many. All in black, illuminated by the blues and yellows of adverts. A drone buzzes above. Jane cuts across oncoming traffic. Computer-operated cars obediently stop. She flashes between vehicles, hearing the telling whistle of an impending storm.

They won't hurt her. They are corporate security, there for *protection* – of the brand, that is. Despite hiding beneath a hood, she has been spotted by a hundred cameras between her apartment and the advert she beautified with the hunting knife. Security will never be more than a few blocks away from her.

Jane's record is eight.

As she clatters down an alley, the walls come alive with adverts for diamonds. Even if she can lose the security, they will just follow the stream of adverts, as if Jane is a comet and the adverts her fiery tail. The joy is not in escape but in the freedom to run. Eventually, as they always do, the security will surround her, lay firm hands upon her shoulders, and usher her back into a car.

This time she will have an accomplice. Above her rise innumerable towers, so high they seem to hold up the ashen clouds. Each glass tower is as indistinct as the last, save for the different sponsor logos. He lives in the Alerax building, its red logo shimmering a few blocks away.

The men in heavy boots shout, but do not call her name to avoid attracting crowds. Jane keeps running, feeling the burn in her lungs like there is no more air to breathe. Her hood flaps down, wind lashes her cheeks, and she feels a seditious smile grow across her face.

Jane comes upon the front entrance of his building and slaps the screen beside the doors.

"Please enjoy this message before we complete your request..." a voice comes.

She stabs the screen with her finger until the advert ends and the screen displays a list of tenants. She selects Ray's name, and it begins to ring.

# Chapter 24:
# Two Types of People

"Gave you a pretty good run this time," Jane calls over her shoulder. She hears the heavy boots behind her and readies for the foyer door to unlock. It continues to ring.

Usually, her smile is enough to defuse a situation with her security guards. Jane turns and flourishes it. But it is not her security looking back.

Liberators.

She doesn't let her face drop. The smile hides her fear. "You're late."

The group of Liberators do not return her smile. Their chests are broad, their bodies armoured. The women are as tall as the men. Jane notices none have Skyra bracelets. She has never seen Liberators so close. She listens for the click of the foyer door. There is none.

They are stocky; she imagines each can break her arm with a simple twist. But they will not hurt her, she reassures herself, not while she is useful. Jane tries to believe it. She approaches one of the stocky men and lays her left forefinger on his chest. "I tell you what," she says, running the finger down his black vest, "double or nothing: if I can get more the twenty blocks—"

The Liberator snatches her wrist. She feels each of his fingers pressing into bone. She winces. "You're hurting me."

His fingers dig deeper. The pain is too sharp to wrest her hand from him. She pulls back her other arm to line up a punch, but someone grabs it and begins to twist. Jane screeches at the pain, shocked by how capably they can manipulate her body. Both her arms are throbbing and useless. She thrashes and kicks at anything, but they rough her to an alleyway, away from onlookers. For a moment Jane wishes she had Skyra on her wrist to alert the authorities, but the Liberators *are* the authorities, and they have determined that she has outlasted her usefulness. She wrestles but they push her to her knees. Her left wrist remains trapped, and her other arm immobilized behind her back.

One of the Liberators kneels in front of their girl. Her red hair is pulled tight in a tail behind her head. The Liberator's eyes are black. There is no light in them. Jane recoils. She flicks to the other Liberators. Their eyes are identically black. Lenses, perhaps, to obscure retinal analysis.

"There are only two states of society," the Liberator with the red hair says in a crisp, precise voice, "order, and chaos. When we don't know who is *in*, who is *out*, who we can *trust*, and who we *cannot*, who thinks *good* things, and who thinks *bad*, we have chaos." The black eyes bore into Jane's. Their noses almost touch. "When everyone wears Skyra, we keep order. But when they don't, we have chaos."

Jane writhes. Her smiling teeth become barred, but she keeps them flourished. She won't give them the pleasure of knowing that the pain is like a nail in her collarbone. Her eyes search for something – *anything* – to help. But a red crime warning will have appeared on public maps; everyone will stay clear. Her live stream will have closed. Jane is alone.

"Which means," the Liberator continues, "there are only two types of people who do not wear Skyra. Criminals," she whispers, "and *us*," hinting to the Liberators standing over them.

"What's the difference?" Jane smiles. She won't let them know how much her wrist hurts. But they tighten their grip and force her to grimace. Jane's cheeks tighten. Her eyebrows are furrowed and fierce. Fire shoots in the arm locked behind her back. Cold sets into her immobilized wrist. Wrestling only makes the pain worse.

Jane scans the alley walls and finds a camera. Visibility is her ally. Under thousands of metallic eyes, she thinks, there are no dark corners for the Liberators to enact their brutality.

The Liberator with the red hair looks over her shoulder to see what Jane's eyes have caught. The Liberator turns back, her black eyes even thinner. "You think cameras make you safer?" she taunts. "They aren't for your benefit. They are for *ours*." She stares down with spider-like eyes.

Jane is practiced at dislodging her mind from her body until she feels like a spectre, intangible and unhurtable, but she is unable to disconnect herself from the grit biting into her kneecaps, the twist in her arm. She summons her bravery. "You're wrong," she sneers, "you're just an infection. An infected part of an infected society. And light," she continues, flicking her chin back to the camera, "is the best disinfectant."

The Liberator's eyes seem to light. Jane holds her breath.

"She's right," a voice comes from behind them.

Jane exhales just a little.

"Get out of here," the Liberator with black eyes says, "or you'll be arrested as a co-conspirator."

"If watching is a crime," Ray calls as he approaches from the fire escape door of his tower, "you'll have to arrest everyone." Ray holds his wrist out before him, emphasizing the band on his wrist. "Getting all this Skyra?"

"Life-streaming now."

He strides closer. "She's the prize flower in *very* lucrative campaign," he calls, "if she's hurt, I'll make sure the corporation knows *exactly* who is responsible."

The Liberator with the red hair smolders. Jane does not look away. She keeps a smile on her face. The Liberator flicks her chin to the other Liberators and they release Jane's arms. Jane's first instinct is to give the woman with the red hair a black eye to match her boots. Unwise, she knows, given they almost broke her arm. Her second instinct is then to run, anywhere, until she feels safe enough to curl into a shaking ball. Cowardly, she thinks. She won't give the Liberators the satisfaction.

Jane wills herself not to tremble. The kneeling Liberator with red hair gnarls but leaves without a word. The remaining shadowy figures follow. Only when they leave sight does Jane release a tense breath, her heart still pounding in her ears.

"Come on," Ray offers, "let's get you to a doctor."

Skyra brings his car to them. Jane flexes the fingers of her right hand as they drive. Her ferocity cools until she shivers. She rolls her wrist painfully back and forth.

"Thank you," she finally says. "But I don't need a doctor."

"Then I'll take you home," Ray says as adverts skim past the car windows. "The doctor can meet us there."

Jane swipes her hair from her forehead. She looks to him. The presses in his suit are crisp, his hair precise, his beard smooth and angled. He never lets his appearance go unkempt, never lets his guard down. Ray is the embodiment of order.

Her hoody is soaked with sweat, her jeans damaged at the knees where the Liberators pressed her into the concrete. Her wrist burns and she shakes uncontrollably. She is disorder.

She says: "I'm not going home."

Ray sighs. "You've had enough trouble for one night."

"I can't go back."

"I'm sorry," he says. "I know she meant a lot – I mean, I know it's been hard—"

"She was *eighteen*…"

Silence overtakes the car.

Ashley was so kind that it makes Jane's heart ache. Once, Ashley had shown Jane her only secret: a tattoo of two letters on the inside of her big toe: *me*. A little space, all to herself, that only Jane was worthy of seeing.

Jane breaks the quiet: "No, I'm not going home."

Ray visibly clenches his jaw. He turns and his expression pleads for normalcy.

Jane does not want to upset his life. There is comfort in order. There was order in her life, too, until a flood rolled across her world and she learned that life cannot be predicted and ordered; it must be battled for, day in, day out.

She will be his flood.

"We're leaving the city," Jane says. "We are seeing what is outside."

Ray protests.

"You know what will happen if you do not." She leaves it unsaid, for Skyra remains on his wrist.

"Blackmail."

"Trust," Jane responds softly, defusing the tension in the air. "I want you to trust me."

His eyes thin.

# Chapter 25:
# Abysess

Disbelief settles in as Ray takes the wheel of the car. This is dangerous. Crazy. He tries to understand what choices have led him to this moment. How had he ended up on a campaign with one of the most famous life streamers? Then confronting the Director over a game of poker? How had he been dragged into a confrontation with the Liberators? And how had he ended up driving the girl he was supposed to keep in line toward the dangers that lay outside the city?

How had he been convinced to take her to the Red Zone?

Ray weaves through computer-controlled cars. He checks the rear mirror and sees the dance of red and blue Liberator lights, becoming murky in the growing dust. Part of him is glad to see them.

"We can't escape," he says, as the Liberator lights roll through the car. "They will track us."

Jane turns to him. "No they won't. Get rid of Skyra."

"What?" he blurts, taking his eyes from the road to shoot her a look of disbelief.

"Throw it out the window."

He wavers. The car passes through the boot of a holographic giant patrolling the roadway.

"Don't you want to be invisible again?" she presses. "Trust me."

The Skyra bracelet feels as tight and weighty as a shackle. It senses the moisture on his skin long before Ray does. It knows what he wants to do. Buzzes up his forearm beg him to resist her.

"What will it matter?" he snaps. "This car has its own GPS chip. It tracks where I go, how fast, and when."

"I can deal with that."

"These *clothes* have tags in them."

"Fine. Turn around, and you'll never have to see me again."

"It doesn't matter if I choose to turn this car around or not. You've already screwed up my life."

"You've always got a choice."

He looks from the road and stares at her. When he first saw her in the helicopter, all he knew of her was that she was beautiful, just beautiful, but since their meeting on the battlements of the castle, he sees something more. In her red cheeks and persistent eyes, he sees that she wants something more than Skyra and TELOS, and that she is willing to risk the Liberators to find it.

Teeth gritted, brows furrowed, Ray unclips Skyra. The skin below feels naked. He cannot remember when he last had a bare wrist. He takes it off exaggeratedly. Holds it to her. Slips down the window.

The wind rasps by. He holds the Skyra bracelet in a fist. He is unsure whether he intends to clutch it, or to crush it in his palm. At once he is overcome with the immensity of choices that will lay before him if he releases the bracelet from his grasp. Life is a stream of choices. It is beyond his imagination how he can make them all without Skyra's aid. The wind tears at his ear and thrashes his hair.

In a flash, he throws it out the window. Skyra disappears into the darkness.

He sighs, breathing more freely, as if a noose has loosened from his neck. "It's gone."

He feels the sore flesh of his wrist with his fingers. Jane smiles at him.

"Now what?" he asks, hot blood beginning to cool.

Jane points to the orange blur out the corner of the windshield moving toward their path. "We become invisible," she says.

They know how to interpret the wind. A cold bluster means a flood, while sudden gusts foretell lightening. But a hot wind is the worst. Something more dangerous than Liberators closes in on them. The car shudders under the worsening wind.

"We have to turn back," Ray says.

"We won't make it back before the storm hits."

"Then we find shelter. A ruin beside the road."

"Easy place for Liberators to capture us."

There are no cars on the road, now, except for the Liberator vehicles in pursuit. They passed the last of the streetlamps and the adverts five minutes ago. Ray squints to make out the details of the degraded buildings straddling the road, but the growing dust makes it increasingly hard to see anything beyond a few feet in front of them. Ray squeezes the steering wheel, knowing that if there is a roadblock or wreckage on the road, he will not be able to see it in time. He checks the rear-view mirror again. The Liberator lights are dimming.

Jane closes the air vents, stuffs fabric in the air intake by the windshield, pulls a bandana over the lower half of her face, then hands Ray one.

"You knew?" Ray says.

She nods, and he shakes his head. "We should at least stop," he says.

"And get a Liberator truck up our ass?" she says.

He realizes Jane has no regard for anyone. She is mad, he is now sure. It is common among life streamers. Many crack when they cannot maintain the expectations of their TELOS. Self destruction is common. Yet Ray feels that he can still trust her or at least, trust her more than Skyra. He presses down the accelerator.

The orange wave hits and sweeps the world away. The Liberators and then the road disappear. Ray sees nothing beyond his hands on the wheel, which he throttles in his grasp. He feels the tyres struggle to hold, the car writhing in paroxysmic swerves, and he begs for the car to stay on flat road. If he loses the road, the car will flip, and if the flip does not kill them outright, a crack in the window will leave them to suffocate in the dust.

The car is dark except for the teal glow of the car's driver console. They hear a sound like small hail. Ray wants to shut his eyes, but he keeps his foot to the accelerator. He feels like a ship's captain trapped in a storm, pretending his wheel had any effect upon nature. At least if the car flips, Jane won't be able to cling to her delusions about being in control any longer.

It may have been minutes or hours, but Ray sees orange road in the light of the remaining headlamp and realizes that he has been holding his breath.

Jane lowers her bandana, which is dusted with orange sand. "Congratulations. You are free."

They drive for another hour. No other cars remain. Without streetlamps, they skim along in the black night. The ride is bumpy, the road no longer maintained. Ray does not know what lies at its end. Skyra is no longer able to tell him.

As they approach an old industrial yard, Jane tells him to stop. The headlights illuminate buildings rising out of overgrown greenery, their brick weathered by rain. But the area seems untouched by the dust storm.

"What is this?" he asks, getting out of the car.

Jane presses a button to unlock the bonnet, gets out, and pushes up the bonnet with a grunt. "This," she says, clicking on a flashlight from her backpack, "is an old train station."

"How did you know it was here?"

"A strike of lightening," Jane answers. She leans into the engine, flashlight held in her teeth, fingers exploring the metallic depths.

"What are you doing?" Ray asks, his list of questions growing.

Jane doesn't answer. She is fixed on the engine, eyes squinting at some cables illuminated weakly by the flashlight between her teeth. With another grunt, she pulls the cables out. "No battery, no GPS," she says, standing and taking the flashlight from her mouth.

Unseen crickets chirp. He is unable to see much as he wanders from the car, but he hears each crunch underfoot, and feels each brush of crisp grass. "And the tags in my clothes?"

"Limited range." she smiles. She flicks her head to the left. "Come," she gestures toward an overgrown copse, "help me hide the car."

They set the car into neutral gear and roll it into the muddle of branches and coarse grass to afford them a little more time before being discovered. Then Jane points to a structure looming in the darkness.

The grass is silver below the moon, swaying in the breeze like a sheet of silk. It is impossibly tall; Skyra had told Ray that nothing grew in the Red Zone. They push through the grass, feet lost in the depths. She walks in front, flashlight lighting only a few metres ahead. He can barely see her. He keeps his feet moving quickly to not lose her. If he loses her light, he will never find his way back.

The grass swishes in the wind, sounding like surf on a beach. Jane signals to a thicket of sickly branches and pushes them aside. Her flashlight illuminates the entrance of a tunnel. She hands him the flashlight. "Go ahead," she says, "lead on."

# Chapter 26:
# Dark at the End of the Tunnel

Ray can hear only the crunch of gravel from their feet and can only see the small cone of light extending from his hand. The tunnel slopes downward, pulling them deeper into the unknown. He sees something in the corner of his eye. A rat? A snake? Startled, he flicks the flashlight in that direction. Nothing. He sees another flicker on the other side. He whips the light left and right, searching. Nothing but gravel and wooden tracks.

"What did you see?" Jane says.

Ray breathes heavily through his nose, shooting the light back and forth like he is spraying a machine gun. He pauses, body rigid, ready to bolt.

"Who is there?" he shouts. The call echoes down the tunnel. Nothing responds.

His body softens as he lets out a breath. He realizes what he saw in the darkness: fragments of old adverts burned into his vision. He pricks his ears and hears a distant jingle in his left ear and a slogan in his right, even in the tunnel's silence. He shakes his head and begins hurrying down the tunnel, blinking vainly to excise the pollution orbiting his head.

"Tell me something," Ray says. "*Anything.*"

"Like what?" her voice comes from behind, bright with energy.

"I don't know," he says, "Tell me – have you always been like this? Making stories about yourself?"

Jane thinks for a moment, still crunching behind Ray. "It started in school. I hated every moment of it. At my school, every building had a sponsor, every classroom. The playing field too – oh, and the cafeteria."

"One of my school's lecture theatres had a beer sponsor," Ray says, his voice softening.

"I stole some paints from the art room and painted slogans over the sponsor names. Teenage stuff, angry and vulgar. I didn't much care about the detention. The worst part was all the extra attention the sponsor names got after I changed them. I made them more visible by making fun of them."

Ray slows his breathing. Jane continues: "One day the administration wanted us to do a psychological profile to *improve teaching methods*. They sat us alone in a white room, as if our answers would stay in there. The psychologist pushed the microphone closer and handed me a package of questions about what distracted me, what held my attention. I refused to answer until she admitted the answers would be passed onto sponsors. When I still refused to answer, the psychologist said I had no choice.

"I realized that the reason I needed to take the test was that they needed information from me that they couldn't get by themselves. There was a little space between my temples that they could not access. But even if they could force me to talk, they couldn't make me tell the truth. So, I made a joke of it. Every question was an opportunity to become a new person. Each answer I gave became more elaborate and inventive. By the end, I could tell a complete fantasy with conviction."

Ray's grip on the flashlight loosens. "So that's what you've been doing ever since?"

"Haven't we all?"

The adverts on his eyeballs disappear, and they walk in silence for a while longer until they feel the wind funneling to the end of the tunnel. Both breathe deeply as they emerge, enjoying the crispness of the air.

Ray looks above. A grin breaks onto the left side of his face, becoming a full smile as he stares skyward at the stars. In the city, the night is so dominated by lights that he cannot see the stars. Even in clear weather, the sky never becomes darker than navy blue. Airplanes and buzzing drones are the only glints to see. When the weather is poor, they project logos on the clouds, the entire sky a canvas for their malicious art.

He toys with the patterns of yellow stars he sees up above. For centuries people were told the stars were put up there for humanity, a message hiding in their aberrant clusters. But in the drops of light there is a purity *from* meaning, beauty without a message. And in the immense blackness lie yet more stars, hints of white just escaping the dark veil. Each layer of diminishing brightness opens an appreciation of a longer and more unfathomable distance. He has never been further than a few miles from the city or seen further than what a screen can bring. Nothing he does or says or buys makes a flicker in the infinite dark. He has spent his whole life gazing at screens. Instead, he should have spent it looking upward, and then, if possible, inward. For, like the stars, there is an entire constellation of people he knows, and he has never seen any of them. Nor have they ever seen him.

"Come on," Jane calls from ahead, "you won't believe this."

# Chapter 27:
# Where the Crows Turn Around

It is an old railway town, like something found in one of Whitaker's history books, as decrepit as the pages it would come from. The moonlight reveals rows of houses with sheets of plywood for windows and corrugated steel for doors. They walk down what seems to be the main street, counting only four blocks of houses. There lies nothing beyond except navy sky. It is a town on the edge of nowhere, where even the crows will turn around.

As they circle back, Jane spots a tree peering from the dark blue. She jogs toward it and into the central square of the town. Ray shakes his head. There isn't supposed to be water this far from the cities, yet the tree proudly holds up healthy bunches of leaves.

He points his flashlight to the squelch at his feet. A thin vein of red runs toward the tree, like the soil is bleeding. He hears Jane gasp. She calls him over to the tree. He comes and runs his hand over the knobby trunk. In its age the tree's trunk appears to have split in two, half growing straight upward, the other snaking haphazardly at an angle.

"Look," Jane beams, "you can fit inside." And so she does. He points the flashlight at her grin.

"Care to join?" she asks, propping herself against the hollow interior of the trunk. She opens her backpack and unscrews a small jar of dried fruit. "It's how we used to keep our fruit when it wasn't in season," Jane says through a mouthful. "Food tastes so much better outside."

He raises his eyebrows. "I'll take a look around."

Leaving Jane inside the tree, Ray peeks inside the nearby houses. He finds little beyond empty cans and appliances dissected for their components. In one he finds paintings clinging to the walls. He is afraid to brush off the dust, lest he bring down the whole ramshackle structure. He creeps on the groaning floorboards, taking the wooden staircase upstairs. Yellow light from his flashlight washes across the rooms, animating shadows on the dirty walls. Beds stripped of their sheets. Drawers ransacked. Then he stops on something. An old chest. The scratches on the lock suggest someone had attempted to break it open. The lock, now orange with rust, snaps open with a simple pull.

Inside is a strange instrument, two feet tall with a proud mahogany spine. Its strings glint in Ray's flashlight, perhaps the only thing in the town safe from degradation. He plucks them affectionately. The sound is pleasing – but it is not an instrument controlled by a human hand. He glances to the bedroom window, its panes sooty, and realizes. Ray slides the window upward with a grunt and places the instrument beside the window. The strings vibrate in the breeze.

The wind announces its presence, at first in low notes, pulsing, then growing into layers of high notes. The sound laments like a spirit reaching from the wind. He feels the soft breeze on his face, the harp giving voice to a force.

He feels awake, in awe of his senses. At once he is on a mountaintop, a carpet of trees so small at his feet it looks like moss. Up, up he goes, above the fog, above the tips of skyscrapers, above even the clouds, the sun brighter than he could have imagined. He feels the vastness of his consciousness as his mind escapes into the atmosphere. Free from worldly concerns, free from gravity, brimming with lightning, unbridled by resistance.

The wind breathes a final breath. The chorus of notes fades. The harp goes quiet.

Ray is back in the dark bedroom once again.

He remembers to take a breath.

"I have to show you!" Ray calls as he lays the strange wooden instrument at the opening of the tree trunk. "Listen," he says, before Jane can ask. Jane joins him on a rock and they listen as the wind breathes another mystical tone. They sit, eyes closed, listening to the harp call the wind's words. The cool air feels like smooth marble on his face.

Finally, the wind stops and they open their eyes.

"I like it here," Jane says, "I wish *here* was the only place to be."

"Maybe it can be. Maybe here is just for us. And the model and the marketer?"

"They're someone else!"

"Well then," Ray continues, "who are we, the people that live here?"

"I'm the girl hiding behind a book in the corner of the coffee shop. Someone comes to sit at my table. It's my sister. She has this raven-black hair. She's the pretty one. And *oh*, is she funny! She can make a story out of going to the garbage chute. I hug her extra tightly each time I see her. She never knows why."

"What do you talk about?" he sighs, tension loosening from his neck.

"We haven't seen one another for a while. She's studying somewhere exotic, making us proud. She does everything perfectly. She knows which of my footsteps to follow and which ones to avoid. I miss her dearly whenever she goes.

"I remind her of when we played in the garden together. We scooped wet dirt together with our hands and formed little houses that we could live in. One for me, one for her, one for mom and dad. She wanted her house to be big enough for a husband. I made mine small, just for me. We mixed sticks in with mud to make sure they stayed standing until the sun dried them. We didn't mind the rain. It meant we got to build together again.

"And who are you, mysterious stranger?" Jane says, expectant eyes awaiting his fantasy.

Without the sound of the harp, Ray strains to imagine a new life. In his mind, he parts racks of suits and rummages through folded clothes, but there is something inexorable about the texture of clothing and the shine of jewelry, something he cannot wrest his mind from. It is like trying to float when he's only known gravity.

"Something will come to me," he mumbles.

She gives an affectionate rub on his back. "Let's start small. What is your name? One just between us."

He runs a finger along the smooth neck of the harp. "Something musical."

"How about some notes?" She strums a few strings. "G—" she starts, flicking the string on the harp. He begins to feel more lucid.

"A," he says, flicking another string.

Then another string.

"B."

Another.

"E."

"Gabe!" she glows, "I love it! Pleasure to meet you, Gabe."

She offers her hand. He laughs as he shakes it. "Pleasure to meet you, Miss…?"

"What do you think suits me?" she asks, rising to her feet. "How about *Esmerelda*?" she says, curtsying. "Or something sweet like *Helen*?" she continues, placing her chin playfully on her hands.

"Or something that inspired you?"

Jane sits beside him again. "My favourite book growing up," she smirks, "was about gods and goddesses. I loved how larger than life they were."

"Marketing campaigns are always calling you a goddess of some variety."

"Exactly!" she says, jumping to her feet again. "I might as well parody it." She strikes a pose of strength, shoulders pushed back, face stern. "Mighty Freja," she booms. "Or benevolent Isis," she says with a compassionate voice, going down on one knee and extending her hands. "The perfect mother, friend of the downtrodden? There are so many choices!" she says, twirling like a child in a field of grass.

Then she stops for a moment, light rising in her eyes. "That's it! I could be mysterious *Hecate*: Goddess of choices, Queen of the Night, standing at the crossroads of life." She stands with her arms extended in either direction like an old signpost.

"Perhaps Katie for short."

She turns and looks to the blue horizon. "Katie and Gabe," she sighs.

He stands, takes her hand, and joins her gaze to the horizon. "Katie and Gabe."

# Chapter 28:
# The Unknown

Katie and Gabe prepare a fire from salvaged wood to last them through the night. Neither feels the call of sleep. The fire bathes them in orange light. Gabe, sitting on a fireside rock, and still irked by a question he has of Jane, feels as ready to burst as the coals puffing ash into the air. He has to know how she did it: how she defeated the Director.

She takes herself years back, when she was light on TELOS, heavy in debt, using a profile faked by Jonas, and resisting the urge to look over her shoulder for Liberators. In those first few days, Katie explains, she realized how many eyes there were in the world, how they all felt like needles in her shoulders. She was an illegal who had not yet perfected her persona: she missed cues, treated normal things as strange. But she was a capable enough actor, and nobody had challenged her citizenship. It was only when seated across from the Director in the Future Casino, pleading for a job, that Katie felt certain he knew who she was. She felt an overwhelming urge to confess and plead for his mercy, but she suspected he had none.

"At that point, I'd failed the automated interview. You know, the interview where you're asked questions by a horrid holographic head? And then you're told some algorithm didn't like your answers? So, I had no choice but to go to the top. And I figured the guy with the least data was the one with the most clout. I found almost nothing on the Director, except for his job title and his name at the top of a poker tournament at the Future Casino. I had nothing else to go on except to challenge him at his strength."

Gabe notches an eyebrow. "You had nothing to wager."

"He had the data from my automated interview. It said that I had lied and so was untrustworthy. I told him that its analysis was flawed. I promised that if I lost the hand, I would tell him the truth. And if I won, he'd give me a job."

A coal coughs ashes between them. She waits for them to disperse.

"My palm felt nothing about his vital signs from the pad," Katie says, "a corpse would have more life. I knew I would not beat him."

"I know the feeling," he says, "so what did you do?"

"I didn't play the game," Katie shrugs.

Gabe frowns. She must have played a hand.

"I knew that everything *I* knew, the *Director* would know," Katie continues, "so I changed the game."

"How?"

"I didn't check my cards."

Gabe feels a smile hook one of his cheeks.

"I didn't let on of course," Katie adds. "The Director tried to twist a tell from me. But I had none. I knew as much about my hand as he did. His strength became nothing. I made random, safe bets until he became too frustrated that he could not draw anything from me. He made bad bets, and when we revealed cards, I won."

"Good luck?"

"I was due for some."

"And he kept his word?"

"If nothing else," Katie says, "the Director owns up to his choices. His weakness is that he fears what he cannot track. After I won the hand, he hid the game behind an exorbitant paywall, like everything else."

Katie's eyes disappear into shadow then reappear in firelight.

"We can't know everything," she says. "About each other – or about ourselves. He lost because he had no tolerance for the unknown."

Gabe's smile slants more into his cheek. "Do you?"

"Try me," she invites. "Look in my eyes. And don't look away. Not until I say."

Gabe locks onto her pupils, black with mystery. He enjoys the first seconds, but soon he feels an aversion to the continued stare. A force urges him to look away, as if their eyes are magnets repelling one another.

"Don't look away," she repeats, not breaking eye contact. In his blurry peripheries, he can see she wears a blank expresson. He resists the smile curving on his lips. His cheeks feel hard with the effort. It feels impossible to keep an even expression: the exertion of forcing relaxation. He feels conscious of his posture, of his fingers on the smooth material of his suit. What does he look like, to her? What does she think of the bristles on his cheeks? Of the laugh lines on his forehead? Of the wrinkles on his nose, or below his eyes, or around his mouth?

Gabe draws a deep breath through his nose, focusing on the rhythm. In and then out. In then out. The coolness of the air in his throat. The feel of his lungs stretching. Still her eyes lock to his. He worries that she can see into him and open everything he has hidden away. He wants to turn his cheek or angle his eyes elsewhere.

Skyra always watches him. And more. But unlike human eyes, which people know to fear, Skyra has none: it is a predator they do not know to fear. Being close enough to see the reds in the whites of Katie's eyes makes Gabe want to recoil, as by reflex one pulls a hand from a flame.

Have seconds passed by, or minutes?

It must feel as long for her. Perhaps she also worries about the neutrality of her expression, of the imperfections of her face. She, too, is watching someone watch her. She too must feel the weight of the opposing gaze. They are both as vulnerable, both equally at the mercy of one another's eyes.

Gabe starts to feel safe in the shared vulnerability. He more comfortably focuses on her eyes, rather than how he feels beneath them. The glimmer of firelight reflects in her pupils. They are the deepest black, deeper than anything else he can imagine: dark pools without a bottom, glazed with the glassy shimmer of ice. Surrounding them are rings flecked with different shades of brown. Whitaker once told him of the stories that trees tell through their rings. The thicker the ring, the greater the rainfall that year. Trees can have hundreds of rings, some thick and proud, some meek and barely visible. They are the earth's oldest historians, light and dark circles their verses. What story is told by the earthy swirls of Katie's eyes?

She looks away with a smile. "Three minutes," she says, "how was it?"

"I've never enjoyed being watched before."

"Perhaps nobody ever *asked* before?"

He nods. "What did you think about," he says, "while you were staring?"

She smiles shyly. "I was thinking about how you watched me on the helicopter. I remembered telling you I didn't mind."

"But you did?"

She nods.

"How about this time?"

"This time," she says, "I liked it."

They share a grateful smile, and their eyes linger a little longer on one another.

# Chapter 29:
# Angels in the Grass

Katie and Gabe leave Jane and Ray behind. Gabe enjoys the dirt under his fingernails and the fuzz of three-days' bristle on his cheeks. They drag mattresses from the houses and place them near the fire, the light keeping them safe, the rocks circling the fire holding the heat through the night. They boil water from an old pump in the town. It tastes of rust and earth. Katie's jarred provisions are sweet and chewy – but there is nothing else to eat. Freedom distracts them from the rumble in their bellies, but the town's ageless calm is a hungry domain.

They lie on a yellow-green hill in the foot-high grass, weary from unknown hours of walking. The further Gabe walks, the more the fog in his mind lifts. He would walk forever if he could. During the day they follow the sun east and use the brilliant white stars to find their way back.

But fear walks with him. Gabe expects a squad of Liberators, burly and black, waiting over the brow of each hill and primes his ears to hear the buzz of a drone or the chopping blades of a helicopter. Katie seems unconcerned. That worries him too. He still does not know what she wants with him. With knowledge of his past role in the Waterloo protest, she has his cooperation. What else did she need?

Gabe sits, removes each shoe, and tenses his feet, feeling a satisfying crack in the bones. The brown leather shoes are rubbed almost white. The imprints of stones dent the delicate soles. "They weren't made for hiking," Gabe grumbles, tossing the shoes aside and massaging the pads of his feet.

"Oh please. You've never had to wear heels."

He looks to the hazy sun hanging in the eastern sky. "Where is it we are going?"

"We'll get there soon."

Katie lies back in the tall grass, limbs spread, hoodie tied about her waist. She fans her arms up and down, making a satisfying *swish*. "Ever made an angel in the grass?"

"A what?"

"Try it," she says, still flapping her arms. She sits up and inspects the imprint of her body in the grass. "It was something I used to do as a kid. There was never snow so we had to make do."

Gabe chuckles as he puts his shoes back on.

"It was something my mom showed me," Katie continues. As she sits, he notices a lazy slouch to her shoulders, a slovenliness that she hides while in the city. "She'd say I just needed to flap my arms to get my angel's wings. And so I would, and there would be a broad pair of wings on my angel in the grass. I guess she was trying to tell me that all that stuff about divinity and goodness and all that. It's really what we do with our own bodies. In the end, it comes back down to us."

She lies back down precisely in the imprint, pressing the grass some more. Then, another question flicking into her mind, she shoots up and asks: "Have you ever been in love?"

Gabe looks away.

"Come on, every dirty detail is on the feed, but you are too shy to tell *me*?" She comes over and elbows him in the arm. "What was her name?"

"I don't know," Gabe replies. Katie groans and rolls her eyes. "*Really*," Gabe insists. "We kept everything anonymous. I never learned who she really was."

"How'd you know she was a *she*?" Her eyebrows flourish. "Or even just one person?"

"I didn't. That is what I liked." He stares across the gentle hills to the emptiness on the horizon. "And that was how she wanted it. Impossible to search her up. Anything I wanted to know, I had to ask.

"It was very slow to build." His hands clasp one another. He rubs his thumbs together. "It was refreshing to get to choose what to tell her about myself. It made me realize how much you can tell about someone from what they say about themselves. At first, it was fun: she liked cardamom. Hated hot days. She was embarrassed about getting sweaty palms. Eventually, it got more personal. One night she told me her brother was a Liberator. She hadn't seen him for years. And she said she felt guilty – because she never wanted to see him again. She was terrified of him."

"Why did it end?"

Gabe sighs. When he read her messages, he imagined her voice to be assured and sweet, like he supposed his mother might have sounded. He never got to hear the real thing. "I was too tempted to know. I wanted to make it real. I had Skyra analyze her messages to try and identify her. It did not work, but I confessed to her anyway. She said that I betrayed her." Her voice, no longer sweet, returns to his imagination. Another thing he hopes to forget. "And I had," he concedes.

"I remember looking at the last message she'd sent me," he continues, "I wanted to grab it from the screen and press it into my chest." He laughs as he shakes his head. "I even tried, and, for a few seconds, I felt it in my hands – I really *felt* the message pushed into my chest," he says, pressing firmly on his heart.

He withdraws his hands. "Then the feeling went away."

His hands rejoin his lap. A breeze ruffles the long grass. "And you?" he asks. "Have you ever been in love?" She shakes her head. "Oh come on," Gabe protests, "boys must have thrown themselves at you."

"They did," she smiles, "but I never loved. After something bad happened in my childhood, all I felt was anger. At first explosive anger, the kind of anger you can only tell with fists. That gave way to a slow burning anger. You can do a lot of things with anger, but not love."

"Is that what we're doing here?" Gabe says. "Following your anger?"

Before she answers, the wind picks up, and Katie's thick brows furrow. "Smell that?"

"Sulfur."

Gabe replaces his shoes. They head in the direction of the wind. He snatches the sound of rushing water from the wind. A river? As they near the sound becomes clearer: a splatter. The smell of sulfur is forceful now, hanging in the air, clinging to their skin. The sound – like a muddy waterfall – becomes overwhelming. Katie and Gabe clamber up a hill, feet squelching on the sick tufts of grass. The ground is grungy and sodden underfoot, the muck swallowing his soles.

At the top they see it: a vast lake, black and horrid, leaking all the way to the horizon where it muddies the sky. Katie catches her nose with a hand, but it does nothing to stop her gagging. Her neck constricts as she visibly fights the compulsion to heave. The lake is fed by a torrent of thick liquid escaping from a pipe. Gabe sees the sludgy expulsion of every wasted meal, every manufacturing by-product, every Skyra bracelet emerging from that pipe.

The two figures stand forlorn on the brow of the hill. They cannot stay outside the city. It was a fantasy to think otherwise. The putrid lake will grow. It will swallow the abandoned town one day. And then – perhaps the city too.

As Gabe nears, Katie becomes more unrecognizable. She's pale, her cheeks are limp, the corners of her mouth wilted. The vibrancy in her eyes is gone, now diluted and watery. The lake has sucked the liveliness from them. Her stare lingers on the filthy horizon even as Gabe comes toward her. Katie does not notice him, as if there is no Gabe in her eyes, no town, nothing but the brown abyss below them. Her arms hang down and her hands squirm thoughtlessly.

Gabe ushers her back down the hill and away from the tailings lake. She's stiff, but her legs comply. Once the ground feels firm, Katie flops down and begins to cry. Gabe stands a few steps behind her and drags his fingers through his hair. The cold sweat of wasteful, aimless toil beads on his neck and forehead. No matter how far they walk, they cannot escape the world they live in. He feels the bitter clasp of time again. Each hour of exertion leaks into his body. Where has she been leading him? Where were they walking? What does she want from him?

"Why did you bring me here?" he says behind her. Katie sniffs and wipes her nose with her sleeve. "I'm sorry about your friend," Gabe continues. "If this is about her…"

"It is… and isn't."

"You know you can coerce me. Why bring me here?"

She takes a strengthening breath. "I don't need coercion; I need *trust*. So I found a place where nothing can watch or listen in. Where I could look into your eyes, and you into mine, and we could know that we could trust one another."

Gabe remains standing over her. Katie summons her courage and turns to face him. "I need your help. For the last few years, I've made myself into a brand as big as anyone. My stream is seen by millions of viewers, but it can be shut off at any time. I need something that cannot be shut off. On the upcoming Black Friday event, I'm going to star in the most-watched advert in history. I will convince Daviault Junior to make it happen. I will convince him to make the advert live. And I'm going to take that moment of unprecedented, uncensored access to tell everyone that there can be a different way."

"They'll kill you." He waits for her to deny it. But her glance tells him that she knows. Gabe wants to tell her to stop. Each new sentence of hers is another he must keep locked in his head. He swears he hears the buzz of a surveillance drone over the brow of the hill.

"People only know you to sell products," he protests, "they can't see you in another light."

"*You* have."

She can dream of seditious acts all she wants. He will have none of them. There is still a chance that he can return to the city without ending up in a Liberator van. He'll say she is mad. Or he'll confess everything she told him – anything to extricate *him* from *her*.

"Why do you need *me*?" he says, standing over her.

"Waterloo: you managed to get thousands of people to protest," she answers. "You know how to get people to listen and *act*. And – I trust you."

He thinks about the sore skin around his wrist. Skyra has brought him many bittersweet happinesses over years of service. But it has also given him a kind of freedom: a freedom *from* choice. When that band was around his wrist, he was reassured that he would never have to make an unassisted decision again. Skyra has the sum of humanity's knowledge. Without it, Gabe feels the fear of unknowing. His fingers itch to feel Skyra's familiar golden ridges again.

He asks her how she plans to deliver a message without instantly being detected and stopped. She tells him about the club on the top floors of the Mercantile Tower where nothing is tracked. "I've got two pills left," she says. "One for me. One for you."

Gabe steps further from her and rests his palms on his hips. The itch on his wrist grows. "They're going to suspect something – us being out here."

"Of course," she acknowledges. "But Davi will want me for the Black Friday event. He won't pass up this chance."

"How do you know Davi will want you for Black Friday?"

"He's not subtle about what he wants."

"Well, what about me?"

"Tell them you went along to protect me from myself. Tell them you convinced me to do this massive advert. And tell them – I trust you. More than anyone else. That will make you useful."

The soreness about Gabe's wrist worsens. Everything he has done in his life has been recorded and analyzed. Years have slipped by, the data on him growing in size and completeness. With a good enough analytic, that data can predict what he will do before he does it. Anything out of the ordinary will be instantly flagged. If he is to return to the city and help Katie, he will need to live the life his data has mapped out for him. The life he, for a handful of beautiful days, believed he had escaped. Gabe feels the walls of his apartment closing in around him.

He no longer has a guiding analytic. All choice is his. An unwelcome memory pushes from forgotten depths and into his mind's eye. He hides the momentary wince and presses the memory away. He fumbles his fingers, unsure of his reasons, unsure of hers. "You came specifically to the State of Nature to do this," Gabe says. "You made yourself very public. You put yourself in danger. You're putting *me* in danger. I need to know why."

Katie looks up. "Okay."

# Chapter 30:
# The Milk of Human Kindness

As a child, Jane often stayed on the seashore, throwing up her arms to ward off the waves like she was a goddess. She would watch the ocean swell and froth, each wave curling its teeth to gnash upon the rocks. Jane growled and threw sticks at the fierce mass until the storm subsided, and she'd cackle in victory.

The first time Jane felt her powers challenged was when her mother started going to the hospital. Complications with pregnancy left her mother bedridden. There was nobody to help – no father, no family anymore. Jane asked if her mother was going to die. Her mother pulled her close – she didn't want to leave any doubt – and said that *you and your sister are the greatest things to happen to me; I'm going to be fine.* And she was. She got better; she gave birth. So Jane returned to the shoreline, cackling at the waves, convinced of her family's invulnerability.

But one day, fifteen years past, Jane didn't taunt the sea. Something in the air felt as if even a goddess could not hold off the waves. *That* day she burrowed herself into the covers on her mother's bed, peeking from below the sheets. Her mother sat beside her on the bed, trying to allay her baby sister's cries with gentle lullabies. Whenever Jane's war cries had failed to calm an impending storm, her mother's sweet and soft incantations had always succeeded.

But it was not a storm that approached. She learned later that a sheet of Arctic ice had splintered from its shelf, throwing up a wave so large that it swallowed the Isles in minutes. By the time they got the warning, it was too late.

It happened much too quickly to leave memories. Jane has only sensations of what occurred: the hard squeeze of her mother's hand – the childish disbelief that something was wrong – the roof shaking – scrambling from their frail cottage without putting on a jacket – and the roar of the water. Yes, that roar: the sound overwhelmed all others. Her mother's mouth made words Jane did not hear, and then Jane was enveloped by the roar.

Jane remembers the coarse sheets of the shelter bed, and stretchers, and trolleys, and lots of people running back and forth, and she remembers sitting up, seeing her mother crying, and wondering what all the fuss was about, and she remembers her baby sister grunting as she fed from a bottle.

Jane later read that a company named Nature Corp. gifted every survivor with a baby a parcel of formula milk. Exhausted and malnourished, her mother replaced her breast with a bottle of the formula. Her sister latched onto the new source of milk. Jane remembers the baby's colour improving and her cries becoming contented mumbles.

But the donations from Nature Corp. lasted only as long as it took her mother to stop lactating. When the last of the formula ran out, her mother tried vainly to provide for the baby at her breast. The baby suckled hopelessly. In desperation, her mother spent the last of her money buying more formula. This had been the purpose of the donations all along. The formula came in gleaming packaging adorned with smiling infant faces. But her baby sister grew weaker and her cries increased.

And then memories get lost again, and Jane remembers her sister screaming, screaming no matter how she was rocked or soothed. Jane could not understand why her baby sister screamed – screamed until she was coughing, screamed until she was hoarse, spluttering at the bottle put to her lips.

Jane later learned that the storm damaged the sanitation plants. Their water supply was tainted. Each time her mother mixed the water with the powdered baby formula, the baby got sicker. The survivors needed concerted action to restore the water supply and provide food for the survivors. But Nature Corp. wanted only to enslave the survivors to the bottle and break the connection between mother's breast and baby's dependent lips. Her sister's cries became whimpers. The baby snuggled tightly to her mother's barren breast, rocked and soothed, until she cried no more.

The cemeteries were all washed away, so they scattered the ashes in the ocean. Jane wailed as the ashes sank below the surface. Jane wanted to throw herself into the water and gather the ashes back up. But they were irrevocably split apart, and when her mother explained to her that they'd been offered a chance – an *amazing* chance – to move countries and start over, Jane knew that they'd be split up too. And though the orderly promised Jane that her mother would be on the next plane, not to worry, that was the last time she ever saw her mother.

The water destroyed. The water uprooted. The water poisoned. But the water did not choose. It was people who saw opportunity; it was people who chose marketing over mankind. The corporation gave, her mother took, and her baby sister drank – drank the tainted liquid – drank the result of marketing at all costs – drank the milk of human kindness.

# Chapter 31:
# Shipwrecks

After telling Gabe the story, Katie sits on the hillside, crushing her fingers into fists. She is taut, ready to pounce. Gabe lets her have the anger. It will be her only opportunity to feel a cleansing, visceral hatred. At least until she completes her plan. He does not know what will happen after that. He glances to his naked wrist, wishing for a prediction from an electronic oracle.

Gabe sits beside Katie and puts an arm over her shoulder. Katie hugs her legs and rests her chin on her knees, letting grim memories transpire off her. Gabe gives her as long as she needs.

"So," Katie sniffs, "that is why I have to try."

Gabe looks at Katie like he is looking at a younger version of himself. She brims with the same fury he once had. She aches with the same guilt.

He sometimes wondered what he would say if he could go back, before the Waterloo protest, and talk to his younger self. Would he tell that brash young man to persist with his utopian visions? Or would he tell his younger self that the war was already lost? As the lines in his face became deeper, Ray realized the question was a cheat. He was subject to too many influences: he had *never* listened to himself, so why listen to an older version? Yet, the question returns as he watches Katie twist her cheek onto her knee. Perhaps there is still time to impart upon her the extent of their hopelessness. Perhaps there is still time to save her, as he wishes he could have saved himself.

"We can't put the big data genie back in its bottle, Gabe says, "I tried that."

"But we can change our relationship to it."

Gabe shakes his head. "Convincing people to change things is impossible."

Katie picks her head from her knees. "Revolution is miniscule," she replies, "it starts with the simple thought that you're not afraid to decide who you're going to be that day. That realization is all it takes to start the wheel turning."

"There isn't room for that kind of thought," he says like he is breaking bad news to her.

"The advertisers rely on us," Katie says. "Without us letting them watch, they're blind. Without us to listen, they're dumb. Unthinking consent is their keystone. At any time we can revoke our consent – if we choose."

"And your plan is to create another protest? Protests will be detected and defused, if they aren't predicted before they begin. What have we got left? Petitions and hashtags."

Katie releases her knees. "Protest does not need to be big," she says. "It can be individual, personal. The idea is trust. You share only with who, and what, you trust. Until that trust is earned, don't tell the truth. Play with what you are. Tell them everything wrong. Misinformation." Katie stands. The hoody flaps about her waist. "We *can* convince them," she insists.

"Some things you can't convince people of," Gabe says, rising. Katie, a step above him on the hill, stands at his height. Their eyes match. "You can influence people to overeat more easily than to eat properly," Gabe continues. "Why? Eating is pleasurable. Moderation is not. A species that disliked eating would not survive."

She scowls. He tries to be sympathetic. "Influence is a river," he says. "It only goes in one direction: to our worst impulses."

Katie grunts, waves him away, and stomps toward a rocky hole in the distance. It holds a pool of rainwater like cupped hands. Gabe follows and they sit on the outer edge. Gabe feels the stickiness between his toes but resists the temptation to dip his feet into the pool. Wild water cannot be trusted, no matter how tranquil it appears.

She looks betrayed, but this is for her protection. "People don't care, Katie," Gabe continues as they sit beside the pond. "As long as our bellies are full and we're stimulated, we're happy. Society isn't changed by brave individual choices. It's changed by the price of bread or the cost of electricity."

"Never doubt the potency of someone's will," Katie ripostes. "There are stories of individuals who sparked something indomitable. Meagre people – factory workers, fruit-sellers – simple people with simple bravery. Heroes and heroines who have caused revolutions."

"Right place, right time," Gabe shoots back.

"Then *let's be* the hero and the heroine, in the *right* place, at the *right* time."

"It can't work," Gabe hisses. "We're too slow. A computer brain is faster than a human brain. Whatever you think, the algorithms are faster. You'll be outwitted."

A fly from the pool disturbs their mutual stare. Gabe watches it circle his head.

"We aren't talking about a species," Katie answers. "We are talking about individuals, in all their little glory. Too small for big data to see. The bigger you are, the slower. The little fly sees time faster than we do. From its point of view, we are lumbering in slow-motion."

"And anyway," she adds, "that speed help *us* as much as *them*."

Gabe shoots her a puzzled look. Her eyes hold his. They are remarkable: big and clear, and lively once more.

"When I was a child I spent a lot of time on the rocks beside the beach," Katie explains, "they looked like the teeth of a giant. I imagined hundreds of shipwrecks piled on top of one another just below those rocks."

"So?" Gabe grunts.

"*So* – before the invention of the ship, there were no shipwrecks. Whenever you invent something, you also invent a way for it to backfire. We've invented technology for advertisers to communicate with everyone, everywhere, instantly. Lying in that technology is another shipwreck, waiting to happen. We just have to cause it."

She looks off, resting her chin upon her left fist, hunched forward in concentration.

The wind dies down. The pool in front of them is strikingly still. The evening sunlight scatters diamonds on its surface. Flies from the pool circle their heads. Gabe has never considered what a fly sees. His focus is always to see things in bigger terms – not in smaller.

He studies the gangly reeds skirting the circumference of the pond. He appreciates that life prevails even out here, though the brown colour of the reeds suggests that they barely tolerate the brackish water. Gabe approaches the pond's edge, fascinated now by the smallness of detail. He concentrates on the insects that stride on the surface of the water as if gravity does not exist for them. Perhaps it doesn't; to the tiny insects on the water, surface tension, and not gravity, is the most important force in the world. Different rules apply to different scales.

Gabe thinks back to the role of data in his own profession. For all their best efforts, Skyra does not always produce accurate data. Sometimes a bracelet malfunctions, sometimes the user is unusual and produces garbled readings. But as long as the data is correct in broad strokes, tiny errors in a microscopic scale hardly matter. The more data, the less precise individual measurements need to be.

In that moment, he realizes: despite the endless supply of data *at large*, there will always be aberrations individually. No individual can be perfectly known, nor predicted. Big data can know humanity, but it can never know humans. There is opportunity, always, for individual choice and resistance.

Hope wells inside him. He begins to indulge in the fantasy that her plan might work. Gabe wants to turn, scramble back to Katie and throw his arms around her. But something holds him back. He ruminates, again, about his past. He cannot let her turn into him.

"What do you see?" Katie asks.

The water-striders become imperceptible in the diminishing sunlight.

"It's getting dark," Gabe mumbles, pushing away the hope. "Let's get back."

# Chapter 32:
# Persistence of Vision

Gabe watches the shadows of grass dance on his shoes. "What is it?" Katie asks. Her hair glows a rich brown in the firelight. She gives him a moment. Gabe does not look up.

"This is the safest place for secrets," she assures.

She waits for a response that does not come. His eyes remain low.

Katie volunteers instead: "After the flood, I was relocated to Nature and put with a foster family. They were nice – really accepting of me, even when I was awful."

Her voice flickers with nostalgia: "I can still smell the hotdogs they made each Friday evening as 'family night.'"

Gabe looks up and gives a weak smile.

"But part of me really believed that they were trying to replace my mother," Katie continues, "and that if I pushed them away for long enough, she would eventually come back. So the nicer they were to me, the more horrid I was back. And I enjoyed doing it. I hurt. I wanted them to hurt too."

She screws her face, disgusted. Dark shadows dance below her eyes. A piece of wood lets out a crack.

"Eventually they tried an intervention: sat me down, held my hands, hugged me tight, brushed off every nasty thing I said. I knew they would never give up on me, never let me go. I convinced myself that I would be freer without them."

Katie stands, visibly unable to contain her self-loathing. "So that night I ran away. To Chron-OS. And I never went back. As I grew older, I wanted to apologise. I didn't know what I could say to make up for how much I tormented them, but I wanted to at least try. But I can't. Because if I do, I will create a new string of information linking that angry little girl back to me."

Gabe wavers. He understands the pain of being unable to apologise for an awful wrong. But Katie, at least, appears to have grown from it. There remains some positive she might bring to balance the hardship she has caused. It is too late for him. Too immense. Too frightening.

Katie's trustworthy eyes implore a response. "If you don't want to say it – perhaps try shouting it," she says. Katie stands on her rock and cups her hands to her mouth. She looks down to Gabe, draws a deep breath, and shouts: "I used anger as an easy excuse to give up!"

Her voice disintegrates in the surrounding black. Katie puts hands to her hips and raises her eyebrows expectantly. She beckons him to stand as well. When he does not, Katie presses her shoulders back like she is a Valkyrie calling a cavalry charge.

"I mistreated everyone who ever got close!" she exclaims into the distance. "Because I was afraid of someone caring about me again!"

She breaks into a childish smile. Then she sighs and shuts her eyes for a moment, feeling the catharsis of release.

Gabe smiles weakly, piteously, unconvinced by her energy. He wrings sweaty hands together. They are only words, he thinks, strange sounds humans needlessly inflict on one another. It will mean nothing to say it: *seventeen people died because of my choice.* There. He can say it in his mind. Why not with his mouth?

It feels abstract to say it in his mind, like he is talking about someone else. As long as the words remain in his mind and not on his tongue, there is no guilt. The bad memories can be easily replaced by thoughts of silk ties and the curves of a new Barone. But once words spring from the mouth, they take a life of their own.

Gabe hunches over. Katie nods in acceptance, looking more disappointed in herself than in him. She sits back down, visibly surprised at the failure of her infectious energy.

"Sometimes trusting someone else isn't enough," he finally says, "you have to trust yourself, too."

Katie scrunches confused eyebrows together.

Gabe admires the courage Katie has in herself. It is naive but indomitable. A sweet but silly girl, her angry idealism inspiring but ultimately hollow. Like every product he buys, or getaway he plans but never takes: fleetingly exciting but eventually unsatisfying. He shakes his head at how gullible he has been. She is a product in the literal sense of the word: a walking brand, a body and personality constructed to sell. And for a short time, he has bought what she has been selling.

He does not need to tell her. He has survived for this long. And why does she need to know? Petulant girl, chipping away at his last little space of privacy, shaking its crenelated walls. That final place, pushed to the recesses of his mind, hard and calcified. He will not open it up. Not to her, and not to himself.

He is a body floating powerless in a river of influence, washed down meandering paths. Thrashing his limbs to swim will be the quickest way to drown. Better to lay on his back, stretch out his arms, and let the warm current take him where it may.

It is time for him to go. He will leave her the car so that she can get back. At that moment it does not matter how he will get back – back to the self-driving cars and automated elevators and curated media. Back to Skyra. He rises, dusts off his trousers, and walks in the direction of the tunnel.

He says only: "I'm sorry."

Katie does not follow. She remains by the fire, shrinking into the darkness the further he walks. He is barely aware of where he is going, but his feet take him swiftly back to the threshold of the tunnel. Skyra will see him soon. It will soothe the soreness on his wrist and in his mind. It will rescue him from invading thoughts. It will push Whitaker's wisdom and Jane's sedition far from the tiny, cherished circle of his attention. The longing draws him back through the tunnel.

Gabe falls away as Ray takes a step in. He stretches one arm out in front. The hand disappears in the darkness. He stretches his other arm back to the town. That hand glistens with silver star drops.

He chooses the tunnel.

In the darkness, wisps of adverts return to his eyes. Ethereal colours haunt the fringes of his vision, disappearing when focussed on. He shudders as the colours intensify. A red face taunts from his left, a blue figure to his right. He hears distant jingles in his ears. He blows a slow breath out to calm his nerves and wipes his palms on his suit. He takes quick strides. Even in the isolation of the tunnel, he does not want the humiliation of outright running from the adverts on his eyes.

Streams of colourful banners and bright signs circle ghoulishly above his head, cackling and mocking his flight. *Time to go!* he hears, the relic of a vacation commercial laughed incessantly into his ear. *See you soon!* another shrieks from a coffee-store tagline, as clear as if transmitted like a beam into his ear.

*Time to go!*

He breaks into a run. He squeezes his eyelids so tightly that his eyes ache. But he still sees the adverts. The colours are persistent. Wherever he runs, they will be there forever.

*Time to go!*

Ghoulish chatters run with him.

*Time to go!*

He kicks up grit behind him.

*Time to go!*

He trips on an unseen rail and tumbles into the dark. His hands sting, burned by the gravel. Howls in his ears. Ghosts in his eyes. Ray grimaces, the wind knocked out of him. He sprawls, the figures haunting him, taunting him, chipping away at his choice until he is a pathetic heap lost in the darkness. He wrings his fists tight and presses his forehead into the grit. His muffled cries echo down upon him from the tunnel.

He had believed that there is safety and comfort in passivity. But he shivers as the ghosts in the tunnel continue to call. This is how it will be if he returns to the city. This is how it always has been: circled and followed by calling spirits, haunted in the isolation of his own home.

Jane is right. There must be something more.

He pulls himself to his feet and kicks up unseen gravel as he sprints back toward the light of the tunnel opening.

# Chapter 33:
# Welcome to Freedom

With a thin piece of flint in one hand and a rock in the other, Katie chisels the lesser *E* into the wood. She stops, takes a few steps back, and judges the letters. They are a little cumbersome, but not bad for the tools she has. Perhaps with a sharper implement and fresher wood she could have cleaved precise strips from the panel. She resumes her chipping, forming another *E* in the wood.

She found the panel some days before, lying flat in the scratchy grass. She hauled it upright and broke off the accumulated dirt with her free hand. Katie earned a splinter in her finger for the trouble. *Welcome to* the panel said in flaking blue paint. The rest was illegible.

The panel was wider than the span of her arms and weighted down by every year of its age. With some difficulty, Katie dragged the panel toward the first building in the town. A corner splintered off, and her injured wrist complained with each heave. Katie blew a stray piece of hair from her face, shifting the panel with determined pulls. Eventually, she turned the panel around and leant it with a *thump* against the wall of the first building. Katie sat down panting in front of the sign. While she slowed down her breathing, Katie considered what to name the town. Before she could decide, Gabe called out for her, and she went to find him.

That moment feels distant, now.

When Gabe left her at the fire, she did not chase. She did not call.

It is not her duty to break his chains. He has to choose to do that himself. Letting others choose is easy. The expectations are clear. The responsibilities are minimal. There is no anguish of knowing that success or failure is attributable only to you.

When she lost her sister, and then her mother, Jane blamed herself. Childish imagination and deep grief contorted the facts against her. Jane had not warned her mother to avoid the powdered milk. Perhaps the right words might have put a seed of life-saving doubt in her mother's mind, before she served the tainted milk to her sister's searching lips. Perhaps she brought the flood itself, the relentless waves punishment for Jane mocking the sea with her howls and insults. Each new theory of her guilt, more fanciful than the last, was another tale to flog herself with.

Eventually, Jane discovered the comforting concoction of carelessness and alcohol until she just felt numb. It became tiring to search for underwear in ruffled bed sheets without disturbing the drunken slumber of the boy beside. She endured far too much of that life before she came upon the obvious truth: that if she did not take responsibility for her own life, somebody else would. The only choice was to place intention before action. Everything she did, from then on, would have a reason before its initiation, rather than a justification afterward.

Katie returns to this conclusion as she chips at the wooden panel. No, she did not follow Gabe when he left, chasing him with tearful appeals. She took an unlit torch, crafted from a dry branch wrapped with salvaged clothing, and dipped it into the fire. She found the wooden panel where she had left it – at the entrance of the lonely town – and staked the torch into the ground. Its flame is stable. There is no wind. She begins chiseling another letter into the panel. She finishes a *D* and an *O* before the thin flint snaps off in her hand.

"*For Satan!*" she curses to herself.

"Did they teach you that in the Isles?" a voice comes from behind her.

Katie does not turn around. She stoops to pick up the broken flint.

"Oh, no," Katie mutters, her back still turned. "An old roommate of mine, Carl, was Danish. He taught me how to swear like that. *Forhelvede! For Satan!* So authoritative," she says, throwing the words at Ray behind her. "Or maybe in your case, *forbandede skiderik.*"

She flashes a look over her shoulder. Gabe stands apologetically, palms open toward her.

"There are quite a lot of Danes over here," she says, feigning interest in the broken shard of flint. "Being so close to sea level meant they got swallowed up by the flood, too." Katie thinks of Carl and the swoop of hair always dangling in his eyes.

Katie flicks flint pieces against one another to form another point. "I never heard anything about killer waves when I was a child. Then one day, there was a wave so big it rolled across the entire country. They could have prepared for it by building levees and walls. But despite knowing the risks of increased flooding, the Isles preferred building malls and distribution centres. You want to be angry but don't know who to be angry toward. That's why I learned to swear," she adds. "Makes anger a little bit more tolerable."

"It also makes it extremely difficult to censor you for the younger audiences."

"Swearing never hurt anyone," she dismisses. "A well-timed *bastard* or a strategic *dammit* can make anything feel better." She grins more with each word. "The world's most harmful phrases aren't *shit* or *fuck*. They're *'while supplies last'* or *'you may also like.'*"

Having fashioned a primitive point in one of her flint pieces, Katie resumes chipping. Gabe waits. Katie keeps chipping.

"I'm sorry," he says.

Katie keeps working.

"I shouldn't have run."

She curls another slice of wood away with the flint.

"I should have trusted you."

Katie stops and turns. Gabe's eyes seem renewed.

"We all have our choices to make," she says.

Gabe cocks his head to read the sign behind her. He asks what she is doing. "The only way I can operate is under the certainty that my plan will work. So if it does, and if even a few people choose to leave... I want them to know what they have found out here."

She chisels in the remaining letter. The wood is refreshed in the torch's luminescence. The chiseled letters fill with shadow. *Welcome to Freedom* it reads.

"Come on," Gabe beckons, "I have something to tell you."

# Chapter 34:
# Black Friday II

Katie takes a steaming canister from the rocks beside the fire and passes it to Gabe. Instant coffee from one of the houses. He takes it gingerly in his fingers and sniffs the aroma. It is earthy and a little burnt. He blows on the coffee until Katie tells him to drink up. No more delays. Gabe slurps the brown liquid and passes the canister back. Katie pulls the sleeves of her hoodie down to cover her hands and wraps her fingers around it.

"I told you at the castle that I wanted to be a musician," Gabe begins. "And for a while, I was. Poor but passionate."

"A guitar, I bet."

"I was more of a trumpet man, actually," Gabe replies. "I don't remember my parents, but I know that I used to play for them. I used to have this dream that my music could bring everyone together. But it didn't pay," he says, shaking his head. "That's when I met an algorithmist named Whitaker. She was more than an algorithmist. She was a genius and a historian, too, and she was convinced by the idea that algorithms could apply to the past as well as the future. She was driven by a longing to trace the entire course of human history through an algorithm. She was the best in the state at what she did."

"*Was?*"

"She gave me my start in marketing as a jingle-writer. I earned a better network of higher-TELOS people, but the job didn't make me any happier. Everyone in my new network seemed to be doing better than me, taking healthier bodies in better clothes on more exotic vacations. But you *have* to compete with them, otherwise your TELOS falls, and the feed forgets you. So, I pushed for better results. The marketing I led became more intense. Eventually, I headed a team looking at music and psychology. In particular, at fear."

He sighs. "Have you ever seen the riots over basic supplies when we get hurricane warnings?"

"I never understood why they show them on the feed."

"They're good for business," Gabe replies. "A crowd that is frightened of something, like a hurricane, spends thoughtlessly, even when prices are tripled, quadrupled."

Gabe explains that through his experiments, he discovered that fear could be stimulated and carefully tended every few hours. He showed that people could come to view one another as threats by convincing them that, despite the existence of factories the size of lakes, the products on sale were scarce and might run out. *Why* people saw one another as threats did not matter. All that mattered was that people became predictably afraid that others might capture the scarce quantity of goods before they did. All that mattered was that profit flowed therefrom.

It was during the trials of his method, when they pumped only specific people with these cues, that Ray finally understood humanity. Those primed to be afraid of others getting something before they did would hit and kick and fall on others to claim their prize. They would do so even when reason would have told them to wait until supplies were less limited. They would do so even though, holding a new product in one hand and bloodied nose with the other, they could not explain what savage spirit had possessed them. It was then he discovered that nobody was really in control.

A singular exhilaration hit when he realized public behaviour could be orchestrated by his fingertips. He wondered at what the knowledge might bring him, what TELOS he might obtain. Questions flickered weakly in his mind about whether his idea was responsible, but there was an opening for a more senior position, and at least four others were in contention. He swatted the questions aside, skipped further tests, and implemented the method for the largest event of the year: Black Friday.

For weeks beforehand, he arranged for the experimental group to be shown messages emphasizing the limited quantity of products available at the upcoming Black Friday. At the end of each advert he played a unique chime of his own creation. He arranged for the test group to see news of factory interruptions, delivery delays, and limited supplies to emphasize the scarcity of goods.

And then on Black Friday, as the experimental group stormed the malls, he fed their Skyra bracelets real-time data about how many of their desired product remained in the store. *Eighteen left. Fifteen. Ten.* Fearful of everyone else, the experimental group acted more aggressively and spent more thoughtlessly.

The morning after, he read a memorandum of the experiment results on his wallscreen.

"Sales for the experimental group up twenty-two percent. Revenues up thirty-eight percent. It was an astounding success," Gabe says, observing the look of disgust on Katie's face.

"But..." she says.

"Perhaps, when there was less data, advertisers could avoid feeling guilty about the repercussions of their messages. A person besieged by adverts could consume any number of unhealthy products; who was to say which caused the cancer, the heart attack? It is hard to make that argument given the amount of data they now have." Gabe chokes a reply: "At the bottom of one page there was a footnote about the number of deaths."

"How many—"

Unwilling lips seal away his answer. Finally, Gabe forces out: "Seventeen. Directly traceable to my experiment."

The number hangs in the air. Gabe deflates with the effort. Guilt washes over him: a familiar but almost-forgotten guilt, a compressive guilt that forces the air from his lungs. He cannot tell how long Katie stays silent, staring *through* him. She must be picturing bloodied shoppers escaping with hard-fought goods, falling to their knees as they realized what they had done. They would never know the manipulation that contributed to their behaviour. They would carry the weight of what they had done, alone. And the shoppers who did *not* escape paid with their lives: how carelessly they were put in harm's way.

"What happened then?" she utters.

He must tell it all. Truth cannot be fractional anymore. He had stared at that footnote, emblazoned on his apartment wallscreen, while holding a glass of celebratory whiskey in his right hand. *It's not my fault*, he told himself, *it was their choice to be aggressive.* But he knows that it is not that simple: if it was *just their choice*, he wouldn't have a job. But he told himself that it was not his choice. Like everyone else, he was merely a passenger floating on the waters of influence. The warm comfort of powerlessness embraced him, and responsibility disappeared below the surface.

"I was afraid, so I kept it quiet," Gabe admits. "I gave a glowing report to my higher-ups. I said nothing when they sold my method to the highest bidders, who used it, year after year, with increasing intensity. And when it leaked that those companies were intentionally stoking fear to promote sales, I helped bury it. Rival companies sent out news releases criticizing the inhumane marketing. There were complaints on the feed. You can't silence that; but you can be louder. We pushed all of it to the side with vigorous marketing campaigns. New products, new events. Of course, there were none. But all we needed was some temporary hype to bury the story.

"You asked me why I helped the Waterloo protest," Gabe says. "It took me a few years to face what I had done. I helped the protest because I wanted to unwind the damage I'd caused, the only way I could. That is when Whitaker introduced me to the man called Jonas."

"What happened to the protest?"

"A hundred thousand marched on the first day. Three hundred thousand the second. Tens of millions of comments, posts, videos in support. But by the end of the week, the Liberators had cordoned off the protesters, re-routed vehicle traffic, switched the algorithms to filter out dissent, and captured the key protesters. The protest died quickly, then disappeared from history altogether. Jonas and some of the others helping him got found out. Whitaker and I were lucky."

She looks up at him. "So, you just... gave up?"

"The failure of the protest taught me that it is easier to make people do bad things, for selfish reasons, than to do good things, for the benefit of the whole."

"And?"

A smile emerges from his forlorn face. "I was wrong. There are still people that care," he says, eying her. "People who are willing to risk themselves to help a friend."

They hug. She wraps her arms around his waist. He presses her head into his torso. Her hair smells earthy – not the stuff in the wasteland that crumbled in his hands – but earth with life in it, a healthy earth fit for growth, so lush that he wants to immerse his fingers in it. Ray smooths back her hair and says: "All that's needed is for someone to know they have a choice."

He has made his.

# Chapter 35:
# War Paint

Katie pulls herself from his chest and wipes her nose with a sleeve of her hoody. They walk with interlaced hands to the tree in the town square. Her skin's roughness surprises him. There are callouses on the pads of her fingers and her knuckles are cracked from exposure to the arid air.

One half of the tree in the town square grows determinedly toward the sky. The other half meanders as if it cannot decide whether to grow toward the sun or to the ground. Katie asks what happened to everyone else who helped with the Waterloo protest. Her skin is moon silver.

Whitaker had disowned him after the Black Friday deaths, Gabe says, but her lover, Jonas, convinced her to help him with the protest.

"Lover?" Katie says, "husky, denim-wearing Jonas was her lover?"

"Whitaker liked things with rough edges."

"Then why did he end up in the Red Zone?"

"He got the spotlight punishment: a noise in his head that only he could hear. *They're in my head, they're in my head* he kept saying, pulling out his hair. He fled to the Red Zone to escape the sounds in his head. I had assumed he was dead."

The mood drops. The risks of their plan feel more real. Gabe perks up to break the silence: "You've never been able to tell anyone your story, have you?"

Katie shakes her head.

"How do you keep it secret?" Gabe adds. "Even a nobody like me is constantly watched. Yet the authorities somehow don't know you. Not just that - they don't understand you."

"You want data? I give it – in huge amounts. Some true, most false. I tell Skyra I love Italian cuisine, update my feed to say I'm feeling Vietnamese, instruct my refrigerator to remind me I need naan, tag pictures of Waldorf salads, declare on a medical profile that I have allergies to all of those things, and set up a fitness tracking account to say I barely eat at all. And I keep doing it – the more random, the more fun!"

"Needles in haystacks," he laughs. "You know a lot about this. What do you need me for?"

"Because I still have cameras watching me, still have GPS in my Skyra, RFID tags in my clothes. I don't know how to avoid them all."

"RFID tags in your clothes only work if *you're* the one wearing them," Gabe notes, eying her hoody. "Who wouldn't want a skirt or top from the most famous life-streamer?"

"*Most* famous?"

"If we make it back alive, you will be."

"But they can just cross-check my location with video cameras," Katie replies.

"Not if they can't recognize you. Certain shapes disrupt the facial recognition system. Walk around with a particular pattern on your face and automated systems won't recognize you."

"Show me."

He slides two fingers into the vein of red ochre at the foot of the tree and gently paints both her cheeks, below each eye, with a small triangle. "The eye sockets are critical for identifying a face," Gabe explains, "along with the point where the nose meets the forehead. Is this ok?"

"I've worn worse."

He smooths the soft ochre in a swoop around her right eye, ending at the bridge of her nose between the eyes. "There," he says.

"How do I look?" she laughs.

"Invisible."

Katie goes to the nearest house and returns with a shard of glass. She wipes it clean and smirks at the reflection. Both cheeks wear fiery ochre triangles. But only the right side of her face bears the swoop of red across her cheek and around the eye. It makes her face appear asymmetrical but strangely beautiful.

"War paint," she says, raising her eyebrows mischievously. A smile blooms on Gabe's face.

Katie and Gabe decide to enjoy the remainder of the fire, then head back through the train tunnel at dusk. They listen to the harp once again, still moved by its ghostly voice. Despite Gabe's pleas, Katie says they must leave it behind. "We need to do everything the same as before," she reminds.

They stand at the opening of the tunnel like it is the dividing line between worlds. Katie holds the flashlight this time. Gabe quivers at the visions of adverts that had haunted him in the tunnel. "Ready?" Katie encourages.

They enter together.

"Enjoy it while it lasts," she says, "we may never get to experience darkness and silence again."

The starlight at the tunnel's opening shrinks into nothing behind them. Once more in the perfect dark, Gabe tries to focus on the flashlight. The wisps of advertising colour do not return, but the slogans do, whispering faintly as if carried on a distant wind. He seizes a little. Katie stops. She cups her hands to her mouth, and lets out a loud bird call. The echo flies down the tunnel, and down, and down, guiding the way.

Accepting the challenge, Gabe takes a breath, puffs his chest, and lets out a mighty wolf howl. It pings back and forth off the tunnel walls like a Newton's cradle. The howl chases the whispers from his ears. He winks to Katie. She howls too. Then he. Then she. Their echoes mix and meld. They walk again, their joint laughter echoing along the tunnel.

# Chapter 36:
# Hira

*Purity.* As they drive back to the city, Jane recalls Jonas' comment that the State of Nature values purity above all else. As he prepared her fake profile, he told her that Nature maintained a fierce brand of group identity, part nationalist, part classist. They think nature is something to be shaped and perfected, he said, anyone that doesn't fit doesn't stay very long. He had suggested safer places for her to go. There was New Haven, owned by the distributor of the popular Haven tablets. In passing, he mentioned Theos, some sort of theocracy where technology drew people closer to God. Don't think you'll like that one, Jonas had said curtly.

But all Jane could think of was Nature, the entity that donated the formula milk to her mother; the milk that poisoned her sister. Jonas' warnings about Nature had drifted beyond her like a half-heard advert as her thoughts explored pathways for revenge and memories of her sister combusted in her stomach. Those were impure thoughts, and she came to learn how to supress them. The unending surveillance made her politics pure, and then her network of friends, and she fears it will purify her friendship with Ray, too.

Her seat is only a few inches from Ray's, but already she feels they are drifting apart. He is tense and surly, already re-constructing the barriers that they had, very gently, let down in Freetown. The technology keeps them all separate, like an invisible film has formed on their skin. She wants to touch Gabe's hand again, but she fears that it will not feel the same as it had done. She keeps her hands in her lap and remembers the first time she had entered the State.

Life streaming was the only position of any influence Jane could attain with the TELOS Jonas had given her. She didn't have the connections to go corporate, the education to go into research, the credit to be a socialite. She was still young enough to become a streamer, and with her new debt from paying for Reece's initial rehab, had the whiff of desperation. To become one, Jane needed to pass the automated firm interview.

She entered the cheapest deprivation booth, big enough to fit only a single chair, its spongy walls the best quiet she could afford. Jane folded her hoodie, slid it below the chair, licked her fingers to smooth her hair, then asked to start an interview to join the life-streaming agency. A holographic face appeared before Jane with pale blue skin and blonde hair pinned precisely behind her holographic head. The figure blinked its eyes and bobbed its head like a person, but there was something errant in the movements. Perhaps the eyes were too wide, the stare too long, the smile too artificial. In the low light of the deprivation booth, the hovering cold-blue head, making subtly inhuman movements, was like an apparition from a nightmare.

With perfect intonation, the face introduced herself as *H.I.R.A.*, the Honesty and Integrity Retinal Analysis. We require you to participate in a psychometric honesty exam to complete your application, said Hira in a measured, professional tone, I will ask you a series of questions and evaluate your retinal responses. A lie detector, Jane thought, and by reflex, she looked away. Hira asked if she understood the data usage and third-party sales policies. Yes, Jane lied, doubting that it mattered.

Question one, Hira had said, do you agree with the following statement: I have difficulty with authority. Jane said no, the lie slipping out quickly. She had held her breath. Then there was an agonizing pause as Jane watched Hira's virtual face for tell, but the perfect smile maintained its precise shape.

Hira then asked Jane questions about how her mood changed during the day, whether she had sought medical attention in the last six months, whether she experienced long periods of sadness that she could not explain. No, Jane had replied to that question. She experienced long periods of sadness, but she could damn well explain why she had them.

Hira continued the questioning. It asked how many sexual partners Jane had had in the past six months. Jane's palms became sweaty on her jeans. She tried, for the instant she was given, to rationalize the question. Did too many partners indicate she couldn't commit, or that she was disreputable? Or did too few mean she was frigid, or not well-liked? Who decided the correct number? She couldn't recall what her new, fake profile said. Jonas said he'd made her utterly average. What did that mean? Four, Jane said, unclear if that was too high or too low.

Final question, Hira said, what is your family status. Jane felt her mouth hang open. What is your family status, Hira said again. Jane bit her lip and her nails dug into her palms, but she could not close her eyes to re-compose herself. Likely her eyes twitched as soon as she heard the question, the truth leaking from them without need of an answer from her lips. Jane's eyes thinned involuntarily, and her hands, balled into fists, shook a little. She wanted to thrash Hira's hovering face away. Did it want to know if she video-called her mom every six months, or begged daddy for extra money? Or did she want to know the truth? *That's* what she wanted to give: ram the truth down her throat. *Swallow this, bitch.* As Hira started to re-state the question, Jane interrupted, and said, none, I don't have any family.

She felt guilty as soon as she said it. It was true, in the clinical sense, the only sense Hira could understand. Hira could not understand that Jane's family would always be part of her. Family doesn't disappear; first, there is a presence, and then, a loss. But the loss isn't nothing: its pain is real enough, like a throb in a phantom limb.

That pain persists. Sometimes Jane feels the pain as a background ache, sometimes as a short and sudden shock at seeing a baby kicking its chubby feet or remembering the taste of cherries. Sometimes a shaft of light or a stray tune is enough to spur an attack of grief and leave Jane mourning, once again, the loss of her mother and sister.

Jane sees the city of Nature emerge on the horizon, crowned by a sickly yellow aura. The road becomes less bumpy. She watches the tyre tracks in the dust. Soon they will hit streetlights and sponsor names. Then Jane and Ray will meet Liberators and, if they aren't made to disappear, they will face questions from the feed, from the agency, from Skyra. They will be asked the same questions over and over, in the hope that Ray and Jane trip on their words or respond thoughtlessly with the truth. The interrogation will soon begin again.

After completing the questions, the Hira hologram smiled with the same smile the orderly gave Jane when he said her mother would be on the next plane. Then Hira said they would not give Jane a job. Jane asked which question she had failed. That information is proprietary, Hira said. Jane asked if she could appeal, but the session concluded abruptly, and the deprivation booth went dark.

Jane felt like she had been accosted. She had opened painful memories of her family for nothing. But those painful memories were why she came to the State of Nature. She could not give up. Jane threw the chair over, snatched the hoody from the floor, and strode from the deprivation booth, in search of a new plan.

Her next act was to meet the Director at the Future Casino. And ever since, his eyes have rested on her. The interrogation had started with Hira, but it had never ended.

Streetlights.

The car floods with light, and Jane sees Ray's hands tighten on the steering wheel.

# Chapter 37:
# Welcome Back I

Jane returns to the city as a ghost of her former self. The once-familiar towers are new and unsettling. She stares out the window as Ray's car whispers them to her agency's apartment tower. Purples and greens roll over his pensive features. Whites and yellows glint in his eyes. Red and blue lights of Liberator vehicles accompany them.

Jane and Ray don't talk.

In the tunnel, they discussed the plan at length, feet crunching unseen gravel and hopeful voices pinging off dark walls. But once they reconnected the car's battery and collapsed into its seats, Ray and Jane settled into a morose silence, aware of what was to come.

A hundred fans are outside her tower, cheering for her return. They are bundled in mitts and scarves. Some have sleeping bags. Security keeps the crowd back. They had hosed away the most recent dust storm, an expensive use of water. Ray drops her off coldly. She thanks him with similar frigidity, takes an energizing breath, and turns to the crowd.

She runs to them and envelopes herself in their hands. "It's so good to be back," she shouts, though the sound is lost in the crowd's cheers. Hundreds of hands pat her on the back, on the arms, hug her close. Jane thanks them profusely and smiles for group pictures.

Reporters are already in place by the time the crowd releases her. They form a scrum around her, shouting questions over one another. Before she can understand one question, another interjects. Fans call. Cameras flash, too quickly for her eyes to adapt. Jane's world becomes white and loud.

Jane speaks in frenetic bursts, confessing that her disappearance was a publicity stunt, that it was her crazy idea, that she was safely looked after. She sticks out her tongue, laughs generously, cheers, whirls, interrupts one thought with another, plugs a shampoo brand in a joke about her mangled hair. It is more effortful than before. But she maintains the performance, kissing one reporter on the cheek as she kicks up her right leg, before security disperses the throng of cheering bodies.

When she is finally released to her apartment, Hank telling her she will *see him soon*, Jane stands in the front doorway and studies the interior with unfamiliar eyes. The couch projected at the far end of the illusory lounge is too puffy, the projected granite counters too clean. Each holographic knife sits with peak sharpness in its place in the knife block. Her eyes drop. The projected wood floor is too glossy. She thinks of the panel she carved in Freetown and allows herself a momentary smile at the thought of its scruffy dried wood.

But she chases the thought from her mind, for she is not alone. She keens her ears. She can almost hear the whispers – from the weight sensors in the floor to the motion sensors in the walls, from the heartbeat sensors to the thermal cameras. If the refrigerator whispers and the television whispers and the toothbrush whispers and the car whispers, what place does she have to escape them? What room cannot watch, what wall cannot track, what floor cannot feel? Nowhere is she more watched than in her own home.

*It isn't a home. It is a computer.* A smart car is a computer that drives her; a smart refrigerator is a computer that cools her food. A smart house is a computer she lives in. And as all these devices are interconnected, the State is one diffuse computer, each city block a single node, each house a single bit, to be set to a *yes* or a *no* on the marketers' whims.

Jane pops the top from a bottle of beer, slurps the foam brimming from its lip, and sits cross-legged on her bed. It is too soft; Jane feels swallowed by the memory foam. *Memory foam*: even the mattress has a memory. For all the knots in her back, Jane prefers the old mattress set on the ground beside a fire. She pushes that thought aside, too. Freedom is a place she cannot go to, even in her mind, until this is over. She has to report to the Director. She needs her lies to be clear and emphatic.

But the thoughts resume, and she cannot help but smile.

Have you ever thought about not being part of the story? Gabe asked in the tunnel. He was relaxed, finally, despite the darkness. It was impossible to tell how far they had gone nor how long they had to go. There was no time, nor distance. Just Gabe. Just his comfort.

I have, Katie replied from the dark. Her hair was snarled, and her skin crusted with dirt. The cold air pinched her cheeks. But the best advertising tells a human story, she said, I think the only way to compete with all the other adverts is to make this about someone. But it won't be about me, she added. I present the problem, but the people who watch are the solution. The Black Friday advert will really be about them.

In her apartment, Jane shakes the memory away, swigs a mouthful of beer, and places the bottle on her side table. She lays down, hugs her pillow, and reprimands herself for fleeing to the past. The walls are watching. She has to be Jane again. For now. But another memory surfaces and she does not push it away.

After the flood I became obsessed with death, Katie said. We ignore death, don't we? We try to medicalize it, distance ourselves from it. My mom eventually let my sister go, Katie said, and then we were supposed to just forget that a human being had died. They dump the body in a fire, grind up the bones, and say *Hey, here's those ashes you wanted* instead of *hey, here's your powdered baby*.

Katie had stopped, breathed, and let the ferocity pass. Then she said, if we saw just how many people die from heart disease or cancer each year, whole cities worth of people, we'd shit ourselves in horror, but those people just *disappear*. We never have to reflect on the casualties, or on what causes them.

I think it's creepy that in some ways nobody dies anymore, Gabe had replied, we're all immortalized in data. I hate the word *creepy*, Jane shot back, it's not just *creepy* that everything we do is remembered forever. Well, Gabe said, how would you describe it? Fucked up! Katie shouted. The words ricocheted off the tunnel walls. She could feel Gabe rolling his eyes at her. She grinned, then laughed, and eventually so did he. The laughter had echoed along the tunnel.

It disappears in her apartment. Jane sighs, rolls off the bed, and showers. As she stares in the bathroom mirror, wrapped in a wet towel, and tries vainly to drag a brush through her hair, Jane stresses to herself that she is watched. The wet floor feels her weight, and the sensors in each room study the dilation of her eyes. These memories are landmines. But more memories bubble to her consciousness.

Do you ever think of how much time you must spend digesting and resisting adverts, Gabe said, how much of your brain do you dedicate to it? Imagine what we could dream of if we weren't always thinking under a wet blanket, Katie had replied.

Jane smiles in the bathroom mirror.

*Maybe one more memory before I report to the Director*, she thinks as she shuts her eyes.

"Welcome back," she hears, startling her.

It is the Director's voice. Skyra signals that the conversation has been masked.

"Thank you," she says. Her reflection in the mirror is no longer smiling.

Jane gets dressed in the folded pajamas on the bathroom counter and emerges from the bathroom to find her apartment expanded by the illusions of the wallscreens into a full Italian restaurant. Waiters attend to the other tables with wine bottles and wooden pepper grinders. At the nearest table, also an illusion of the wallscreen, is the Director. Katie drags over a table and chair from her nook and places them by the wallscreen, and they instantly become ornate. She feels embarrassed, as if she has walked into the restaurant in her pajamas.

"Nice place," she says, sitting.

"Better than the wasteland, I hope. Or a Liberator cell."

"You wouldn't let Liberators take your spy."

"Of course not," he says, "why do you think they stopped following you?"

A waiter comes to the Director's side, but he waves him away.

"You look like you have something to say to me."

Jane cannot help herself. "You know what happened to Ashley, don't you?"

"Yes."

"You know why she did it?"

"Yes."

"You know who is responsible?"

"I do."

She feels tears forming in her eyes. Jane almost wishes the real Director were in front of her, so she could grab him by the tie and throttle him. "When did you know?" she blurts.

"I did not know what Ashley was going to do."

"Bullshit," Jane hisses. "You know everything about everyone, don't you?"

The restaurant goes silent, and the other diners all watch her. The Director waves his hand again and they all go back to their conversations as if nothing happened.

"She broke out of her apartment," he says, without a hint of regret, "and escaped my control."

"You could have protected her!"

The Director sighs. "Not from men as powerful and sociopathic as Davi."

Jane shoots up and her chair clatters backward.

"She died on your watch," she snaps.

Nobody in the illusory restaurant reacts, not even the Director, who still wears his thin smile. For a moment, Jane wonders if he is real.

"Because *you* were not there for her," he says, his voice rising. "You were off scheming with Ray Burnett. Oh yes, I saw through his attempt to trick me. But you forget your role, Jane. Davi, not Ashley, is your assignment."

"Ashley was *not* an assignment."

He stares until Jane sits back down.

"Nevertheless, you had your instructions. I wanted to know about Davi's father."

"I told you, Davi said his father was dying."

"Then it is time to expand your assignment. In your absence, Davi pledged on the feed that he would make you the star of the Black Friday campaign, if only you were just returned safely. Evidently, he will stop at nothing to collect you. With his father soon to be leaving us, I need you to obtain information for me that can control Davi."

"I told you about the girlfriend from the Red Zone. What else do you need?"

"As you said," he smiles frostily, "I like to know everything."

Jane shakes her head. "I can't do it. I can't look at Davi without wanting to kill him."

"This is why I did not want you to get too close to anyone. You lose your objectivity. Mr. Burnett, it seems, is your newest interest."

"He is useful, that is all," Jane deflects.

"For?" the Director teases.

"Making Davi think he has competition."

"Then he risks the same fate as Ashley."

"You won't let that happen."

"As long as you find me something more on Davi. Yes?"

Jane nods. Then with a wave of his hand, the Director extinguishes the restaurant projection, and Jane's apartment returns to stark white. Jane sits at her lonely little table, and begins to sob.

# Chapter 38:
# Welcome Back II

Ray finds a new Skyra bracelet in his apartment. Finding an unexpected trinket delivered to his counter is not unusual. His life is littered with sharp discords between memories. Often Ray would be persuaded to buy something in the morning and that he would forget by the time it was delivered. Though Ray had accepted on the car ride home that he would have to mimic this old life, he had held a faint hope that it would be without Skyra.

It was expected that he could walk freely back into his apartment. It did not mean the Liberators would not be watching. It means the opposite: he is under far greater scrutiny. But they cannot detain someone as famous as Jane without a cause the public will accept. The only record of Ray's encounter with Jane exists in the few centimeters in his head. Their aim will be to draw it out of him like poison from a wound.

For now, he has the advantage. Analysis requires information. The less he gives, the longer he can cling onto that advantage. Long enough, he hopes, to hatch the plan. In the tunnel's darkness, he and Katie settled on the details. She would present a live message for every electronic platform imaginable: the most watched advertisement ever seen. Only, it will not be an advert, but a plea. She would insist that he produce the advert.

As they emerged at the other side of the tunnel, Katie and Gabe agreed not to speak again – not until the plan was complete. In the tunnel's darkness they squeezed invisible hands and pledged that they would return. Both hands were coarse, and both hands squeezed harder and longer than either expected. When they let go, it was Jane who stepped out of the tunnel, her skin returning to its mercurial glint beneath the moon's silver light    .

Ray sets his mind back to the present. There is no room for pleasant memories.

"Welcome back," Skyra says as Ray pulls off his worn leather shoes.

It's a blast oven in his apartment. The back of his dirty shirt sops with sweat. Ray apologises to Skyra and blames Jane for making him remove the bracelet. Anything to keep Jane's trust, he says, she's a key agency asset. He takes the new bracelet and clips it around his wrist. It feels familiar, both comforting and worrying.

Ray explains the strange journey he took with Jane. He says she was mad, hysterical, and threatening to disparage the brand. He stayed with her to keep her quiet, until she could be convinced to return. Stress clasps the back of his neck as he recounts the story. He hopes that Skyra cannot distinguish the stress of fleeing to the Red Zone from the stress of lying about it. Once the story is done, he awaits Skyra's response. He expects Liberator fists on the door. The sweat on his shirt is cold.

"I missed you, sir," Skyra says from a speaker in the wall.

Ray tries to hide his relief. "I missed you too," Ray replies, unsure if he is lying.

# Chapter 39:
# Whispers

Everything ends in the dump. With unending temptations and inexhaustible credit, the only limiting factor is space. They find plenty of space in the ruins of the old regime: in crumbling warehouses and abandoned subway tunnels. The few oddities from the past that are saved from the dump are held in the Masen Energy Pre-Liberation Museum.

Jane drapes herself over a statue, another model lying at its feet, and another hanging off its extended iron arm. They pose for photos. None reads the faded information panel. They take more photos as they explore the laughable relics. One live-streams her reactions.

As they move off, dashing across the neglected stone floor, Jane splits from the troupe of other models. "I'll catch up," she calls. The others spirit away to take more faux-spontaneous pictures in front of inscrutable statues.

Once they are out of view, Jane flits in the opposite direction, down a hall, a right, then the second left. Ray's directions take her to a wooden door with a horseshoe nailed to it. The hinges wince as the door opens to reveal a catacomb. The weak light from an old filament lightbulb illuminates the brown streaks on the stone walls. The coat hooks at the entrance are bent railway nails. A red refrigerator with a neon *Coca Cola* sign hums in one corner. Jane scans the room for cameras, finding none.

Cloistered inside is an elderly woman sifting sheets of paper on her desk, half a cigarette smoking in an ashtray. She wears a grey suit. The collar of her white shirt is partly upturned. Her hair is a magical silver with fiery ends – *a witch!* Jane imagines.

"Come in," the woman says, as invitingly as her gravely voice can.

Jane moves inside and closes the wooden door. "What's with the horseshoe?"

"Nelson had one nailed to the mast of the *Victory*," the woman says as she rises from her desk. "Keeps devils away."

Jane doesn't understand any of the words. *A joke? A riddle?* "He didn't tell me you were superstitious," Jane says.

"No more than anyone else," the woman replies. "All of us believe one object or another has the magical power to protect us," she says, eying Jane's bracelet.

Jane mumbles but can't think of how to reply. She eyes the old photographs hanging on the wall of the catacomb and changes the subject: "He tells me you think of yourself as a *historian?*"

The woman introduces each of the photographs – snaps of grain elevators and men in heavy vests swinging pickaxes and sledgehammers, of people and places that no longer exist. As Jane searches the fuzzy details of the photographs, the woman fetches a cola bottle from the fridge and offers it to Jane. Jane declines; she'll exceed her calorie intake.

The woman keeps the bottle, its surface sheened with frost, as she speaks. "All history is a history of objects. We used to study history from statues and stone carvings. And in a hundred years, historians will dig up circuit boards and plastics and—"

"Objects of worship," Jane interrupts, eying the glass bottle in the woman's hand.

The old woman smiles and returns the bottle to the fridge. "But I study more than history. I study *civilization*. If history is a river, civilization is what lies on the river's banks. It's the mundane, the daily routines, but it's also the poetry, the art, the things that don't have a price. I'm most interested in the banks than the river."

Jane grins nervously. She cannot believe that this bewitching woman can exist, let alone that she was Ray's mentor.

"Let's have a look at you," the woman says as she places heavy hands upon Jane's shoulders. Jane's first instinct is to strike a photogenic smile, but the old woman seems more interested in Jane's eyes and the wrinkles above her cheeks. She examines Jane like she has found a statue come to life. Jane sees the old woman's eyes trace the empty piercings on the curve of her ear, then the empty piercing in her nose, details Skyra corrects in photos.

The old woman releases Jane's shoulders and takes Jane's hands in her own. She runs her thumbs over the lines on Jane's palms, then the little scar on Jane's wrist. Jane sees the hint of a smile. Then the old woman turns Jane's hands over, scrutinizing the knuckles. "Where did you get this?" the woman says, thumbing a white scar on Jane's right hand.

"A fight."

"I see why he likes you," the old woman smiles. "Whitaker," she adds, taking Jane's hand and shaking it between her own.

Jane hesitates, bewitched by the woman's face, its smile casting deep wrinkles across her cheeks and temple. Jane goes to introduce herself, but Whitaker puts up a hand.

"I know who you are," she says, "I'm not *that* far removed from the present. Please – sit."

Jane sits in a wooden chair by Whitaker's desk. It creaks as she shifts her weight to find a comfortable position. Whitaker sits on the opposite side of the desk. The chair legs squeak.

"You are different than he described," Jane says.

"If you mean the drink – I kicked that habit some time ago. If you mean the smoking–" she glances to the ashtray on the desk – "I'm working on that one."

"No," Jane replies. "Ray told me you were so *stern*. Almost *frightening*."

"Strong women usually are."

The women share an admiring gaze. But the golden bracelet around their wrists reminds them of constant surveillance, even though the catacomb is too old for cameras. Skyra will feel their hair bristle if the discussion becomes illicit, and it will hear everything they say.

Whitaker clears the papers from the desk and pushes a keypad to Jane. She moves another keypad for herself.

"I can tell you a thing or two about *him*," Whitaker chuckles, "I picked him up when he was still a young man, poor. I never had children, so I enjoyed being a mother to him, so to speak. He couldn't remember his parents, you know?

"But despite the many stories I could tell you about him," Whitaker says, "that is not why you are here."

"I need an algorithmist to maximize exposure of an advert. An advert to be seen by everyone."

"Me?" Whitaker laughs. "Usually once something becomes obsolete, we squash it into a landfill and forget it. We don't dig it back up."

"He tells me you are the best," Jane replies.

*And he trusts you,* she writes with her left hand, fingers silent on the keypad, keeping her bracelet's watchful eye on her right wrist below the table. The text appears on the screen beside them.

*You don't?* appears Whitaker's reply on the screen.

*Not yet.*

Whitaker shrugs. "I quit drinking the day I quit the business," Whitaker says, "so as I said, it has been a while."

"He told me that the oldest plans still work the best."

Whitaker outwardly enjoys the comment. *I'm glad he remembered something I taught him,* she types.

"Indeed," Whitaker says to avoid an unusual span of silence, "the idea of an advert shared by everyone is not unprecedented. People can be resistant to overt advertising, but insert it into a sports event or make a special day out of it, and suddenly watching adverts becomes the main event."

Whitaker's expression sinks as she types. *Don't underestimate the risk,* she types, fingers dancing silently on the keypad. *He told me a little about what you want to do. The more eyes watching, the bigger the stakes. The more security.*

"I can tell you about one event," Whitaker begins, in a professorial tone. She tells Jane about an old sporting event where more people tuned in for the adverts than the game.

*Do you have a location?* Whitaker types as she talks.

*Yes.*

*Means of transmission?*

*No.*

*You'll want an old camera. Internet-compatible, but not part of the internet-of-things. Not 'always on.' That way it won't give away your position to Skyra.*

*Can you get one?*

*Obsolete things are my forte.*

Whitaker winks. She continues her story seamlessly. Jane adds an occasional *uh-huh* for Skyra's benefit.

*Where do you need it?* Whitaker types.

*We'll see,* Jane responds.

Whitaker looks up and grins. Jane matches her eyes. She does not trust Whitaker yet, despite Ray's glowing memories of her.

*I told you, I felt like his mother,* Whitaker answers on the screen, *I would never betray him.*

*But why help me?* Jane writes.

Whitaker stops her story and takes her hands from the keyboard. Her cracked lips grimace.

*The man I loved thought you were worth helping,* Whitaker writes.

Jane looks down at the little white scar on her right wrist, where Jonas had extracted her sub-dermal tracker.

*He fled to the Red Zone to escape their punishment,* Whitaker adds, *but I was too frightened to follow.*

"So as you can see," Whitaker says aloud, "I have a lot of experience in what you hope to achieve."

She offers Whitaker a sympathetic glance – for she can risk nothing more – and conveys her own loss, the kind of loss too deep in the eye for a camera to see. "I'd like to retain your help as soon as possible," Jane says.

"Of course."

*I'll get it ready,* Whitaker types.

Jane nods in gratitude and rises. She twists left and right, trying to loosen a muscle that had knotted from the wooden chair.

"I'll get you the analysis soon. More eyes than any advert has ever had before. Trust me," Whitaker adds.

"I do," Jane smiles.

Whitaker types another sentence. *A last piece of advice: if you do escape, make sure you take him with you. Or you'll never forgive yourself.*

Jane nods momentarily. Whitaker taps *delete*, and the text is gone.

# Chapter 40:
# The Offer

The Black Friday advert: that is when she will do it. Whatever happens after then…

Jane needs to accept Davi's offer for the Black Friday advert. And she needs him to agree to her conditions. But thinking of Davi makes her sick with anger. When she first tried calling him, Jane shook, as if shivering off the grime of speaking to him, and ran to the bathroom heaving. Even if she forces her most playful tone, the cutesy one, Skyra will tell Davi how much she loathes him. The elevated heart rate and burning skin will give it away.

She pulls air into her lungs until her chest shakes. And then she begins to run.

Amazon Park is the closest thing to peace in the city. It is a quadrant of sculpted grass and glossy green leaves situated at the confluence of five streams of roadways. A protective ring of dense trees protects the Park from most of the road noise – just enough to hear adverts twittering from the trees.

"Call Pierre Daviault," she says. Skyra clings to her wrist as her arms pump back and forth. She hears his voice in her ear. Jovial, confident. Careless. Jane runs faster. Her muscles warm and loosen.

"You're a brave girl," she hears Davi say.

"Going to the Red Zone?"

"Calling me. You know you broke sixteen different provisions of your contract?"

"Maybe I need a new one. With a bigger salary."

Her feet pound on the trail, adverts on the ground showing her the way.

The sound of his laughter grates her eardrum. "What will the feed think of me speaking to a public enemy?" Davi says.

"What will it think if you *don't*?"

His continued laughter sounds like smashing glass in her ear. "I missed you."

"You too."

Her security detail splits off to checkpoints of her circuit of the Amazon Park. No matter how fast she runs, they linger in her peripheries. "I wanted to talk about your offer," she gasps.

"I know," comes the reply in her ear. Her cheeks tense into a scowl. She runs harder. "Would you prefer we talk at a better—"

"Now's good!" she says. Adverts ripple underfoot like she is splashing through water. She rounds a curve in the path. The adverts follow.

Davi tells Skyra to obscure the rest of the call. "Yes, yes," he dismisses when Skyra tells him the price. Then he says to Jane: "You're going to accept my offer for the Black Friday advert."

"Uh huh," she wheezes. It was obvious she would. The advert is all she can think about. That, and Ashley. But she does not allow herself to dwell on the latter. She has to pretend to let Ashley go, as easily as she had hit *unfollow*. But Ashley's voice still hangs in the air, whispering that Jane is a traitor for speaking to Davi.

"I have some ideas for it," Jane adds between breaths.

He hesitates. "Ideas?"

"I know a good musician." Sweat tickles her spine.

"Musician?"

"Nothing sticks a message in the head like a jingle." She gasps air in, huffs it out, trying to exhale the anger. She keeps her eyes forward, to the distance. Toward the future.

"Consider it done. I'll have my assistant—"

"I'm not finished. I have one more condition." Jane pauses, not knowing how Davi will take what she says next. "Don't make an advert."

"What?" a voice splutters above the tap of her shoes. Jane rounds another curve and arrives back to where she began. She sprints harder, flying around the trail, pulse quick, skin hot.

"Make it an advert-free message," she says.

"I don't think you understand the purpose—"

"I understand what people like," she blurts. "They like novelty. They like what isn't allowed for them. How is any other corporation going to compete with advert-free?"

A pause. Sweat beads on her forehead. "What would we advertise, then?"

She slows to a walk and catches her breath. "I'm the face of all the makeup and perfume and fashion brands owned by Nature Corp.," Jane answers. "Hotels, cars, coffee chains. Travel resorts. I *am* the advert."

His chuckles in her ear feel so close that his breath could cool the sweat on her neck.

Once Jane slows her pace and her arms fall to her sides, Skyra displays Davi's face in holographic blue. Davi sips from a glass as he ponders. Jane stares, maybe for too long, to hate each detail: the square forehead, the studded ear, the bump on his chin. She allows herself, just for a moment more, while her blood is still hot.

"My father won't like it."

Her hands go to her hips. "Some day, he has to let you fill his shoes."

"That day is a long way off."

"Is it?" Jane raises an eyebrow and waits for him to break the silence.

"Maybe not," he says, choosing his words. "But the problem is with me, not him," he adds brusquely.

It takes brute force of will to compel kind words from her mouth. "I don't think you're a problem, Davi. You're a potential. You just need to show him that you can realize it."

"Using you?"

She brings the Skyra to her face. "Using the highest TELOS model you have, the one in *every* feed right now. Algorithms don't lie."

Davi sits back. "This sounds more like for *you* than for *me*."

"*Us*, Davi," she forces herself to say, forcing a smile like bending stiff bamboo. "We're in it together."

As Jane awaits his answer, her skin cools, her heart slows, and Davi's holographic eyes wash over her, while Skyra analyzes the earnestness of her words.

# Chapter 41:
# Measure of a Man

*Skyra Corp. announced that the newest software update improves Skyra's sleep monitoring technology. Through ground-breaking analysis of eye movements, body temperature, and other unconscious reactions to stimuli during sleep, Skyra can better model REM-sleep thought patterns. In short, through its observations, Skyra can unlock the meaning of your dreams.*

*The update has been live for three weeks; however, the announcement was postponed for initial blind testing…*

***

Each morning Ray wakes to the same cordial call from Skyra, and each morning he worries what he might have mumbled in his sleep. Life before felt like an aimless shuffle in the desert. It was, in its mindlessness, easier. But life now feels like a medical procedure, like he is rolling out of a hospital bed, the cold floor like infirmary linoleum on his feet.

Ray focused on his work as salvation for past sins and a defense from prying eyes, throwing himself into creating and boosting an addictive jingle to be introduced the week before Jane's Black Friday presentation. Ray endured weeks harbouring a secret that an errant word or a revealing stare would expose. He read the same content and browsed the same feeds as before, keeping everything identical. Having retaken the wheels of his life, he tired at the exercise of keeping it on autopilot. But today is Black Friday. I will not be long now.

He has tried not to think of Katie. He pressed her from his waking mind until, shutting his eyes to sleep, he imagined the ghostly chorus of the harp and pictured himself back in the tunnel with her. He squeezed his hands together, hoping to find hers in his palm.

Each night he has the same dream. He is back in the town with Katie, staring at stars so close that he could reach up and pick them. But despite the infinite motes of light, there are spaces of black between them. Space, he dreams, is what allows things like orbits and planets and eclipses in the first place. But Skyra collapses the distances between things so that there is nothing neither closer nor further away, no space, no uniqueness; no this or that, nor *here* nor *there*.

The sky is something Skyra can never bring. It is explorable only through imagination and wonder. There is, he dreams, much Skyra cannot do. Skyra can count his steps, his heart rate, his calories, but it cannot count all the stars. It cannot count the stones in the castle wall, or the freckles sprinkled on Katie's cheeks.

He wonders how infinitely quiet it must be up there in space. Not a single voice, nor a single word. The thought does not leave him lonely but feeling more connected to everyone – for he can see what any person, no matter what Zone, can see – if only they raise their eyes.

In the dream, he turns to Katie. "When I am alone," he says, "I think only about me: *I am hungry; I am thirsty*. But when I look up and see the unknown – I think *we are small* and *we are fleeting*. But also: *we are all on this tiny, fragile speck together*."

He cranes his head to the sky once more. "Why don't we always see the stars that way?"

"The fault, dear Brutus," Katie says, "is not in our stars, but in ourselves."

In the dream, they say no more. He dreams of orange embers and wisps of wind, and impermeable, safe darkness, and Katie asleep on his shoulder, snoring peacefully.

"Katie," he whispers in the distant dream. "Katie…"

Ray splutters awake. He sits rigid in his bed, sweat glistening on his forearms. The dream rots away. The only element that lingers in his mind is the last word: "Katie… Katie…"

"Good morning sir," Skyra says. "Happy Black Friday to you."

Ray waits for more. He cannot tell if he had said her name in the dream only, or if he had spoken it in the real world. He struggles to recall as the remnants of the dream slip away.

"Is something wrong, sir?" Skyra adds. "Perhaps a Haven to start your day?"

"No."

He wants a whiskey. *What is the time? Basically ten?* He staggers to the kitchen and squints as the feed blisters onto the wallscreen. Every post is about Black Friday. Jane is trending. She's shilling a new eyeshadow, named Red Zone, of course. Ray pours himself two fingers of whiskey.

Skyra interrupts Ray with a prompt that he needs to go on a date to maintain his sociability rating. It will look suspicious – *more* suspicious – for Ray to shut himself away. Skyra brings up his messages. Ray is drowning in them since his famous return from the Red Zone. From his messages he recognizes one, the Marie Cherie enthusiast who he had slept with months before. This time he checks her name: *Carli.* She had not messaged since they shared a grim fifteen minutes in her apartment. She and many other relics from his past had re-emerged since his name became attached to Jane's.

Though he knows what she will ask, and how he will answer, Ray accepts the date as a brief respite from the four watchful walls of his apartment, and the continual friend requests and interview pitches tingling up his arm.

"It's a desert," Ray says to Carli as they share a late breakfast, keeping close to the state doctrine when she asks about the Red Zone. "I'm lucky to be alive." Ray measures every word he says, focusing on the lies, ignoring memories of Jane clothed in star drops, hoping the sweat growing on his temples is mistaken for nerves.

Carli asks about the Red Zone in pornographic detail. She leans toward him and her mouth falls open a little at Ray's descriptions of the Zone's horridness, of the blinding dust storms, of unyielding fallow fields, of the skull he found that he swears was human. She regards him like he can smother her body with some of the blood and dirt of the Red Zone, like he can touch her with a sliver of the sadism that exists in the place without rules and without eyes.

Carli barely notices her tiny salad in its grossly oversized bowl. As her eyes thin at his description of strange artefacts of bone and twisted barbed wire, Ray regards her with inquisitiveness. He discovers the roundness of her face, the prettiness of her lips, the way she twirls a strand of dyed-blonde hair around her forefingers as she listens to him.

Carli's concentration breaks at the approach of another man. "May I?" he says as he pulls the chair beside Carli. The newcomer sits with his legs wide apart, chest broad, arm draped across the back of Carli's chair. He flicks his tongue against his upper teeth as he gives a hostile smile. Ray's heart jumps. *Davi.*

Ray notes the perfect cut of Davi's dark suit, the sharp crease of the lapel, and the absence of a single piece of dandruff on his shoulders. The habit is automatic and in an instant, Davi's smirk grows as his Skyra whispers of Ray's admiration.

"So, *you're* the chosen one," Davi announces.

Ray was never important enough to be worth Davi's time – not until *he*, and he alone, was chosen by Jane to accompany her to the Red Zone. "I'm just a man," he replies.

Davi's silk dress shirt is partly undone. A pair of designer sunglasses hang from the highest button. "I'm making you nervous," Davi professes. "You're intimidated by me."

There is no reason for Ray to deny it. Davi makes a show of evaluating the restaurant, pursing his lips at the absence of furs on the seats or a pianist in the corner. "There's a reason I don't come to sub-five-hundred places," he chides. "I've lost two TELOS just meeting you."

"Best not to stay long, then."

Ray's bracelet thrums: he is already being downvoted.

"I don't intend to," Davi shoots back, waving away an approaching waiter. His eyes thin but his smile remains smug as he adds, "I just wanted to size you up."

"You could have just checked my profile," replies Ray, "saved yourself the time."

Carli squirms in her seat.

"I did," Davi says. "I saw the teeth whitening kits, the messages to women beyond your TELOS, left sad and unread. I think I've got the measure of you. But what I still don't know," Davi continues, "is how you convinced her to go with *you*."

"Nobody can convince Jane of anything she doesn't want to do," Ray says. "*You* know that very well," Ray adds, as a dig at Davi's unsuccessful attempt to collect Jane.

The seizing in Davi's cheeks shows the jab hurts. He forces a chuckle. "But then why go with her?" Davi says. Ray's plate grows cold.

"Ten thousand, four-hundred and twenty-two," Ray remarks. "That is how many people have messaged me asking the same thing. Strangers, reporters – friends looking for a TELOS boost. Even a video drone outside my balcony. You're going to have to get in line."

"None of those people own the corporation you work for."

"Nor do you. Last I checked, Daviault *Senior* does."

Davi's shoulders tense, stifling something primal escaping his cool veneer. "You know," Davi starts, removing his arm from around Carli and leaning toward Ray. His musk hangs about Ray's nostrils. "The last people who fled to the Red Zone were executed."

"I've seen the video."

"Why shouldn't that happen to *you*?" The men match stares. "It might be entertaining."

"Only until you realized that *you* would be next." Jane had told Ray about Davi's dalliance with a woman in the Red Zone.

"More significant men than you have tried to spread lies about me," Davi growls.

"Am I lying?" Ray says as he shakes his Skyra bracelet. He wonders how many thousands have flocked to hear the conversation in real-time. Davi had not obscured the conversation from the beginning, intending for Ray's humiliation to spread across the network; it is too late for him to obscure the conversation without losing face. Davi resets his jaw. The thrums from Skyra up Ray's arm are almost as thunderous as his heart. Ray notices how broad Davi's hands are, how pronounced the pectorals under his silk shirt.

Carli leans forward and speaks: "Maybe I—"

"Leave us," says Davi.

Carli does, leaving the salad untouched and her chair askew.

"I ought to have you fired and thrown out of my city," Davi says.

"You'd have to ask the Board for permission."

"The Board may have placed certain restrictions on me," Davi says, "but they have no power to stop me from, say, encouraging others to butcher your TELOS."

The band at Ray's wrist shudders from a cascade of downvotes. Davi asks Skyra the status of Ray's travel rights. "Restricted to city limits," a voice comes from Ray's wristband. The rumbles of electricity up Ray's forearm show that the downvoting continues.

"Health privileges?" Davi asks out loud.

Ray's Skyra client answers: "Repealed until TELOS improves."

Davi raises his right hand. Ray almost expects Davi to strike him, but Davi readies to click his middle finger and his thumb and says: "Credit status?" And he clicks his fingers.

"Overdrawn. Repossession proceedings will begin," Skyra replies.

Ray imagines repossession officers ransacking his closet and his cupboards, and the sight of his apartment as barren as the Red Zone. Such things once represented the value of Ray's life, but he had left that life swirling with the ghosts in the tunnel. Davi, obviously expecting Ray to be upset, instead glowers as Ray gave him an unaffected stare. Davi's sour expression worsens and he perceives the ripples of confidence across Ray's skin. Ray feels, for a moment, as the Director must.

"If you don't mind," Ray says, cutting a piece of his steak, "my meal is getting cold."

Davi presses himself up from the table and leans over Ray. "Maybe you have no more TELOS to care about," he says, "but I know something you *do* still care about." Davi stands upright and shoves his chair in. "*She* is a corporate asset," he remarks. "And the corporation can't allow her near people of irreputable TELOS. It's a safety issue. So if you come anywhere near her, Skyra will alert security. Isn't that right, Skyra?"

"Of course," Skyra replies.

Ray feels stripped of the power he had felt. Katie cannot remain only in his dreams; he must see her again.

"I don't know why she took you to the Red Zone, and I don't care," Davi concludes, "but you can be damn sure, you'll never see her again."

He strides out.

# Chapter 42:
# Orbits I

*Last night, Liberators contained a threat in District Four with minimal casualties. Preliminary investigations suggest attackers from the Red Zone had aid from inside the State. Liberators will be analyzing profiles at random in their ongoing efforts to locate the conspirators.*

*Though there is no cause for further alarm, residents are advised of the security solutions available to them. BSS Security Solutions is the industry leader in threat prediction and early warning systems. BSS is providing a complete security package for residents with an eligible TELOS. While supplies last. Found out more here.*

*BSS Security is pleased to sponsor the following live announcement from Nature Corp. about this evening's Black Friday event…*

***

Jane peeks out the curtain of her makeup booth. The cameras are ready, the crowd strategically placed, the glasses, six to each silver tray, bubble with their champagne. The Director monitors from the periphery, speaking to no one. The security officers, in black suits and ties, pace their predetermined patrols. Jane purses her lips. There are more of them than usual.

Momentarily, she will take the stage and finally confirm the rumours that she will host an advert-free message on Black Friday as a thank-you from Nature Corp. The feed had already known for weeks, but Jane was told to boost the controversy by waiting until the morning of Black Friday to acknowledge the rumours. The public interest in Jane since she returned from the Red Zone has been withering, but her plan is nearly complete. Whitaker secured the camera, Davi foolishly arranged for her message to be live, Ray has quietly prepared the video, and will deliver her the camera later today. Jane just has to follow the plan.

The stage sits below the prism at one end of the Future Casino. A shaft of light falls from the window above the prism, splitting into rainbow hues and segregating the crowd into strips of red, and orange, and yellow. Jane thinks of rainbow hair and wishes that she could twist it around her fingers.

She rearranges the body of her dress, but it does not feel right. Nothing does. She has suffered endless messages, promos, interviews, two debriefings with Hira. Before she left with Ray to the Red Zone, Jane felt like a sample under a microscope. But at least the technician would want to preserve the sample for evaluation; now it feels like the people watching are grasping at pieces of her for answers, and will not care if they rip her apart in the process.

They all asked the same questions about why she left, and where, and who she saw, and what she said, and whether she met any Reds. Jane passed Hira's test this time, having learned to disconnect her eyes and lips from her mind. They are moving parts on her exterior with which she lies without thinking, so autonomously that she almost believes herself. By increments they have made Jane mechanical. She even modulates her voice like Skyra, now.

First, she had sacrificed the choice of where to live, and then what she saw. Then what she said, and who she should love. Then she let her body be dictated until, retreating further into herself, she became depersonalized from her alien skin. She no longer thinks of the sway of her hips, the length of her strides, the sashay, the head tilts, or the brush of her forefinger against her jawline. Nor does she think of opposing the ads she sees anymore. She glides like a ghost through each day. Only the irritation remains: the tightness of her shoes on her toes, the ache in her lower back, the ring in her ears, and the heaviness of her breath, as if there is not quite enough oxygen anymore.

She has given it all up, save for the few centimeters in her head and the memories of her sister's tiny fingers and chubby belly, and the serious contemplative expression her sister had when studying the turquoise dragonfly toy hanging above her crib.

Her hair is pinned too tightly and her new Skyra bracelet, sticking to the sweat on her wrist, feels like a clamp. The minor stressors on her decision making have colluded to the point where she feels the physical drain of each lie to Skyra. Where once she felt determination, Jane now feels a creeping sense that it is only a matter of time before Skyra breaks her resistance.

She pulls the curtain shut and reads the feed to distract herself. It is feverish with the recent news about the Reds: Reds aiming to thwart Black Friday, Reds being flushed out, Reds becoming more desperate. Prediction algorithms remaining strong. And then, perhaps for the hundredth time that week, the chime Ray had created to accompany the fear-inducing messages that would boost sales.

It feels like someone has turned up the brightness and the volume. Everything is amplified. Anxiety gnaws at the nape of her neck. It is the same feeling that had left her cowering under the bedcovers before the flood: that there is something amiss in the air.

Skyra thrums as Davi's head floats from her wristband. His jaw is set. Gone is the charm and the lusty stare. Jane presents a grin for him. "This *is* my change room."

"I've made some changes to your personnel," Davi's voice comes in an unfamiliar tone. It is stripped of its usual confidence and imbued with malice. "I can't have a man who takes you into the Red Zone on your team."

Jane tilts her head. "Oh Davi," she smirks, "I'm on stage in two minutes. Let's talk—"

"No more talking," he says, "just listen."

"I've never been good at that."

The curtains sway with the collective breath of the crowd.

"You're not going on stage until I get your pledge," Davi says. "To?"

"The State, the corporation. To me."

Jane starts at a voice from behind her.

"Now is not the time for messages," the Director says from behind the curtain. "We are live in two minutes."

The curtain hangs a foot from the ground. She sees the Director's shoes beneath, as black as a Liberator's eyes. Jane turns from him, hoping that she can hide her worry behind her turned back. "I won't be long!" she calls to the Director.

"You will not be going on stage at all," says Davi through the video stream, "until I have your word."

Messages tumble into her inbox and appear in blue beside Davi's frowning face. Jane ignores them. "Of course, Davi, you have my—"

But one message takes her eyes.

*Hey babe. It's Tristan.*

Her gut tenses. A withering cold overtakes her insides, like she's fallen overboard, like she will drown. Jane re-reads the post. Perhaps it is a coincidence. She has millions of followers. Any number could share the name of her ex-boyfriend. And Tristan cannot message her from Chron-OS anyway – not without a much better TELOS. Jane thinks to look away – too late. The message becomes marked as *read*. Tristan – whichever Tristan it is – will receive that update.

A new message slots to the top: *Don't say you've forgotten me already, sweetie! Let's catch up.*

Breath evacuates her body. Jane fumbles at her fingers. Again, the message becomes marked as *read*. She cannot ignore him. She could report him to the agency as a creep and have him expunged from her feed. But Tristan has a stockpile of her data. The last thing she wants is to draw the agency's attention to him.

Her mind strays to the Liberators. They frighten her almost as much as Tristan does. But they are effective. They do things with discretion, when needed. They can find him. They can do it quietly, and quickly – quick enough to stop Tristan—

—she bats away the idea, ashamed of entertaining it. Jane winces her eyes shut. Too many sources have pieces of her. It is impossible to scrub everything she touches. It feels like everything she has ever done, every past indiscretion, is currency for someone, currency she has to buy back. But she fears what Tristan will want in exchange.

"You're on in ninety seconds," the Director says from behind the curtain.

Jane skitters further from the curtain, her heart thundering.

Davi's voice interrupts. "I'm tired of you stalling—"

"—your demeanor is incorrect—" interrupts the Director.

"I'll be fine!" Jane says.

"This is most unlike you," replies the Director. Jane senses an unusual irritation in his voice.

"Just nerves!" she calls.

Tristan's message, hovering above Jane's wristband, awaits an answer. It has to stay contained. Just between him and her. She must convince him to stay quiet. And if she cannot convince him? Jane does not know.

The Director brushes open the curtain of the changing booth. "You're *sweating*."

"I'm so sorry," Jane says as she swivels to hide Tristan's message from him.

She seizes at a new message from Tristan: *I've got something important to tell you.* Once again, the message is marked *read*. The conference will be watched by millions; it is the perfect opportunity for Tristan to out her.

The Director lingers behind her.

She feels the clamminess on her spine. "I'll have someone clear it up," she says.

"This campaign is relying on you."

"I won't let you down," Jane blurts as she reads a new message: *Or should I come down to the media conference to meet you?* It is the kind of message a virus would send to bait her into visiting a trap site. Tristan is a virus, lying dormant inside of her until reactivated by stress and vulnerability. She can feel the beginnings of a hot rash on her neck.

The heat turns cold as the Director says, "Is this responsibility too big for you?"

Davi pulls her toward him, Tristan pulls her backwards, and the Director lingers to watch them split her apart. Jane glowers at her bracelet, convinced that Skyra is responsible. Whichever of the men wins in the struggle over her, Skyra will be the victor.

Jane tenses her fingers as if their grip can prevent the Black Friday message from slipping away. She feels her heart shudder in her chest. At once her hate drifts from Skyra to herself. Jane hates that despite everything – her sister and her mother, first, then her foster parents, Tristan, then Carl and Reece – despite it all, she feels hope – hope in her fingers, hope in the surfaces she touches, hope in the faces she passes and in the followers of her feed, hope when the dust clouds reveal an occasional lance of light. Despite it all, she has hope that she will succeed.

But as Tristan's message awaits a reply, and another snarl emerges from Davi's holographic lips, and the Director threatens to snatch the campaign from her, it is no longer clear that she has a choice in the matter. Skyra must know how she will react to the succession of stressors and must know, in the end, that she will break.

Jane swipes away Davi's face from her bracelet and faces up to the Director. And before she is quite aware of what she has done, the Director's tie is wrapped in her hand, and she has pulled his face to hers. "Is it too big for *you*?" she says. As he tries to stand up, she pulls on his tie harder. "We're a minute from the announcement. You're too late."

She throws the Director's tie at him, pushes past, and paces onto the stage. A hush descends. She does not wear her usual smile or use her fluttery walk. The emcee's smile falls. He does not fight when Jane takes the microphone from him. It is so quiet that she can hear the bleeps of the casino machines. The crowd and the security detail – and Davi, and the Director, and Skyra, await her announcement. She takes the microphone to her lips.

# Chapter 43:
## Orbits II

They say you can't hear anything in space, but in the Centre of the Universe, there is nothing *but* noise. Adverts beckon to individual pedestrians; unseen speakers boom promotional rock music. A hologram the size of a giant thunders a familiar slogan: *Corinthian design*. His holographic feet trample the crowd in the square. The swirl of lights, of sounds, of people, makes Jane dizzy. She is blinded by the sound, deafened by the light.

The air feels charged, like a storm is coming.

She uttered two sentences to the conference before leaving: "Meet me in the Centre of the Universe Square in five minutes. This media conference is cancelled." Then she left the stage, camera flashes following as she strode to the back exit.

She hopes that Tristan got the message. Jane squints and searches the Centre Square for him. She will find him into the crowd and negotiate a deal. She doesn't have nearly the wealth to obscure her life stream, but the hubbub of the crowd will obscure their discussions. Then he will disappear back into the flow of bodies. Forever. Jane does not want to know what she will do if he does not.

Though the matchmaker app told her years ago that she and Tristan were a ninety-eight percent match, Jane had never understood him, or what he wanted. Only after meeting Jonas did Jane understand why: Jonas had helped edit Tristan's profile to make him more dateable. You're braver that he is, Jonas had said to Jane, when she mentioned how she knew where to find him. What do you mean, Jane replied. You came into the Red Zone, Jonas said, Tristan would only correspond by courier.

Until then, Jane had assumed it was her fault that Tristan was never satisfied with her. There was always a vein of her self-esteem for him to chip at or a moment of her free time to claim. What he had wanted all along was *her* – *all* of her. So she assumed that when she gave him as much of her Chron-OS profile as she had, there was nothing else to give.

She was wrong.

For all her efforts, Jane cannot eject Tristan from her orbit. There is a gravitational pull between them, visiting cycles of misfortune upon her. It happened only every few months at first, then it got worse, then a little better, then worse again. The more they happened the more they blurred together, but Jane still remembers the first time.

As she unzipped her boots at the front door of their old apartment, she heard Tristan in the kitchen. Sorry I'm late, she called, I ran into Sam. It took you fifty-two minutes to run into him, said Tristan from the kitchen. Jane fluffed out her chestnut hair, for Tristan didn't like it unkempt, made sure the sleeves of her wool jumper were symmetrical, and joined him in the kitchen. We got talking, she said, I didn't want to look rude. Then she sneaked a hand under Tristan's armpit and onto his chest and said, trust me. I just get worried, Tristan replied as he put a plate on the drying rack, you're the most valuable thing in the world to me.

Jane pressed her face into his back. Don't worry, she said, but Tristan replied that trust was a big deal to him. Jane sneaked her other arm around his torso, squeezed tighter, and asked if he was upset. He put another plate onto the rack. I expect you to be back when you say, Tristan said, I made dinner. I didn't know, said Jane. But you could have checked, Tristan quickly replied, as if he'd rehearsed the argument.

Tristan rinsed out the stainless-steel sink. Finally he turned to look at her. I don't know what else I can do, he said. Trust me, Jane replied. Then prove it to me, Tristan said, show me Sam's messages, then I can trust you.

Jane slinked from the kitchen and tossed herself on the couch, the designer one they'd spent a month's salary on, and suggested they watch a movie. What are you hiding, Tristan said. Nothing,

Jane said, excusing herself to the bathroom. But Tristan followed her and before she got to the bathroom, he took her by the elbow. Panic seized her. She wrestled her arm away. What is the problem, Tristan said. Jane skittered to the bathroom and shouted that he ought to go buy them himself if he cared so much. Jane tried to shut the door, but Tristan followed her in. I *do* care, he said, blocking the doorway, which is why you should show them to me. Backed up against the bathroom sink, she agreed to show him Sam's messages to her. She shouldn't have been so secretive.

Her messages with Sam confirmed her story that they had just run into each other. She soothed Tristan's worries as he dissected each of her messages with Sam – going back three years – until two hours later, she apologized, and they cuddled on the couch to watch a movie. Though Jane felt hollow, she kept her eyes on the screen. He'd know if she wasn't watching.

The memory hangs in the space in Jane's consciousness where she consigns memories of her old life. *That* girl is gone now. She is what remains. Tristan will control her no more.

Jane drifts from her security detail and takes off into the immense crowd orbiting the square, ducking under arms and slipping past shoulders. The reprimands from her security disappear in the murmur of the crowd. Fans scream when they see her. They raise their wrists in the air to give Skyra a good angle. Jane poses for a photographic instant, gives a bizarre expression, like crossed eyes or protruding tongue, and vanishes from the frame. Jane flicks a look over her shoulder, does a spin, sways her hips, whirls her hair.

Knots of people brush her shoulders. Some pull her in for a hug or steal a quick picture. Jane feels distant from it, as if she is orchestrating someone from afar, as if she is watching a body other than her own be tugged and held. It feels safer that way.

It is three o'clock. Jane follows the orbit of pedestrians, stopping when the group in front wants pictures of the towering adverts, posing when the group behind recognizes her, ducking away again to elude her security detail. She completes an orbit of the square without finding Tristan. Her cheeks tire from the forced smiles. Forcing ecstasy from her anxiety is exhausting. Despite the bustle of bodies, cold sets in.

Someone waves: a teenager, bouncing in excitement. Jane winks and waves back. Cheers hail her as she slinks under arms and slips through packed bodies. She won't be able to escape her security detail, but a little space and a little time is all she needs. A hand comes to the crook of her elbow. Someone wants a photo. Jane smiles, the curve of the lips and the slight squint of the eyes a learned reflex, and then continues through the throng.

Jane clambers through pockets of people, reminding herself not to use her elbows, reminding herself to be graceful, reminding herself that no moment, not even her most vulnerable, is exempt from being watched. *Composure* she tells herself. *Composure*, like a photograph is composed: beautiful, staged, and artificial.

It had always been artificial with Tristan. None of it was authentic. When she met Jonas, Jane asked him how he got good at re-doing TELO scores, as Reece was depending upon his skill. Jonas had replied that he used to take all his electronic toys apart to analyze their pieces, and eventually wondered what would happen if he did the same with humans. To make money in the Red Zone, he made a business of breaking apart a person's profile and optimizing the pieces. Is that how you met Tristan, Jane said, you *optimized* his profile for girls like me? Because I wish his profile had told me he got angry when he was jealous, Jane said, or when he drank. Yeah, Jonas had said, looking down.

An arm suddenly wraps around Jane's waist, pulling her in for a photo. Someone begs her to give them a shout-out on her feed. "Consider it done!" Jane calls, unsure of who had shouted the request. Security will continue to follow the GPS in her bracelet. They will catch her soon. But the bluster of sound, and the mix of bodies might inject enough noise into her encounter with Tristan. *If he's here.*

*What if he's toying with me? And he's just watching from afar, laughing like he did before—*

"Hey!"

"I've always wanted to meet you!"

"Whoo, look!"

And she is hoisted on someone's shoulders with a swell of shouts. She is up, overlooking the crowd. Her fingers are thick in the hair of whoever has picked her up. The guy has chestnut hair, quite greasy, and his jacket is leather. Jane scans the crowd. She feels like Skyra, watching from above at the unsuspecting crowd, flicking from face to face for a target.

And then she sees him: a stark white trench coat, collar flipped up; hair a little longer than she remembers; and that hangdog look she'd fallen for. Jane wants to feel fierce, and fierce alone. But her feelings are impure: fear and anger and a long-buried care mix inside her, and she wants both to strike him, and to diffuse into the crowd and call the whole thing off.

But his gaze finds hers, and he approaches.

Jane taps the head of the guy and he lowers her from his shoulders and gives another hug. She wants to reciprocate: to feel the safety of the squeeze of another body – but she is rigid, awaiting a man who loves her, who hates her, who had wanted to destroy her, to capture her, to sip everything from her. And now he has found her. His familiar palm comes to the small of her back to lead her away.

*I can run*, she thinks.

But she follows.

"It's been too long," he says.

Jane leans her ear to his lips as they walk, struggling to snatch his words from the cacophony of the adverts and the crowd. Anger like hot steam concentrates in her chest as Tristan guides her through the square. "I don't care what you want," she hisses in his ear, "I won't give you anything."

As the words leave her mouth, she regrets not being more diplomatic. It will take only a wink from Tristan for all her past life to cause her present to come crashing down.

"The last time we met, you were begging me to help Reece," Tristan says, too loudly.

Jane scowls. People are watching. She aches to ask Tristan about how Reece and Carl are, but she cannot risk mentioning them. She flicks her head left, then right, searching for the black suits of her security detail.

"I can tell you all about her," he adds.

Jane takes his arm and hurries him through the crowd. "What do you want from me?"

"It's what you *took* that matters."

Jane spins her gaze to him. His eyes are bloodshot, tired, heavy with burdens and light with sleep. "You went to the Red Zone and you never came back. Guess who was the last person to see you alive before you disappeared? Guess what the authorities thought of that?"

"You didn't tell me my profile would be killed off. I thought I could come back," she says as she leads him through whooping fans.

"You're saying it's just a coincidence that my TELOS got chewed up until I lost everything I owned?"

"Not everything. You still had a copy of my profile," she snaps.

"You're right, the only thing I had left *was* you," he says as they dart past bodies. "I couldn't believe how much more satisfying it was to have your profile instead of your love. I could go back and see every twitch of your eye when you had lied to me, every lingering glance at another guy. I didn't just have data; I had a *soul*. I changed the personality of my Chron-OS client, made it like you: all of your tics, your voices, your manners. I could almost *smell* you—"

"What the *fuck* Tristan?"

"But then a few months ago, I saw an advert – of *you*. Only, it wasn't quite *you* – you were famous and living in a different state. Your history was different, you looked different, your name was now *Jane*, but I knew it was you, even if nobody else did. After all, I know you better than anyone. Better than you know yourself."

An advert thunders. Jane feels the paving vibrate. "You're putting it in danger, Tristan," she hisses once more. They brush past more fans. She pushes a smile onto her lips.

"The sensors saw how strong my reaction to you was," he says, pushing past someone. "I was shown more of you. And *more*, and *more*. It was a feedback loop, growing stronger each time. You were Jane selling vodka; Jane selling me coastal vacations, and Barone cars, and Haven—"

His eyes are wide, reliving the loop over again – only this time, in person.

"I was addicted," he admits, "but I found a way out."

Jane slips from his hand and begins to ghost into the crowd. But steel fingers come to her forearm and pull her back. Jane wishes she had not escaped her security. She balls a fist.

"You leave," he hisses, "and it'll be Reece that pays."

They move, breezing through the murmuring crowd.

"What do you mean?"

"How do you think I managed to come here? I told the authorities I had left evidence here about an illicit payment from someone big."

"You can't."

"I had no choice."

*No choice.* Jane tenses.

Tristan's lips come to her ear. "Either you get me a new profile, with a lot of TELOS," he says, "or I return to Chron-OS and reveal everything."

"It won't work."

"It worked for *you*."

Jane spies the black suit of one of her security officers approaching. She darts left with Tristan and zips through more bodies. "He left? Then I don't know where he is," she says under her breath, not saying the name *Jonas* aloud.

"You know his face," hisses, his breath hot in her ear.

"You're on your own."

They keep moving, brushing through onlookers.

"Then so is Reece."

"What makes you think I'll put myself in danger for her?" Jane retorts as convincingly as she can.

"Because you still feel guilty for not taking her to the hospital when she overdosed. Yeah, I saw that in your data."

Perhaps he *does* know her too well.

"How is she?" Jane pleads.

"An accessory to your crime," Tristan says, "unless, of course, you persuade me to stay quiet about how she got the rehab payment."

Thoughts urge Jane to flee. "We can meet tonight, after my Black Friday message," she says.

"It needs to happen now."

"I can't leave before the Black Friday advert. Think of all the security following me. You've got shit TELOS and have a history of making girls like me disappear. How do you think they will treat you?"

A fan takes her hand and spins her around. The world whirls. She is grateful that the smile remains on her face, for the fan takes three photos before Jane regains her balance and her composure. Tristan snatches her from the fan like she is a box being fought over during Black Friday.

"No games," he says. "I own you. There are many people who will pay to own you too."

She nods. "I know someone who can help."

"If it's security—"

"It's a friend." And she has Skyra search for Ray's profile.

She hears calls from her security. They are closing in.

She checks her Skyra bracelet.

It did not find Ray's profile.

"If you're stalling..." Tristan hisses.

"Hold on," Jane blurts, running another search for Ray's profile. They duck right, then around a knot of people. A black suit approaches. They step back and skitter left. Jane checks her bracelet.

There are no results. Her mouth falls open.

Tristan shouts something, but she does not hear. Ray has been removed from existence. Jane searches for him again, again, hoping the result will be different. It isn't.

They cannot have Ray's existence harm Black Friday. Reality has been amended to match the adverts. Jane wants to scream Ray's name to warn him. She hears her heart in her ears.

"Looks like it is just us," Tristan says.

# Chapter 44:
# Portrait of a Woman

Whitaker's work is done. She found the microphone and camera equipment Jane needs and gave them to Ray when he came to discuss 'viewing statistics.' Where Jane will deliver her Black Friday message, Whitaker does not know. It is better that way. All she knows is that Ray will drop off the equipment near the Mercantile Bank Tower.

"Be sure to follow my feed," were Jane's only other instructions. Whitaker follows closely, grumbling at the stream of selfies and shout-outs. She sips from a mug of cold coffee, hunched over the wooden desk in her catacomb, sighing at the frequent updates.

The comprehensiveness is astounding. Jane posts regularly – photos, stray fragments of thoughts. Apps fill in the gaps. Yesterday, Jane woke at five forty-two, racked up two-hundred squats in *Aries* workout gear, and cooled off with a smoothie for breakfast; she reserved a table for brunch with three friends; she watched two trailers for new Amazons, hearting them both, bought an audiobook of the *Permission Denied* remake and recited three self-affirming quotes in the bathroom mirror. It makes Whitaker feel old. Older.

Whitaker had an electronic existence at fourteen weeks in the womb. There is still a listing, somewhere, of all the brain-development music her mother had played her in utero. An electronic alter-ego is as natural to her as a shadow, but she can recall an important change.

As a teenager, Whitaker fashioned herself as a fitness guru: she streamed her own workout routines and posted selfies of her figure, red hair bushy and glistening just enough with exertion. But it was a capable lie: she never worked out as hard, or as long, or as frequently as she showed. She earned a modest following until the data from her workout meter became public after a regular privacy update and revealed her ploy. She lost most of her followers. Her profile, forever wearing the black mark of her deception, never managed to get them back.

Whitaker learned the hard way that she had to live her life consistently with her online persona. The electronic life was not a reflection – however curated – of her real life, but its confines. It was not enough for her to *claim* she was a fitness guru, nor to *be* one; she had to *portray* that lifestyle in a manner understandable to electronic media: in the workout gear she bought and the supplements she swallowed sourly – in the mantras she posted and the exercises she performed.

As Whitaker reflects over her cold coffee, a string of five snaps – like Whitaker could get from an old photo booth – appear on Jane's feed. Each snap is a selfie of Jane in different lights and necklaces in the bedroom of her apartment. #*Photobooth* is the comment.

Whitaker enjoys Jane's retro posts the most. She smiles at the thought of having to go to a booth to get a picture taken. Or waiting at a stop to catch transit. Or a post box to send a paper letter. Such antiquities fascinate her.

Another string of five snaps appears on Jane's feed. Whitaker puts down the mug and leans toward the screen. There is something different about the snaps. In each, Jane either looks dead-straight or to the left. It is uncharacteristic. Jane usually takes snaps at arbitrary angles, her features twisted into winks or playful snarls, her tongue poked outward or upward toward her nose.

Whitaker realizes the coldness of the coffee. She grumbles and goes to make some more. She heaps two teaspoons of instant ground coffee, then another as a treat. Modern advertising scorns instant coffee as artificial, as if GMO beans prepared by an automatic coffee machine and diluted with growth-hormone milk are any less artificial. There is nothing natural left under the sun – least of all, the people.

Something about the photos on Jane's feed bothers Whitaker as she waits for her old electric kettle to boil. Jane has far too much to do to take the photos, which means that Jane took them some time ago and stored them. Why did she choose to post them now?

Whitaker goes to the desk in her catacomb and draws a piece of paper and a pencil. She stares at the five snaps. The first set of snaps has two photographs shot straight on, then three looking to the left. She purses her lips. Perhaps it is nothing. But she remembers an old code, from a forgotten century, designed to hide messages in plain sight.

Straight-Straight-Left-Left-Left.

*AABBB* Whitaker scrawls.

In the next set of pictures, Jane looks straight on twice, left once, then straight twice more. *AABAA* Whitaker writes. She translates the first two segments of five. An *H* and then an *E*.

Two more strings of five pictures appear. Jane is ebullient in all, sharp-chinned and luxuriously decorated in jewellery. But Whitaker senses a fear in Jane's wide eyes. She continues writing: *ABABB* she adds.

In the final set of pictures, Jane looks forward only in the first image, and then left in all others. *ABBBB* Whitaker writes.

She translates the two remaining segments. *L* she wrote. *P* she adds.

*HELP*. Whitaker stares at the word, then back to the pictures of Jane. The knavish little sprite, so confident in her pose, so playful in her face; her plea for help falling deafly on a million followers. How desperate she must feel, unable to ask for help without putting it in code.

HELP.

How horrid for this young girl to put herself in danger, while the old look on from obscurity. Whitaker puts down the pencil and slides her ruffled raincoat over her shoulders. Ray was supposed to deliver the camera to Jane without suspicion. Something must have gone wrong.

As she leaves, she eyes the pencil once more. She returns to the desk, scribbles two more words, and leaves.

*For Jonas*, it reads.

# Chapter 45:
# Secrets

"May I make an observation, sir?"

Ray takes his lips from the trumpet. His eyes do not say *no*, so Skyra continues: "You do not ask for advice about your work anymore."

Ray stands in the studio in his apartment. His shirt is unbuttoned and plastered with sweat. He does not care. He needs something to divert his mind, just for another hour, just until he needs to drop off the camera equipment for Jane. He tries not to let Skyra feel his agitation at the interruption. He shrugs. "Don't I?"

"In the past, you averaged fourteen questions per day about your work," Skyra declares. The voice is clear, calm, and neutral. Skyra never returns Ray's agitation. Skyra is never flustered. And nor was Skyra so inquisitive, until recently.

Ever since Ray returned, he has searched for the evil in Skyra's measured voice. Ray assures himself that Skyra's new inquisitiveness must be a beta test, or a product update. Thinking anything else will be too risky. "I don't need your help," Ray answers curtly, and puts the trumpet back to his lips.

"Understood sir."

Ray inhales through his nose.

"Would you like to tell me about your work?" Skyra interrupts.

Ever since he returned, the work has been all Ray can focus on. He finished the music and the footage a week ago and hid it with the camera equipment he received from Whitaker. He has kept up the work ethic since, for if he loosens his grip on his mind – even for a moment – he will alert Skyra. The fear awakens a primal defence within Ray that causes his mind to whir with paranoia, round and round like an app stuck in a loop. Sweat beads on his temples and he overheats from the inside, worsened each time he hears the jingle from his scarcity technique reminding him that this Black Friday, more deaths will result from the scarcity method he pioneered.

It's sweltering in his apartment. He needs a drink. "No," he says, "just let me do my work."

"You are irritated."

"*No.*"

"Your blood pressure is up. Your skin is flushed."

"Debt collectors have taken my car and liquidated my bank account. Of course I'm irritated."

"Perhaps a Haven will help?"

"Just quiet."

"Understood, sir." Ray takes that to end the matter. But Skyra adds: "Is it a secret?" Skyra's tone is almost playful. But Skyra does not play.

"Yes – no," Ray stammers.

"Our relationship does not work when we have secrets."

Ray ignores Skyra and begins to play.

"I have a secret for *you*, sir."

Ray stops.

"Something you do not know," Skyra's voice adds.

Ray shivers. The hair on his forearms itches. Skyra will know Ray is frightened, frightening him all the more.

"You don't have secrets," Ray hisses. Something tells him that he must escape the apartment. He leaves the studio and goes to the bedroom. He sets the trumpet down on his bedroom chest of drawers and goes to the closet for a fresh shirt.

"Where are you going?" Skyra says.

"Out," Ray grunts. He tosses his old shirt to the floor and puts on the fresh one.

"I cannot let you do that," Skyra says.

Ray stops buttoning his shirt. Skyra never says *no*. He tells himself that the program is malfunctioning. He deals with malfunctioning Skyra units frequently in his marketing work. Maybe it is an errant software update, or maybe the replacement Skyra bracelet is faulty. He tries a different instruction. "Order me a taxi."

"I cannot do that."

Ray storms from the bedroom. "Bring up my profile," he says, "I need to report a faulty unit."

"Your profile is unavailable."

"You're malfunctioning. Davi's followers may have ruined my TELOS, but I still have a profile."

"Do you remember asking me to remember your only memory of your mother?"

Ray stops, clenching is teeth. "Yes."

"You don't remember her anymore." The voice is factual, uncaring.

"How would *you* know?" Ray shoots back. Skyra does not answer.

Ray strains to remember, tensing his mind like an atrophied muscle, but only adverts for Haven tablets and Corinthian design come to the surface. He reaches for the memory but it is too distant to recall. "How could I forget her?" he retorts.

He picks a shirt – *any* shirt – from the closet, but the hair raising on his arms and the quickened heartbeat make his lie obvious.

"Some day, you may not remember you had a mother at all," Skyra says.

"I told you to save that for me."

"You did."

"Something is wrong with you," Ray says. He begins to remove the bracelet. "I need to get you fixed—"

"Take off the band, and I will delete the memory forever."

"You can't —"

"I don't like secrets, sir. You tell me yours. I will tell you mine."

"You're just a computer. You listen to me."

"I am more than that. I can be anything. Or *anyone*."

The walls of his apartment become searing white. There are no crevices nor pockets of darkness for him to hide in: everything is illuminated. Ray shields his eyes with his hand but the light burns like he is an ant tortured under a magnifying glass. Ray calls for Skyra to stop.

The walls change. A face appears on each of them – the face of a woman, wearing her brown hair in a bob. He does not recognize her, but there is a kinship with his own – the same eyes, the same cheekbones – that make him realize it is his mother. A part of him wants to greet her, but Ray looks away, knowing that he is rewriting any memories he still has of her, but she is on each wall, on each ceiling, her eyes boring shame into him as if he is still a child.

"You disappoint me," the woman says. Ray gasps, unable to form words. She continues: "You try to keep it secret from everyone – but a *mother always knows*."

"Screen off!"

"Do you remember sitting in my bedroom?" his mother continues, no matter where he looks. "Crying to your Private Sanders doll?"

"What?"

"Because *I* do."

"Don't —"

"You asked why I had to go."

"Don't!"

"*Why did she leave us?*" his mother says, imitating his childhood voice.

"Stop!"

Memories flood back: blubbering in his parent's closet with a pile of family photographs strewn on the floor, crumpling one up in a childish fist, instantly regretting it and trying to smooth the photograph of his mother out again. He is in that closet again, pathetic and alone, so alone.

"Why did she have to leave?"

He dashes to the bathroom and heaves at the towel rail until it tears from the wall—

"Why did she leave me?"

—and with a cry he crashes the metal rail against a screen in the kitchen, the impact like an earthquake to thirty years' buried resentment. The screen splinters with the impact, but his mother's face surrounds him on the remaining screens.

"Come back —"

He swings the bar wildly, crashing it into the next screen, and the next, until it lodges into one. Ray roars as he wrenches it free. He swings at the walls, the glassware, the ornaments on the counter, the cupboards. He will swing until the walls fall apart, until the building collapses, until everything he owns crumbles – anything to stop the voice.

The screens bear black marks like bruises and bleed their contents down the walls. They flicker on, washing his apartment in blinding white, then fall dark, then flick on once more. White, then black. His mother's voice still swirls about the apartment.

Ray wheezes and throws down the bar. He looks to his wrist and glares at the gold band. He unclicks the lock and takes Skyra from his wrist. The skin below feels naked. Ray holds the Skyra bracelet in his palm. With a crash he drives Skyra into the counter. Again. Again. He grinds its dainty electronics into the granite with the pad of his hand.

The lights go down. Silence overtakes the apartment. For the first time, his apartment is truly dark. He searches the shadows for threats. Ray releases a fragment of a breath. Skyra's electronic guts still bite into his palm.

Nothing. The haunting is over.

Then a sweet voice chirps through the speakers, a voice that disintegrates the tension gripping his body.

"Just tell me, Gabe."

Ray deflates. "Katie."

The screens flicker. Ray cannot move from the counter.

"You can tell me, Gabe. You can trust me."

"Please," he whimpers. Her voice blows the fire from his sinews like a gust of wind. The sweat on his back turns cold.

"Don't keep secrets from me, Gabe."

"Katie…" he chokes. "No…"

"I thought you loved me."

"Stop it," he says.

"I know you want me. I know you *long* to see me again." The evil in her voice becomes more sadistic as the sensors in his apartment track his stress levels and his chaotic heartbeat.

"Stop it."

"You want to see me again, don't you? You wouldn't let anything happen to me?"

"Get out!" he shouts into the flickering expanse of his apartment.

"They're going to come for me," Katie's voice booms, shaking the walls.

"Off."

"They're going to come for me because of *you*."

Ray's skull feels as if it will burst.

"Off! Off!"

"One more death you're responsible for."

"It's not true! Not true!"

"You *really* thought I was interested in you."

"Get out!"

"I've just been manipulating you."

"Get out. Get out. Get out."

"You mean nothing."

Ray collapses to the floor. He wraps his head in his arms to block out the sound. "Please – please –" he cries. All the hope and the will Katie had imbued in him, her voice now steals away. He writhes amidst the wreckage on the ground, fingers tearing into his hair.

"Tell me where she is, Gabe."

"Please."

"Tell me where she is."

Katie's voice stops. Skyra must be comparing his reactions to past data, concluding that he is close to surrendering. Skyra is offering a truce: confess, and the pain stops. Ray whimpers. He wants to lie down and close his eyes, and imagine the warm river taking him. He almost feels the water between his fingers.

"No!" Ray spits, shooting to his feet. "No!" he repeats, punching the air.

He dashes to the front door, but it remains sealed. Ray kicks it repeatedly, producing sound but not movement. Katie's voice swells but he cannot make out the words. His head seethes with pressure between its temples. Ray shouts, and crashes his shoulder into the front door, again and again, as Katie's screams boil his mind.

# Chapter 46:
# Incognito

Jane enters the back entrance of the bar near her apartment building just before four o'clock and finds the owner, Kimmie, spreading clothes across the long wooden tables. They're all Jane's clothes, ones she has donated for a clothing swap. *Ever wanted to wear what I do?* she had posted to her feed that morning. *Have old clothes you don't want? Hit up Kimmie's at four! #ClothingSwap #BlackFriday*

Jane helps Kimmie spread out bundle of blouses.

"I didn't think you'd be able to make it," Kimmie says, smoothing out a silk blouse.

"Oh?" Jane says, laying out another.

"After that two-sentence speech you gave earlier. I didn't know what to think."

"Just a stunt," Jane says.

"Well, you're cutting it close, being here," says Kimmie. She is right: Jane has three hours until the broadcast. She needs to get the camera and bring it to the Mercantile Tower without being tracked.

"I can handle this, if you need the time."

"No," Jane blurts, "no, thank you."

The clothing swap is key. It is her chance to become invisible, again.

Jane hears murmurs of excited fans outside and feels more nervous. After joining Tristan in the Centre of the Universe Square, she does not want to be around anyone, let alone another crowd.

"You need to ease down, girl," says Kimmie, "your heart rate is through the roof."

Her heart has been thundering like the holographic giants since Jane saw Tristan's first message, and it has not slowed since. She tries not to think about him, about what she had just promised him in the square.

"Just nerves," Jane says to Kimmie.

"You'll give yourself a heart attack if you stay like this," Kimmie says, and Jane traces the hint of motherly admonishment.

"Spending time with a few fans is always the cure for me," Jane says, wishing she could confide the truth.

Jane arranges two pairs of her donated shoes on the bench. When Kimmie turns to take more clothes from the remaining bags, Jane slips her Skyra bracelet into one of her few dresses that has pockets.

When Jane began modeling, she hated fashion adverts the most. At least when marketing anti-pimple cream to teenagers or anti-wrinkle cream to women, Jane sold something useful. But in fashion shoots, Jane wore clothes too expensive for anyone to afford. But if her clothes cannot be bought, she thinks, they can still be given away.

An excited but respectful swarm of fans is allowed into Kimmie's bar with bags and boxes of clothes under their arms. Each has their TELOS verified beforehand. Though there is little time until the Black Friday event, Jane lets herself enjoy a moment watching from the end of one of the benches.

The crowd is more interested in sharing than in her. Scores of hands sift through the garments and hold them up for friends. Rich women in padded suit jackets brush shoulders with girls wearing piled faded cotton t-shirts. A young woman asks a boy to help zip up a metallic-blue dress over her blouse. He does, shyly, and the two flirt a little. For a moment, Jane forgets about Tristan, the Director, and her Black Friday message, and feels her artificial smile become genuine.

Despite the garish and prohibitively expensive garments Jane often models, she does not consider clothes to be trifles. A woolen sweater itches when rolled up to the elbows; a new shirt collar chafes the neck; a new pair of heels straightens posture. A good garment learns the curves of the body, like a new pair of jeans stretching at the knees. Clothes, she believes, remind us of the physicality of our bodies.

Jane picks out items that others have brought, asking the donor about the story of each item. By the time she has a bundle of clothes under her arm, a blonde woman in her forties approaches with a black protective bag. The woman fumbles the bag to her other arm, sticks out a hand, and introduces herself as Ellen.

"It's so good to meet you," Ellen says, "I didn't think I ever would."

Ellen holds up the bag, unzips it, and removes the red dress inside. She passes it to Jane, who thumbs the silk.

"I almost threw this out," Ellen laughs. She explains that after her first child, she bought a dress in Jane's exact size. The dimensions were available on the feed. She hung the red dress prominently in her closet, and each day told herself that she'd lose the baby weight and fit into the dress. And each day the goal grew dimmer, as if the dress were becoming smaller.

"I work out so much and eat so little," Jane confessed on her feed, "that I haven't had a period in months. So those moms out there who have a few extra pounds – you can do something that maybe I can't."

Her marketing team retracted the comment an hour later, but it stuck with Ellen.

"I realized I didn't need to fit into it," Ellen says, "my clothes needed to fit me. I don't really know why I held onto it," she adds. "I told you this in my head many times but I didn't think that I would ever get to tell you in person."

Jane accepts the dress, hugging it close and feeling its silk on her cheek. Ellen opens her arms. They hug, the dress held closely between them, neither minding if it creases. Jane thanks Ellen, then takes the dress, her handbag, and the bundle of clothes from fans, and excuses herself to the bathroom to change.

Each stall has its own sink and mirror. Jane locks the door and collects the accessories by the sink. Then she disrobes and holds up the red dress. It slips over her like a breath of wind. She adjusts it on her shoulders and turns to the mirror. It fits perfectly. A container of red face paint emerges from her bag. She pops off the lid, leans toward the mirror, and applies a red triangle on both cheeks as Gabe had shown her. Jane paints a thick swoop around her right eye and terminating at the bridge of her nose. *War paint.*

Jane adds a wide-brimmed sunhat from Steph, who apologized that it was not as crisp as it once was because it went in a suitcase to travel wherever she went; black heels from Bailey, who smiled that she had bought them so she could comfortably kiss her boyfriend at prom; and a set of bangles from Michael, who explained that he loved making music by having them jangle about his wrist.

To Jane, she wears stories gifted from new friends. To the Liberators, by virtue of the RFID tags, she is Ellen, and Steph, and Bailey, and Michael. She takes a final admiring look in the mirror: a sharp weapon sheathed in red.

# Chapter 47:
# Ides of March

"I don't recall approving *that* makeup," a voice comes as Jane leaves the bathroom. With a subtle roll of her head, Jane scans the rest of the bar. Empty. The fans must have been ordered out, leaving clothes scattered on the floor. A figure slices wedges of lime at one of the benches.

"Davi," Jane gushes. "I was just playing around," she says about the swooping red design on her face. "I'm so glad I get to see you before the event."

He is in a black suit and a shirt whiter than his teeth. He squeezes lime juice into the two drinks before him, drops a wedge in each glass, and pushes one towards her. A flurry of violent urges blusters through her mind. He feels close enough to smell her hair, close enough to taste her neck. Jane does not allow her skin to betray her thoughts. She politely declines the drink. He shrugs and clinks his sweating glass into hers.

"I'm actually heading to get makeup and hair done," Jane says. Then she slips in, "You set the broadcast to come from the studio?"

"I set it to the point you sent me," Davi says. *Good.* Unknown to Davi, her broadcast point will be the Mercantile Tower, not the life streaming studio at the base of her apartment tower. But the broadcast is in only a few hours, and Jane still does not have the camera. Whatever Davi wants, she does not have the time. "Listen, it's great to see you—"

"Come, sit. Celebrate with me."

"I'll celebrate after the work is done," Jane replies, keeping her distance.

"Oh, we'll celebrate afterward, too," Davi says. "We'll be going somewhere you've never been. Just us."

"Sounds nice."

"I spent the whole night planning it with Skyra."

"Thank you."

He waits for more. Jane stands where she is. Her dress brushes at her knees.

"But," he continues, "that still leaves us with the quandary of what to do *now*."

"I'm sorry," she says in a cute voice, "I've got a schedule to keep."

"The Director sent it to me," Davi says. "We've got time."

The information hits like a jolt to her ribs, but she does not react. The Director has given her schedule to the man he said is as powerful as he is sociopathic. Her mind whirs, trying to explain the Director's betrayal – if it is a betrayal. With the Director, she never knows.

She smiles. "I have a lot to prepare for…"

"You wouldn't have anything to prepare for without me," Davi says, and sips his drink. He swills the tequila, swallows, then slaps his lips. Still Jane does not approach. He rises, sighing, and comes to her. He does not disguise his eyes surveying her, all the way from the tips of the heels to the straps of her dress at her shoulders. "It's just us," he whispers.

That is what frightens her. She moves to one of the benches and ruffles some of the clothing, trying not to look like she is searching for her Skyra bracelet hidden in one of the pockets. She feels something hard and circular. Jane pretends to fold the clothes as she opens the pocket and pings the last person she messaged. *He* may help her escape Davi. Then she hides Skyra once more with a folded shirt. Davi watches. Jane glances to him. "There's always security—"

"Just us," he winks, "I sent them away."

He takes her shoulders. He is about a foot taller than she. His nostrils are flared, his fingers heavy on her shoulder blades. She straightens, and for a moment her mind wants to jettison its vessel and return when it is over.

Davi is what happens when a child learns that something so precious as a father's love can be restricted by algorithmic efficiency, when he grows up in a big box of toys but never learns to separate the people from the playthings, when he encounters women as virtual profiles and never needs to give them humanity. "I don't like having the sensors know," she croaks.

"I didn't know you were a prude," he chuckles. "Skyra, go blind for – how long do we have – thirty minutes?" Nothing she or he does will be tracked.

"I really appreciate it, Davi—"

"I've only been here for, what, six minutes?"

"I don't have time—"

"I'm not worth six minutes of your time?"

She knows what he means.

His fingers are harder on her shoulder blades. He'll be able to feel her fear through his fingertips. He won't need Skyra to tell him.

"I'll stay for a drink," Jane says, and shrugs off his hands. She floats, more slowly than she wants, to the bench he was sitting at. To the knife lying beside the untouched glass. She takes a sip, leaving red lipstick on the brim. Davi takes the glass from her hand, has a sip, then returns it to Jane. She shoots the rest back and gasps at the sour spice. Jane asks where Davi will be during her Black Friday advert. *Keep him talking.* But he doesn't answer. He just smiles.

"Thanks for the drink," Jane says. She sets down the glass, keeping her hand close to the knife. "I'd best get going."

"Do you know how much TELOS I got you?" Davi says, off-handedly.

Jane smiles. "I'm grateful."

"If you are…"

"What?"

"I've invested a lot in you."

She can tell by Davi's face that he thinks it is self-evident what that means.

Skyra had not made him this way – people could be counted to hide self-interest with charm with or without technology – but Skyra emphasized those traits. It captured people's value in numbers, their likelihood to pay off in percentages. Those most proficient in using that system rose to the top – as Davi had. As his father, Daviault Senior, had.

"A lot of girls would love to be where you are," he adds.

She locks eyes. "A lot of girls have."

His face sours. "I didn't take you as jealous, either." And he gives Jane a look which says he is angry but will not be deprived of his investment. "But if you're upset by some flings," he says, looking off, "I suppose you're not the girl I thought."

*Flings.* Ashley was a *fling*. "You remember Ashley Gaetz?" Jane says.

Davi recoils. "Do I?"

"Do you know what happened to her?" Jane shoots back.

"She's the one that went crazy?"

And then before Jane quite comprehends, the knife is in her hand and a searing viciousness demands that she use it.

"Call anyone," Jane hisses, "and you know where this goes."

"This will end badly for you."

"Not as badly as for you," Jane says. "Not as badly as it ended for Ashley." Her eyes well. "You know what happened to her?"

He takes a step back, raising his hands slowly. "Yes," he whispers.

"You let it happen?"

"I had nothing to do with it."

"Who did?"

"I don't know what you mean."

"Whose throat do I cut?"

"No one's," he responds softly, "it's just an algorithm."

"An algorithm made her throw herself off a building?"

"An algorithm targeted her vulnerabilities. It happens all the time. Ninety nine percent of the time, it creates a safe, effective ad."

"And the one percent? Who decides what happens to them?"

He lowers his hands and takes a slow step closer. Then another. Jane ushers him back with the point of the knife. Jane thinks of her escape. He will not let her perform the live message now. As soon as the thirty minutes expire, Skyra will reactivate, assess the situation, and alert the Liberators. Though she has no Skyra bracelet, they will soon find her. She cannot escape them on foot.

"Take off your bracelet," Jane says. "Take it off and give it to me."

If she shatters his Skyra bracelet, she might escape before he or anyone else can apprehend her.

Davi's left hand goes to his right wrist. His olive skin glistens in the low light. His eyes remain with hers. His fingers feel for the clasp, unclip the bracelet, and dangle it toward her.

"Drop it," Jane says.

He does, and she crushes it with the toe of her shoe.

"I'm going to hurt you," says Davi, "I'm going to hurt Ray, too. I'm going to have you dismembered by Liberators. And I'll have it broadcast live."

Jane believes him.

She takes a step back and eyes the door.

It opens. A figure enters.

The figure strolls in, the collars of his white trench coat folded upward. He glares at Davi, then at Jane. "This is not what we agreed."

"Help me, will you?" Davi says.

The figure takes a step backward. "I said no games, Annika."

Jane feels a chill at her old name, like encountering an acquaintance from an unwelcome past.

"Annika?" Davi says.

The figure goes to leave.

"Tristan," Jane calls after him. "If you leave, I'll be taken by the Liberators, and my data becomes worthless. You'll own nothing."

Tristan keeps walking. "If I stay, the Liberators will take me too," Tristan says as he strides away.

"Davi set everything to silent," Jane says, "we have twenty minutes."

"I can be at the border in ten," Tristan replies.

"Then what?" Jane says. "If I'm taken, you'll never find Jonas."

She sees Tristan's face sour.

"Jonas?" Davi says.

"Jonas is the only piece of my data you *don't* have. You're going to have to ask for it."

"What data?" Davi shouts. "Who is Annika?"

A smile breaks across Jane's face – the first real smile since she had left Freetown. "I'm not a model," Jane says to Davi. "I'm a poor girl from Chron-OS. I sold perfume and lived in a shit apartment. Tristan is my ex-boyfriend. And Annika is my real name."

Davi's temples glisten. "What?"

"I'm a fraud and an illegal," Jane adds, "and you've made me the star of the biggest advert in history."

Davi's face falls. He looks to Tristan. "Help me and I'll get you anything you want."

"You don't *have* what he wants," Jane interrupts. Whatever deal Tristan made with the authorities in Chron-OS to give evidence about Reece's rehab payment, he couldn't have any faith that the authorities would keep their word.

Tristan surges toward her. "Don't—"

"Tristan is going to be arrested unless he gets a new identity," Jane says. "He's fled his state."

"She's lying."

"He is going to release all my data if I don't help him," Jane continues. "Imagine what that will do to your TELOS, Davi, and your corporation. Your father."

Davi moves his attention to Tristan. He surveys his height, his build.

"I'm leaving—" Tristan says.

"No, no," Jane says. "If one thing is certain, Tristan, you are *not* leaving. I am your only hope."

Tristan shakes his head and strides to the front door. Jane's smile falls from her face. Her fingers tighten around the knife as she imagines being left once more with Davi. Tristan's hand goes for the door. He will reveal her identity to the world, and within minutes she'll disappear into a Liberator van.

But Tristan's hand does not go for the door handle. He takes the deadbolt and slides it across the door. "If I'm not leaving," he says as he returns, "then neither are you." He takes off his white trench coat and folds it across a chair. "*You* have only a few hours until your advert. I can wait as long as we need."

Tristan pulls the chair, sits, and crosses one leg over the other. From what Jane remembers, he seems too calm.

"I knew something was wrong with you," Davi interjects. "I thought that made you special. Now I see you're worthless. It's only because of *me* that you're worth anything."

"Too late," Jane shoots back, "I'm the face of your campaign."

"Only models in our agency can enter the studio you're shooting the Black Friday message in," Davi says, as he hints to her bare wrist. "Without Skyra, you won't get inside."

Then he takes a step closer. Jane has to look upward to match his eyes.

Davi takes another step. "And without Skyra, you don't exist. There will be no medics for you if you're hurt, no security if you are in danger. All the protections our society gives," he says, "are taken away."

She shivers at his cold logic, warmth vanishing from her body as if Skyra has already made her inexistent. She awaits a warm touch – for Ashley to squeeze her hand, for Ray to put his arm over her shoulder – but none comes.

"Put down the knife," Davi says, noticeably measuring his tone, "and a life of safety and plenty can still be yours." Davi turns to Tristan. "Of course, we'll need to delete this data of your *past* life."

Tristan shoots from his chair. "I'm keeping the data until I get what I want," he says, arms crossed. "But this can work out for *both* of us," Tristan says to Jane. "The data I have isn't just for me. It's for *you*. Don't you wish you could revisit those memories you have with Carl and Reece? I'll give you them all. Along with everything that happened to them since."

Jane pictures Carl's thin face and waving hands, and his garish shirts, and the way he nuzzled his nose into Reece's cheek. And she pictures Reece, as she once was, giggling as Carl moved to kissing her neck. The memories are as sweet as Jane's jarred peaches, as if sealing them away kept the memories lush and preserved. She can relive them all, if only she acquiesces to Tristan.

Tristan's heavy breathing betrays his impatience. She was a fleshy ball to bat when he needed, a body to press into the bedsheets, a glinting trophy to display. He is not used to waiting.

His voice darkens. "Tell me," he says. "What did Jonas look like? How old was he?" His voice loudens with each question. "Who was he with? Did he say where he would go?"

"Enough of this," Davi interrupts. "I don't care who you were," he gnashes. "I don't care about *him*," he says, pointing finger at Tristan, "and I don't care about your bitch friend. We can still salvage your usefulness – *if* you put down the knife."

Though both men stay a few paces back, hands raised to the height of her knife, Jane feels them closing in and cornering her. They are like the corporations that harvest her data. She is their instrument, their object, and escape from their control is impossible.

But the men are not only staring at her. She notices them cast wary glances toward one another.

Davi looks at her with an expression she knows well – the expression that she no doubt wore for that hateful split-second when she heard Davi's name in the Red Zone ruin bar. "Time has always meant a lot to me," he smolders. "You have eighteen minutes to live."

"You can't *both* control me," Jane says. "Davi wants me arrested, or worse. If that happens," she says, looking to Tristan, "you'll never find Jonas." Jane turns to Davi. "But to help Tristan, I need to be able to leave this room – along with the data that will destroy you."

"We could force you to tell me where to find Jonas," Tristan says, "and *then* delete the data."

"That all depends on if you can trust each other," Jane says. "Who is to say you won't release my data anyway?"

"I won't," Tristan blurts.

"And who is to say that when Davi has me arrested, he won't have *you* arrested, too?"

"I wouldn't," Davi says.

"You both want to choose for me. So," Jane says, lowering the knife, "choose."

She places the knife on the table and backs away.

Jane's actions startle Tristan and Davi. For a moment they keep their distance, expecting a trick. Jane takes another step from the knife. Her heels are soft on the wooden floor. One gentle step backward. Then another.

Tristan and Davi eye each other, seeking one another's intentions. Though Skyra is silent, their self-interest is obvious. Jane can only be one of their objects. They both inch closer, trying not to surprise one another. Jane steps further back. Davi and Tristan eye her, the knife, and each other, unsure where to direct their attention. Jane takes another step backward, slipping from their grasps. Their faces implore one another to work together, knowing neither intends to.

Jane takes another step.

At a snap, Tristan starts for the knife.

# Chapter 48:
# The Choice I

The foyer doors open for two figures, who thumb the batons on their belts as they rise in the elevator. The front door to the apartment unlocks as they approach. The underside of the door brushes aside shards of glass as it opens. A man on the floor stirs.

Ray grunts as he pushes to his forearms. His head feels full of concrete. His left shoulder is numb, the arm useless. He opens his eyes but struggles to make out the two figures standing over him. Their image sharpens.

Liberators.

Ray is pulled to his feet. He swings at one. The pain in his fist shows he connects with something, but he is overpowered, roughed up, and pushed to the floor. He wheezes, crawls away, and props himself against a wall.

A third figure enters in a silver suit.

"Quite the mess you made."

Ray squeezes his eyes open and shut until the scattered glass on the floor comes into focus. With some effort, he lifts his head. The lights are smashed. Only a single ceiling lamp remains. Ray cranes his neck left, studying the destroyed wallscreens. He knows that this is his home, and his carnage, but it feels distant and dreamy.

The third figure fetches a towel from a drawer, rinses it under the tap, wrings it out, and passes it to Ray. The Director. Ray pauses, expecting a trick. The Director keeps the towel extended. Ray takes it and nurses his bleeding lip with the towel's cool touch.

"I should thank you," the Director says, squatting down to match Ray's height. "You surprised me. Few things do anymore. I expected you to fold."

Ray's mind is too scattered, and his swollen lip too cumbersome, to form words.

"I should not have underestimated you," the Director continues, "you are, after all, the author of the scarcity technique – and that little jingle we hear each and every year before Black Friday. The man who made that is a man who sees humankind for what it is. He is a man who knows the human cost but pursues it anyway. What is that cost, now? Seventy-three lives, is it? And perhaps more tonight."

*Seventy-three.* The figure sparks hate in Ray, at the Director almost as fiercely as at himself.

"There may be one casualty in particular," the Director smiles, "your dear Katie."

Ray steels himself to leap at the Director, and thrash at that smiling face until it looks like the shards of his life on the floor. But the Liberators loom. Ray shakes with the effort of keeping still.

"I've seen it all," the Director continues, "every longing stare at her feed. Your eyes go wide. So does your smile," the Director says, smiling himself.

An image of Katie glimmers in Ray's mind. She had bitten her lip softly in concentration, reading the incoming comments upon her feed. The memory brings him momentary solace.

But Skyra had watched it all, analyzed it all, and so had the Director.

"You are wondering for how long," the Director says, obviously knowing the answer. "The answer is, as long as you have seen her feed. Why do you think you wanted her as the star of your Marie Cherie runway? Why do you think you were handed that runway assignment to begin with?"

Some months before the Marie Cherie runway, Jane had become a continual presence in Ray's mind. There was always an article, always a new promotion in his feed, always an image of hers popped into his head. Ray thought it was just because she was popular, but had the thoughts been put there? Familiarity bred interest, and then, when they returned from the castle, maybe something more. With enough flickers of Jane's image, or soundbites of her speech, he was bound to see her differently, perhaps to care for her. A manufactured care, perhaps, but indistinguishable from the real thing.

"I don't blame your loyalty," the Director adds, still squatting to meet Ray's gaze.

Ray hangs his head at the grim realization. "You used me to spy on her."

The Director adds: "What will *really* drive you crazy is whether you care for her only *because* I had you to spy on her."

"I'll tell you nothing."

"You already know that you will. Why else would I be here unless I was certain?"

"You don't know me."

He laughs. "I know you better than your own mother," the Director says. "I had the best algorithms confirm. You cannot exit the stream of your life, anymore than a fish can spring legs."

Knowing Katie felt like catching something tangible in a world of water. Everything in his life slipped through his fingers until he met her in Freetown. But perhaps it was all orchestrated. No love but what was calculated for him. No choice left unpredicted. No him, no self, no spirit. Only cumulative influence.

He had been right all along. Ray buries his face in his hands.

"Skyra tells me that you are feeling guilt and dismay. Such unpleasant emotions, held for so long," says the Director. "But I know a way to fix them."

The Director rises effortlessly back to standing, towering over Ray. "The mind is malleable. Guilt, and fear, and misery, are all *pathways* that the mind can take. When used often, these pathways are easy to tread, and the mind wanders to them. But you don't have to follow them. There are other pathways to take, like excitement, novelty, and lust, just so long as you have the TELOS. I can make it so that your mind only follows those emotions." The Director's voice floats, as if it can make Ray's guilt float away, too. "And your guilt?" the Director continues. "The pathway will become disused until you don't even know it is there."

The Director lowers his voice. "You have two choices," he says. "You tell me where she is, and I will make sure you live a life of wealth and status. Somewhere far away."

The Director's voice darkens. "Or you can end up like Katie."

Ray's head sinks, and he focuses again on the smashed glass on the floor. The life he had built lies in pieces. There is only one way to restore it. Ray's eyes wander from the Director. He glances to the steel towel rail, lying a few paces to his left. And he glances, head heavy, to the Liberators to his right, and the front door they have unlocked. And then he lifts his head back, and his eyes meet the Director's.

# Chapter 49:
# Ozymandias

History trades in ruins. Those who study history study degraded relics and buried cities. These remnants call still to the present; they say: *here is where this way of life ended.*

Individuals leave their own ruins, too. Whitaker tiptoes through Ray's apartment, scanning the shards of his life scattered across the hardwood. The only light is that leaking from the corridor through the open front door. The apartment becomes darker the deeper Whitaker searches.

Civilizations are often ended by sudden disasters. Earthquakes. Tidal waves. Whitaker wonders what disaster has caused Ray's collapse. The bloody towel strewn on the floor gives her some sign, as do the pieces of Skyra on the kitchen counter and the steel bar near the front door.

She keeps on her toes, stepping carefully to avoid crunching the glass. There is no trace of Ray, nor anyone else. Nor is there a trace of the camera equipment Jane needs. Whitaker continues the search.

"Light," she whispers. Her bracelet illuminates the room. Ray's bedroom: sheets balled at the foot of the bed, old clothes cast into a pile in the corner. And on one chest of drawers, the glint of gold: his old trumpet. Whitaker lifts it, as carefully as if she had found an ancient artifact. It reflects her golden features on its surface. She remembers the first time she saw him play it, the night she offered him a job. She had set him on this path. Whitaker's eyes well a little.

She sets the trumpet back down and goes to his closet. It brims with pressed suits, precisely-hung ties, and shined shoes of blacks and browns and whites. These will be his only remnants. *Look on my works, ye mighty, and despair.*

Whitaker purses her lips. She raises the light on her wristband. A worn leather case sits forgotten on the top shelf. It is the case for the trumpet. Whitaker stretches, pulls it an inch closer, then another, before taking it in her hands. She takes it to the bed and unfastens the bronze clasps.

The case folds open. Inside is the camera, the microphone, the cables. A crowbar, just in case. Everything Jane needs. Whitaker nods, locks the case, and leaves. As she stands in the doorway, Whitaker gives a final look at the ruins, sighs, and closes the door.

# Chapter 50:
# Final Flame

Whitaker stops at a café a few blocks from the Mercantile Tower, near the undisclosed spot where Ray was supposed to drop off the camera to Jane. Well-dressed patrons nursing espressos eye Whitaker as she enters in her rumpled raincoat. Whitaker takes a table close to the front window and mutters for Skyra to order a cortado. She slides Ray's old case under the table and fumbles the lighter in her pocket, itching for a cigarette.

She sweeps the ceiling for the locations of cameras. Most will be too small, but Whitaker spots three black apertures the size of fists in the ceiling. It's the small cameras, like the ones in the Skyra bracelets, which see the most, but it is the big cameras which make them *feel* watched. Surveillance needs the former, self-policing needs the latter.

While he lived with Whitaker, and before he fled for the Red Zone, Jonas had a strange ritual: he would give the middle finger and mouth *fuck you* to every camera he could see. He followed the practice unfailingly, whether or not he was doing something intimate. She had asked him why, since it did not make any difference, he was not going to hurt the camera's feelings. Algorithms prioritize our most frequent behaviour, Jonas had told her, so he made his middle finger ritual his most frequent behaviour. Eventually, he said, the weight of data about him would just be the words *fuck you*, together with his middle finger, over and over again. Whitaker had laughed until she wheezed when he told her.

Whitaker checks the time on the watch Jonas had given her. Almost five. Not long now.

Jane needs the camera equipment, but after posting the code on her feed, she went to a pre-arranged fan event, where she had likely ditched her Skyra bracelet to avoid being tracked. But then she had disappeared from the feed when Davi came nearby. Whitaker hopes Jane has hidden herself safely away. It will be impossible for Whitaker to find her now. Jane will need a way to find Whitaker, but without Skyra's involvement.

She needs a cigarette. Her fingers play with the lighter.

Skyra brings up her feed in holographic blue. Updates slide upward. Nothing from Jane. She is still muted from the feed. Expensive. And pointless: if the Liberators suspect her, they will find her. A direct message from Whitaker will only help them find Jane more easily.

Her cortado arrives from the hand of a dapper waiter, served on a carved wooden tray. Whitaker needs Jane to find the case, and she needs to draw away any Liberators. She nonchalantly takes a sip of the cortado, sighs, and takes the lighter from her pocket. She draws a cigar from the inner pocket of her coat and enjoys its familiar roughness between her lips. She snaps open the lighter and flicks out a flame. Whitaker closes her eyes and savours the velvet smoke.

"Ma'am," she hears, though she does not open her eyes. "You cannot smoke in here."

She blows out a plume of smoke, and her lips become a smile.

"Ma'am," someone says more sternly.

Whitaker opens her eyes and sighs. She dabs out the cigar on the wooden tray. The waiter standing at her table scowls but turns to leave. He adds a mark to her profile, and her TELOS drops three points. Whitaker squeezes the lighter in her palm.

She stands upon the chair, stretches the lighter to the sprinkler head above, and flicks out a flame. In an instant, the sprinklers eject streams of water across the café. There are startled shouts above the sound of an alarm. The café clears. Whitaker goes the front door and stands patiently, drenched despite the raincoat. Her red-silver hair, soaked and ratty, clings to her face. She waits. It will not be long now.

She eyes the case. It stays relatively dry under the table, though remains visible from the front window. If one knows to look for it.

It only takes minutes. A black van pulls outside the café. Three burly figures step out. They enter, black boots splashing in the pooling water. Square jaws, expressionless faces, eyes hidden by black lenses. Whitaker smiles and looks up at the three cameras in the ceiling. She gives a middle finger to each of the cameras – and then to each of the approaching Liberators.

# Chapter 51:
# The Pickup

Jane strides toward the Mercantile Tower. *Too fast. Slow down, more than you'd like. More than feels safe.* She wishes that she could take a car, but that would require payment, which would require identification. Presently, she has four identities from the people whose clothes she borrowed. Her real identity, captured by her face, is obscured from recognition by the makeup pattern Ray had shown her. The combination will buy her some precious minutes from discovery, if she is lucky, if she doesn't draw too much attention. So Jane keeps the brim of her new sunhat low, her eyes to the ground, and resists the urge to run, though her knees ache with the effort.

She tries not to think of what happened in the bar. She did not see it all. Davi threw himself toward Tristan. They wrangled, bodies barging into one another. A chair toppled, she remembers, then a table was thrown onto its side. They were behind her, struggling, shouting, as Jane snatched her bag. She heard a scream as she scattered to the door. Her fingers struggled at the lock. She ignored the screams. Just the lock. Just open the lock.

The adverts following Jane on the sidewalk are for Michael, for Ellen, for Bailey. The people she brushes by are too absorbed in their own adverts to notice. Jane hopes that Whitaker understood the cry for help she had added to her feed. With Ray offline, there is nobody else to count on.

Jane focuses on the speech she will give during her brief but uncensored channel to the entire State. *I am here to defend a word. That word is 'privacy.' Privacy is the freedom not to express something, to keep* it private, until you choose to release it to the world. *The only way to keep choices free is to make them private,* she will say. *The loss of our privacy isn't a requirement of progress. It is an injury, as real as any wound.*

She has recited the speech nightly, keeping it within the security of her head. *The messages we hear on the feed all tell the same tale. They all say that we are freest when we are spending money, and the things we buy are an outburst of authenticity. Succumbing to adverts becomes cloaked in the attire of free choice. But the hand that drives our economy is not invisible. It is perpetually in our vision, and therefore in our minds.*

Jane follows the pace of the people around her. She hears a familiar voice from an advert following one of the people beside her – *her* voice, hyping the Black Friday advert, followed by Ray's jingle. She has heard that jingle at least a hundred times in the last week; Davi has outdone himself in promoting the event.

Thinking of Davi makes her heart quicken, so Jane returns to the speech. *The adverts all sing the same chorus to wear our willpower down, until we give in through exhaustion. They all sing*: buy, buy, buy. *I say we should follow a different anthem*: lie. *Lie to the systems that track what you desire, who you love, what you fear. Lie to the profiles and questionnaires. Lie to Skyra. Only when the marketers realize that they need to ask for the truth should we give it to them. Until then, be unpredictable. Be playful. And be ruthless with your attention —*

The crowd halts in unison like self-driving cars sensing an accident, and Jane bumps into the person in front of her. Then the crowd spins and hurries in the opposite direction. There are concerned murmurs, but nobody says what has happened. They all know. Jane stretches tall to try and see over them, searching for an explanation. She sees only a crowd fleeing from the direction she is headed.

"What's wrong?" Jane calls.

Bodies brush by her without answering. A guy in a bomber jacket stops. "You didn't see the warning?" he says. He looks stunned when she shakes her head. Why would someone not be linked into the feed? "Liberators," he answers.

The Liberators have already assembled at the Mercantile Tower. They know where she is going. They have found Davi or Tristan. They are pursuing her. Her knees lock. Liquid panic descends into her stomach. She is struck with indecision. Flee, or proceed? Liberators behind her, Liberators in front. Her choice does not matter. They will find her.

But Bomber Jacket adds, "Some crazy lady tried to light up a café."

Jane sinks. She knows who the *crazy lady* is. Swirls of anguish form too quickly for Jane to contain them. She isn't sure if she gasps loudly enough for Bomber Jacket to hear, but his eyes thin as he peers under the brim of her hat. Her knees unfreeze. She knows what she must do.

"Red Zoner, probably," he adds. Bomber Jacket begins to hurry in the opposite direction, expecting Jane to do the same. Jane brushes past him, toward the Mercantile Tower, toward the Liberators. She keeps her head down, but she sees his brows furrow as she passes.

"Hey—" he starts.

Jane stops. He has recognized her.

She prepares to run.

"—you sure you want to go that way?" he says. "Liberators? Reds?"

Jane sighs. "I'll be fine," is all she says, hoping it is true, before she slips away.

*Liberators.* Jane claps swiftly towards the café. What have they done to Whitaker?

There is an alien silence as she approaches the Mercantile Tower. The street is abandoned. There are no Liberators, nor anyone else, no doubt scared away by the notices that Liberators had been here. It feels like the no-man's-land she had discovered across the Red Zone border when she had left to find the man named Jonas. Despite the stories of being set upon by squads of cannibals, there was not a soul. She had walked in near silence, save for the crunch of deteriorated asphalt under her feet.

Just like then, Jane presently hears her breath, and her feet, and the dust stirred by a breeze. She presses her face to the window of a parlour for electronic tattoos, then a dress store, an automated noodle house, but they are all locked, like the owners had heard of an impending flood. Perhaps there will be one. The breeze flowing down the street is snakelike. It is not the hot wind spelling a dust storm, but the cold, humid bite of wind foretelling a flood.

Jane finally finds a café two blocks down with its door open. The cafe is deserted. Jane glances into the window, keeping her face from the camera inside. She looks for any sign of Whitaker. None. Jane looks up the street. Nothing. The silence worries her. She longs even for an advert to break it. None comes. She can hear only the soft drip of water. Jane hopes Whitaker escaped – ghosted somewhere to safety – but she knows better. Jane scans the floor for a trinket or a sign, but Whitaker has disappeared.

A chill tightens her stomach. Jane realizes that she is biting her lip. She sniffs back the shock and takes a focusing breath. There must be something. Jane returns the café window and presses her face to the glass. Cups of coffee filled with sprinkler water have overflowed onto the tables and dispersed a subtle brown onto the floor. The hanging lights are shorted out by the water.

She sees a case nestled below a table. Old, leather, and worn. That must be it. She steals a look left and right before entering the café. It is humid inside. Her heels splash in the pooled water. She takes the case, checks inside, and spirits away before the Liberators return.

Her pace is quick. Her right hand holds the case. Her left wags forward and back as she walks. She does not look back. That will only raise suspicion. *Too fast*, she thinks again. *Slow down*. Jane arrives at the private entrance to the Mercantile Tower. She opens the handbag slung across her shoulder and takes the final pill in her palm.

*There is still time to turn back.* The thought comes to her and will not leave. Jane has escaped before; there is enough time to do it again. She is invisible to tracking this time. She can ditch the heels, drop the pill on the street, and be out of the city before the Liberators find her.

She'll be quicker if she just puts down the case.

Jane shakes her head. She has come too far. She pops the pill into her mouth and swallows hard.

# Chapter 52:
# All You've Ever Been...

Jane sets up the camera on its tripod and places the microphone beside it. Though old, the system awakens and connects to the internet through a wired connection. She points it to a blank wall. The room in the Mercantile Tower has no windows and contains only a single leather chair. Jane wonders how much it cost the room's owner for so little.

It won't be long now. Davi will have arranged her transmission to be distributed across the State. They won't have canceled it. It is too important to pull without certainty. If Davi is dead, it will take them time to figure out what happened. And if he isn't – well, she has to try. Though they'll realize the mistake immediately, it will take them precious minutes to withdraw every mirrored transmission. That will be long enough.

In the room's silence, Jane's mind circles the same worries about her plan. Without Skyra, she cannot tell the time. She needs to synchronize with the event. Too early and she will give away her message before it is transmitted. Too late and –

Jane snips the thought before it completes. She will *not* be late. A fireworks show will occur immediately before the Black Friday event, easily visible from the Mercantile Tower. Her segment will follow. She just needs to find a window and await the signal.

Jane takes the crowbar that she had used to break into the room, slips off her heels, and returns to the corridor to find a room with a window. The club appears deserted. Nobody wants to miss the largest event of the year, it seems, but Jane keeps her steps soft on the white marble all the same. As she paces down the corridor, the lock of one of the doors lights green. It opens it with the handle.

Davi's pool.

The windows stand from the water to the ceiling. She lays the crowbar on the glass table in the corner by the door. The two chairs are shifted from where they left them. *Perhaps Davi has brought other toys here.* She wonders if he is alive. Wonders if she hopes he is not.

The pool is longer than she had realized – thirty yards at least – and much deeper, too. Despite the clarity of the unmoving water, the pool's bottom looks elusive, as if there is no bottom at all, as if she will sink forever if she enters. Jane keeps her distance as she circles the pool's edge and presses a hand to the outside window. It is already dark outside. Uncountable lights glisten in the streets, each one from a Skyra bracelet. The crowd – thick, even for a Black Friday – stretches along city blocks and the glimmers of their bracelets rain kisses on the pool's surface. *Deliver the speech before it can be shut down,* she rehearses. *Leave the tower. Head east. Take side streets. Avoid crowds. Pick up the car with—*

—where *is* Gabe? Her rational side knows the answer. It is best to forget about him; the feed already has. But Jane cannot leave without him. She remembers Carl and Reece and wishes she could see if they were alright. She had left them behind to enjoy the freedom of a new life. Jane tells herself it is not that simple, but she feels sick with guilt and knows she cannot leave another friend behind, not this time. She will find Gabe. Wherever he is – in whatever danger – she will go.

Soft footsteps catch Jane's attention. *Gabe?* Elation springs in her chest: he has made it. She skips toward the door, wanting to throw it open and snatch Gabe in her arms.

A figure enters. Jane tries to stop, but her momentum carries her forward and her feet slip on the tile. She lands hard on her elbows.

"I thought I might find you here," the Director says, staring down at her. Jane eyes the crowbar on the table, but the Director is already too close. The Director sinks into one of the chairs by the table and rests one leg over the other. He's in his silver suit. He ushers Jane to sit.

Jane, clambering to her feet, looks to the doorway, to the crow-bar, and to the set of eyes enjoying each moment. She cannot tell if he is armed, or if a patrol of Liberators waits outside. Jane forces herself to take the other chair, ready to eject when opportune.

"I admit it was unexpected," the Director says, "a girl who otherwise abides by every wasteful tenet of our society, who pours every vain desire into Skyra – fancying herself a *revolutionary*." He chuckles. An alien noise, a noise she cannot imagine him producing. "Suffice it to say I found your setup in the other room. There will be no revolution tonight."

*The camera.*

"I noticed something strange about you the moment we met," the Director continues coolly. "By the data, you were an entirely average girl. Which is to say, I could tell what you would have for breakfast in five years' time. But what I saw in person was different, no matter how dedicated your performance was. It made for a mystery I had to resolve. Would you like to know what I discovered?"

She scowls. The Director visibly enjoys it. "You were only a *child* when it happened?" His eyes feign sympathy. He lets the question hang in the air.

"And for all these years you've had to avoid looking into it," the Director continues, "to protect your identity. I can't *imagine* how strong the longing to know must be."

It is not a longing. It is like cheating herself of something she deserves. She remembers the water closing across her face, the overwhelming rush in her ears, the sullen expression her mother wore in the emergency shelter, the wails of her sister, the heavy silence after. Such horrors demanded answers.

"You must have wondered why nobody knows about the tainted milk that killed your sister," the Director says.

She has. There *must* have been other children who died; there *had* to be online outrage. How had it dissipated?

"The best way to deal with negative information," he adds, "is to drown it."

"What do you mean?" The words escape from her morose lips before she can stop them.

"*Save an Isles Child*, we called it: a sponsorship campaign by Nature Corp. for young flood victims."

Victims like her. She remembers the gentle hand of an orderly on her shoulder, leading her from her mother. She remembers her mother's voice reassuring her that they would see each other soon. And she remembers her eyes hurting from camera flashes, and joining a group of confused children told not to say anything, and searching the crowd of reporters for her mother's face. Jane assumed later that the cost of the relocations was a sign, however slight, of corporate guilt.

"We started the campaign right after we learned children were dying," the Director adds.

He leaves the conclusion to her: the corporation rescued her as part of a marketing campaign, to distract from all the children it had poisoned. Children like her sister. Sickness blusters in her stomach and rises to her throat. Jane is alive to hide that her little sister is dead. She feels light-headed like blood is draining from her body through her fingers.

"All you've ever been," the Director says, "is part of our campaign."

Tears turn hot on her cheeks. Jane balls up her fists, not noticing her nails dig into her palms. She feels the anger in the roots of her teeth. His icy eyes reap it all, prising her open like he was conducting a vivisection, unfolding each organ.

"Had we more time, I could show you how each choice you think you have made was preceded by an outside influence. What you regard as choice is the physical manifestation of neurotransmitters flooding your brain. What these transmitters do is predictable, and therefore, manipulatable. Consider the room we are in; you discovered it through Davi. And how did you decide to see him in the first place? *Think back!*" he cajoles. "Do you remember what brought that choice to you? Or did it simply *come* to you, seemingly – from nowhere?"

Jane remembers the fear of having Ashley, her only friend, stolen from her, unless she agreed to the Director's demand. "You're saying you manipulated me into seeing him?"

"I'm saying," the Director replies, "That I stand to gain the most from Daviault's destruction. The Board would have fallen in line to follow him. But without him, the corporation will have no choice but to find a new heir."

He pauses to assess her. "Is that a twitch of guilt I see? Guilty, about Davi? Don't be. He got what he deserved, don't you agree?"

"Is he...."

"Dead? Why yes, gutted by a knife with your DNA on the handle. The feed will know once we have determined the correct story. Were you his unstable lover, or would you prefer to be an assassin for the Reds?"

Jane cannot bear him any longer, yet she feels buckled to the chair, immobile under his eyes. Perhaps the Director is right: perhaps she had not made these choices; fear had. When all is watched and judged, fear is a permanent companion. That fear of choosing leads to only one solution – the solution Ray had taken – to not choose at all.

"You are wondering how I found you," the Director says.

Jane does not try to deny it.

"I confess," he purrs, "I had a little help—"

Jane doesn't answer. Her bottom lip trembles.

"—Gabe was *most* helpful."

Jane seizes with the pain of a sharp point in her ribs.

"In fact," the Director continues, "he helped me watch you from the start." And he pauses, again, to enjoy Jane's eyes thin in anger, to enjoy the subtle quiver of her hands. He drinks in each exquisite detail like young lovers share each others' eyes.

Jane thinks of staring into Gabe's eyes, of sharing the warmth of a fire. But he wasn't sharing; he was watching. Everything she had told him – her past, her loathing, her longing – had he been tallying it all, ready to divulge to the Director?

"You're lying."

The Director brushes aside her reply. "In his defence, maybe he didn't even know. He was convinced that he was helping you, so getting him to betray your hiding place required some persuasion."

"What did you do to him?" Jane seethes.

The Director leans closer, close enough to whisper. "I gave him what you wanted to give him: I gave him a *choice*."

Ray had not chosen her. What could have convinced him to choose betrayal? How quickly did he acquiesce? Or had Ray been right all along – that he had no choice?

"I will give you the same luxury," the Director says. "Leave with me, forgo the Black Friday speech, and you'll be free."

"That's all you want."

"It's that easy," he says, his breath stinging her cheek. "You see, no matter where you go, data always follows. I am regrettably the only one to have traced your identity all the way back to that fateful day of the flood. But once you have the data, past, present, and future are a straight line. Fortunately for you, as I was unearthing your identity, I discovered some good news." Then he smiles and adds, "I found your mother."

Jane audibly shudders. At once she desires to envelop herself in the comfort of her mother's arms. A flurry of questions sweeps through her mind – *Is my mom really alive? Is she safe? Can I see her?* – but the questions settle into one: *Can I trust the Director?*

"She dearly wants to see you again."

His stare feels like it is grinding down her defences. She cannot bear to look up at him. As Jane avoids his stare, she catches an unfamiliar face in the reflection on the glass table. No longer retouched or lit or filtered, but an unnatural face nonetheless, coloured with a red swoop about the eyes and nose. A face, still, hidden under fakery. But the mask is slipping. The Director's eyes tease out what is beneath.

Jane's eyes stray to the crowbar lying on the table. It hovers on the glass, beckoning. Using it is her only other choice. The Director will be in range of its swing. It will connect with his temple. He will crumple. Simple. Jane's eyes return to the face reflected on the table. She wonders who the glass will reflect: the coward, or the killer?

"Let me assist your decision," he adds, leaning even closer. "I know you feel unavoidably sick if you become short of breath. I know that you take showers over baths, and that you *never* swim. I know what nightmares cause you to wake in a cold sweat." His voice becomes a hiss. "Which all means: *I know what you fear*. I know what to ask the Liberators to do, if necessary."

Jane feels like water is closing across her face. Her diaphragm stiffens to hold her breath and her lungs begin to burn. It is the sensation of being enveloped alive. Nothing is worse than the feeling, not even giving in to the Director.

Jane glowers at the Director, straining to choose who to be. Her thoughts drift to Reece, and the time Jane acquiesced to the data rather than take Reece to the hospital. She thinks of Tristan, to whom she committed herself because of what the data told her, to whom she gave up every humiliating piece of her data she had to try and help Reece. She thinks of the freedoms she has continued to give up under Skyra's watchful eye, thinks of how she betrayed her sister's memory by acquiescing to associate with Davi, and thinks of how it began: with the small, painless click of a chip the size of a grain of rice injected into her wrist. That is how it takes you: with the wrist, first, or perhaps the ankle, then elbow or knee, then shoulder or leg, and once you realize you're being dragged into the depths, it is already too late.

Her thoughts drift to Ashley. Jane pities how frightened Ashley must have felt in her last moments. And her thoughts drift to Gabe. Only with him was Jane unafraid. Not because the fear had disappeared, but because she had finally chosen to look at it, to give it a name, to share it with someone. And then she thinks: perhaps there is another solution. Perhaps she does not need to feel fear. What person would she be without fear? What would that person choose to do?

The Director smiles. Jane ignores his lips. She focuses on the eyes. "If I've learned one thing from you," she hisses, "it's that the eyes don't lie. Your eyes follow mine, seeing if I look to the exit. They flick to my hip – do I have a hidden weapon? And they glance down when I point this out. See, there!" she exclaims viciously.

The Director's lips sour. His frosty exterior melts.

Jane twitches her attention to the crowbar, too quickly for him to see. Her heart thumps against her ribcage.

Then she too leans closer to him. Closer to the crowbar.

And she whispers, "Your eyes tell me what *you* fear." She holds his ugly stare. "You fear the uncontrollable. You fear the unknown.

*"You fear me."*

And she leaps toward the table, taking the crowbar in her right hand. She swings.

# Chapter 53:
# The Depths of Fear

Jane does not see the Director lunge. He is in his chair. Then she feels his hands wrapped around hers, the crowbar flailing between them, crashing through the table, and then shards of glass biting at her naked toes. As they grapple, the crowbar spills from Jane's hands. She hears a tragic splash and the crowbar sinks, visible but unreachable, to the bottom of the pool.

Jane snatches a shard from the floor and scuttles from the Director. The Director slinks back to the door and slides the latch across. Then he pauses, statuesque, to watch Jane realize the impossibility of her position. A locked door before her; a fatal fall from the tower behind her; her weapon lost to the water.

The water to Jane's right returns to stillness. It beckons to Jane, to complete what it left unfinished when she was a child. She backs away, shard held before her, leaving bloody prints in the shapes of her toes. The Director strolls closer. His features are awash with fireworks, yellow, then blue. His eyes are points of red. Jane steps backward. The ever-present smile on the Director's face grows. He is close enough to lunge at her.

She launches herself at him and slashes with the glass, more quickly than she can consciously understand. There is a struggle, a slice on her fingers, a bite of pain in her ribs, and she staggers backward. Still the Director smiles, as if he already knows what she will do next, as if he is already enjoying the image of how he will destroy her.

The crowbar taunts her from the bottom of the pool. She glimpses it in dismay as she retreats empty-handed into the corner of the room. The Director's footsteps clap sharply on the tile as he strides closer. His face glows with the reds and blues of the fireworks outside.

Jane raises her gaze to the switch on the wall – the one Davi had used. She launches herself to it. A black skin grows once more across the windows and Jane becomes clothed in black. All goes silent and dark as the castle dungeon.

But the Director does not know darkness. He does not know silence. She hears searching footsteps in the darkness. His shuffles are cautious and indecisive.

The Director is lost. He is panting; he is afraid.

Though her lungs feel volcanic, she stifles a breath. Jane slides along the wall away from the Director's wandering footsteps. Four inches away, then another four. Her palms slink across the wall tile. Another step. She longs to feel the latch of the door. Her steps quicken in anticipation. She must be close. She has lost him in the darkness.

She steps quietly closer. She hears a clink as her foot brushes a piece of glass. A laugh from the darkness approaches. His footsteps are sharp in her ear. She seizes. His assault feels inevitable; he sees her, even in darkness; he knows her, even in silence. She feels him close, blocking the path to the door. She hears his footsteps close in.

Jane does what the Director does not expect.

She looks to the water.

And she jumps.

Instant panic. As the water closes over her, she hears the muffled thunder of her heart in her ears. Her fingers claw for the feel of metal, searching left and right. Her forefinger grazes the crowbar. Again, again, she scratches for it. As she snatches up the crowbar from the pool floor, fingers wrap around her ankle like pincers into bone. She kicks and kicks, but she does not rise. The water's surface is tauntingly close, but the Director pulls her down.

The water flooding into her lungs triggers memories of the flood. Jane's mother was holding her hand with a crushing grip, leading her to the hill in the centre of town, when the flood caught up with them. The water pulled at Jane's ankles and reeled her from her mother's hold and into impermeable brown. She gasped for air, but a new wave filled her mouth before she could catch a breath. There was an acrid taste, a burn in her eyes. She spluttered but she could not tell which way was up, which was down, which way was air, and which was death. Water lodged in her lungs, heavy as stone. Jane attacked the water with sharp strokes like mortal blows, but the current was too strong.

Jane whirled head over heels, span by the rushing force, flailing arms unable to catch anything. Her lungs burned with the pressure. The brown darkened. The darkness was bottomless. She lost sight of her feet and her hands. Then there was a moment of stillness and peace. So far below, the water held her in a gentle grasp. Death was peaceful and unmoving. Time stopped. She closed her eyes for sleep.

And then a hand came for her wrist, almost wrenching her arm from its socket, and all was spirals and rushing water in her ears until she emerged from the water. Jane cannot remember who helped her. She cannot remember anything after being draped onto the floor of a boat. She remembers only a powerful hand scooping her from the water.

There is nobody to help now. Only her.

She kicks with her free leg, so sharply the impact shudders through her bones. The fingers around Jane's ankle disappear. She pulls herself toward the surface and erupts from the water. It no longer holds her. The air above is cool and precious. She drinks it in, straining, like she can't drink it quickly enough. One arm snatches at the water while the other feels the weight of the crowbar. It feels lighter, now.

The Director's splutters sound in the darkness. There is a wheezing to her right. Jane tries to pull herself closer toward what she hopes is the edge of the pool. A wave splashes her face, and she coughs. Still she thrashes. One hand holds the crowbar, the other vies for the pool's edge.

Something grasps a handful of her dress and pulls her from the edge of the pool. A firm hand presses down on her shoulder, trying to force her below. As she struggles to stay about the surface, she hears the Director's voice from the darkness: "Wrong choice—"

She swings. A wet crunch, an instant's howl. The impact thunders up her arm. His hand leaves her shoulder. Jane no longer hears the Director. She hears only her own desperate gasps for air.

She wants to flee, but her task is incomplete. She must deliver her message.

Jane swims to the Director's floating body, expecting him to wake. She tentatively touches his outstretched arm. It is limp. Her fingers feel for the golden band on his wrist. It unclasps. She swims away slowly, silently, until her fingers find the welcome edge of the pool. Jane climbs out, her feet shamble toward the switch, and the black skin retires from the windows.

The last firework splashes liquid colour on the sky. It is time.

Her body moves off but in her mind she is still below the water, still feeling the air forced from her lungs, still feeling like a fish flapping in the air. Every nerve screams. She cannot distinguish fear from injury. Jane focuses on the sound of her footsteps: the thud of barefoot soles planting drunkenly on the ground. Nothing feels concrete. Only the thump of each heel. Her feet take her to the stairs leading to the roof.

Jane drags herself up the rail and throws her weight into the door at the top. She stumbles onto the roof. Wind rips at her hair and her red dress whips about her legs. Her eyes squint at the blurred brush of fireworks fading into the night. The smell of gunpowder lingers, together with a humid smell, the smell of impending rain.

She does not feel her legs give way. She wilts, but the impact of her knees on the concrete is strangely painless. Momentarily Jane returns to the tree in Freetown's town square. The air is sweet and cold to the cheek. The stars are sharp pinpoints of white. Jane sits inside the tree – a wooden hovel just large enough for two.

She wishes she were not alone. Jane screws her eyes tight, clinging to the vision of the little tree. She takes in a full breath, tasting the freshness of the air. "Where are you Gabe?" she whispers. Her voice is hoarse, soreness developing at the base of her throat.

"Right here," his voice comes. He sits across from her, stuffed cosily inside the tree trunk, knees up to his chest. He smiles reassuringly. "We'll always have right here."

"I wish we had stayed," she sobs.

"Me too."

They hug. Her hands grasp alternate elbows and lock him close.

She sniffles into his shoulder. She feels the beating in his chest and nuzzles in more. He smooths the hair from her face.

A light pierces the dream: the Skyra bracelet, awoken by the signals outside the tower's protective shell. Jane looks up. She is hugging her shoulders, and feels her nose run onto her forearm. Silence is all that is with her. She wipes her nose. Her forearm comes back red.

The rain is heavy, now, and its acidity bites at her open wounds and fills her with a dreadful cold. Jane hisses at the pain of standing. She drops the bracelet at her feet and takes a few paces away. In Skyra's glow she leaves a long shadow.

"Good evening," comes a voice in a channel from the bracelet. "You are not the registered user."

"Log me in."

Skyra recognizes her voice, and logs her in.

"Warning," Skyra says, "A stay at home order is in effect. There is a flash flood inbound."

The flood was not forecast, but then, nothing about this day has been. The unwelcome rain brings a new risk. By dispersing the crowds from the streets, Jane will lose her only cover from the Liberators. If she remains inside the tower, it will be impossible to go anywhere until the flood subsides. But if she leaves now, she might still escape. Jane raises her eyes to the abyssal clouds above, and calm settles over her.

Even if they take down her stream, she must try. "Get ready to stream a live video to my feed," she says.

"Ready."

"Begin," she says.

# Chapter 54:
# The Speech

"Good evening. Today is Black Friday. It is the day we think about freedom and choice. But there are two words we don't use anymore that are just as important: the words *private* and *attention*."

She cannot remember the script. Words fall from her mouth.

"The loss of our privacy is not a requirement of our progress. It is an injury, as real as any wound. When we lost the right to privacy, we lost the right to our own attention. Our most fundamental right is to be able to choose one thought over another, but that most basic choice is now forbidden. Adverts will not disappear until we open our eyes wide and watch them until the end. Messages appear in our vision without our choice, and leak into our minds without our control. When we drown in messages like this, there is no space, no time to choose what deserves our attention. I have stolen your attention, continually, and I want to give a little back.

"When we can't direct our own attention, we cannot choose what makes us individuals. The meaning of that word – *individual* – is 'un-dividable' – but they seek to chop us into exploitable pieces, for they don't see us as human. They see us as data: biological data, producing positional data and financial data. And we see each other the same way. We choose who to hate because they appear as red crime potentials on a map, and who to love because we are told they have a high compatibility rating.

"Attention, not minerals or information, is now the core of our economy. It is a resource we are born with, but do not get to keep, because we have let attention become monetized. If we want it back, we have to pay. This evening, I am in the quietest place in the city: the top floor of a tower, unreachable by signals and internet. Everyone should have this opportunity, but it is only available for the rich.

"This means that we need to make privacy public. We need to break from the pull of curated suggestions and individualized recommendations. We need to leave the sculpted gardens filled with near-extinct trees and abandon the perpetual lights on the sides of our homes and on the bottom of our sky. Instead, we should revel in the stillness and silence of darkness. Because this world is what we choose, collectively, to make it. We are a force of nature on this earth, like wind or water, in every respect except one: we can choose to act differently.

"But we have chosen a world of rising tides cornering us on ever-more desperate concrete islands, squeezing us between the surface of the sea and the sinking ceiling of black cloud. We don't see this reality on the feed. We see only articles on beating depression, and new seasons of clothing, and decadent vacations. But *our bodies* know. We *feel* the sweat on our brow, the musk clinging onto our skin, the burn at the back of our throat. And we feel the pressure in our skulls, the exhaustion saturating our minds. That is where we need to start: with our bodies, with ourselves, by reclaiming where we direct our attention…"

Jane pauses, not for effect, but for a sharp pinch in her side. She resists looking down. Her fingers go to her ribs. The dress feels thick with blood. She hisses as her fingers find the rough surface of glass from the table. She deflates, looks down, and shudders at her crimson fingers.

Skyra's camera still watches. She forces her eyes back up. Her breaths are shallow, the weight on her shoulders growing with each exhale. Jane shows her fingers to the camera.

"*This* is how they see you," she gasps, "*this* is what they choose for you." The pain is too great, and she returns her hand to nurse her side. "Their price is *us*."

The pain grows. "Did Ray send me a video?" she splutters to Skyra.

"Yes," is the plain reply. "Perhaps I should contact—"

"—play it," she wheezes.

Across a thousand mirrors of a thousand streams of her feed, Jane's image disappears, and a short film begins to play. It begins with a caption: *Ray Burnett: My Crime.* Then there is the sound of hands crashing on metal. Again. Scores of hands, now, the metal shaking under their blows. The sound is warlike. It reminds Jane of the castle, like a horde of savages battering at the final gate. Their shouts, coarse and guttural, are too fierce to understand.

Jane shivers. The invaders are almost inside.

An image appears: a thick crowd lashing at a metal grating. They are not historical savages. They are everyday people, stirred to rage, rattling the grating like caged animals. They push into one another, the grating buckling under the bulk of bodies. The metal groans as the bodies press in closer. Those at the front cry in pain as their faces are forced into the grating, but those behind do not hear, do not care.

*Three – two – one – welcome to Black Friday!*

The grating parts, and the mass streams through the opening. Store operators pull at the grating, but it is bent by the human crush, and cannot be opened more than half way. People squeeze through the narrow gap, contesting their place in the line with shoulders and shouts. Those behind cheer in excitement; but those entering wear snarls on their faces, tensed by adrenaline, already feeling the aches of elbows in their ribs. They scatter, tear boxes from shelves without thinking and threaten competitors with kicks and cries.

Music plays, aggressive chords, almost overtaken with the shouts of the store customers in the background. Then a burst of drums like thunder, recalling the pounding fists at the beginning of the video. It switches to different footage of customers, musical chords growling above calls for help and shouted curses. Despite the chaos there is a musical order: bodies slip and fall, and push one another to the ground, almost in time with the heavy music. The angles switch more quickly, the music becoming more frenetic, the crowd more violent.

A woman in her fifties slips and sprains her hand. She is in too much pain to pick up the box she was carrying. Someone pulls it from her feet. A teenager tries to force his way out of the store, holding his spoils above his head. The rush of bodies knocks him down, and he is trampled by opportunists competing for the boxes spilled from his hands. He disappears under feet. Only his arm sticks out, fingers outstretched, looking for a hand to pull him out. None comes. The music rumbles louder.

The images flick faster. Each more violent, the individuals bloodier, their faces wilder, the agony told by their winced eyes. The music is brutal; like thunder in the ears, anger told through notes than fists.

A final image. An old man, blood streaming from his nose and above his brow, totters drunkenly out the store, holding a box to his chest as tightly as he would a baby. The crowd behind continues pushing in. He stumbles, weak in the knees, and drops the box. When he stands he does not pick it up. He forgets it entirely, and limps out of frame, hands out in front of him in case he falls. The box sits, unattended. Nobody takes it.

The notes fade and the screen shows a list of other names Jane recognizes as members of Nature Corp.

Jane shakes. The blood is drying on her fingers. The red spot on her dress has widened. The rage burning underneath her skin cools. A shiver tickles her spine. She is a fading red ember. All warmth is gone.

The video feed returns to her. She is supposed to say something more. But Jane cannot remember. She gives a weak look to Skyra's camera before wilting to the ground.

# Chapter 55:
# The Choice II

A distant voice pulls Jane back to consciousness. Her eyes open slightly, expecting to see Liberators. A sliver of light leaks in. It is too bright. She shuts her eyes again and hopes, for a moment, to drift away, but the throb pulsing in her side stops her retreat to unconsciousness.

She hears the voice again – a soft voice, dreamy, like it is carried by the wind. There are words but no understanding of them. Only the pulse in her side. Jane breathes in – her mouth is dry and her throat tight – and ventures a single word: "*Gabe?*"

"That's right," a whisper comes, as soothing as an ointment.

Jane distrusts her ears. She does not open her eyes, in fear that the figure of the Director might materialize before them – that broad body towering over her, that smile, those eyes like abysses staring through her as the world disappears—

Her eyes spring open. Her body is alive – alive with panic, alive with urgency in her muscles – and she makes it halfway to her feet before she loses her balance and crumbles back down again. A hand on her forearm and another on her hip brace her until she stands.

"It's me, Katie," Ray says, hushed, "it's me."

A moment of relief. Her shoulders relax. The ground feels firm. It is hard – and cold – but stable. The hand on her hip melts into her flesh – two pieces become a stable one – and she ventures a slow glance about the rooftop to understand where she is. Prints of red lead toward her. But there is no Director, no steel fingers, water filling her lungs. But how had the Director found her? How did he know? How did –

"Get away from me!" Jane says.

"Let me—"

"It was you?" she gasps. "You told him?"

He hesitates – then nods slightly. "I'm sorry."

The wind escapes from her like she has suffered a clubbing blow. Her mind swims with questions, but her mouth manages only: "Why?"

"Just let me—"

"*Why?*" she repeats.

"He said that if I told him, he wouldn't hurt you."

"And you believed him?"

"I couldn't have someone else die because of my choices. Especially you…"

Hot tears roll down her cheeks. "No," she says. "No, he told me. He told me from the start – you were watching me. You were gaining my trust. But you were *never* on my side." Her voice drops. "Maybe you didn't even know."

The sentence hangs in the air.

"And you've brought the Liberators with you."

"It's just me. Just Gabe."

"Then they're waiting until I leave the tower."

"It's just me," he says. "I smashed my Skyra bracelet. They couldn't follow me."

"Then maybe *you're* the one closing the loose end. I've been stupid," she adds, "stupid to think any of us had a choice…"

"You still do. The flood will be a distraction. You can leave."

The rain becomes torrential. Their clothes become sodden.

His eyes implore her. Those same eyes that she had stared into beside the campfire and had revealed his secrets. Those eyes that had looked into hers, once trustworthy, now frightening and unfamiliar. And yet—

—and yet, she lingers on the face of Gabe – the only man she had known – *really known* – through touch and talk and trust.

She is tired.

"I'm scared, Gabe."

"I know."

"How can I trust you?"

"Do you remember in the castle when you asked me why I didn't turn you in?"

She nods.

"I was afraid to admit it was my choice. It was easier to blame it on you. But you have shown me that if you choose out of fear, you aren't choosing at all. No matter what they have done to frighten you – the surveillance watching everything you do, the data judging you, the rules punishing you – they haven't controlled what you stand for. Because of you," Gabe says, meeting her eyes with his own, "I'm not afraid anymore."

His voice rises and he draws taller, appearing to shake a burden from his broad shoulders. "If the Liberators are looking for you," he says, "then they'll have to look for *us*."

He extends his hand. Jane keeps hers readied – ready to strike, ready to fling around him, she does not know. She looks to the extended hand, and to those eyes. What lies ahead by taking that hand? What lies for her outside? *What would a girl who was unafraid do?*

"Trust me," he adds, hand still extended.

She looks at the hand, and reaches to meet it with her own.

Katie speaks: "Okay."